THE
BREACH

THE
BREACH

DIANE/DAVID MUNSON

The Breach

ACKNOWLEDGMENT

Many thanks to our dear readers, friends, and family who continue to pray for us and our writing. Thanks also to Micah House Media and those supporting them for bringing to fruition this story of courage and faith in such turbulent times. We need God's truth and help more than ever.

John 3:16 (NIV) is a wonderful promise for us to cling to: "For God so loved the world, that He gave His only begotten Son, that whoever believes in Him shall not perish, but have eternal life."

We give a special thanks to Pam Cangioli for her expertise in editing and great support for our endeavor. And we thank Rik Hall of Wild Seas Formatting for his excellent interior design, and the ever-patient book cover designer, Luisa Pereira. We are grateful and blessed by those who because of the sensitivity of their assignment in the intelligence community or station in society can only be acknowledged by their first names. Thank you, Ada and Scott.

Each of the Munsons' Stand-Alone Thrillers May Be Read in Any Order.

Facing Justice – ISBN-13: 978-0982535509
Confirming Justice – ISBN-13: 978-0982535516
The Camelot Conspiracy – ISBN-13: 978-0982535523
Hero's Ransom – ISBN-13: 978-0982535530
Redeeming Liberty – ISBN-13: 978-0982535547
Joshua Covenant – ISBN-13: 978-0-983559009
Night Flight – ISBN-13: 978-0983559023 (Young Adult and Grandparent Suspense)
Stolen Legacy – ISBN-13: 978-0983559047
Embers of Courage – ISBN – 13: 978-0983559061
The Looming Storm – ISBN – 13: 978-0-983559085
North by Starlight – ISBN – 13: 978-1-732582309
The Breach – ISBN – 13: 978-1-732582323

Chapter 1

"**G**uilty! Darin Hilton is guilty!" Judge Reginald Ginsburg pronounced the verdict in such a loud voice, his words bounced around the crowded courtroom like a boomerang.

"The defendant is guilty on all counts!" the judge bellowed again.

"I think Ginsburg likes saying the word *guilty*," FBI Special Agent Griffin Topping whispered to the federal prosecutor sitting beside him. "But not nearly as much as I enjoy hearing it."

An eerie silence filled the federal courtroom. Finally, the truth seemed to sink in, with the bevy of court watchers coming alive and gasping, "Arghh!" all at once.

A shrill female voice shouted from behind Griff, "Darin, no!"

"Quiet in the courtroom!" Judge Ginsburg commanded. "Or you will be cleared."

Griff had been the case agent during the swift two-day trial, and was seated at the prosecutor's table on the other side of the courtroom from Hilton and his defense lawyer. Reporters dashed out to file reports before the noon news. Griff suppressed a smile in the midst of the swirling chaos.

He glanced at Patrick O'Rourke, the Assistant U.S. Attorney (AUSA), who'd just chalked up another conviction.

"Ginsburg gave me fits that he might find Hilton not guilty," Griff confided to Patrick. "I kept track of how many times he ruled for the defense during the trial."

The way Patrick stared straight ahead without flinching, Griff decided the AUSA expected the guilty verdict all along. Then Patrick surprised him by saying, "Me too."

Patrick clenched his hands on the table, his knuckles white, which told Griff the guilty verdict also caught the seasoned AUSA off guard. Griff had even shared with his wife over a hurried cup of coffee this morning that he was concerned the judge might let Hilton off. Dawn shone with her usual beacon of encouragement.

Her words, as she'd filled his coffee mug, floated through his mind: *Take heart, darling! I'm praying the judge will discern the truth of the evidence and find justice.*

Griff's wife often prayed for him to be safe while doing his dangerous job, and she lived out her faith in the trenches, too. As a federal probation officer, she worked for Judge Ginsburg and other judges in the courthouse to ensure convicted defendants adhered to judicial orders of incarceration and supervision. Dawn would be thrilled to know her prayers were answered.

His mind was so preoccupied he nearly missed Judge Ginsburg saying in a steely voice, "Defendant Hilton is remanded to the U.S. Marshal. Sentencing is in thirty days provided the pre-sentence memorandum is complete."

"Your Honor." The defense attorney rose to her feet. "My client runs a company. People rely on him for their livelihood. We ask he remain free on bond until sentencing."

This got the courtroom buzzing, and the judge banged his gavel. Silence instantly blanketed the room.

"Ms. Stone, your client won't remain free on bond," Ginsburg intoned. "He's a danger. Too bad he failed to consider those depending upon him before he threatened Senator Cambridge Easton. The senator couldn't be here this morning due to an important vote on a new trade bill. The defendant's also a flight risk, given his past travel overseas to meet technology customers."

Attorney Madison Stone launched a fresh argument. "Your Honor, Mr. Hilton already surrendered his passport to the court."

The judge dropped the gavel even louder, saying, "Court stands adjourned."

Murmurs flooded the courtroom. Griff looked around. Something was missing. Oh yeah. The jury box was empty, meaning Ginsburg had no men and women to thank for their service. The judge swiveled his high-back leather chair, preparing to leave the courtroom.

Darin Hilton jumped to his feet, yelling, "I'm not guilty!"

Blood vessels in his forehead bulged. He pounded the table with giant fists and hollered, "You presided over a farce! I'm innocent and you know it!"

Griff leapt to the floor, ready for action. Ginsburg banged his gavel several times, signaling he wasn't taking any guff from the convicted man. Madison Stone tugged her client's suit jacket and pulled him down to his seat with a loud thud. Griff saw a despairing look sweep over the face of the normally cool and calm lawyer.

"Madison is beside herself," Griff quipped to AUSA O'Rourke. "I doubt she picked a bench trial. Hilton strikes me as a guy who wouldn't trust a jury deciding his fate."

O'Rourke drew his litigation bag onto his lap. "I'm glad Hilton put his life in this judge's hands. The entire legal community knows Ginsburg is erratic."

"Your Honor." Hilton's lawyer again scrambled to her feet. "Excuse my client's outburst. It's a grueling time for him and his family."

The judge stood erect in his black robe and gathered his dignity along with a thick file. He stopped to study the defendant. Griff imagined the judge's look telegraphed something to Hilton like, *Buddy, get ready to serve the maximum time in prison.*

Judge Ginsburg relinquished his laser-like stare at Hilton and stepped down from his bench.

Hilton began spouting, "You'll be sorr—"

Madison Stone clamped a hand over her client's mouth.

Had the judge heard his threat? Griff wondered. The deputy U.S. Marshal apparently did. Looking like a beefy football linebacker stuffed in a business suit, he reached the defense table and, in one giant motion, yanked Hilton from the chair. He wrestled his hands behind his back and handcuffed him.

The judge, along with his black robe, disappeared through a door behind his bench. Unfortunately, Griff was familiar with that infamous door leading to Ginsburg's chambers. He'd recently been on the receiving end of a severe tongue-lashing back there by the fickle judge.

Griff leaned over to Patrick. "Do you think Ginsburg heard Hilton threaten him?"

"Nah, Stone shut him up just in time," Patrick replied.

Madison's cheeks reddened to a purple hue. She wiped her forehead with her hand. Not until the deputy marshal hauled her client from the courtroom did she approach Griff and Patrick.

Sweat beaded on her upper lip. Her eyes revealed a haunted look. "I'd hoped this judge would better understand computer technology than a jury."

"Apparently, he did." AUSA O'Rourke wore a lopsided grin on his lean face. "After all, Judge Ginsburg's appointment to the bench was confirmed years ago by a majority of U.S. senators led by, you guessed it, Senator Easton. Jurors, some of whom may not approve of Congress, likely would have found your client not guilty."

"Your instincts are spot-on," Griff told Madison, one of the few defense attorneys he respected. "On my last fraud case, the jury got hopelessly deadlocked because they couldn't comprehend the financial angle."

She sighed, clinging to the handle of her litigation bag. While Griff was thrilled for the conviction, he felt sorry for her.

"I told Mr. Hilton a jury might acquit him," Madison said. "He insisted on Ginsburg. He'll appeal, claiming I gave ineffective assistance of counsel."

Patrick turned in his wheelchair, and gathering files from the prosecutor's table, he stuffed them in the lit-bag on his lap. Madison left the courtroom.

"Well done, Griff." Patrick shook his hand with vigor. "You make my job easy. Thank the other agents, analysts, and crime lab techs for me."

Griff nodded. "I will. And Madison said it herself. They would've had more success with a jury of non-legal experts. It makes no sense."

"Get ready for his appeal," the AUSA said, rolling his wheelchair from the courtroom.

Griff held open the waist-high gate to let him scoot through. This weird case was finally at an end. Relief washed over Griff like a cleansing rain after a grueling hike.

Senator Easton's chief of staff, Li Chen, had called Griff daily since Hilton's arrest demanding updates. As the trial drew near, Chen called twice a day. Griff detested the pressure.

Madison stood by the elevator. When the door swished opened, the trio rode down in silence. It wouldn't be right for Griff to blurt out, "Sorry your client gambled and lost."

Rubbing salt into a gaping wound wasn't his style. Instead, Griff began mentally to write a report documenting Hilton's conviction. He'd have to wait until the sentencing to find out if Ginsburg actually heard Hilton's threat. In either case, Griff believed Hilton deserved a longer sentence.

He waved good-bye to Patrick and Madison before hopping into the government vehicle, ready to sink his teeth into something more meaningful and less politically charged. All his current investigations for the FBI's Joint Terrorism Task Force (JTTF) seemed mundane. He despised down time and thrived on action.

Was Griff losing his passion for doing justice?

No way. He started the car, forcing political cobwebs from his mind. A new thought burned.

What about his recent meeting with Special Agent Eva Montanna, his JTTF partner from Immigration and Customs Enforcement (ICE) and Drug Enforcement Administration (DEA) Agent Brett Calloway? They were all concerned about China flooding the U.S. with explosives and illegal drugs. Griff intended to find a case worthy of their combined fifty years of investigative experience.

With renewed purpose, Griff sped to the office weaving in and out of traffic, completely unaware of the peculiar phone message waiting there for him.

GRIFF LISTENED TO THE VOICEMAIL a second time, suspicion growing over what he'd just heard. Where was Eva? He wanted her take on the troubling message. Griff trusted her instincts more than any other agent he'd worked with.

Her office cubicle was stone-cold quiet. The lights were off. So was her computer. Her desk sat empty, except for the photo of Eva and her family. Griff sensed something was wrong and went to the breakroom.

"Where's Eva?" he asked Sosa Garcia, their boss.

"You aren't up to speed." Sosa poured his coffee. "She's up on the Hill."

Griff frowned. "Why? She didn't tell me of any meeting with Congress."

The group supervisor slowly dumped sugar into his cup as if he had no cares in the world. "Nah, nothing like that. She's up there with Scott."

"Right. She's having lunch with her husband." Griff's mind tumbled to his last conversation with Eva. "That's what happens when you get wrapped up in a trial. Your life's on hold. Ginsburg found Hilton guilty on all counts."

"Speaking of Darin, he must be short a few brain cells to want that wacko judge deciding his fate," his boss said, stirring the coffee with a tiny red stick.

Griff considered asking him to hear the voicemail, then changed his mind. He helped himself to the last of the coffee and returned to his desk where he replayed the message. Every detail seared into his mind. Not recognizing the man's voice, he played it again:

"Agent Topping, it's Alan on Senator Easton's staff. The senator thanks you for your professionalism. He's sending a commendation to the FBI Director. You'll also receive an invitation to his annual charity ball."

Click.

Commendation letter? Charity ball invitation?

Griff was tired of getting annoying calls from Easton's office. So what if he'd been instrumental in solving the case against the man who threatened Senator Easton? It wasn't about a senator's importance. Griff handled the case as he would for any other victim. He bristled at the idea of a commendation. This wasn't even a major case.

He didn't want his superiors thinking he'd personally helped the senator or solicited praise. Easton had no business inviting him to a charity ball like some kind of payoff.

Griff smoothed his open palm over his moustache, his mind demanding he act. But do what?

Maybe Senator Easton played fast and loose with Hilton, failing to help him on an important matter. Or perhaps a grudge propelled Hilton to make violent threats against the senator. Those details hadn't surfaced at trial. Still, Griff couldn't help making the leap all the same.

Easton seemed like many of the one hundred senators on the Hill. Each one believed they were the most important person from their state, when in reality, they mostly wrote letters praising and schmoozing constituents. Griff would let Easton know he didn't need or want his praise.

His blood boiling, he picked up his cell phone to call Eva to see if she was heading back to the office. Spotting an unread text, he opened Dawn's message sent two minutes ago:

Sweetheart, are you free for dinner?

Thoughts of his wife brought immediate calmness to his mind. She answered his call right away.

"You are quick," she said chuckling. "Darling Griff, is it a date?"

The way she said his name, Griff pictured her smile beaming from across the four miles from his office to hers. He exhaled every misgiving.

"Dinner sounds great," he said. "I've got good news about my case."

He heard his wife catch her breath in his ear before saying softly, "We'll celebrate, and keep an open mind. I have a surprise for you."

"What surprise?" he demanded.

Dawn laughed lightly. "If I tell you, it won't be a surprise, will it? You've been so busy at your trial, I haven't said lately how much I love you."

The words *I love you too* stayed stuck in Griff's throat as Sosa sauntered by his cubicle. Griff cleared his throat, telling Dawn in his most professional-sounding voice, "I'll get back to you."

"Super! I've gotta run," she chirped. "My one o'clock is here. Let's have Italian."

She hung up, leaving Griff to fume. He'd had enough surprises for one day. He shrugged off irritation and called Anthony's to make reservations. He waited on hold, his mind combing every important date to find a clue for Dawn's surprise.

Eva Montanna entered her cubicle waving at Griff.

He held a hand over the phone receiver. "I'm making dinner reservations. Dawn says we celebrating her surprise for me."

"Oh?" Eva dropped her purse onto the desk. "Any idea what it is?"

"No. Are you involved somehow?"

Eva shook her head. "Don't look to me for help. I passed two accidents on the way to the office. Texting is involved, I'm sure."

"It's not my birthday or hers," Griff said. "It's not our anniversary."

He set the reservation for seven, then asked Eva, "How's Scott?"

"I had my own surprise." Eva blinked. "He wants a new job. Political wrangling as press secretary for the Speaker of the House has gotten to him. Sec Def is lobbying for him to return to the Defense Department."

Griff whistled. "What do you think about the change?"

"I'm not sure. He agreed to decide after we return from the fundraiser I'm organizing at the Biltmore."

"Give yourself time," Griff suggested, powering up his computer.

Eva walked over. "Is the jury still out?"

"It was a bench trial and Ginsburg found him guilty. Hilton's going to prison for a long time."

"Way to go, partner," she said.

They traded high fives, and Griff asked her, "Do you think China is trying to create havoc inside the U.S.?"

"You read my mind," Eva replied. "Mark your calendar We're set to meet Brett next Tuesday at noon. He's briefing us on how China is disguising shipments of illegal explosives and drugs coming over the border."

"Sounds like a plan," Griff said, ready to tackle a new challenge. "Listen to this voicemail I got from Easton's office after the verdict."

He hit play and watched Eva's eyes narrow. Then she shrugged. "After what Scott shared about highly political nutjobs on the Hill, I advise you to forget it and do what you do best. Pursue the bad guys."

"I was pretty steamed, Eva," Griff admitted. "Your advice is good as usual."

Chapter 2

Griff held Dawn's hand as they walked along a slippery sidewalk into their favorite Italian restaurant in Manassas, Virginia. He'd tucked an umbrella under his arm in case the skies opened up again. Smells of tomato sauce simmering with garlic tickled his nose. His mouth watered. Candles flickered on the tables. Griff ignored the romantic setting because his mind was stuck on something else.

What surprise was Dawn hiding? Maybe she was about to lose her probation officer job due to federal budget cuts.

The hostess took them to a cozy table in a separate alcove. She put down two paper menus saying, "This must be a special occasion. Our alcove is usually reserved for parties of six or more."

Griff pulled out a chair for Dawn, telling the hostess, "My wife and I are celebrating, so yes, it's a special evening."

He took a seat across from Dawn, concerned by shadows flickering through her tired, dark eyes. She brushed a lock of rich, ebony hair behind her ear. Was that a sad sigh he heard?

He reached for her hand and smiled his most winning smile. Griff beat down guilt pangs for not showing her these past few weeks how much he cared. He'd been too involved with Senator Easton's case. The love of his life sat across from him and Griff intended to make up for his unfortunate misstep right now. First things first.

He pressed her hand with his fingertips. "You have a surprise for me. Tell me if it's good or bad. Then we can enjoy our meal with no clouds over our celebration."

"It's perfectly sunny in my corner. No clouds." Dawn stifled a yawn. "I'd rather save my news for dessert. Tell me about your day."

Griff squared his shoulders and flipped over the menu. "You insist on holding me in suspense. Let's order an appetizer to tide me over. I'm swimming in coffee."

The server arrived and took their order for zucchini fries with marinara sauce and two diet colas with extra lime.

Griff squeezed Dawn's hand the moment they were alone again. "I'm thrilled to be with the woman I love and respect."

"Hahaha." Dawn's face crinkled into a smile. Tiredness vanished from her eyes. "I'm on to you. You think praising me will get me to tell you my news, right?"

Griff pulled back his hand to unfold his napkin. "Such a thought never crossed my mind. Every word I said is true."

"I love being here with you, too. We're celebrating your case?"

"Yup. Hilton's trial for threatening Senator Easton ended today."

His wife had a way of cutting to the chase. "Guilty as usual? Did the trial reveal his reason for making threats?"

"Not really." Griff shrugged. "I think the senator's office knows. I've long felt Easton's staffer, Li Chen, showed too much interest in the case."

Dawn lifted her pretty chin. "Are you alleging something?"

"Perhaps. Easton is chair of the Foreign Relations committee. He assigned Li Chen to work on the subcommittee on Asia. We received an anonymous tip that Hilton bribed someone on Easton's staff to insert an amendment into a trade bill to benefit Hilton. Maybe he never got what he paid for."

"What does his company do?"

"He develops computer chip technology. Hilton was working with Chen to get an exemption on a tariff bill."

"Is that why you objected to Chen's excessive attention?" Dawn smiled. "Always the enforcer, trying to keep the playing field level."

Griff looked around for a server to bring him a refill, telling her, "Hilton put on one witness, his wife. She testified he had an alibi. She lied under oath, saying her husband couldn't have sent the senator a threatening email because they were eating lunch together at Crabbies on the River when it happened."

"Wow!" Dawn's hand flew to her mouth. "We might have eaten there at the same time. Oh, not for lunch. We last had Crabbies' famous blue crab cakes for dinner."

"I've learned to respect your memory."

Her recall continued to amaze Griff, though it shouldn't. After the server refilled their drinks, Griff told Dawn more of the trial, including how Hilton's wife testified he never used his phone or computer during their lunch.

Griff sipped his cola, adding, "Because the judge recognized Hilton's computer expertise, I'm sure he realized even a novice could have typed and disguised the origin of an email while sending it from his smart phone and dining with his wife."

The server brought them a tempting platter of zucchini fries and mega-sauce.

"At last," Griff muttered under his breath. He dropped his voice and said with a zucchini fry in his hand, "I caught a glimpse of his attorney's twisted face. Believe me, it wasn't her idea to have the wife testify."

"What do you make of it?" Dawn asked, dipping a fry into the sauce.

"It makes me appreciate your excellent qualities. You'd never stoop to lying for me, even though I know how much you love me."

Dawn flashed him a dazzling smile. "Honey, I married you knowing you'd never put me in such a position."

"It was awful," Griff said abruptly, scowling.

Dawn dropped her fry and looked around for the server. "If you don't like the zucchini, let's order something else."

"No, these are good. I mean the bench trial. The sympathetic look on Ginsburg's face while Mrs. Hilton testified made me squirm. He was buying her line and I knew then we were about to lose the case."

Dawn held her zucchini in midair. "I considered watching from the back, but I didn't want to pressure you. So I'm guessing you're sorry you lost? If so, what are we celebrating?"

"Hold on a sec." Griff wagged his finger. "The threat to the senator happened last November, right? When Mrs. Hilton testified that is when they ate at Crabbie's, I wrote a note to Patrick O'Rourke that said, *Crabbie's closes for the season at the end of October.*"

"Brilliant! Now whose memory rocks!" she said, smiling.

"Dawn, if you could've seen Patrick getting the wife to say repeatedly, 'Yes, sir, I'm dead certain of the date, and I don't mean maybe, baby.'"

"She actually said that in court?"

Griff chuckled and squeezed lime into his soda. "Perhaps I embellished the *baby* part. Anyway, when Patrick reminded her Crabbie's was closed during November, she deflated like a leaking balloon."

"My hero." Dawn touched his cheek. "How did Judge Ginsburg react?"

"Madison objected, claiming Patrick had no evidence of the restaurant's calendar. Ginsburg asked for proof and I figured he was on the verge of caving. Patrick asked for a recess to check Crabbie's website. The audience started rumbling and a reporter shot straight outta the courtroom."

"Griff, to hear you tell it is like having a front row seat."

"As a probation officer, you sometimes do. Want to hear what happened next?"

Griff finished off the appetizer before she said, "Absolutely!"

He picked up where he'd left off. "Ginsburg demands quiet in the courtroom, and waves off any break, insisting he will determine the veracity of the wife's testimony and its weight."

"Sounds reasonable," she said.

"Still, I didn't trust Ginsburg, and can't put my finger on why. In the end, he found Hilton guilty. The guy erupted like a tornado let loose."

Dawn gave him a lingering look. "Here's something for you to mull over our spaghetti and meatballs, which I hope arrive soon. Do you hear my stomach growling? I ate no lunch today."

"You should have said. Here's me eating all the zucchini and talking nonstop. Tell me about your day."

"Nothing unusual at work. Here's something wonderful." Dawn's eyes shone like a bright sunny day. "Pastor Crandall is leading a trip to Israel. They have four openings, and I want us to be two of them."

Griff stared in disbelief. "A trip to the Middle East? How soon?"

"Before you say no, we both have plenty of vacation time stored up. Since hearing of the tour, I've been praying and waited for your trial to finish."

"Thanks, because I'd like to pray too."

"My heart says we should go. Griff, you know I've wanted nothing more than to spend time with you in the land where Jesus lived."

Griff couldn't deny it. She'd been telling him since last Christmas how she wanted them to travel to the Sea of Galilee where Jesus taught while on earth.

Should we even go there? he wondered.

Israeli news reported violent tensions escalating, especially in Jerusalem. Missiles being fired at nighttime. Riots on the Temple Mount.

He hedged. "Ah ... sounds great. I suspect our passports have expired."

"Don't try that excuse. I looked this morning. They're good for five more years."

Their eyes met. Dawn returned his probing look. Delight danced in her eyes. His heart turned. Suddenly he wanted nothing more than to give his wife the desires of her heart. He couldn't say no.

Besides, Eva would cover for him if anything urgent erupted.

Griff clasped Dawn's smaller hands into his larger ones. "As I said when we sat down, you're an amazing wife. When do we leave on our incredible adventure?"

Chapter 3

The following Tuesday morning dawned fine and clear with no storms in the April forecast. Eva Montanna rode the elevator to her office at the FBI Joint Terrorism Task Force, recalling her fun family times. A smile reached down into her heart. She'd spent a pleasant weekend with Scott and their three children, yet Eva looked back upon Saturday and Sunday with more than simple gratitude.

All her family was safe and sound with no trouble landing at her door. Before she could prevent it, a seed of doubt sprung up like a vicious weed she needed to pull.

What about Kaley?

Eva could see in her mind's eye Kaley pushing away pancakes and dashing off with her friend Lexi on Saturday morning. The teens had huddled in the den to finish homework when the phone rang. Eva could still hear Kaley call out, "We're going to help Fred set up the new iPad his daughter gave him."

The door had slammed and *poof!* Kaley and Lexi disappeared to help old Fred across the street.

Anxiety for her soon-to-be nineteen-year-old daughter's future roared through Eva like a speeding car with no brakes. Kaley would start college this fall. Eva hardly saw her now as it was. What might happen when she was out of Eva's sight and control?

"Kaley reached out to a neighbor. Quit being so negative," Eva muttered to herself as she exited the elevator, the heavy purse weighing on her shoulder.

She turned her thoughts to yesterday's worship at church. Her pastor's message about praying in times of trial had lifted her spirits. She shouldn't let fears over the future dampen her joy. Scott had declared her chicken dinner a "sumptuous feast." His words of praise made her giggle. Yet her mind wasn't ready to relinquish her right as a parent to worry.

She passed Griff's office cubicle asking him, "How was your weekend?"

"Exhausting."

He quit looking at his cell phone and strode toward her.

"Are you doing remodeling I don't know about?" she asked.

"Dawn and I shopped Saturday for new luggage and gear for our upcoming trip to Israel. I'm worn out before we even leave."

"I'd love to return as a tourist," Eva said without a touch of envy. "You and I have been to Israel for work, not pleasure."

He fiddled with his cell phone. "Don't let Dawn know I'm on

edge about our safety. Hey, forget I said anything. How are Scott and the kids?"

"I should follow your lead and quit dwelling on problems," Eva replied. "Scott worked on the riding lawn mower with Andy and Dutch. He wants our boys to handle yard duties this summer. I think they're too young."

"And Kaley?" Griff stared at his cell as if distracted.

When it rang, as if on cue, he ducked over to his desk to take the call. Eva dropped her purse into the desk drawer with a thud, debating if she should accept a recent invitation. Irene DeVroom, a friend at church, wanted Eva to attend a half-day prayer event for women at church. Women were being urged to come pray for their families and the nation. Concerns about Kaley and Lexi loomed large, prompting Eva to turn on her office computer and send Irene an email accepting.

That done, Eva picked up her travel mug to get more coffee and nearly ran into Sosa Garcia, the FBI group supervisor hurrying into her cubicle.

He raised his dark eyebrows. "Eva, two inspectors are here from ICE's OPR. They're waiting in the conference room. I hated telling them you were late."

"A multi-car accident on the freeway snarled traffic," Eva replied, scowling. "I had no idea OPR would be here or I could've left earlier."

Eva's palms began sweating. She gripped the insulated coffee mug. Agents from the Office of Professional Responsibility were the "felony squad" of internal investigators who went after ICE employees for engaging in improper conduct. They had no reason to probe her cases. She set down the coffee mug, wanting her hands free to deal with whatever these "suits" had in mind.

"What do they want?" Sosa drew his brows together.

"I have no idea." Eva forced a shrug and gathered her wits. "If they're investigating another ICE agent, I haven't worked with any since joining the task force."

"Their being here worries me, Eva."

He blocked her from leaving. On a whim, she slid open the drawer and grabbed her purse just in case she needed her cell phone. Also, her .40 caliber Glock was nestled in it. She hoped she didn't need her gun.

She faced her boss. "To quote my Grandpa Marty, 'Don't borrow tomorrow's trouble.' I'll let you know."

Her boss backed away and went over to Griff who hung up from his call. Eva strode to the conference room, head held high. She entered the room. A man and a woman, both dressed in business attire, stood and extended their hands.

The female agent took the lead. "Agent Montanna, I'm Tiffany York. Stan Houseman and I are assigned to OPR at ICE Headquarters."

Like clones, they each presented leather credential cases, their shiny gold badges affixed to the covers. Eva pressed her lips together, and taking York's case, she flipped it open. The photo and description confirmed Inspector Tiffany York was indeed an ICE headhunter. Anxiety grew. Inspector York had broad authority to intimidate the accused.

Eva must stop thinking like this. She wasn't accused of anything.

She handed York back the credentials. "Just like mine; however, mine still says 'Special Agent.'"

"Hmmm." York's eyes narrowed behind enormous glasses. "Right."

Inspector Houseman offered Eva his credentials, which she refused. "Inspector York just vouched for you. Take a seat. How can I help?"

Both inspectors sat grimly across the long table from Eva. York pulled a paper from a valise, which she passed across to Eva, whose heart thumped when she saw what it was—an "Advice of Rights" form.

Eva glared at the interlopers. How dare they? Her blood pressure skyrocketed.

"Inspectors York and Houseman, I suspect I have as many years, if not more, on the job than you both. I know my rights. I'm aware of what Title 18 of the U.S. criminal code says about lying to a federal agent. I suggest you come right to the point about your reason for this unexpected visit."

"Agent Montanna." Inspector Houseman slid his chair a bit closer to the table. "Then you know it's a formality."

Eva surveyed him before shifting her eyes to York. "I interview many suspects alone, and take along a witness and advice of rights form when I'm looking for usable evidence. How about dealing with me as your equal and I'll decide if I sign your form and talk further."

"Fair enough," Houseman said. He took her hint and began again. "We're here to interview you because the FBI wanted to, and our ICE director wouldn't let them."

"I note you use 'interview' for 'interrogate,' but go ahead," Eva said, smirking.

Houseman smiled sheepishly. "Instead of the FBI, Inspector

York and I are here to interview you."

"That makes sense." Eva leaned back, relieved. "I'm on the FBI Joint Task Force and work mostly with FBI agents. Does one of them have a problem I can help solve?"

"No." York shook her head vehemently. "The FBI is interested in *you.*"

Eva sat erect. Concern assailed her mind. "Why?"

"Do you, or does anyone you know, use the name Kaley Van on social media?" York asked, her tone gruff, unfriendly.

"Because someone using that name made derogatory comments about a member of Congress running for re-election, right?" Eva replied.

York nodded, holding Eva in her glare. "Was it you?

"No. I'm interested in knowing why you think it was me."

"The social media account used a computer or iPad with an IP account issued to you," York declared.

Eva put her hands palms up on the table. "Let me tell you a story, which should answer your questions."

York immediately began making notes. Eva had no problem with that. She'd do the same.

"My husband Scott and I have three kids. Our oldest daughter Kaley is about to graduate from high school. If you have kids, you know they yield to social pressure and therefore MUST have a smart phone and whatever social media accounts and apps are currently cool."

Eva studied Stanley Houseman's face wondering if he had teens. She read no clues in his unwavering steely-blue eyes.

She drew in a deep breath. "Because my job is sensitive, as is my husband's, we didn't want Kaley on social media. However, we relented to her constant pleading when she agreed to use the name Kaley Van. My maiden name is Vander Goes."

"Two words, ending in Goes?" York clarified.

"Yes," Eva said. "Kaley agreed I'd have her password and review her content. All was fine until a friend from church who has a similar agreement with her daughter called to warn me of the untruthful posting about the senator appearing on Kaley's page."

"You're aware of it?" Stanley interrupted his notetaking to glare at Eva.

"Of course." Eva stared back. "What kind of investigator am I if I don't know what my kids are doing?"

"What did you do?" York probed, her voice sharp.

"First, I logged into her account and found no such posting. My friend sent me a screen shot of what appeared on her page purporting to be one of Kaley's posts."

"You're claiming Kaley didn't make the post?" York asked.

"Exactly," Eva said. "I concluded Kaley's password was compromised and some Russian bot started launching lies in hopes of effecting the upcoming election. I changed the password. We've had no problems since."

Having given her explanation, Eva stopped to study both inspectors. When they finished their notes, she asked, "That's what you came to see me about?"

York looked up and adjusted her glasses. "Basically, yes."

"It doesn't seem like a matter demanding two inspectors and an advice of rights warning," Eva said in a belittling tone.

Inspector York laid down her pen with a loud crack. "Our chief inspector insisted on obstructing the FBI from talking to you. You know why? Because he discovered the FBI went to ICE asking questions about you, your career and address. So our chief went to the FBI's OPR chief to insist we take over."

Eva was about to ask why when York laughed out loud. "It was kinda funny. At first, the FBI denied they were snooping around in our agency, but later apologized."

Eva had no words. What was going on at the FBI?

"We kid you not." Stanley smiled at Eva. "We received a call from Department of Defense. Guess what? The FBI also inquired about your husband, and when they asked about you in a roundabout fashion, the DoD Inspector General finally notified us."

Shock coursed through Eva. Before she could respond, Tiffany took up the story, "We didn't realize your husband is press secretary for the Speaker of the House of Representatives. He used to be press secretary for the Secretary of Defense. Our chief inspector is concerned political activists within the FBI might leak it that your husband is sabotaging opponents. That's why we insisted on taking over the FBI's investigation of one of our own."

The tips of Eva's ears burned hot. All she could manage was, "Do you know which group or office of the FBI is behind the smears?"

"Eva, it took us a while to figure out," Tiffany explained. "It's not an office we typically work with. Turns out, the Counterintelligence section at the FBI Headquarters is behind it, which is why they held it so tightly in their system."

"Don't get me started," Eva grumbled. "I won't waste your time. I've had little respect for CI agents during my career. They shouldn't be called agents. In truth, they're more like intelligence analysts. Most of them never sign a search warrant, make an arrest, or can investigate their way out of a wet paper bag."

Stanley didn't stop smiling as he nodded in agreement. Eva leaned forward, surprised the inspectors had suddenly grown friendly.

"What next?" Eva asked.

York shoved pen and papers into her valise. "We talk to our chief inspector. We won't give them anything you said today, or they'll leak it to the press to help their political friends by embarrassing the Speaker of the House."

"I never dreamed Scott would be dragged into this," Eva replied, upset Kaley started the social media account.

Tiffany winked at Eva. "Leave it to us. Now that we know it's bots, we'll stall and obstruct the FBI. Meanwhile, Kaley should get a new social media identity. You all be super careful to safeguard your passwords."

"My sentiments exactly, Tiffany," Eva replied with force.

She shook their hands before leading them out of the JTTF office. She sensed this visit from Tiffany and Stanley, her new OPR friends, had revealed the tip of a very dangerous government-wide iceberg, one meant to harm Eva and her family.

AN HOUR LATER, AGENT GRIFF TOPPING LISTENED to his new voicemail message a second time. No doubt the distinctive voice and accent belonged to a secret agent with Israeli Mossad. Griff had met Judah Levitt in Israel previously. Judah, failing to identify himself, stayed true to his secretive ways.

The Mossad agent's words and possible meaning behind them troubled Griff. He tapped replay and listened again: "Griff, call me tomorrow at ten in the morning, your time, from a secure phone. You and Eva should avoid using your cell phones. Turn them off."

Short and sweet and loaded with intrigue. Griff pulled his cell from his pocket and inspected it, wondering if it was looking at him.

What was it doing? What was it capable of doing?

He prepared to turn it off, but decided to first call Dawn and also Eva. Nope, that would be a mistake. He quickly shut off his cell. Eva's cubicle was dark. He wanted to warn her, but where was she?

To find out, he strode into his supervisor's office, demanding Sosa tell him where to find Eva. Sosa didn't bother looking up from his computer screen. He appeared to be reading an agent's report on his computer. It looked like the one Griff submitted after Hilton's guilty verdict. Not wanting to rattle Sosa before he approved his report, Griff waited, giving his boss plenty of time.

Finally, Sosa glanced up. "I hoped you'd tell me. After those two ICE OPR inspectors interviewed her, Eva rushed out of here without saying boo."

"Yikes," Griff said, puzzled. "OPR interviewed Eva?"

Griff's mind whirled. Why were OPR inspectors after Eva? Given Judah's cryptic message, his unease doubled. He resisted asking his boss. He'd find out from Eva's own lips.

Sosa had other ideas. "Okay, out with it. You and Eva work on tons of stuff together. You must have some idea of why she's aroused OPR's interest."

"Me? I can shed no light." Griff flinched at the very mention of OPR. "You know Eva is a straight arrow. Maybe they interviewed her for a character reference."

Sosa glowered. "Come on, Griff. You know it doesn't take two inspectors to conduct reference interviews."

"Your point is valid." Griff ran a hand down his moustache. "I'm heading to a noon conference with Agent Calloway. Eva's supposed to be there."

Griff left Sosa's office frustrated that Eva hadn't left a note. Judah's warning prevented him from calling her cell phone. He supposed she'd be at their lunch meeting with Brett. If she failed to show, he'd know something serious was brewing.

Chapter 4

Eva knew nothing about Judah's ominous message to Griff and forgot about her noon meeting. She stopped at a red light. With the hands-free feature on her cell, she phoned Kaley. Her daughter's phone simply rang.

The light turned green. Eva raced to the Trumpet's Call where Kaley volunteered. She was prepared to hang up when Kaley answered, sounding breathless.

"Mom, I'm sorting donations. Is everything okay?"

"Meet me in five minutes, outside. Bring your phone."

"My phone? Why?"

"Just come outside."

Eva ended the call. The sight of Kaley's cute lime-green Beetle Bug in the parking lot gave her pause. Why let OPR inspectors cause division between her and Kaley? She needed to calm down. In that moment, love for Kaley filled Eva's heart.

Her smart and vivacious daughter, a senior in high school, volunteered twice a week at the Trumpet's Call to raise money for orphans and children in foster care. School credit for an independent study was a bonus Kaley didn't care about. She longed to help those in need.

The idea to repurpose clothing and household goods had been the brainchild of Irene DeVroom and her husband Fritz. The couple had raised more than forty foster children, adopting several into their family.

Eva enjoyed her church friends, though today she wouldn't go inside to greet them. Kaley hustled out the back door, her long brown hair blowing in the breeze. Eva pulled up alongside and motioned for her to climb in the passenger seat.

"Kaley, sorry to be curt. Remember when we changed your password?"

"I can't forget." Kaley sighed. "A hacker posted a creepy comment on my page like it was from me."

Eva held out her hand. "From the two inspectors who quizzed me today, it's regrettably front and center again. Give me your phone."

"Mom, I thought that was over. You can't have my phone," Kaley insisted.

She stared at the cell in her hand as if Eva had asked to take away her favorite puppy, and gripped it fiercely.

"I'm not fooling around. Give it to me. Before Dad and I buy you a new one, if we ever do, I need to uncover the problem with your account. Someone may be trying to get me or Dad fired."

"That's terrible!" Kaley's eyes grew wide. "Who would do such a thing?"

"I have no idea. I'll be trying to solve it the rest of the day."

Eva had a funny feeling someone was staring at her. With a start, she looked out the side window. Irene stood by the side of Eva's car, her face blossoming into a crinkly smile. Eva lowered the window.

"Kaley said you were here. I wanted to say hello," Irene said. "Many thanks for helping our daughter Cora plan the Trumpet's Call fundraiser."

The two women chatted about details for the upcoming event at the Biltmore Hotel in Asheville, North Carolina. Their conversation was cut short when Kaley's phone rang in Eva's hand.

She checked the screen. "Kaley, it's Lexi. Let her know not to call this number again as you're getting a new phone. Then hang up."

Kaley took back the phone, and Eva whispered to Irene, "You and Fritz come for dinner Friday night. We'll finalize the Biltmore plans."

"We can't," Irene lamented. "We're taking some of our belongings to Cora's that day. She wants us to move into the guesthouse behind their Middleburg home."

Eva patted her hand out the window. "Your move is sooner than I realized. Middleburg is true horse country and beautiful."

"Cora insists we downsize. She contacted an agent to sell our townhouse. When Fritz and I moved from Pennsylvania three years ago after Cora's marriage, we had no idea his heart problems would turn serious. She wants to keep an eye on her daddy. On me too, I suppose."

Eva nodded at Irene. "We ladies in the prayer group will pray for God's help in your move, and that He will bring you a new beginning."

"Ah!" Irene declared. "'See, I am doing a new thing! Now it springs up; do you not perceive it? I am making a way in the wilderness and streams in the wasteland.'"

"That's a Bible verse in Isaiah, right?" Eva asked.

Irene nodded, her eyes getting a faraway look. "Those verses mean much to us. We prayed those over our foster children when they came to live with us, Cora included. You are encouraging me greatly."

"I am?" A smile spread across Eva's lips. "I came here for another purpose."

Irene replied with her own smile. "I believe God is using you to fulfill His purposes. As He is using Cora to nudge us into His perfect plan."

"Don't forget Christ strengthens you to do all things," Eva assured her friend.

Irene wiped tears from her eyes and Kaley finished her phone call, telling Eva, "Lexi's on board. She'll wait for my new number. Here's my phone."

LATER THAT EVENING, Eva served a quick supper of chicken tenders and sweet potato fries she'd picked up on the way home. Her fifteen-year-old son Andy helped by loading plates into the dishwasher. Her younger son Dutch labored over math problems in his room.

Eva headed for the family room to join Scott when the house phone rang. It seemed only solicitors ever called their home line. Eva checked the muted TV screen to confirm her suspicion. This time she was wrong.

"Hey, Griff, you never call from your landline phone," Eva said. "What gives?"

"Eva, you tell me. Is everything okay?" Griff barked, dispensing with niceties. "I heard about your unwanted visitors today at the office."

"I'm all right and will explain in person, not over the phone."

Griff grunted. "Roger that. I wondered because you blew off our meeting with Brett."

"Yikes, that was today? Those two unwelcome visitors wiped my memory clean."

"I figured something like that happened," he replied. "I would've called sooner, but I've been out buying a new cell phone. It took hours."

"Why do you need a new cell? I have to get Kaley a new one tomorrow after what happened to me."

"Won't say more," Griff said abruptly. "Turn yours off, pronto. Keep it off. Meet me tomorrow at the office first thing. We're calling our biblical friend from a SCIF."

Eva's mind went full bore wondering what Griff meant. She wouldn't ask any more because he wouldn't say.

Finally, she managed, "Is it related to the unwanted visitors today?"

"No more talk," Griff ordered.

The line went dead. Eva weighed his words, assuming tomorrow they'd phone Israeli Mossad Agent Judah Levitt from a

Sensitive Compartmented Information Facility, or SCIF, at FBI Headquarters. The reason must be ultrasensitive.

With the kids occupied in their rooms, Eva thumped down next to Scott on the sofa, telling him, anxiety ringing in her voice, "Today, OPR harassed me over the derogatory comment posted from Kaley's phone. Now Griff orders me not to use my cell phone. Are we in trouble here?"

Husband and wife looked into each other's eyes seeking answers. Eva saw the unmistakable flicker of worry in Scott's eyes. They needed each other. They needed to think clearly. Scott rarely succumbed to emotion.

He pressed her hand into his. "Eva, these inspectors can't believe you, a highly respected agent, wrote derogatory comments on social media about a U.S. Senator?"

"It's pure garbage. I'm sick of it." Eva squeezed his hand, absorbing his strength into hers. "What I'm trying to decipher is how and why does it involve my phone as Griff just warned? Are Kaley's social media postings causing us more problems?"

A disturbing hush engulfed them until Scott asked, "Is it your personal cell, or your government phone?"

"Good question. I'm not sure. I think my personal one."

"Eva, it makes no sense for you to carry two phones," Scott sympathized.

"I don't. That's why I forward my work phone to my personal one. I can tell from the incoming call if it's related to work."

Scott held on to her hand. "You're one wise woman. What else did Griff say?"

"He and I will make an important call in the morning. Then I should know more."

Her brain firing on all cylinders, Eva added, "Kaley and I need new phones and numbers. We'll create new contact lists, rather than transfer old data to the new phones. What about yours?"

"I wonder." He swiped his cell phone from the side table. "You've got me concerned about mine."

"Since OPR ambushed me, I've thought of little else. Griff's cautionary call gives us plenty to worry about. Where's the threat coming from?"

Scott fiddled with his cell phone until Eva placed a hand over it.

"Do you trust FBI agents you encounter?" she asked softly.

"What?" he demanded. "You work with them every day. Griff's our good friend. Are you suggesting he's gone to the dark side?"

"No, not Griff. It's something else ..."

Her voice trailed away. Eva debated if she should voice all she was thinking.

Scott grabbed her hand. "If it's classified, I don't expect you to tell me. This sounds like it involves our family and I'd like to know."

"Here goes." She exhaled. "I work with some of the best investigators in the world. There's nothing I wouldn't do for most FBI agents, but Scott, the FBI is investigating you and me to see how we're connected to Kaley's phone and vulgar comments about a U.S Senator. They should've warned us that we're being targeted by someone."

"Honey, you're believing the worst. Maybe they were being thorough before approaching us."

"No. There's something I didn't tell you. Even worse than the FBI never telling my agency of their interest in me, the FBI was sneaking around the Department of Defense trying to uncover more about you and your family."

"Me?" Scott thrust his thumbs into his chest. "They're coming after me?"

Eva swung her arms around in the air. "Exactly! Ever since I left their interrogation, I've been trying to discern what's really going on."

"I need to get up to speed," Scott said. "It could be routine, but I don't want our lives in the hands of agents I don't know or trust."

His eyes burned as they locked onto Eva's.

She wasn't finished. "They seem to believe Kaley targeted a senator she's probably never heard of."

"It's unbelievable."

Eva agreed and fought for control. "They don't know how thoughtful and nice she is. Hopefully, they'll follow logical leads now that I've sent them looking elsewhere."

"Our daughter is too compassionate," Scott said forcefully. "That kid her friend Lexi hangs out with. What's his name? Conman?"

"Funny. His name is Conner. He's a year older than Kaley and graduated last year in Florida. What about him?"

"You make my point. Why is Conner hanging around with younger girls? I don't want Kaley in his company."

She stood. "Fine. I don't like his casual attitude toward Lexi either. He acts like he's a rock star."

"He peeled out of the driveway last time he was here," Scott complained. "Andy and I had a tough time getting his black marks off the cement driveway."

"As her dad, you go tell her. She'll take it better from you since

I took her phone away," Eva said with a wave.

Scott picked up his cell phone again. "I'll turn this off tonight. Good thing we never disconnected our landline."

"I'm treating myself to a hot bath and reading a devotional on prayer," Eva said.

"You deserve to relax." He hugged her tight. "We make a pretty good team."

"It helps talking challenges over with you," she said. "Let's hope tomorrow we're more in control."

Chapter 5

Ensconced in the SCIF, Eva temporarily put aside misgivings about being inside the FBI Headquarters. She refused to become paranoid. She and Griff waited for a security technician to connect their call to Mossad Headquarters in Tel Aviv, Israel. Neither she nor Griff had activated their cell phones since Judah's ominous message to Griff yesterday.

What does Judah know that we don't? Eva thought, sitting and watching a desktop telephone with Griff.

The technician stepped into the soundproof booth and pointed to a flashing light. "There's your call."

He left, closing the heavy door.

Griff punched the hands-free button and said, "Hello. This is Griff Topping."

As clear as if he were in the same booth, Judah's familiar voice and heavy accent replied, "Boker Tov."

Eva knew enough Hebrew to know Judah had just told them, "Good morning."

"Eva's here too," Griff said. "We're eager to hear what you need to tell us."

Judah greeted Eva and said, "I miss the times when matters of mutual interest permitted us to break bread together."

"Judah, perhaps this is such a matter." Eva edged her chair nearer the phone. "Griff implies we have a security lapse."

Griff interjected, "You and I may break bread soon, Judah. My wife signed us up to tour Israel. We're visiting Galilee and Jerusalem next week."

"Your tourist dollars are welcome." Judah's laughter filled the SCIF. "Could you travel a day early and see me in Tel Aviv?"

"I'll try arranging it and let you know," Griff promised.

"Good. I would meet you both, but it is unwise to be seen together in public," Judah cautioned.

Griff told Judah that Dawn would understand, adding, "She, too, is in the business, as we like to say."

"You should stay at the Shalom Hotel in Netanya. Not only will you have beautiful views of the Mediterranean Sea, you are close to my Tel Aviv office. I will come to your hotel and reveal the data prompting this call."

"We fly out Friday," Griff replied.

Eva tired of their back-and-forth. "Must we wait until then? Won't you share any info this morning?"

A pause, then Judah said, "Here is the important thing. You and

Kaley need to change your phone number. Reset your phones to the manufacturers' factory settings, which will clear your cell of any bugs and reload your information manually."

"I'm buying her a new phone," Eva shot back.

"That is good. It appears one of your phones is compromised. I guess, Eva, it is yours. Although, Griff, you should get a new number and reset yours also."

"My phone is compromised?" Eva protested. "Why mine and not Griff's?"

Judah cleared his throat. "I must be careful. Some information in a Chinese operative's computer fell into our hands. I received data to analyze because a certain number was called from my phone. I found phone numbers for people in your part of the world, including one for Eva Montanna."

"Wow," both agents replied in unison.

Griff glanced Eva's way. "Judah, any idea how Eva's data was obtained?"

"I think from contact data stored in a cell phone. It puzzles me because there is mention of Kaley, but no other contacts or of Griff."

"How can that be?" Eva wanted answers today and not after Griff went to Israel.

"Have you traveled to China or Asia lately?" Judah asked.

"Ye–es," she answered, thinking back to a previous trip. "A year ago, I flew to Hong Kong to meet Customs officials from that region."

"Did the Hong Kong border agent demand to see your phone or turn on your computer?"

"No. I did not take my computer and no one took my phone. I was careful to charge it only in my room at night."

Griff began asking, "Is it possible—" when Eva cried, "Oh no!"

She waved her hands in the air. "I used the phone charger in the airline VIP lounge while waiting to depart Hong Kong."

"The Chinese have developed software that sweeps your phone and copies your data," Judah said, his voice gruff. "They have such software on public charging stations. Did your Customs conference include the subject of importing agricultural products from China?"

"No ag imports," Eva said with confidence.

"We will not solve this today," Judah declared. "Griff, you and I will put our heads together in Tel Aviv. Meanwhile, clean up your phones and plan to see me the day you arrive. Send details. Shalom."

The light on the phone went out. Griff stood to leave the SCIF. "We've had more complicated cases, Eva. We'll piece it together with Judah's help."

"You and Dawn leave on Monday. Scott and I are heading out tomorrow with the kids, going to North Carolina for a special event for the Trumpet's Call. Keep me posted on your travel plans."

"I will," he said, reaching for the door.

Eva put a hand on his forearm. "Let me tell you what happened with OPR yesterday."

Griff resumed his seat and Eva quickly told him everything.

When she finished, Griff cautioned, "Eva, we must be extra vigilant. Yesterday, an FBI agent in Los Angeles faced angry Marxists with signs and megaphones screaming on her front lawn because she arrested one of their sympathizers. Someone doxed her, posting her address all over social media."

"I find that chilling," Eva said, putting on a brave face.

"There's more," Griff declared, his voice solemn. "The Commies kicked in her door. She managed to hold them at bay with her Glock until the riot squad showed up."

Sweat pooling on Eva's brow, she cried, "How awful! I have three precious kiddos at home. What should we do?"

He looked as alarmed as Eva felt as he said, "I'm installing another dead bolt on our front door before we head to Israel. The local police chief promised he'd have a cruiser drive by the house while we're gone."

"I'll have Scott get another lock too," Eva said. "Try and put the wackos out of your mind, but Griff, make sure Judah holds nothing back. This is serious."

"You can count on me, Eva. I'll reset my phone to factory settings as Judah suggested and change passwords."

He rose and she followed him from the SCIF, saying, "I'm shopping for a new phone after we meet Brett and will text you the new number before we leave town."

ON FRIDAY AFTERNOON, Eva struggled to banish from her mind the violence happening to other federal agents. Scott had put in another dead bolt at home and Eva's neighbor Fred was keeping an eye on things for them. Plus, Eva had obsessed yesterday over the strange happenings with OPR and her phones on their drive to Asheville.

Time was getting away from her. Eva was determined to enjoy the fundraiser in the gorgeous mountains, and rushed up a red brick walkway on the Biltmore grounds where the Vanderbilt family lived decades ago. The palatial home and its plush gardens drew visitors from across the country. Eva and Cora chose this beautiful locale for the Trumpet's Call annual fundraiser.

In God's sovereignty, when the DeVrooms moved from Lancaster to be closer to Cora in Virginia, they chose Eva's church, and before long, she and Scott met them at a Wednesday night service. She counted their friendship dear and so jumped in to help make the fundraiser a success.

The packages she carried in large paper bags tugged on Eva's shoulders. Cora had gone to rest so Eva would finish decorating by herself. She could use Scott's help, yet he seemed nowhere in sight. She'd seen him in the parking lot by the SUV, and wondered how he disappeared so quickly.

Eva strode toward the conservatory. Though she was physically away from the office, her thoughts focused on the briefing Brett gave her and Griff on Wednesday about the recent influx of drugs across the nation's southern border. Smugglers were flooding America with cocaine, methamphetamine, and fentanyl.

The JTTF worked to stop the flow of illicit drugs because terrorists around the globe used drugs to finance their terror. Much fentanyl came from China. Eva was planning a way to identify these drug cartels when her ankle twisted beneath her. Her high heel dug down into a crack between the herringbone brick configuration. She almost fell!

Eva reacted quickly, flinging out an arm to steady herself against a waist-high stone wall. Only she miscalculated. In trying to save herself from a nasty fall, she crushed a huge shopping bag filled with gifts against the brick wall.

She straightened her back and flexed her ankles. Fortunately, she felt no stabbing pain. From her many years as a federal agent, Eva wasn't easily shaken by missteps. She picked up packages of special napkins and bows that spilled out. One of the gifts looked badly squished.

"Could've been worse," she said aloud.

"What could have been worse?"

Scott ran up alongside her, his forehead beaded with sweat.

"It's beastly hot," he puffed. "I thought mountains were supposed to be cooler."

"I almost fell over, but never mind. You vanished like our kiddos do instead of finishing their chores." Eva gave Scott her full attention. "It is stifling. Why I wore jeans and a long-sleeved top to finish the setup, I can't fathom."

"Here are the flower arrangements you made for the head table." Scott adjusted two boxes, one under each arm. "They look nice, Eva."

She smiled at his compliment. "We'd better hustle. Folks will arrive soon."

"Fritz called," Scott said, breathing hard. "He and Irene have checked in. They're tired and will nap. I'm surprised they drove through the mountains at their age."

Eva collected the shopping bags. "Fritz wasn't behind the wheel. Their son John Lapp picked them up."

"Have I met him?" Scott asked, following Eva into the plant-filled conservatory.

"No. John lives in Ohio. Their youngest adopted son is quite the computer geek, or so Fritz says. He visits often. I saw him once at church, but we didn't actually meet."

Eva gazed around the towering building made of brick and glass. "It's as gorgeous in here as the online photos. The palms trees are lovely."

"So are the masses of flowers." Scott grimaced. "Why did we haul yours up here?"

Eva's heart sagged. Vases overflowing with magnificent roses of varying hues were on every table around the room.

"They look amazing," she said. "Perhaps Cora ordered them from a local florist."

"What now?" Scott sounded as baffled as Eva felt.

She quickly decided. "My informal flowers will be perfect on the outside tables."

Eva walked toward the open area when a movement caught her eye.

She stopped in her tracks, telling Scott in a hushed tone, "Someone's poking around in the corner. Who is that? The party doesn't start for two hours yet."

"Hello there," Scott shouted. "Can we help?"

A young-looking man straightened his back. As he faced them, Eva relaxed. She recognized his reddish hair, although he wore it sticking up in pieces and had the beginnings of a new beard. The man held one hand firmly against an ear.

Eva set the gift bags on a chair while Scott lowered the boxes onto another chair.

"Are you Irene and Fritz's son John?" Eva asked, holding out a hand.

"Yes. I'm John Lapp," he said, his eyes lighting. "You are?"

"Eva and Scott Montanna," she said. "We're friends of your folks from church."

They shook hands, and John immediately resumed nosing around in the plants.

"A palm branch yanked my Bluetooth from my ear," he explained, sounding sheepish. "It dropped into the ground cover, right here. I hoped to find it before the crowd comes in. Do you see it?"

The three of them scouted around. Scott used his cell phone to shine its bright light into the foliage.

"Ah ha!" Eva spotted something gleaming and scooped up a small earpiece. "Yours, I think."

"You found it! Thanks." John placed the device back in his ear.

She gazed around. "We're going to arrange the tables. Will you help?"

"Sure," he said pleasantly.

Eva asked Scott to check on the musicians. He fired off a mock salute and returned his cell phone to its holder.

Leaning close to Eva, he whispered, "What was John really doing back there in the plants? And what's with the weird chin beard? He has no moustache."

At her shrug, Scott added, "Something to consider," before hurrying off.

She turned her mind to something she could solve. John placed a table along the outer perimeter for Eva to exhibit various items for tonight's auction. Meanwhile, she set her flower arrangements on the patio tables while keeping an eye on her wristwatch.

Time was ticking. Andy and Dutch were upstairs supposedly showering. Kaley had been in the middle of blow-drying her hair when Eva and Scott hurried to their SUV for the gifts and flowers.

A sudden scraping sound made Eva flinch. She spun around. John was lifting up a patio table in one hand, and in the other he held a small object.

"Look here," he hissed, beckoning her across the patio. "Is this part of a listening device?"

"I've never seen one like it," Eva replied, after examining it.

"Have you seen many?"

"Perhaps you don't know. I'm in federal law enforcement, which leads me to question who planted this. What inspired you to check for spyware?"

John lifted his bearded chin. "Simple. The wire scratched my hand as I moved the table."

Eva narrowed her eyes, thinking of the unknown persons hacking into Kaley's phone. Were these same people tracking their movements to North Carolina? What if the same Marxists who assailed the FBI agent in LA were here and ready for Eva?

Her pulse galloped. This was not the celebratory evening she'd hoped for.

She lifted the gadget toward better light, inspecting every angle.

"Hmm … it has mildew here." Eva pointed. "See, on the side between the magnets, which held it to the table bottom."

He leaned closer, squinting. "What are you implying?"

"I don't think this bug is meant for us," Eva opined. "These wires indicate it's a battery booster for a listening device. From the mildew, I suspect it's been here a year or more. Someone probably retrieved their bug and left the booster behind."

She pressed hard to slide open the battery compartment. Two tiny batteries were both badly corroded. "Look. It's really dead."

"I'm glad I showed it to you," John said.

Eva handed it back to him with a grin. "I guess it's your souvenir."

He followed her outside to the patio. Eva noted the winds picking up and she didn't like the look of clouds swirling in a darkening sky. Scott handed her a vase of silk flowers, interrupting her concerns.

"I found this in the car," he said crisply. "Irene phoned me after leaving you a message. She wants you to call her."

Eva patted her jeans pocket. "I never heard mine ring. John and I found something unusual."

"Oh?" Scott's eyebrows shot up and he gave Eva an *I told you so* glance.

John opened his hand, revealing the battery case.

"You've got me curious," Scott said. "What is that funny-looking thing?"

"John found part of a listening device attached to a table," Eva explained. "I believe it's been there a long time so I'm not worried. The batteries are corroded."

"Whew!" Scott lifted his eyebrows. "For a minute there, I thought we might have a new Spygate on our hands."

John pocketed his find. "Any ideas how it got there?"

"Maybe high-level White House or diplomatic meetings were held here last year," Scott suggested.

"Or a company listened in to some competitors' conference to get an edge. Industrial espionage," was Eva's idea.

Thunder rumbled, echoing in the hills. Her eyes flew skyward. Threatening storm clouds whirled closer. Eva expected rain might fall any second and catch the people outside in a soggy mess. Should she move everything indoors?

Before hauling in the tables, she lifted up an earnest prayer asking God to hold off rain until *after* the festivities. It might be a small matter, but not much escaped Eva's prayer life. She had witnessed the power of bringing her requests to Almighty God.

Chapter 6

When drops of rain tickled the hairs on her head, Eva resisted panic. She lifted her eyes to the skies and stood amazed. The clouds were lessening and scattering west across the valley. She grabbed her phone to check the radar. Sure enough, the map showed the "green" rain moving rapidly west.

She whispered a prayer of thanks. Scott joined her, and she said, "God heard us. We're safe leaving the tables out here."

John began hurrying back down the walkway. Before he rounded the corner, Eva saw him speak to a tall, well-dressed man wearing a suit, then he handed him something. Moments later, both men disappeared around the bend.

Scott's caution seeped into Eva's mind and she wondered what John was up to, and who was the man? Given the unusual way he found a battery pack to a listening device, she wanted to investigate further.

Scott distracted her by asking, "Did you return Irene's call?"

"Oops, I forgot," she admitted, quickly phoning her friend as she and Scott walked to the hotel.

"Irene, sorry I didn't call sooner," Eva said as she pressed the elevator button. "Are you ready for the celebration to begin?"

Irene sighed into the phone. "Fritz is lying down. The long ride through the mountains has tired him out. John is so kind. He called before you did and is bringing us hot tea from the refreshment station."

The elevator doors opened. Scott dashed in and held the door open to let Eva finish the call. "He's one busy guy," she told Irene. "He's been helping me. Do you need anything?"

"No … yes. Cora wants to commence the program. Do you mind?"

"Not at all," Eva replied, curious why Cora hadn't told her. "See you—"

The phone disconnected, and Eva stepped into the elevator, fixing a penetrating look upon Scott.

"Honey, Cora wants to give remarks. I'm going to have to alter what I say."

"That shouldn't bother you, Eva. After all, she is their daughter."

Eva touched his shoulder. "Cora can take over being the emcee as far as I'm concerned. In fact, I asked her last week to do that very thing. She declined. Said she'd be too teary-eyed to say a word. I'm worried about some unwanted surprise."

"Ah." Scott nodded as if he understood exactly what she meant.

"You do have extra-special intuition. Like when you sensed my sister Viola was nearby and she called later that night to say she was in town."

Eva forced a smile. "I think of Viola as my sister. She and I have gotten so close through the years."

"Because you lost your sister Jillie in the Pentagon on 9/11," Scott whispered, holding her close. "Viola fills the gap we both feel."

Eva leaned against him. "Thanks for reminding me of Jillie. We should plant a new azalea in her memory when we return home."

The elevator doors slid open and they hopped out with Eva saying to Scott over her shoulder, "Let's hope no storms or anything else ruins this evening. I want Irene and Fritz to have a blessed and successful fundraiser."

TWINKLING LIGHTS STRUNG OVER the patio emitted a warm glow for the festivities. All traces of a lingering storm vanished. The sun slipped down in the west, painting the sky a vivid pink. Eva found the meal delicious and warm breezes uplifting.

A cellist began playing "Be Thou My Vision." This was Eva's cue to walk up front to start the program. If only she could have talked over this next phase with Cora, but Irene chatted with her daughter during the entire meal. It was too late to rehearse now.

Eva leaned over, asking Cora, "Are you ready to say a few words in tribute to your mother and father?"

"I think so. How long do I have?" Cora looked at Eva, her hazel eyes starting to tear.

Eva patted her hand. "Take as long as you'd like. Is everything all right with your husband? I never met him and he didn't join our table."

"Just as we reached the conservatory, he took an urgent call on his cell." Cora yanked a tissue from her purse and dabbed her eyes. "He's catching the shuttle to the airport and leaving for China."

"I'm sorry he'll miss you honoring your folks. If you're ready, I'll introduce you."

Eva walked to the dais, and using her command voice over sounds of murmurs and clinking of silverware, she said, "Thank you for coming on this special evening."

She lightly clapped her hands. A hush fell over the group. Eva gathered the love she had for Irene and Fritz and asked them to stand. They did, holding hands.

"And now, will all of you who were raised by these two wonderful people stand along with them," Eva said pleasantly.

Slowly, one by one, thirty men and women rose to their feet.

The guests began clapping softly at first and then a tremendous burst of applause resounded, lofting up into the sky that now turned pure gold. Eva motioned for everyone to resume their seats.

"Irene and Fritz, you've opened your hearts and home to many children the Lord brought to your path. Over the years, you've fostered more than forty children, raising many to adulthood. You've known your share of joy and grief, yet both remain steadfast in your devotion and Christian faith."

A smattering of applause interrupted Eva's train of thought. She inhaled, and continued when things grew quiet.

"Fritz and Irene never planned to be foster parents. After the unexpected death of their daughter Lizzy at age seven, a wise social worker from their Pennsylvania church found a way to refocus their pain and grief. Thirteen-year-old Cora Allison was a ward of the state after her mother was killed in a car accident. Cora was already missing her father who died much earlier in a SEAL team training accident."

A few murmurs prompted Eva to pause. She smiled warmly at Cora, telling those assembled, "Because Cora was a teenager with no known relatives, the social worker encouraged Irene and Fritz to take her home. It was a good match. The loving couple had boundless energy and Cora was like a prickly cactus. The more she resisted their love and care, the more they tried."

Eva spotted Cora sliding a tissue over her eyes. Irene patted her hand.

"Cora's friends can testify to the miraculous transformation in her life," Eva said. "She bloomed under the kindness and structure Irene and Fritz showed. The hurting teen became a love sponge, and an 'A' student, popular with classmates. The day the judge finalized the adoption of Cora by the DeVrooms started a long parade of boys and girls who received a loving family. Many, but not all, have their own success story."

Eva turned her attention to Irene and Fritz. "We gather here, not only to thank you for your incredible investment in the children and for heeding God's call on your lives, but also to raise money for the Trumpet's Call, your thrift shop that helps foster children and families in need."

More applause. Eva ventured into an area she hadn't been sure she would share. She lifted an arm across the many tables of smiling people who had flown and driven to the Biltmore from around the country.

"We're guests tonight of Cora and Marlow Bryson, who not only picked up the tab for this event, they also paid travel and lodging costs for some. Unfortunately, Marlow was called away this evening. Cora, please say a few words."

Cora walked to the microphone, her fine tailored jacket and long silken skirt a far cry from her impoverished early childhood. She raised the microphone as she stood even taller than Eva.

Her smile at her parents brought a rich glow to her pretty face. "Mom and Dad, it's your unfailing love and faith in God I remember most. You influenced my life while shepherding me through college and into a career as a teacher."

"Mark," Cora nodded at her foster brother, "you and I were there as we went from an expanded dinner table to the large picnic table. We supervised younger kids in setting the table and re-setting it for a second dinner shift. For each of us, there was a period of fear and mistrust as we tested our new foster parents. Most quickly we discovered Mom and Dad showed us more love than we'd ever known."

Cora laughed. "They imposed strict rules about homework and bedtime. Each Sunday, we loaded into two family vans and were taken to church. They didn't demand we follow their religion, but by going with them, we discovered the source of their love. We sang songs of God's love and our parents insisted we show each other kindness. When I went to college, I wasn't religious, but I recall being offended when my professor quoted Karl Marx who wrongly believed religion was the opium of the masses."

"Mom and Dad." Cora looked at them lovingly. She placed a hand over her heart, and her voice cracked as she said, "I feel badly for what I said when I first came, that it was silly going to church on Sundays. Being with you here tonight encourages me to rekindle my faith and return to church. Brother John, you were nine years old when I returned home after college graduation. Look at you now."

John waved and Cora wiped more tears gathering in her eyes.

"I'm blessed to have been placed in your home and to become your daughter, Mom and Dad. I love you both from the depths of my heart!"

Cora stepped away and then as if she had another thought, darted back to the microphone. "Cards and checks have been placed in a 'Blessing Box' by the cake. The silent auction has already raised $50,000.00. Items are still available for bid. You are all so generous with your giving tonight!"

Eva couldn't have been more thrilled. She and Scott served the cake, and when the last piece was taken, the two of them walked onto the patio. Under the sparkling lights, she held his hand. They stood looking up at the stars to the strains of a cellist playing

"Amazing Grace."

"If only you and I can give such a Christian heritage to our children and their children someday," Eva said softly.

Scott squeezed her hand tightly in his. "That's my prayer too, my sweetheart."

AFTER MANY FAMILY MEMBERS lingered and talked, the crowd thinned. Eva and Cora began removing centerpieces and gathering decorations.

Eva smelled a purple rose, telling Cora, "These are the most stunning roses I've ever seen."

"They're from my rose garden in Middleburg," Cora said, sounding wistful.

"You grow roses," Eva replied, marveling. "What else don't I know about you?"

Cora reached for the vase. "Since you asked, I'm a master gardener. Tomorrow, these flowers will be delivered to the local children's hospital and nursing homes. The Queen Elizabeth roses are my favorite. Do you have room in your car to take some?"

"We do. Please bring my silk flowers with your deliveries," Eva insisted.

She moved a chair as she reached for Cora's arrangement. The chair banged against a table leg and fell over. Eva couldn't believe her eyes. A man's leg protruded from beneath the table!

Eva nudged his leg with her foot, demanding, "What are you doing under the table? Who are you?"

The man, on hands and knees, backed out from beneath the table. Cora's brother John scrambled to his feet, holding up a small black device with wires sticking out of it.

"I was sitting at this table while Cora was speaking and felt something scratch the back of my hand," he said.

Cora squinted. "What is that horrid-looking thing?"

"Another battery pack," Eva observed. "I find it most strange."

John frowned. "It's very strange indeed, but this one looks like a quality device."

Scott strode over to study the battery in John's hand. "Are you sure it's not the same as the other one?"

"If John says it's a battery pack, it must be." Cora stepped close to her brother. "We must believe him. He's a tech guru and Ohio college professor."

Scott gave Eva a funny look while Cora patted John's back.

"He's famous for refurbishing used computers," she said, complimenting John. "Though he was young, he had the older kids in our house wired up like a computer lab."

"You're convincing me," Scott quipped, and wandered off to clear tables with Cora as if the incident held no further interest for him.

It did for Eva. She lowered her voice, "John, what will you do with it?"

"Throw it in my trunk," he said with a shrug. "Never know when I might use it."

"Mind if I ask you a question?" Eva stepped closer to him.

"I'll try answering it." John stowed the battery pack in his pants pocket. "Are you looking to buy a new computer?"

"I saw you talking with a man and handing him something. Is your meeting with him related to the weird battery packs you keep finding?"

"Not sure who you mean." John rubbed his short beard. "Was it after we found the first device?"

"Yes."

John tilted his head as if thinking. "I spoke briefly with Cora's husband, Marlow. He had a business proposition for me and I gave him my business card."

"Cora said he's on his way to China," Eva said. "Do you know what his company does?"

"He imports and distributes food. Since I teach agricultural courses, we may have things in common I can help him with."

Eva decided not to ask any more questions. John seemed a decent and caring young guy with a proclivity to smell out technical problems.

Instead, she asked, "When are you driving your folks to Virginia?"

"Cora offered to take them since Marlow isn't going along. Fine with me. Summer classes start Monday so I'll leave at first light."

Eva smiled, wished him a safe trip, and collected her vase of roses. All in all, she felt satisfied the evening had gone beautifully with few hiccups.

John turned to leave, and Irene beckoned him over to her. Eva watched. Though she couldn't hear their conversation, she saw Irene give him an envelope. Looking puzzled, he began to open it until his mom wagged a finger and shook her head.

John inserted the letter into his shirt pocket and hugged Irene before departing. Eva admired the young man, suspecting the DeVrooms were still helping him financially.

Kaley ran up, and sounding out of breath, chirped, "Mom, my new cell phone is acting up. Lexi's been trying to reach me all evening. When do we get back home? I'm invited to go with her and Conner to the Wolf Trap concert."

"How much do you know about this young man Lexi is seeing?" Eva asked. "To your father and I, Conner is at loose ends."

"He is. Lexi is helping him, and I'm helping her. Conner has huge potential," Kaley insisted.

Eva stood there, vase of roses in her hands, and understood the learning opportunity for Kaley as she observed her friend trying to rescue a man. Ever since she first held her beautiful daughter in her arms, Eva had made it her life's mission to protect Kaley. Tonight, she'd tread lightly. She handed her daughter the vase of rare flowers.

"Will you take these special roses from Cora inside? I don't want them crushed."

Kaley took the vase with a free hand, airing a new complaint, "What about my phone?"

"We'll deal with your phone and the Wolf Trap concert when we get upstairs," Eva said. "Your dad will have ideas. He is Mr. Techie, you know."

She took one last look at the Conservatory, ready to begin the drive home early in the morning. Her task-oriented brain was already processing her upcoming work week. Not only would Eva have her own work, she'd be subbing for her partner because Griff and Dawn had already left for Israel. Eva hoped it would be a trip of a lifetime for them both.

Chapter 7

Israel

Griff deplaned with Dawn from their long flight across the Atlantic at the Ben Gurion airport. He guided his wife by the elbow as if on an important mission.

"We must clear passport control first," he told Dawn.

She trilled a laugh. "I can't wait for our visit to the land of the Bible to officially begin."

After a few questions about why they arrived before their tour group, the officers allowed them to proceed to the next phase of their arrival in Israel.

"Hold on a second," Griff told Dawn.

He wandered close to a window and pulled out his recently-restored cell phone.

Because his new number would be unknown to Judah Levitt, he texted: *Griff here. Just landed. En route soon to Shalom Hotel, Netanya. Available rest of today.*

Dawn came over and gripped his elbow with her fingers. "Dearest, we've no more than left the plane and you're back at work. Will it be like this for our entire trip?"

"This involves the matter I spoke of," he said in low tones. "Once I get that out of the way, you'll have my full attention and then some."

Dawn's smile was radiant despite the grueling flight, with tiny snippets of sleep on the plane. "That's what I hoped you'd say. Let's retrieve our luggage and clear customs. This is one busy airport."

After finally leaving the customs area with their luggage, large blue and white signs welcomed the Toppings to Israel. Griff managed to hold his cell phone in one hand to see its screen while pulling the suitcase behind him with his other hand. The leather backpack swayed on his back.

He glimpsed Dawn sailing past him, rolling her suitcase, and saying, "Wow, we're here! I'm really here!" every few minutes.

Security officers marched by with search dogs. Griff didn't bother with them. He kept his eyes focused on his phone. Had Judah received his text? Or did he already know Griff was here through other means, like the security officer who cleared him through customs?

Dawn pointed out the taxi window at various sites during their ride to Netanya, giving Griff a running commentary as if she were a tour guide. He nodded, his mind elsewhere. Finally, his phone vibrated in his shirt pocket.

He snatched it out and read Judah's text: *Will meet in private at your room in two hours. I made dinner reservations for you and Dawn at the Bistro on the Med. Get back with your room number.*

Things in Israel were definitely on a roll. He reached for Dawn's hand, telling her, "Judah is meeting me in our room in a few hours. Maybe you could check out a café for a bite once we get settled in. I'll join you after."

Her eyes sought his before roaming to his cell phone screen.

Giving him a curt nod, she said in a firm voice, "Fine and dandy, but don't forget your promise."

A MERE TWO MINUTES AFTER Dawn left their hotel room with a plan to stroll along the Mediterranean, Griff heard a tap on the door. He checked through the peephole with one well-trained eye. He instantly recognized the man with whom he'd worked dangerous joint ventures in the past.

Griff pulled open the door and Judah pressed past him with a finger to his lips. He lifted out something from a valise he carried. Griff hurried to lock the door. He watched with interest as Judah held up a black box and plugged its electrical cord into the wall. The device instantly emitted a sharp hissing sound.

Judah clasped Griff's hand, saying in his heavy accent, "My friend, it is good to see you. I have fond memories of working with you and Eva."

"Likewise." Griff nodded at the black box. "Is everything okay?"

Judah answered with a wry smile. "A precaution. We do not know if you were expected in this room, or who was here last. I assume the worst."

Griff stepped close to visually inspect the nondescript box. "Is it effective?"

"We should keep our voices down just in case," Judah replied with a shrug.

Griff opened a sliding glass door leading to a narrow deck, which overlooked the blue Mediterranean Sea. He stepped outside and motioned for Judah to follow. Judah shook his head.

"We must not be seen together," he hissed. "It could have disastrous results."

Griff stepped back inside. "I'll leave the door open for more ambient sound."

Pulling some colorful brochures from his valise, Judah offered, "A few suggestions for today's tour where guides do not usually take tourists."

"Thanks," Griff said. "I'm sure we have more important things to discuss."

"Yes, and my time is limited."

Judah dug into his leather valise and presented Griff a list of printed phone numbers. "This list is important. It contains the phone number for 'Eva Montanna – FBI.' And has the phone number for Kaley Montanna, who is Eva's daughter."

Griff held Judah's sheet toward the sliding glass door for better light. "This is why you wanted to see me in person. I can't figure why it says Eva is with the FBI. She's with ICE and I'm the FBI agent."

"Yes, I know this." Judah reached for a chair, positioning it near the open slider.

Griff followed his lead. The two agents huddled close and spoke in whispers.

Judah tapped the printed list. "Israel's Airport Authority employed a local electronics firm to install cell phone charging devices at the Tel Aviv airport, where you just arrived. That contractor then hired a Chinese company to provide the software and install a demonstration portion as required by the contract."

"You learned they installed software to steal people's data," Griff guessed.

"No." Judah shook his head fiercely. "Their installation worked well and safely."

Griff arched his eyebrows. "What am I missing?"

"Mysterious things happen in our business. You can imagine that certain USB drives the Chinese contractors kept in their hotel room fell into our hands. It seems the contractor intended to safely install the software. Then, after the contract and installation were approved, they were going to install secret software and steal all data including apps, programs, contact lists, and photos from every cell phone plugged into our airport's charging stations."

Griff fluttered the paper containing Eva's phone number. "And these?"

"One USB drive contained data stolen earlier from unsuspecting cell phones. Our analysts told me I had called one of the numbers on that USB drive. That was Eva's phone number. She called me and I returned her call when she was previously in Israel. Her phone is compromised. Yours is too if you are in her contact list. Thus, I warn you."

Griff's mind whirled. With a downward stroke, he smoothed his mustache. "We must assume the Chinese Communists possess everything in Eva's phone."

"There is another issue I did not want to mention from the SCIF. Our analysts found a phone number from your U.S. Senate. It is for the Foreign Relation's Subcommittee on Asia. Do you or Eva have dealings with them?"

"Not really. Eva's husband Scott works on the opposite side of the Capitol, for the Speaker of the House of Representatives."

Judah waved his hand as though swatting a fly. "No matter. Our electronic intelligence experts have shared what they learned with your government. I was not sure the info would reach you in time so I called you at the SCIF."

"We are indebted to you, Judah."

"Griff, it is far worse than you can imagine. The Chinese are very active. They have opened naval bases in the Middle East, India, and Africa, which greatly concern us. They send their spies into Israel as students or visiting professors, and also to the U.S. Many study for advanced degrees and are spying at the same time."

"Thank you for this." Griff folded the paper. "When I return to my office, I'll analyze the data and take corrective action. I'll send you a secure communication or arrange another SCIF meeting if necessary."

Judah stood. "I have kept you and Mrs. Topping from your touring far too long. Sorry not to meet her. You understand and will square with her."

"Perhaps one day you and Dawn will meet. She arranged for our trip to Israel."

"You and she will find harmony in the land. This evening enjoy a fabulous dinner by the sea. You will be well taken care of, my friend."

That said, Judah walked to his device, yanked the plug from the wall, and shoved the gadget into his valise, whispering, "Greet Eva for me. Shalom."

He fired off a mock salute before disappearing down the hall. Griff removed his shoe and pulled out the insole. Folding the list of compromised numbers, he inserted it into his shoe before returning the insole. Next Griff put on his shoe, checked his watch, and sprinted down to the promenade to find Dawn.

What was he thinking to let her wander alone outside? Hadn't there been a recent stabbing in the city? Griff had a sudden urge to make sure she was all right, and raced from the lobby.

Chapter 8

Griff made a beeline out of the hotel. He spotted Dawn out front, looking at the sea. Relief coursed through his veins. All was well. Then a different emotion cascaded over him like crashing waves. Her long black hair billowed over her shoulders. In her dark sunglasses and wide-brimmed hat, standing by the sapphire blue water with bits of foam splashing in front of her, Dawn looked like the subject of a painting by a master artist.

In a flash, Griff saw her with new eyes. All of Dawn's special qualities unfolded before him. His heart filled with fresh love for his wife.

She is a wonderful woman! he thought. *And beautiful too!*

He strode to her side, and slipped his hand into hers.

"Hello, my lady," he whispered in her ear. "How about joining me for lunch?"

"This is heavenly, Griff. I can't fathom why it took us so long to come here. The next ten days will speed by and I plan to cherish each moment here with you. And yes, I'm starving."

They had a merry laugh over not eating for nearly eight hours.

"Who cares about food when I have you in my life?" Griff said, grinning.

They walked into the hotel holding hands. Pleasing smells of baked bread and freshly brewed coffee from a small café tempted them to bring food up to their room. They shared a roast beef sandwich and cucumber spears with hummus. After resting awhile, Griff arranged for a cab to drive them to the national park at Caesarea, which Judah had recommended.

They paused near the entrance to read a sign that explained King Herod built the ancient city in 20 B.C.

"Because Caesar Augustus Octavian gave Herod this shoreline, Herod named the seaport after him," Griff read out to Dawn. "The king built the Hippodrome, a palace, and aqueduct to bring water here from Mount Carmel up north."

Dawn drew his attention to a walkway. "This will take us right to the ocean. Let's go see the water."

He took her by the arm and steadied her on the path made of stones and sand. Husband and wife stood together enjoying the azure blue Mediterranean Sea. Strong waves crashed against massive rocks piled along the shore. Awed by the breathtaking sight, Griff caught Dawn's enthusiasm for Israel. Her laughter was infectious.

"Griff, breathe in this air! We're standing in the land where

Jesus walked and lived," she said softly.

He stepped closer to better hear her say, "Pontius Pilate's stone …"

Her words lofted skyward in the rising winds. He leaned down, and pointing past brick ruins, he spoke in her ear, "We have reservations at the bistro in that fantastic-looking stone building. We should head that way. I sense a storm is brewing."

She agreed. They took their selfie with the tumultuous sea behind them. Then Dawn snapped a photo of a stone with Pontius Pilate's name inscribed on it.

She pulled a guidebook from her fanny pack, saying, "This stone is a replica of the original found in 1961. It contains the dates Pilate ruled over Caesarea. Pontius Pilate was the Roman ruler who ordered the crucifixion of Christ."

They reflected on the enormity of the discovery until a rumble of thunder overhead broke the solemn moment. Griff saw storm clouds sweeping in.

"Let's hurry," he said, guiding her elbow so she wouldn't slip on the gravel.

They hurried toward the distant restaurant set upon a rock at the water's edge. Ten minutes later, they were tucked safely inside a glass enclosure where they had a stunning view of the expansive and ever-moving blue sea.

"How did you find this gorgeous eatery?" Dawn asked, her eyes wide in wonder.

Griff smiled. Judah, Mossad agent and friend, had come through once again.

"I have my sources," he replied. "And Judah strongly hinted we should order fresh salmon with roasted vegetables, and Rustico salad. You choose the appetizer."

"What's a Rustico salad?"

"I'm not sure." Griff picked up a blue and white menu written in both English and Hebrew. He frowned. "Veggies and feta cheese."

"Hmm …" Dawn hesitated. "The salad sounds light. I know my Griff. You need something more substantial."

She looked over the menu. "Does butter shrimp with garlic and herbs sound tempting for an appetizer?"

"Shrimp wins my vote every time," came Griff's reply, his mouth watering.

The server appeared at their table dressed in black slacks and shirt. He took their order without writing anything down.

"You have chosen well," he said with a slight accent. "Our orange juice is fresh squeezed to order."

He turned on soft-soled shoes and headed back to the kitchen. Before Griff could finish telling Dawn a hair-raising story about a dangerous case he'd once worked in Tampa, the server returned, bringing them each a large glass of orange juice over crushed ice. A split strawberry balanced on the rim.

Griff ate his strawberry and watched Dawn gaze at the sea. His eyes followed hers. Was she as happy as she looked? Waves kicked up, tossing white foam high into the air and he imagined vacationing together by the water for a longer stretch.

"Good thing we're inside," he said, enjoying the moment. "I've heard storms on the west coast of Israel race in rapid-fire. We should have brought an umbrella."

Dawn pulled a small collapsible one from her purse. "No worries."

The tantalizing shrimp arrived and Griff let Dawn sample the first bite. She smiled, her dark eyes gleaming.

"It's fascinating," she said, her face a portrait of a woman at peace.

"The appetizer?" Griff reached over with his fork. "How about saving me a bite."

Dawn shook her head. "I mean the ancient stone is fascinating. It was found with Pilate's name carved on it. That stone corroborates the biblical account of Pilate's existence at the time he caved in to the crowd's demands to crucify Christ. Though Herod built this harbor thousands of years ago, I noticed constant winds eroded much of it away. Yet, God's truth remains eternally."

"Very well said. We'll see more of this historic land tomorrow when pastor and the group arrive."

Griff tore a piece of warm pita bread from the basket and dipped it into the hummus drizzled with oil. Before he could eat one bite, his cell phone vibrated in his pocket. Across the table from him, the way Dawn kept chewing her bread, Griff figured she hadn't heard it. He'd ignore the call. The buzzing started again. He'd have no rest unless he answered.

He yanked the phone from his pocket. "Sorry, Dawn. Let me see who dares to interrupt our dinner."

It was a text message from Judah: *Alert for your trip. New discovery. Sending link.*

Griff navigated to the link to sounds of Dawn's perturbed sigh.

"Really, Griff?" she quipped. "What's so urgent? Can't Eva or your team in D.C. handle whatever?"

He couldn't help laughing. "You have it all wrong. Judah's letting us know about a new archaeological discovery. The Church of the Apostles is being excavated near the Sea of Galilee."

"Sorry I scolded you," Dawn said, smirking. "Tell me everything."

Rain began pelting their glass cocoon, which forced Griff to raise his voice. "The church ruins are in Bethsaida."

"It's thrilling the church has been found," Dawn replied, taking out her guide book. "This says Bethsaida is the small village where Jesus' disciples Peter, Andrew, and Philip were from, in northern Galilee. I seem to remember that's where Jesus healed a blind man and fed the five thousand with five loaves of bread and two fish."

Griff read from the link on his phone. "Archaeologists from Israel and New York worked on the dig and believe the church was built over the homes of the apostles Andrew and Peter."

"Amazing." Dawn briefly shut her eyes, and opening them, she looked at Griff with a burning intensity. "The apostles lived and ate with Jesus and saw His miracles. They were in the Garden of Gethsemane when Jesus prayed before His crucifixion. John stood with His mother Mary when Jesus hung on a cross. From their eyewitness testimony, we know the absolute truth of Jesus' sacrifice for us."

"In the church ruins, they uncovered marble from a chancel screen and bits of small glass blocks from mosaics on the church wall," Griff told her.

After Dawn finished the last shrimp, she told Griff, "History comes alive before our eyes. I'm trying to decide what it means for our future."

"Here's something interesting," he said. "Early Christians mentioned this church, and a Christian named Willibald wrote about it in the year 725 A.D."

Griff put away his cell phone just as their dinners arrived piping hot. Their conversation turned to lighter matters until Griff suddenly stopped eating, fork poised by his mouth.

"Wait. What do you mean the church discovery impacts our *future?*"

Dawn's eyes twinkled at him as she ate her salmon and gave no answer. Why was she purposely ignoring his question?

"What about our future?" he insisted. "Is there something you aren't telling me?"

She laid down her fork and touched his arm. "Honey, what I mean is, being here in Israel is deepening my love for Jesus at warp speed. It's like I once saw the Bible in black and white letters on the page, and now ..." She paused to sip her juice.

Dawn continued, her face aglow, "Jesus' love and power are

more real to me. It's like I see Him in vibrant technicolor. You and I must return here someday, that much I know!"

AFTER DESSERT, GRIFF ORDERED a rideshare back to the hotel. The night was dark. Though rain stopped falling, on the way back to Netanya, lights from passing cars reflected off the wet pavement. Griff began chatting with the driver.

"From America, yes? A big place like New York?" the man asked over his shoulder.

"We live in Virginia," Griff replied. "Have you spent time in the Big Apple?"

"Once. For a family gathering. Now let me tell you something. I will be your guide wherever you want to go. I take you to Bethlehem, the desert of En Gedi, and Hebron, where you will see the tomb of Father Abraham."

Griff glanced at Dawn. "Thanks for the offer. We join our group tomorrow. The first place we will visit is the Jordan River, where God led the Israelites, His chosen people, across to their Promised Land."

The driver stared at them in his mirror. "The land already had people. My people. God give my people this land."

As though she were a teacher, Dawn pressed forward, "Scriptures tell us God promised the land of Israel to the Jewish people."

"AGGH!" the driver cried like a petulant student.

He slammed on the brakes so hard Griff's head snapped forward. Dawn strained against the seatbelt.

"What's going on?" Griff demanded, looking for some obstacle in the road.

"Get out!" the driver ordered.

"What?"

"I said, get out of my car!" he shouted, and started blowing the horn.

"No." Griff folded his arms. "I insist you drive us to our hotel. You can't order us out because we're in a tour group and won't hire you to be our guide. It's unethical."

Dawn clung to his hand. "Honey, please stay calm."

"I said leave! You offend me with your talk about our oppressors being chosen." The driver reached down under his seat and pulled out a knife and waved it at them. "You leave. Now!"

"Okay, okay. We're gone."

Griff swung open the door and dove out, pulling Dawn by her hand, which felt cold as ice.

"Wow! He truly meant to harm us!" she cried, straightening her back.

The crazy driver spun away in a huff, his tires throwing stones and road debris behind him.

"Unbelievable!" Griff yelled after him. "He leaves us stranded miles from our hotel on the side of a wet and slippery road."

One car after another whizzed by, forcing Griff and Dawn into the weeds. Griff did some fast thinking. He could always call Judah, but then another idea lit in his mind.

"Fortunately, I have the rider app in my phone. I'll request another driver. It's too far to walk."

Dawn drew close to Griff and pulled on her sweater. He punched in redial, sensing she feared their trip was going sideways in a bad way.

After the operator assured him a car would come soon, he hung up, telling Dawn, "All is well, honey."

"I'm standing here, praying God will help us," Dawn said, her voice agitated. "May He send a normal person and not a wild man!"

They waited in the ditch for a good twenty minutes before another car and driver finally arrived. Griff stepped to the roadside, and shining the light from his phone, waved him down. The car rolled to a stop. Griff used his light to illuminate the rideshare logo on the windshield.

He opened the door, stating in a firm tone, "I asked for a ride to the Shalom hotel in Netanya. Are you the driver?"

"Yes, sir," the older gentleman with graying hair answered.

His reply and his bearing reminded Griff of a military man, so he felt secure climbing in and gently easing Dawn in behind him. She snuggled close.

Griff had learned his lesson. He said nothing to the driver except repeating the hotel name, and asking, "Do you know where it is?"

The man nodded and hit the accelerator. Griff realized Israel was a steaming pot of escalating emotions. He'd be more careful from now on. They exited the car under the well-lit portico. Griff caught Dawn's hand in the lobby.

"Sorry for opening my big mouth back there," he said, searching her eyes for lingering signs of anxiety.

She brushed a lock of hair from his eyes. "Hey, buddy. I don't blame you for one second. It was me who set him off. Let's hurry to our room before discussing it. Send Pastor Kenneth the link for the apostle church and maybe he'll arrange for us to visit the dig."

Griff had no desire to argue with her ideas. He kept a protective arm around her all the way to their room.

Chapter 9

Eva battled fatigue on the treacherous drive to the office. Her hands dripped with sweat as she held onto the wheel passing one accident, then another with three cars, and finally, dodging a car on fire. All hope for a quiet Monday morning evaporated.

Thankful she reached the office in one piece, Eva dropped her heavy purse in the bottom drawer and trudged to the coffee station. She filled up her travel mug and took a long, well-deserved sip.

"Ah," she said, dropping into the desk chair.

Her mind and body were grateful for a pause in the action. Griff's cubicle across from hers was dark and silent. Right about now, he and Dawn were exploring Israel.

"Good for them getting a break from work," Eva muttered, then navigated on her computer to read Brett's update on his recent drug smuggling case. A small part of the report revealed a cooperating defendant who told Brett about driving a Syrian mobster to Baltimore's harbor area and returning with boxes they delivered in D.C.

Eva found an intriguing clue and sent Brett an email:

Brett, you're a drug agent who's thinking drugs. I note your snitch complained about the Syrian who was a smoker himself, yet insisted the driver not smoke in the van. Could be the target was smuggling explosives and not drugs. Is it possible the snitch would take us on a drive to retrace their steps? I'm happy to work with you in hopes of identifying suspects in D.C. and Baltimore. Let me know your thoughts, Eva

Needing a boost of energy, Eva reached into her big purse and found a roll of candy. She relished the peppery flavor of a Wilhemina peppermint on her tongue.

"I said, Agent Montanna!"

A raspy voice shouting her name gave Eva a start. She lifted her head with a jerk. Sosa Garcia stood at the entrance to her cubicle wearing a deep scowl.

He muscled his way in. "Eva, get down to security. A woman's demanding to see Griff and refuses to leave, despite the guards advising he's unavailable."

"Who is she?" Eva used her tongue to push the giant peppermint to one side of her cheek.

Sosa handed her a slip of paper. "Jennifer Tuttle is her name."

"Jennifer Tuttle? That's all you know?"

"Just go," Sosa snapped. "And convince her to leave."

"Okay, boss."

He headed off with a swagger.

He could've already gone down there himself, Eva fumed, leaning down to lock her bottom desk drawer. Oh well, this was her baby now. She knew being forewarned was to be forearmed.

She removed her purse with her weapon, the mighty Glock, from the bottom drawer. This she shoved over her shoulder before walking with determination to the elevator. Her mind considered what possible beef Jennifer might have with Griff. Was she a new secret informant?

Eva approached the security kiosk, noticing a mid-thirties-something woman with long auburn hair and dressed in business attire. Eva observed something odd while the woman cooled her heels in the lobby. She wore no heels. Purple running sneakers adorned her feet. Eva concluded Jennifer had walked in athletic shoes from a parking lot or commuter station.

Jennifer talked in animated tones to the security officer, and gestured wildly with her hands. From the angry look on her heavily made-up face, Eva imagined steam was blowing out of her ears and choice words were flying off her tongue.

Without missing a beat, Eva pressed the big purse to her side and strode up with bravado. "I'm Griff Topping's associate. Can I help you?"

Jennifer spun toward Eva, then stepped back as if seeing a ghost. Eva saw definite fear in her eyes. The woman quickly recovered and looked Eva over from head to toe.

"Who are you?" she demanded.

Eva observed the security guard's attention shift from his computer screen to Eva. She nodded hello at him, then told Jennifer, "I just told you, I'm Agent Topping's associate. You've asked for him."

"What is your name?" the interloper insisted on knowing.

Eva straightened to her full height and shook her head. "No. It doesn't work that way when you show up unexpectedly. Let me see your ID."

Jennifer paused to assess Eva before reaching into a small purse dangling from her shoulder. Eva tensed. She'd respond with firepower if necessary. Jennifer took a driver's license from her wallet, which she gave to Eva.

Eva studied it, made a mental note, and said crisply, "Jennifer Tuttle, from Silver Springs, Maryland."

Eva slid out her leather credential case, a gold and blue badge attached to its cover, and flipped it open displaying her photo and name.

"This proves I'm Eva Montanna, an ICE Special Agent, and Griff Topping's partner. How can I help you?"

"He's an FBI Special Agent, right?"

"Yes, and his partner is me, an ICE agent. You know he isn't here. Was Agent Topping expecting you or does he know you?"

"No to both," Jennifer said apologetically. "I have information I can give only to him. What time will he be available?"

"That depends on what I tell him about you. He may never be available." Eva stared hard at Jennifer, evaluating her true motives.

Jennifer glanced at the guard who seemed distracted by his computer screen. She stepped further away and motioned for Eva to follow.

Her bottom lip trembled as she asked, "Does Darin Hilton mean anything to you?"

Eva instantly recognized Hilton's name. Griff had celebrated his recent conviction for threatening U.S. Senator Easton. Eva suspected Jennifer might be a scorned girlfriend.

She leveled a stern gaze at Jennifer. "I know of Agent Topping's case involving Mr. Hilton. Why do you care?"

"I'm a messenger," she said, her voice low, "whose been told to speak with your partner and no one else."

Discovering Jennifer wanted to talk about Hilton's case softened Eva's attitude.

"Agent Topping is out of the country," Eva said. "It's appropriate for you to speak to me."

"Out of the country," Jennifer repeated as if processing that fact.

Eva nodded. "Are you concerned you're at risk of arrest?"

"No. I can't decide if I should tell you."

Eva took hold of Jennifer's arm. "Look, I have a top secret security clearance. I'm an expert at keeping secrets. I've been a Special Agent for years, and never had a complaint filed against me. You can trust me to listen and give your information to Agent Topping upon his return. Would you like to speak privately in our office?"

Jennifer's eyes pierced Eva's eyes for a blazing second.

"Yes," she whispered.

FIFTEEN MINUTES LATER, Eva had searched Jennifer's purse and patted her down for a hidden weapon. The two sat across from each other at the conference room table. Eva gave Jennifer a bottle of water, then folded her hands next to her idle pen and pad. "Tell me what you'd like Agent Topping to know."

"Um ..." Distrust shot through Jennifer's wide eyes. "First, I need assurance I won't incriminate myself or my brother."

"Do you think that you're at risk of being charged criminally, or your brother is? I don't even know who your brother is," Eva added.

"Oh, I'm sorry. I didn't tell you. My brother is Darin Hilton."

An "ah-hah" moment exploded in Eva's mind. Jennifer Tuttle was more than a messenger from a convicted felon. Eva hoped her surprise wasn't apparent to Jennifer.

"Let's do this," Eva said, without touching her pen. "You tell me a story about some other persons. We both agree none of the hypothetical people in your story are you or your brother. Does that work?"

Jennifer paused. "I can't get in trouble that way?"

"As long as you're not trying to waste my time or that of Agent Topping."

"Okay." Jennifer's shoulders slumped and all her bravado seemed to fade.

Eva encouraged her to drink some water, and then picking up her pen, said, "A lady's brother is in jail facing prison time. He asks his sister to deliver a message to the FBI agent who arrested him. Is that a good beginning?"

"How do you know all that?" Jennifer asked, blinking furiously.

"Many of these stories begin the same way." Eva smiled. "Tell me, am I right?"

"We're still not talking about me or my brother, right?"

"Just hypothetically."

"Okay." Jennifer dropped her arms from the table into her lap. She sounded less strained telling Eva, "That man would be very angry if he was convicted by a judge, even though the man paid the judge an enormous bribe to find him not guilty. Now his entire technology company has gone bust!"

"Oh, that would make me angry too." Eva offered an understanding nod.

Jennifer coughed out a sigh and began fidgeting with the water bottle. "I'm not sure how much to tell you."

"Let me ask this," Eva said evenly. "Did the man pay money to an imposter who wasn't really the judge? There are lots of hustlers around."

Jennifer's eyes widened. "Oh no. Maybe so. Is it possible?"

"Anything's possible." Eva shrugged. "You need to tell me more."

Jennifer remained silent as if thinking. Then she burst out, "No! No! There is evidence it wasn't an imposter."

"Go on," Eva urged, picking up her pen to take notes.

"It all started when the make-believe man received a phone call offering to fix his case. The caller on his cell phone was a woman. He didn't know what else to do besides listen."

"He should have a number from whoever called," Eva suggested.

Jennifer grimaced. "It came in a blocked number."

"Not surprising. Tell me when this happened."

"The day after the pretend-man's preliminary hearing. The man was scared FBI agents were trying to set him up, so he ignored it."

Eva set down her pen. "So that's it? Nothing else happened?"

"Are you kidding?" Jennifer defended. "Don't you know how mad he got after his conviction?"

"We're talking about Darin Hilton now?" Eva shot back.

The sister's hands flew to her face. "No! I forgot. I mean, the man was upset when the judge convicted him without a jury, because he paid off the judge."

"The hypothetical man, right? I thought you said he suspected the woman's phone call came from FBI agents."

Jennifer stared at Eva with large watery eyes. "He did at first. Then the woman called again. She said for a half-million in cash, the judge would acquit him."

"Wasn't he still suspicious?" Eva probed.

"Ye-es, the man was," Jennifer sputtered. "The woman explained he should ask for a trial with no jury. The judge would decide the case. When the man told her that he didn't believe she was speaking for the judge, she said there was a way for him to know. The judge never wore bowties. To prove she spoke for the judge, the woman promised on the man's next motion appearance the judge would wear a bowtie."

"Did the man tell anyone about this?"

"No. Not even me. The woman warned him not to mention her calls to a single living soul, especially not Madison Stone, his lawyer."

Eva nodded. "What happened next in your hypothetical case?"

"Like the woman said, at the motion hearing, the judge wore a bowtie above his robe. I was there and remember seeing it. The man searched photos on every legal listing he could find, you know, like Internet sites. The judge never wore a bowtie in those."

"Explain how he paid the money," Eva said.

"The woman called again, demanding to know if he believed

her. When he said he did, she said his lawyer should file a motion for a bench trial, and after the judge saw the motion, she'd call again and he would need to deliver the half-million dollars."

Eva quietly wrote a few notes and folded back a sheet of paper. "Do you know what happened next in our pretend case?"

"Yes, because it involved me. The man's lawyer filed the motion and the man gave me the money. Well, he gave me a bag to deliver. Sure enough, the woman called him, and I took the bag to her at the Red Dragon Chinese restaurant not far from here."

"You met her there?" Eva asked.

Jennifer looked tense as she said, "She looked so much like you. In fact, when I first saw you downstairs, I thought you were the woman and that my brother … ah … I mean, the man was right and it was a setup."

"You mean the woman is about my age with blond hair?"

At Jennifer's nod, Eva asked for a better description of her height, weight, and eye color.

"Like you." Jennifer relinquished the water bottle from her grip. "Blonde, striking blue eyes, your height and weight. She dressed business casual, maybe in her late thirties."

"Did the two of you talk?"

"She sat alone at a corner table. When I walked up, I asked if she was Susie, and she said yes. I gave her a shopping bag taped shut at the top as instructed. I said, 'I was told to give you this. You know what to do with it.' Then I left."

"How did she respond?"

"She didn't. Absolutely nothing but that word 'yes.' I didn't know at that time what was in the bag, or what she would do with it."

"When did you discover—"

"Wait!" Jennifer interrupted, her brow creased with concern. "I already said too much. I don't want to answer any more questions."

Eva tapped her pad with the pen. "Jennifer, what do you expect me to do with this information?"

"I'm not sure." Jennifer glanced around as if ready to flee. "Am I in trouble for what I said?"

"Honestly, if you're the sister of Darin Hilton, and what you've done here," Eva stopped short without answering. She was deep in thought as she tapped the pad again. "Then you may have broken some laws, but more than likely, you and your brother are victims of a grand hoax. We don't normally prosecute victims."

"Whew." Jennifer sighed. She reached for the water bottle like it was a lifeline to keep her from sinking.

Eva added, "I'd like to pursue the facts further, but that would require you and maybe your brother to truthfully furnish more information."

"I'm afraid to say more," Jennifer whispered, studying Eva's face. "What if someone comes after me? Or my brother in jail? I'm worried for his safety too."

Eva understood her concerns and sought to soothe her anxiety. "We wouldn't do anything to put you at risk. I promise not to use anything you've just told me against you. Without your help, I can't determine if you're a victim of a dishonorable judge or thief who conned your brother. I want to find out and Agent Topping will also."

"Will you tell him?"

"Of course. He seeks to right wrongs as do I."

Eva wrote her name and phone number on a sheet from her pad, which she handed to Jennifer. "Call with questions, or if you recall anything important. When Griff returns, I'll inform him of our conversation."

"Please don't contact my brother in jail. He said it's too dangerous with his sentencing coming up soon."

Eva shook her head. "No. We know how to proceed. We might ask you to pass messages to him, or ask him questions during family visits."

"Okay, I can do that." Jennifer sounded relieved.

"How about a phone number where I can reach you?" Eva asked, holding her pen.

After a pause, Jennifer gave her cell number. Her knees seemed to buckle when she stood and she had to lean on the table to steady herself.

"You did the right thing by coming," Eva assured. "I'll escort you downstairs."

At the building entrance, Eva thanked Jennifer and hurried back to her office. She secured the empty water bottle in an evidence envelope just in case she needed DNA or fingerprints. She recorded her notes in the computer.

Eva wanted to be ready to discuss the evidence with Griff, so she got busy researching Jennifer Tuttle's social media pages and computer databases to uncover as much as possible about her. Before she left for home, Eva had every reason to believe Jennifer's hypothetical story was true.

Chapter 10

Israel

Griff and Dawn stayed up to the wee hours sharing their hopes and concerns for the future. She confided how the political wrangling in her office exhausted her. Sometime after one a.m., they finally fell asleep. When the early alarm buzzed, Griff sat up startled.

The truth set in, and he whispered in Dawn's ear, "Rise and shine. Our chariot arrives in about an hour."

They were off and running to eat breakfast. With a few minutes to spare, they rushed down to the lobby with their luggage, making it just in time to join their tour group. Griff and Dawn slipped into two empty seats on the bus, which whisked them to the dry and desolate Judean desert. Here they saw caves in high and barren rocks where David once fled from King Saul. A sparkling waterfall and bubbling springs at En Gedi took them both by surprise.

Griff floated alongside Dawn in the salty Dead Sea, and he rode a crowded tram to the high peaks of Massada. His claustrophobia didn't once rear its ugly head on the way up or on the way down, which was some kind of amazing result as it had plagued him for years. But no longer!

After lunch at a cafeteria specializing in warm pita bread sandwiches, Griff and Dawn grabbed their seats back on the bus. His stomach began churning on the ride to Tiberias, so he leaned his head back on the seat and closed his eyes. He listened to their pastor give devotions over a microphone about Jesus' ministry in Galilee.

Griff opened his eyes as Pastor Kenneth declared, "Along the shores of this sea and by the high hills, Jesus turned water into wine in Cana. He also brought a dead girl back to life."

Dawn took notes in the seat beside him. Griff succumbed to an urge to look at his cell phone. Ah ha! Judah sent another text, checking on their trip.

With his thumbs, Griff answered: *Going well. Nearing Tiberias.*

Judah quickly wrote back, *Which hotel?*

The Ahava. Why? Griff asked.

I have good reason for asking. Stay in tonight. Will say no more. Write when you leave and head for Jerusalem.

Okay, Griff typed back.

It was all very cryptic. Griff grew tense. Judah must have

discovered something since their meeting in Netanya. Griff would have to trust in God to keep them safe, but he'd overheard some in their group mention they planned to walk around town after they ate dinner.

Griff sent a quick text to the pastor: *We will stay inside the hotel tonight. I've reason to be concerned about local safety.*

They soon reached the hotel, and after a short rest, Griff escorted Dawn to an enormous buffet dinner in a special room for their group.

"Being in the fresh air sure makes me hungry," Dawn said, heaping her plate with salads, grilled beef, and pita bread.

Griff took a few spoons of meat and potatoes, skipping the smoked salmon spread. He nibbled at his food, perplexed by Judah's warning. Dawn fed her hearty appetite laughing and conversing with another couple from church. She sampled a special dessert called chocolate babka. A word-of-mouth message passed among their tour group. Pastor Kenneth suggested everyone remain in for the evening and get rested up.

Griff felt easier and dug into dessert, managing to down several cups of fresh coffee. That turned out to be a huge mistake. Long after his wife fell asleep, he read the tour book using his cell phone light. He stared at the ceiling for hours listening to Dawn's soft breathing. His mind kept turning over her heartfelt desire to return to Israel and other hoped-for changes to their future, including more mission trips.

He sighed, his thoughts gravitating to Judah's vague message and possible danger lurking come morning. No answers revealed themselves in the heart of the night. Griff decided he'd be prepared for whatever came, then rolled onto his side, willing himself to sleep.

The sun crept into their room with Dawn shaking Griff awake.

"If we aren't downstairs in ten minutes," she said, "you'll miss breakfast. You know how you love Israeli breakfasts."

He jumped out of bed, changed swiftly, and grabbed his cell phone from the charger. Homemade omelets tempted his growling and empty stomach. They filled their plates from the plentiful buffet, eating quickly. Griff waved off coffee. He chose a cup of orange juice instead.

Thirty minutes later, he helped Dawn step from the hotel dock onto the wooden tour boat with a canvas-covered top. An Israeli flag fluttered in a slight breeze from a pole in the stern. All seemed tranquil on the aqua water fed by snow melts from Mount Hermon to the north.

Griff had studied this body of water, and knew the sea lay just below the headwaters of the Jordan River. To the south, the Jordan flowed downhill into the Dead Sea where Griff and Dawn visited yesterday.

The captain started the engine. The boat slowly got under way, rocking slightly beneath them. Griff walked to the boat's side and gripped the railing. He breathed in the fresh air as Dawn joined him.

"The hills around us are heavenly," she said, her voice hushed.

"I can't believe we can see the other side," Griff remarked. "I thought the Sea of Galilee would be much larger."

"Shh. Our tour guide is talking."

"The Sea of Galilee is shaped like a harp," the guide explained. "It is called Lake Kinnereth, which derives from the Hebrew word for harp. Below us, it is very shallow and teeming with fish. The sea is 200 feet at its deepest point, just like your Lake Erie."

Griff yawned from lack of sleep for two nights. He heard Dawn marveling about the spiritual importance of this waterway, yet he didn't see it. Water was water, wasn't it?

Glancing down, he envisioned swarms of fish swimming below waiting to be caught in large nets for his lunch.

His thoughts rewound to a biblical account he'd read on his phone last night. The disciple Peter, along with John, James, and three others, had fished all night on the Sea of Galilee without catching a single fish. In the early morning, a man stood on the shore telling them, "Throw your net on the right side of the boat and you will find some."

In this moment, it was like a video began playing before Griff's eyes. He could envision Peter tossing a net over the side of a small fishing boat, and instantly having so many fish he couldn't draw in the net. It was then Peter recognized the man as Jesus and jumped into the water. He ran to the Lord in the water without stopping. When the other disciples came ashore with the catch to join Jesus and Peter, they found a fire burning and fish cooking over the coals and some bread. Jesus, who had risen from the grave after His crucifixion, said to them, "Come and have breakfast."

Dawn nudged Griff's side, and he rubbed his eyes, forcing his mind to the present. He now knew she was right. Being in Israel was unlike any other journey he'd made in his life. He was meeting Jesus, the Miracle-Worker, the Son of God, his own Savior, close up.

Griff whispered to Dawn, "I'm visualizing the miracles Jesus performed here. Are you?"

She flashed a knowing look and before Griff could reply, the guide lifted his arms, saying loudly, "Join me in this exercise. Face the shoreline in front of the boat. Now, point your left arm to at ten o'clock and your right arm to one o'clock. You may be surprised to know Capernaum is in this area between your two arms and is where Jesus spent more than eighty percent of His ministry during his lifetime."

"We're heading right there!" Dawn chimed, voicing the excitement Griff shared.

He grasped her hand. "I didn't know Jesus performed so many miracles in such a small area. Jesus calmed a storm in a fishing boat right here on the Galilee."

"Oh dear, it's getting cloudy. I hope it's clear sailing until we reach the other side," Dawn said, shuddering. "Our bus will join us over there and I forgot my jacket. I'm suddenly cold."

"I'd give you mine, but it's on the bus too," Griff said. "I've read storms on the sea can be quite violent."

"Thanks for that," Dawn said, clasping both arms around her.

The tour guide was explaining, "Jesus focused His ministry here because Capernaum, Bethsaida, Tiberias, and Magdala were crucial hubs for fishing. People from around the world walked the ancient roads near the sea. The sick came to the sulfur springs near Tiberias for restoration."

As if the winds had heard Griff mention the very idea of a storm, they began gusting harder. The guide talked louder to be heard, "We're seven hundred feet below sea level. The hills beyond are two thousand feet high. The drastic change causes storms to erupt without warning."

"He's right," Griff told Dawn, sliding an arm around her and drawing her near.

Darkness descended over the water in seconds. Winds howled and roared as if a tornado was bearing down on them. Griff clutched Dawn in his arms. They rocked from side to side. The wind turned cold and fierce.

"Take your seats," the guide bellowed. "Grab the sides!"

The boat rolled as if a giant sea monster was trying to push it over. Griff hobbled and steered his wife to a seat in the midst of a mad rush by their group to take cover.

Pastor Kenneth called to the guide, "This is frightening. Can you get us to shore?"

The guide groped along the side until he reached the captain. Immediately, the boat began to turn.

"Our only hope is to make it to Tiberias!" the guide yelled.

The boat turned broadside into the waves. They tipped farther down. Waves crashed against the side. Cold water sprayed the scared tourists. Griff covered Dawn's head and face with his arms. He heard her muttering under her breath.

An elderly woman was thrown against an awning support. Clinging to it, she cried, "Don't let us die here!"

The boat lurched to the other side. A loose chair slid along the deck.

Griff shouted at the pastor, "Call the bus driver! Tell him we turned back to Tiberias." Next, he grasped Dawn's shoulder. "Don't worry. This boat is substantial."

"Pray with me, Griff! We need Jesus to calm the sea!" Dawn hollered.

He yelled back, "I am praying!"

Griff looked over Dawn's head just then to the northern hills, and spied an opening in the clouds. Blue sky peeked through. It seemed the waves weren't as strong. The winds were ebbing. He was about to turn his eyes away when a burst of light blazed through the sky. Lightning? No!

These streaks were more brilliant. Griff saw a trail of smoke lifting skyward, rising like contrails. This was no natural occurrence. It had to be a missile.

The distant contrail ended high in the sky with a puff of smoke. Because he heard no sound, he decided not to alert Dawn or the others. He wondered if this missile launch could be related to Judah's warning.

The ride back was rocky. He and Dawn were thankful to walk safely off the boat uninjured. They boarded the bus and headed for Jerusalem, not getting to see Capernaum. Dawn nestled in the seat next to Griff wrapped in her jacket.

"I'm checking my phone," she said. "That looked like a tornado."

She pulled her cell from her fanny pack and scrolled down the screen. "Here's breaking news! Rockets were launched from Syria into the Golan Heights. Israeli Defense Force says the Iron Dome stopped many, but one landed near the Galilee."

Griff grasped her hand and drew close to her ear so no one else could hear. "That proves it. The storm made us turn back, and God used it to protect us. I didn't want to scare you any worse back there, but I saw a missile launch right after the captain made the turn on the Galilee. It must have been the Iron Dome."

"Wow!" She stared at him with wide and knowing eyes. "I'll never think of Israel again without always being aware of the danger they're in. Will you pray with me?"

He did, folding his hands over hers, with thankfulness for God's protection.

Griff pulled out his cell phone, found Judah's last text, and typed: *Thanking the IDF for the fireworks we saw this morning. Good job.*

Griff hit the send button, wondering what else God had in store for them here in the land of Israel.

GRIFF DIDN'T WAIT LONG to find out. As the bus driver unloaded bags at the Jerusalem hotel, Griff stood to the side reading his cell phone. Judah had written back: *Dawn is heading into the lobby. I am here in the area. Wait five minutes, then walk to the coffee cart across the street. I will hand you a cup. Keep walking.*

Griff noted the time on his phone. He stepped around the massive tour bus and gazed across the street. Sure enough, he spotted a food cart with a colorful umbrella. No one was around except a bent-over woman wearing a shawl, who hovered by the cart.

Seconds ticked by. Wondering what Judah had up his sleeve this time, Griff strode over to the cart when the five minutes were up. Before he said a word, the elderly woman handed him a to-go cup. She waved off any payment with a gnarled hand. Griff turned and a man dressed in khaki slacks and shirt strode toward him on the sidewalk.

He wore sunglasses on a cloudy day. Passing by Griff, he muttered, "Take the cup to your room and look inside," and sped away.

Griff hurried to his room with the cup. Dawn was napping. He carefully removed the lid from the empty cup and pulled out a small scrap of paper.

His eyes scanned a typed message: *Destroy after reading. The fireworks you saw were caused by a breach. Can't say more except look to the same enemy who invaded your partner's phones. It's time for action.*

Griff agreed. But what action did Judah mean?

Chapter 11

Eva walked into Griff's cubicle one morning after he'd returned to the office. He was typing feverishly on his keyboard.

"If you can break away, I've got something to tell you," Eva said. "Bring your coffee and join me in the conference room."

Griff grabbed his cup and hurried in behind her. He shut the door, saying, "It's great to be home. Before you begin, let me tell you what happened on the Sea of Galilee. Syrian rebels fired missiles into Israel. We were right in the line of fire until a fierce storm arose suddenly on the sea. We were forced to turn around and were saved."

Eva's eyes rounded. "Whew! Thankful you're safe. I imagine Dawn was upset."

"She was, more than I." Griff paused. "I'd already met with Judah and he warned me of possible hostilities."

"All in all, was the trip everything you both hoped for?"

Griff sipped his coffee. "Absolutely. It was exhilarating to be in places where Jesus ministered. Brings Him to life in ways I never imagined."

"I'd love to travel there with Scott sometime," she replied.

"Eva, I'm impressed by how Israeli Defense Forces and Mossad protect their people."

"Did you spend time with Judah?" she asked. "What did he tell you?"

"Not much, but it was well spent."

Griff then explained what Judah told him about China's successful hacking within Israel and elsewhere.

"We've seen the results firsthand," Eva declared, tapping a finger on the table.

Griff nodded. "Yeah, and each time Judah told me of possible danger, his warnings were spot-on. His last update said it was 'time to act.'"

"What do you think he meant?"

"After we landed at Dulles, I saw on TV Israel sent elite troops into Syria and wiped out several terrorist encampments." Griff arched his eyebrows. "If you poke Israel with a stick, you'd better expect Judah's people to impale you with a phone pole."

Eva finished her coffee and set down her travel mug. "We can learn lots from them, and you can learn a thing or two from me if you're ready to listen."

"I sense trouble brewing," he replied, grimacing.

"Just the opposite. I took good care of your cases and

developed a new informant for you." Eva watched for Griff's reaction.

He wiggled a bent finger. "Out with it, Eva."

"The morning you flew out, a woman showed up downstairs asking to speak with you. She wouldn't leave, so Sosa sent me down to quiz her."

"Who was she?"

"I invited her up and we talked in here. Turns out she's Jennifer Tuttle."

Griff shrugged. "Name means nothing."

"It will." Eva grinned. "Darin Hilton's sister Jennifer delivered half-a-million bucks in a bag taped shut to a woman named Susie, who claimed she could guarantee Judge Ginsburg would acquit Darin if he waived a jury trial."

"Ha!" Griff exploded in laughter. "That didn't work so well, did it? I can't believe Darin was that dumb, but it does explain his anger."

Eva raised a hand. "There's more. On Susie's phone call to Darin, she told him to prove the judge was agreeable, he would wear a bowtie at Darin's next motion appearance. And the judge did."

Griff folded his arms, grinning from ear to ear.

"What's so funny?" Eva demanded. "Do you know someone named Susie?"

"Don't you see the irony? One crook gets conned by another crook. Better they victimize each other than innocent law-abiding people."

"You don't think Judge Ginsburg wanted to throw the case?"

Griff shook his head. "Bottom line is, he didn't. The judge found Hilton guilty and the evidence supported his verdict. While it's true Hilton threw a temper tantrum in court, it doesn't mean the judge is corrupt."

"The whole thing smells like moldy cheese," Eva objected. "I know it's your case, but people don't usually waive jury trials."

Griff stared at Eva, and she could almost hear his mental gears turning, albeit a bit slowly. She checked her notes, giving him time to catch up and get over his jet lag.

He sipped his coffee before saying, "It's possible the culprit is someone in the justice system, like a lawyer or clerk in the courthouse. It bears our scrutiny."

"Ginsburg isn't off the hook in my eyes," Eva cautioned. "We can't rule him out."

Griff yawned, prompting Eva to hide her own yawn behind her hand.

"If you don't mind, Griff, we should search courthouse security videos to see if Ginsburg actually wore a bowtie on Hilton's motion day."

In reply, he pointed at his phone, suggesting, "Try April twenty-first."

"Why that date?"

"Perhaps you don't recall. The night of April twentieth, I played softball on the U.S. Attorney's baseball team against the judges."

"How does that help us know if Judge Ginsburg wore a bowtie?"

Griff's eyes shone. "Oh, I guarantee he wore a bowtie the next day."

"Did you already know about this and check it out?"

"You really have no idea, do you?" Griff mocked.

"No, and I'm getting tired of your game."

"Eva, it's an annual tradition," Griff told her. "The U.S. Attorney's office, assisted by me and other borrowed FBI agents, played their annual softball game against federal judges who recruited deputy U.S. marshals to help them."

Eva spit out, "And?" her frustration dripping.

"And this year the judges and marshals lost. So, as is the custom, they had to wear bowties to work the next day. It's always been that way."

"You can't be serious."

"Oh yes. I thought you knew. One day each year, you can walk into the federal courthouse and either the prosecutors or the judges will be wearing bowties. Men and women alike. This year it was April 21."

Eva lifted both hands and leaned forward. "Griff, think about it. If Judge Ginsburg is crooked and solicits bribes, he can't provide as an assurance he's going to wear a bowtie on a certain day when he doesn't know which team will win the game the night before the hearing."

"Right." Griff narrowed his eyes. "Nor can any trickster who works in the justice system at the courthouse. This is a real dilemma." He paused, before coming up with, "Maybe Hilton lied to his sister. You did say the shopping bag was taped shut."

"Jennifer said so." Eva wanted more coffee, yet hesitated to interrupt Griff's train of thought.

"Hilton may have his sister out running drug drops to raise money to pay his lawyer," he muttered. "He is a convicted felon."

Eva had to admit he made a valid point. There was a way to find out.

"You meet Jennifer and talk with her," Eva said. "Check the

motion hearing date to see if it was indeed the day after your bowtie ball game. Meanwhile, I'll keep combing my brain to find ways to solve this puzzle. I don't think we should mention this explosive allegation about the judge to anyone. Not yet."

"I don't intend to." Griff stood up and stretched his arms above his head. "I'll follow your suggestion and phone Jennifer."

IT WAS NEARLY FIVE O'CLOCK on Saturday afternoon when Eva pulled into the parking lot of the Trumpet's Call. Kaley's VW Bug was in the garage waiting for a new fuel pump, and Eva had to fetch her in time to feed and deliver her to a church youth group event. Eva reached the entrance just as Kaley's friend, Lexi Dawson, walked out.

"Hi, Mrs. Montanna," she said, waving.

"Hello back, Lexi. Is Kaley done with her shift?"

Lexi opened the door to her parents' van and slid in, saying, "Yeah. I donated a bunch of clothes. She's sorting them now."

"Are you going to the party at church?" Eva asked.

Lexi beamed a smile. "Yes, with Conner."

She waved again before slamming the door. Eva went inside, amazed by the rows and rows of folded and hanging clothes. Irene DeVroom stayed behind the cash register to help a customer. Kaley tossed a pair of jeans into a bin.

"Mom, I have to pay for this before we can leave," Kaley said, grabbing her jacket and a small battered suitcase.

Eva shook her head, scolding, "Your luggage at home is nice. You don't need that old thing."

"But I do." Undeterred, Kaley set the "old thing" on a counter and opened it. "Look! It's perfect for storing my American Doll and her accessories."

"I guess it's better than the tired cardboard box Molly's in now," Eva admitted. "Grandpa Marty will be glad to know you're still interested in the doll he gave you."

"Mom, I love how Molly is from WWII. You took me to the Netherlands where Grandpa Marty served in the war."

Kaley slid her fingers into a silky fabric pocket on the side. "Look. I can put her mini-doll in here. In this small pocket along the back, I'll keep her tiny books."

"Very nice," Eva said, relenting. "Let's get going or you'll miss supper."

Kaley pulled something out. "Hey, someone left old pictures in here."

"Please pay for the case." Eva checked her watch. "You can

look at those later."

After setting the suitcase on the countertop, Kaley said, "Mrs. DeVroom, I want to buy this, but I found two colored pictures inside."

"That's four whole dollars," Irene replied, entering the sale into the register.

Kaley dug in her pocket for money while Irene inspected the photos. Eva noticed a quizzical look pass across her friend's face.

"I can't believe I never found these," Irene said, looking wistful.

Curious, Eva leaned in to have a look. "Do you know those people?"

"I do," Irene said, touching the photos. "When I brought this suitcase from my home, I didn't remember its special history. It belonged to a young dying mother who asked us to raise her son. In this suitcase she had packed his clothes."

"Irene!" Eva exclaimed, her eyes stinging. "That's so precious and sad."

Irene held the pictures in her hands as a treasure. "You met our son, John Lapp, at the Biltmore. We adopted him, but it was his mother's desire for him to keep his father's last name. Recently, we gave him a letter she'd written for him just before her death. This is the first I've seen these photos."

Irene handed Eva one with worn edges. Kaley stood by, gazing at them with tears hovering on her eyelashes.

"I'm surprised to see a photo of this Amish teenager as they normally don't pose for pictures," Irene said, pushing a strand of hair behind her ear. "There's no mistaking it. She is Johnny's mother, Sarah. Notice the wooden chair, plain dress covered with an apron, and her starched white bonnet."

"See, Kaley? She's pretty without makeup and blow-dried hair." Eva flashed a tight smile.

Irene handed Eva the second photo. "This large castle-like building with the arched entryway is in Lancaster. Sarah is kneeling down and Johnny is the young boy standing with his arms around her neck."

"Both look very happy," Eva remarked, her heart touched by John's history.

"Kaley, do you mind if I don't sell you this suitcase?" Irene's voice cracked. "I'd like Johnny to have it. He's never seen a likeness of his mother. He was only five when she died. He'll cherish the suitcase, I think."

"What a sweet story." Kaley wiped her eyes. "Please give it to him. I know he'll treasure it always. I would."

Eva laid a hand on Kaley's shoulders. "Let's give Irene time alone."

They slipped outside with Eva mentioning on the way to the car, "I saw Lexi leaving a few minutes ago."

"She and her mom cleaned out their closets and donated tons of clothes," Kaley explained as she opened the passenger door.

"Lexi said she's going to the party at church with Conner." Eva hoped Kaley would reveal more about her plans.

Kaley buckled her seatbelt, saying only, "She's going to pick me up."

"Are her parents taking her?" Eva asked, starting the SUV.

"No. Connor's driving and will come for me after Lexi."

"Dad and I will take you just the same. Andy wants burgers at the root beer stand where we used to go. Sounds fun. Then we'll drop you at church."

"Mom," Kaley protested. "Why can't I go with Lexi? You guys refused to let me go with them to Wolf Trap's opening concert."

"One simple reason. You and Lexi have been friends for years. Her friend Conner is new to us, moving up here a few months ago from Florida. Your dad and I aren't comfortable with him."

Kaley slumped in her seat and folded her arms in defiance. Eva sighed inwardly. Her daughter had such a stable outlook for her life until recently. Why the sudden change? Two words burst into Eva's mind.

Conner Kosta.

That kid was a bad influence in spite of any "potential" Kaley thought he had. Eva saw right through him. The kid used his charming ways to play on Kaley and Lexi's desire to help the downtrodden and lost. She switched on praise music she knew Kaley liked, and drove away from the Trumpet's Call with a heartfelt prayer God would protect her children from the evil one's schemes.

To Eva's surprise, Kaley raised a new subject of conversation. "Mom, do you think I could be a lawyer?"

"A lawyer? Sure! You're smart and determined. It means three years of law school after college."

"A lawyer donated beautiful clothes today. She's about my size so I tried on one of her suits. I looked like a lawyer ready to do battle in court for my clients."

Eva smiled, pulling to a stop at the red light. "Kaley, you can do whatever you put your mind to. Dad and I are praying you'll find God's plan for your life."

"Thanks, Mom. Oh, the lawyer knows you. She defends people in federal court. I said maybe you arrested one of her clients."

"Be more careful telling people about me. Who is this woman

attorney?"

"Madison something. Mrs. DeVroom said she's very nice and brings in lots of quality clothes."

"Oh, you met Maddie Stone," Eva said, turning down their street. "It's fine she knows you're my daughter."

"Yup, that's her name. She says you're a super good agent."

Eva eased into the garage. "Just be aware I don't want most defense attorneys knowing anything about me or our family."

"I'm careful, Mom, especially after the weird things with my phone."

As they walked into the house, a question plagued Eva, which had nothing to do with Madison Stone or her client Darin Hilton's shenanigans.

Kaley was at a turning point, needing answers for her future. Eva reminded herself to ask Scott to talk with their daughter before the youth group party tonight. She refused to stand idly by and let her wonderful Kaley slide down to Conner's level.

Chapter 12

Griff Topping drove with gusto on Monday morning. He reached the JTTF parking garage early. He spotted Eva in her car already waiting for him. She'd agreed to meet him in the garage and go with him to conduct an interview. She was in for a surprise and Griff couldn't wait to gauge her reaction.

He parked his Bu-car next to Eva. She motioned him over like she wanted to drive. Good idea. He could brief her as she drove. Griff slid into the passenger side of her government-issued Fusion and secured the seatbelt with a wide smile.

She sat watching him. "You were unusually brief on the phone last night, saying this interview relates to Hilton's case and now you look like the cat who caught a mouse."

"Susan Brockman's office is fifteen minutes away," was all he said, enjoying keeping her in the dark a bit longer.

"You're stonewalling. What gives?" Eva pressed.

He slid his cell phone from his pants pocket. "Turn left at the street."

"So that's how it's going to be," she griped, pulling the shifter into gear and heading down the garage's exit ramp.

At the bottom of the ramp, she glanced past Griff and accelerated while making the left turn. His head snapped against the headrest.

"Whoa, Eva. Didn't you see that car coming straight at us?" he grumbled.

Eva looked furtively toward Griff and changed lanes. "Of course. Why do you think I took off like I did? No way I wanted to be stuck behind that super slow guy."

"Okay, here's the skinny for our interview." Griff settled back in his seat, hoping Eva would take it easy. "You met Jennifer Tuttle, who delivered a half-million dollars to a woman at the Red Dragon for her brother, Darin, right?"

"Jennifer was afraid she'd make trouble for him because he insisted she talk only to you. I met with her because you were in Israel," Eva declared, sounding apologetic.

Griff waved off her concern. "You were right to interview her, and pronto."

"We go straight here, right?" she asked.

"Yeah. It's not too far ahead."

Eva passed a car and zipped into the right lane just as the traffic light turned yellow. She stomped on the brakes, skidding to a stop at the crosswalk. Griff slid forward in his seat. The seatbelt tightened at his lap and squeezed across his chest.

"Easy, Eva! You drive like you're on a racetrack."

She laughed. "Griff, you're a basket case. You need more experience riding shotgun. I never complain about your driving."

"I don't drive as recklessly as you."

"Yes, you do. We both drive like we're used to tailing people. The only difference is, I'm always prepared for your sudden moves."

The light turned green and Eva sped off. Griff grasped the hand grip above the window. She apparently wasn't done razzing him.

"You don't complain when Dawn drives, do you?"

Griff simply checked their route on his phone and didn't respond.

"Silence," Eva said, tailgating the car ahead of them. "Maybe you don't let Dawn get behind the wheel. Is that it?"

"I can tell by your aggressive driving, Scott does most of the driving in your family," Griff offered in his defense.

"*Au contraire*," Eva barked. "Between me and Kaley, Scott gets very little time behind the wheel."

"Truthfully, do you want Kaley driving like a crazy woman?"

Eva continued speeding in the right lane. "When she becomes a federal agent, I do. Course, that may not happen now that she's met Madison Stone."

"What? Maddie talked her out of becoming an agent?" Griff asked. "Weird."

"Yeah, it's strange. Kaley is set on law school and being a lawyer like Maddie. My daughter has wanted to follow in my footsteps and become a federal agent for as long as I can remember."

"Life sometimes throws us curveballs when we expect sliders," Griff said. "Turn right at the next light."

She did so with ease. Griff decided it was a good time to redirect her attention.

"Back to the reason for the interview. Jennifer's claims shed light on why Darin blew a fuse when the judge pronounced him guilty. Since I returned from Israel, I started wondering if the money was delivered to the wrong woman."

"You never mentioned that to me," Eva snapped.

"I am now. Today, you and I will meet Susan Brockman, the woman who might be the unexpected beneficiary of a possible error."

"And you think I drive fast. How did you identify her so quickly?"

Griff felt Eva was impressed and chuckled. "I had help. Last year at a financial investigation seminar, I met an IRS agent who is liaison to social media companies."

"What did he do to help?" Eva asked, braking at the red light.

"They honor our subpoenas for our active investigations when there's evidence in a person's social media postings," Griff replied. "I issued a subpoena for an unknown subject living in Virginia and D.C. zip codes."

"Looking for what? I don't understand why you didn't tell me before about this."

"I wanted to see if I could put it together first. Guess what? Someone claims to have found or received a lot of cash," he told her with a smirk.

"Susan Brockman?"

Griff checked the map on his phone. "Another mile. A few days after Hilton's cash is delivered to the Red Dragon, a woman named Susan sends a private message to her sister in Atlanta saying she's behind in her car payment, but an angel surprised her with a gift of money. She used many dollar signs indicating mega-amounts of money."

"Hmm." Eva pointed ahead. "The office we're going to is near the Red Dragon where Susan eats lunch, right?"

Griff nodded. "Her sister answers back, 'How much?' Susan writes she can now buy whichever car she wants."

"This should be fun. I'm predicting she's quite pretty." Eva sported a grin.

"Why?"

"Because Darin's sister Jennifer said she gave the money to a woman who looked very much like me."

"Ha." Griff chuckled. "You've got that right."

Griff gestured to Susan Brockman's office building, and Eva pulled to a sudden stop.

"According to the website, Susan is on the real estate office staff," he explained.

"Let's see if she's even here." Eva swiped the keys from the ignition. "And not on an island vacation somewhere, spending all of her newfound money."

"Or maybe she's the new CEO because she bought the company."

He hopped out and slammed the door, ready to find out if his theory was right.

GRIFF PRESENTED HIS GOLD FBI BADGE to the receptionist. She shuddered and looked at the front door like she wanted to get out of there.

Griff asked her again, "Is Susan here?"

"Ms. Brockman is in her office," the rattled receptionist said. "Come this way."

She rushed to the firm's conference room without another word and left Griff and Eva to wait for Susan Brockman, who had apparently been summoned.

"Looks like your witness is sticking around town after all," Eva kidded her partner after five minutes. "She sure is taking her time. Maybe she's calling her lawyer."

Griff held onto his badge. "I'll lead off the questioning. Watch her closely, Eva. She may try to lie her way out of a jam."

Susan stepped timidly into the room. She wore a casual outfit and kept her hands folded in front of her. Griff flipped open his leather credential holder to reveal his photo and shiny badge.

"I'm Agent Griffin Topping, FBI." He nodded to Eva. "This is my partner, Eva Montanna."

"Hello," Susan said, shaking their hands.

Griff lifted his chin at Eva, signaling he noticed the woman's striking appearance and her vivid blue eyes. Her light blond hair was nearly the same shade as Eva's. However, Susan wore plenty of makeup and eyeliner, which Eva did not.

"Susan, thanks for meeting us," Griff said in a lighthearted tone. "May we ask you to close the door?"

A look of fright spread across her face, though she did as he asked. Susan remained standing with her back against the door. She pointed to chairs along a table.

"You can sit down. I really don't know what this is about."

Before Griff could answer, Susan began saying nervously, "Has something gone wrong with one of the houses? Was something stolen? I just sit in the open houses, you know. I don't know anything about anything, except what people might tell me as I walk them through the house."

Griff snagged a seat at the far side of the table where he could watch the door, as he always did. Eva sat beside him. Susan slowly perched across from Eva with her back to the entrance door.

Griff sensed Susan was hiding something the way her clasped hands quivered.

"Ms. Brockman," he said, his voice growing stern. "Is it true you've eaten a midday meal at the Red Dragon in the last six weeks?"

He saw an instant reaction in Susan's eyes. Fear once again swept across her face.

She swiped a hand across her forehead. "Ye-es, that's true.

How did you know?"

Griff leaned slightly toward Susan. Eva made notes on her pad.

"On how many occasions?" he asked.

Susan's hands flew across the table in front of her. "I eat there every week. It's close to the office and the food is good. Does it matter where I have lunch?"

"We understand on one occasion you received an unexpected gift while enjoying the good food." Griff fixed his eyes upon hers.

She stared at him for some time as if grasping for the truth. "Am I in trouble?"

"It depends on why you received the money," Griff replied. "If you're involved in a crime, like ransom money, bribe payoffs, or blackmail, then you could be in serious trouble."

Her eyes moistened. "I did nothing wrong. I'm a struggling single mom with three kids and unpaid bills. One day, an angel comes in the restaurant and hands me a gift that covers some of my big expenses."

"What did you do to earn the money?" Eva interjected.

Tears trickled down Susan's cheeks. "Nothing. Absolutely nothing. I don't know why she gave me the money."

"Did the angel call you by name?" Griff asked.

"Yes, she did," Susan then shook her head. "No. Wait. She asked me if my name was Sue and I told her yes."

"Tell me how the money was packaged," Griff said.

"In a shopping bag. It was taped shut at the top." Susan wiped her cheeks with the palm of her hand. "She simply gave me the bag and left."

Eva asked a question of her own. "Did you look into the bag?"

"Not at first because it was taped shut. I took a steak knife and cut through the tape. When I looked inside, I couldn't believe the huge stacks of money."

"Use these," Eva said, handing Susan a small pack of tissues from her purse, adding, "Describe your angel for us."

Susan dabbed her eyes with a tissue. "After what she did for me, I will never forget her. She's my age, on the tall side, and long auburn hair past her shoulders."

"How much money was in the bag?" Griff asked, striving to find out if Susan was telling the truth or involved in the bribery scheme.

She stiffened in her seat. "Do I have to say?"

"Are you concerned about paying taxes on the money because you really earned it somehow?" Eva blurted.

Susan's eyes darted from Eva to Griff for an uncomfortable time. No one said a word.

Finally, she cried, "Five hundred thousand dollars! The angel gave me five hundred thousand dollars!"

Griff didn't blink. It must be a staggering number for a working single mother. Giving Susan time to consider what else she should confess, he stayed mum. Eva stayed occupied with her notes. He imagined her mind was also revving over their next steps.

"Am I going to jail? Can't I keep the money?" Susan gushed like a fire hose.

Griff settled back in his seat, and started talking again in an easy tone, "Susan, it's like this. If you did nothing wrong, you've nothing to fear. You're in trouble if we learn you were in fact an accomplice to a crime."

"I'm not an accomplice to anything wrong," Susan insisted, her eyes sparking fire. "The gift came from out of the blue … from above, if you like."

Eva set down her pen hard on the table. "You may believe God answered your prayers. I'm all for His miracle-working power being revealed in people's lives. Agent Topping and I are tasked to ensure justice is being done here on earth. We may want you to take a polygraph exam, to test if you're telling us the truth."

"I am telling the truth and will take your exam now if you want me to," Susan vowed, her voice no longer shaky.

Eva picked up her pen and waited. Griff assumed Eva was signaling she was satisfied by Susan's reaction. He'd probe a bit more to determine if she was being truthful.

"We will get back to you about the polygraph," Griff replied. "Do you have the money someplace safe?"

"Yes."

"Where is it?" he asked.

"I hid it."

Eva held her pen in the air and went on the attack. "Susan, you need to get that money out of your coffee can or from beneath your mattress and secure it in a safety deposit box. Don't tell anyone else you have it. And don't post about it on social media."

"You mean you're not taking it from me?" She sounded incredulous.

"It is possible the government may demand you surrender it at some point. Then again, that may never happen," Griff admitted.

"Do you know why it was given to me?" Susan asked, her brow creased.

Griff stood. He was done asking questions. "Perhaps you were mistaken for someone else. It could be the money was intended for use in a crime. You appear to have received it innocently. My advice is don't spend it and pray you can keep it in the end."

"Will I ever learn if I get to keep it?" she asked, clasping her hands together.

Eva smiled. "We should be able to advise you in a few months, or at most a year."

Susan handed the tissue pack back to Eva, who waved it off, telling her to keep it.

Griff gave Susan some final advice. "Tell your co-workers we were looking for witnesses to an incident at the Red Dragon. Just say we were vague when it appeared you couldn't help."

Back in the car a few minutes later, Eva started the engine and turned to Griff, asking, "Susan's description does match Jennifer Tuttle. Do you have a next step?"

"Darin's sister delivered the money to Susan, all right," Griff replied. "She just gave it to the wrong person."

Eva tugged on her seatbelt, voicing a concern, "If we let this go, we may never know if the judge was involved in the attempted bribery or if Darin was scammed."

"Good point. I can brief Patrick on this unexpected turn of events and see if he wants us to investigate further before Hilton is sentenced."

Eva pulled the selector into gear and drove off, asking, "What about the money?"

"I'm curious where Darin got so much cash to make the payoff," Griff said. "We might discover it's the proceeds from a criminal act."

Eva changed lanes. "Then we seize it for whatever other crime he committed."

"Sounds like a plan," Griff answered, scrolling on his phone.

"But wouldn't we be diverted from investigating the terrorism cases we're supposed to be doing?"

"Uh huh," Griff mumbled, checking his messages. One caught his eye.

"Griff!" Eva barked. "Put your phone away and listen."

He clipped the phone back on his belt, saying, "Sorry, Brett texted me."

"We shouldn't be tempted to go after the bribery money," Eva proclaimed. "We might not be able to seize it, and shouldn't forget our task force mission."

Griff turned slightly in his seat. "Eva, that's wise counsel."

"I hope Susan can keep the money," she said, turning left when traffic cleared. "I like her thinking it was a divine gifting. So no more investigating the money?"

They rode in silence while Griff gathered his thoughts. He

trusted Eva's instincts, yet a part of him wanted to hammer Hilton for daring to bribe a federal judge. What if Ginsburg had improper motives in finding Hilton guilty?

He mentally reviewed the evidence against Hilton, and when they reached their parking garage, Griff said, "We had the goods against Hilton. Ginsburg can enhance his sentence for the threats Hilton made in court. We don't need to investigate the money any further."

"You're a trusted agent, Griff," Eva told him in the parking garage.

"So, I agree," he said, grabbing the car handle. "We do our assigned job and let Susan Brockman be blessed."

Chapter 13

The next day, after a demanding work schedule, Eva zoomed home. She had just enough time to bring Kaley to the garage, pick up the green Volkswagen, and get home to fix a quick dinner. She tried putting time pressures aside because she really enjoyed being alone with Kaley.

As they sped to the garage, Eva told her, "Finally repairs are done. Will you be glad to start driving your little green Bug again?"

"I like driving your old car, because it was yours," Kaley chimed. "Just like I loved the trip with you and Dad to Europe to see where Grandpa Marty served in the Army. It gave me fresh perspective about what he did in World War II."

"Dad and I have been talking about visiting Grandpa in Michigan this summer before your college starts," Eva said, passing through a green traffic light.

Kaley let out a high-pitched scream and cried, "Mom!"

Eva's eyes darted left! Then right! At the same time, her foot lifted off the gas and searched for the brake pedal.

Seeing no danger, she hollered, "What?!"

"You passed a wrecker back there." Kaley pointed over her shoulder. "It's hauling Connor's car!"

Eva checked her left mirror and saw a wrecker completing a left turn and hauling a badly-wrecked red car.

"I'm calling Lexi." Kaley began punching on her cell phone. "That's his car. I saw his Bucs decal on the rear end."

"A Bucs decal?" Eva caught her breath from hearing Kaley cry out.

Kaley sighed. "Tampa Bay Buccaneers. He's from Florida, Mom. Lexi isn't answering."

Eva heard Lexi's voice message click on. Kaley shouted in her phone, "Lexi, I saw Connor's car all smashed. What happened? Please call me back!"

"See how fast things can turn sour?" Eva cautioned. "Which is why your dad and I don't like you driving with friends in your car. They're too great a distraction."

"I hope Connor isn't hurt," Kaley worried aloud. "Or Lexi."

Eva swung into the parking lot at the auto repair shop, her mind flooded with concern for Lexi. She told Kaley so, adding, "Did Lexi plan to be with Conner today?"

"Every day, Mom." Kaley kept her eyes glued to the phone. "Connor was picking Lexi up at school."

Eva spotted her old bright green VW parked near the street,

ready for pickup. She handed Kaley a key to transfer her backpack and gear into the Bug while Eva paid the bill. A few minutes later, she returned with Kaley's key.

"You're staring at your phone as if that will make Lexi call and tell you she's okay. Until we hear back, Kaley, please find courage. You have dreams of being a federal agent or maybe an attorney. With either one, when presented with a frightening or challenging event, you have to determine to respond logically and not emotionally."

Kaley wiped a tear from her cheek.

Eva gave her a hug. "Come, I'll follow you home. Take a deep breath. Drive carefully, honey, and be brave."

"I will," Kaley said, hugging Eva.

At home, Kaley beat her mother into the house. Eva entered the kitchen and saw Kaley run straight to her room. Eva set down her big purse, and was about to wash her hands when she spotted a light flashing on the answering machine. She pressed 'play' and stood close to listen.

"Eva, it's Yvonne from the church prayer chain. Trish Dawson is heading to the hospital. Her daughter was injured in a car accident. Please pray for Lexi!"

Eva replayed the message as Kaley scurried into the kitchen.

"I heard her say Lexi was in a car accident! I knew that was Conner's car!"

Kaley sounded frightened and looked terrified. Eva fought panic. She could be on the way to the hospital if Kaley had been in the car with that wild kid! Suppressing her fears, Eva sought to comfort her daughter.

"The church prayer chain is sending alerts asking us to pray for Lexi. She was in an accident, probably with Connor. You and I can pray—"

"Mom!" Kaley interjected. "Call Mrs. Dawson and find out if she's okay! I'm going to the hospital."

Eva kept her voice low and firm. "Honey, let's wait to call Trish. She's busy with Lexi at the hospital. Prayer is the most important thing."

She grabbed Kaley's hand. They stood close together in the kitchen, and Eva whispered, "Father God, please help dear Lexi and Conner in whatever they're facing right now. Give wisdom to the medical team and comfort to Lexi's folks and Conner's too. May they receive Your protection and healing. Strengthen our faith as we wait on You. We ask in Jesus' name."

Mother and daughter said "Amen" in unison. Kaley opened her

eyes and looked at Eva. She sniffled.

"Mom, that was a beautiful prayer," she said. "What should I do now?"

"First, give me a hug." Eva wrapped her arms around her daughter, and when they released each other, she told her, "You and I will both trust the Lord with all our hearts." Kaley slumped in a kitchen chair. "It's hard not knowing."

"There is power in prayer," Eva assured Kaley. "Go splash cold water on your face. Then we'll concentrate on dinner. Dad will be home from work soon. He and your brothers will want to eat something even if we aren't hungry. This is when our faith in God must be stronger than our fears."

DINNER ENDED with Scott dashing into the garage to pump air in the bike tires. The boys were clearing the table when the phone rang. Eva recognized Yvonne's number on the caller ID.

"Is this about Lexi?" Kaley asked, hovering behind Eva's shoulder.

"We'll find out."

Eva pushed the phone's speaker button to let Kaley hear.

"Trish called and it's fairly good news," Yvonne said excitedly. "Lexi has a concussion, and no broken bones. She'll miss school and work for a few days, giving time for her concussion to heal."

Tight strain released from Eva's neck muscles. She blinked back tears, and glanced at Kaley whose bottom lip was trembling.

Eva told Yvonne, "We've been praying for Lexi and her family."

"They feel the prayers. Trish asks us to pray for the boy whose car Lexi was riding in. His name is Connor. He's hospitalized with a severe concussion, and has broken ribs and a fractured tibia."

Kaley wiped her eyes and nodded.

"We will," Eva promised. "Kaley knows Conner from a youth group meeting."

Yvonne cleared her throat. "The police found methamphetamine and fentanyl in his car. They think Conner took a mixture of the drugs and passed out while driving."

"How awful," Eva said, trying not to overreact within Kaley's earshot.

At the mention of illegal drugs, Kaley spun around and bolted toward her room. Eva turned her attention to her prayer partner and friend.

"I'm concerned Lexi and other young people are at risk from his erratic behavior," Eva told Yvonne. "Do you know his parents?"

Yvonne did not. "Nor has Trish met them. They live in Florida.

I think Connor moved in with his grandmother not too far from my house."

When Eva hung up, she headed straight into Kaley's room without knocking and demanded, "Tell me, did you know Connor is into drugs?"

"No way!"

Kaley stared at her cell phone. "He kept distancing Lexi from her friends, and especially from church activities. I hope she hasn't tried drugs. That would be the worst."

"Kaley, talk with me without looking at your phone," Eva insisted. "I told you before I sensed something was wrong with him and you wouldn't listen."

Kaley dropped on her bed, still clutching the phone. At least she looked at Eva.

"I felt I had to be with them." Kaley sighed. "To stick with Lexi so he didn't turn her away from her faith in God. I've been praying he'd lose his influence in her life."

"Sweetie." Eva sat beside Kaley. "May God use this trial to begin answering your prayers. You and her parents will encourage Lexi to be wiser in choosing friends."

Kaley leaned against Eva's shoulder before lifting her head to gaze in her eyes. "And I should be too. God protected me from going with them and getting in the accident. You're always right, Mom. I'll talk with Lexi when she feels better. She must cut Connor loose. If she won't, I'll concentrate on what the Lord has for my future."

"Sounds great, kiddo. I'm here for you always."

After giving her daughter a loving pat on the shoulder, Eva went to find Scott in the garage and share the news.

"We shouldn't delay having a serious talk with our three kids about the dangers of drugs," Eva said, hands on her hips.

Scott held his air pump and stared back at her. "Dutch is still pretty young,"

"I need your wisdom on this," Eva said in earnest. "Don't let this teachable moment escape. You and I've seen the damage when people make bad choices."

"We'll have our family meeting, and then go for ice cream. My treat."

Eva smiled at her husband and left the garage, thinking of Conner's parents and how their son had gone so wrong. Conner was messed up and apparently gave no thought to hurting Lexi. Disgust at his selfishness assailed Eva's mind. Darin Hilton was no better. Not only had he tried to bribe a federal judge, he ensnared his sister Jennifer into a web of deceit in making the payoff. God had intervened. The cash had gone to a struggling single mom with three children.

If Susan Brockman kept the money and used it for her children, to Eva, that sounded like sweet justice. She went in the house to find the kids, her heart brimming with a burning desire to keep them free from criminals and safe always.

Chapter 14

It was a sweltering Thursday night. John Lapp turned on the overhead fan and prepared for bed in his tiny Ohio apartment. He returned an hour ago from a technology conference on the East Coast. After unloading his pockets, he placed his wallet and keys on the nightstand next to his bed.

He took a business card from his front pants pocket, the one Marlow gave him at the Biltmore. Cora had bragged up John's computer skills to her husband, who then urged John to call him.

"Is it too late to try him now?" he wondered aloud.

So many weeks had passed. Should he even bother? John examined the card:

Marlow Bryson, CEO of Occidental Organics Inc.
World's leading wholesaler of Organic Foods

Marlow must be boasting he was the "world's leading wholesaler." John considered himself an expert in organic food production and never heard of Occidental Organics until Cora married Marlow three years ago. Though dog-tired, John's curiosity surged. He logged onto the computer to explore Occidental's website.

Sudden hunger pains forced him to first heat chicken nuggets in the microwave. He brought his meager supper to the computer and spent time browsing the company's history. Marlow's product diversity and distribution system intrigued John.

Eating his nuggets and fighting exhaustion, he ended up with more questions than answers. He closed his laptop and prepared for bed. Much later, after he crawled beneath the quilt Mom made him for Christmas, John dreamed happy dreams of living on an Amish farm.

JOHN'S ALARM STARTLED HIM AWAKE. Morning light streamed through a crack in the room-darkening curtains. He sat up in bed, looking around the room. Oh right, he'd made it back home from the conference. His apartment on campus of the State College of Agriculture was situated midway between Columbus and Cleveland, and hardly a real home. The college provided most of the furniture.

Because he taught a class this Friday morning, he needed to "rise and shine," as Pop loved to say when he was a boy. John needed to be on the road by noon for a meeting in Walnut Cove, where he hoped to help Eli Miller start growing certifiable organic produce on his Amish farm.

John slid his feet into his shoes, and tucking the laces in the sides, he shuffled across the efficiency apartment to switch on his coffee pot, a recent birthday gift from Pop. He turned on his computer and straightened the bed covers. Having so few possessions to call his own didn't bother him. He kept too busy as an associate professor to make his dwelling more home-like.

He stepped to the window to pull back the curtains. The sight of the wide green campus lawn with students bustling to class filled his mind with good thoughts. He loved spending time out-of-doors, and could hardly wait to visit the Miller farm.

An important task drew his attention. He removed a letter from an envelope and re-read it. John brushed a hand over the simple handwriting of his birth mother. His eyes moistened just thinking of his mommy writing such tender words before her death. Mom DeVroom had preserved the letter for John and presented it to him at the Biltmore.

He'd already duplicated the letter so he could create a screen saver of his mother's favorite flowers, which adorned the top and borders. The letter he kept in his resume file for always.

John checked the clock. Five minutes wouldn't hurt, he decided. Though he was expected soon in class, he wanted to read her letter one more time. He tapped gently on the miniature letter so it enveloped the entire screen. An arbutus stem reached across the top of the stationary and into his heart as he read:

Dearest Johnny:

By now, you have received this letter from Fritz and Irene. I am writing as it's my last chance to love and encourage you. Irene gave me this beautiful paper with my favorite flowers of all, arbutus. She and Fritz agreed to grant my greatest wish, to raise you and love you. The doctor says I do not have long to live.

While I have many regrets, my faith in God remains sure. I was raised by a loving family in a supportive community, which I hope one day you will discover. My people are plain people who chose a simple life, avoiding conveniences to depend more completely on God, the One whom they and I love and trust.

My life there holds precious memories. Feeding an apple to Nellie, our sweet mare. Helping Mama can tomatoes. Seeing stars twinkle on the farm at night. And most of all, I think of you, my beautiful and strong son. Now I see you would have thrived in the community. Because of hurt feelings, I took you and moved to the city after your father died. I am sorry you missed the closeness of our families. It's too late to correct that, and I hope you find your father's parents someday. They will love to know you.

Even though I knew as a young girl God loved me, it's what I learned in the DeVroom's Bible study that grew my belief in Jesus and His sacrifice for my sins. Irene showed me in Scripture how God secured our future when He sent Jesus to be crucified and raised Him from the dead to fulfill prophecy.

Johnny, I pray you will accept Jesus' wonderful gift of salvation so we can be together in heaven one day. Listen to all the DeVrooms teach you and choose Jesus, Who gives us life after death with Him. Follow His path and you will grow into a godly man. My dear son, I love you with all my heart! Your ever-loving Mommy.

Tears stung John's eyes and he flung them away with his hand. The other day when he'd read his mother's letter, he'd also cried. He longed to assure her how important Jesus was in his life. He did want to know more about his father's parents. If only he could find answers to the constant question that plagued his mind, night and day.

John wanted to know where he was supposed to live his life. Previously, he'd been told his father died when John was a toddler, his mother moved to the city where she met Mom and Pop, and they adopted him before he turned five years old. He'd recently found out he'd been born to Amish parents on an Amish farm.

Should he be living among the Amish? John also wanted to know if he could reconcile his chosen profession of working with computers and technology every day with a plain way of life.

Time was speeding by and he must get to class. His problems would have to wait. As he closed the computer lid, a kernel of hope grew that his work at the Miller farm would provide the answers he so desperately was seeking.

In the closet-sized bathroom, he lathered his face and shaved his lip and cheeks, carefully following the outline of his new Amish beard. He intended to be on the lookout at the Miller farm for more ways to identify with his heritage.

He was hurrying to class when a visiting professor walking toward him raised a hand as if wanting John to stop. John recognized this man who was from China and taught advanced computer courses.

He introduced himself to John as Mao Peng, adding, "I teach class in the same labs where you teach."

"I am John Lapp and teach agriculture classes and an elementary computer class."

"Yes." Professor Peng dipped his head. "I know. I am here on fellowship and return to China next year. I wonder, can we have lunch together? I could tell you of a chance to study and teach in China, and could sponsor you for a fellowship there."

"Really?" John was astonished by Peng's suggestion. China was a far cry from living on an Amish farm.

He thought a moment, telling Peng, "I never thought of going to China, let alone teaching there."

"We have lunch together." Peng smiled. "I will tell you more."

"I suppose it can't hurt," John replied, smiling in return.

Peng bowed slightly. "I will locate your name on the school website and send you the email with possible times."

"I'm late for class now," John said, wanting to hurry. "It was nice to meet you."

"Me too." Peng waved and walked on.

IT WAS NEARLY TWO O'CLOCK when John turned into Eli Miller's gravel drive. His spirits soared at the thought of finally arriving at the Amish farm. This one seemed like many other Amish farms John passed along the drive to Walnut Cove, a tight-knit community that many plain people called home. The Miller's large, plain white house with its several additions represented something more to John, and his unknown past rose up to greet him.

He parked the car and gazed out its front window. Sure enough, no electrical wires ran to the house from poles along the road. Three white outbuildings and a windmill revealed a simple life. Two black buggies, parked outside the good-sized barn, made John wonder if his mother might have lived in a similar home.

John beeped his horn before getting out and strolling over to the barn. Gravel crunched beneath his sturdy black shoes as he walked along. Being here in a white cotton shirt and bibbed coveralls, he almost felt like a plain person.

Mr. Miller strode from the barn, looking like the Amish farmer John remembered, wearing work boots, dark pants, grey shirt, and straw hat. His blue eyes sparkled above a long shaggy beard. He extended a hand, and John grabbed it, noting he wore no gloves. The farmer's gnarled hands gave evidence to a life of hard manual labor.

"Hello, John Lapp," he said in a friendly tone. "Welcome to our farm."

John sensed he was a kid again meeting his new teacher and used a formal tone.

"Hello, Mr. Miller. As I explained last month at the town meeting, the college encourages us to help organic farmers. I'm keen to know your challenges. I brought kits for taking soil samples and literature for organic farming."

"Good. First things first. John, because we are working

together, you call me Eli."

"Yes, sir. I mean, Eli."

Eli nodded, and then called over his shoulder, "Thomas, come."

John watched Eli's son, who he'd also met in town, run out of the barn. The fourteen-year-old was dressed the same as his father, had peach fuzz and no Amish beard.

"Hello again, John Lapp." Thomas extended a firm hand. "Did you leave your wife at home? Are you here to go hunting?"

"No. I'm here to share information about organic farming with your father. I'm not married."

Eli pointed to John's beard and smiled. "Thomas is joking with you. Amish men do not grow a beard like yours until they marry. We wear bibs only when we hunt."

"I didn't realize. I don't want anyone thinking I'm married," John lamented.

"You are right," Eli said, chuckling. "You will scare away every prospect in the county."

John didn't find his mistake funny. When Eli spoke to Thomas in their traditional Pennsylvania Dutch language, John had no idea what he said. This visit may prove more challenging than he'd realized.

Eli gestured to the barn, telling John, "We have a guest room for you in the barn. First, Thomas gets the buggy, and you drive your car to town. Park at the general store. My friend, John Nolt, is the owner and lets you keep your car there."

"You ride back with me in the buggy," Thomas said, his eyes glowing.

"You know we do not drive cars," Eli said. "It is best if your car is not here overnight. I have young daughters."

"No problem."

John went to open his trunk. He and Eli carried several boxes into the barn where John inhaled deeply. The spacious place held a collection of unusual odors and sounds. Sweet aroma of dried hay mingled with the rank odor of cow and horse manure. He enjoyed a soft whinny coming from a brown horse, which Thomas was leading outside.

Eli opened a rough-sawn wooden door with a black metal latch and said, "Here is your room. We trust you will be comfortable here."

John looked around his new abode, believing his time here would be adventurous. The sparse room was swept clean. Simple wooden floor boards matched wooden walls. A small window, trimmed with plain white curtains, gave him a view of a green pasture.

He wondered if his mother lived in such a room, or if he was born in such austere surroundings. A small stove stood in the corner, its black chimney pipe rising up toward the wooden-board ceiling before turning and extending through an outside wall. He spotted a twin bed like the one at his apartment and felt at home.

"Thank you," he told Eli. "You've given me a washbasin and water pitcher. I have seen such battery lanterns online. This is very nice."

Two white towels dangled from a towel rod. More importantly, John noted the absence of anything electronic including a TV or electrical outlets. He would have to monitor his cell phone use to keep its charge until he got back to his car.

Eli's vigorous nod set his beard to quivering. "You eat with us tonight after Thomas brings you back in the buggy from town."

John climbed into his car and made a U-turn while Thomas hopped into the buggy. John drove to town, recalling his earlier visit to Walnut Cove farmer's market with the college's agricultural team who were promoting organic research. That's where he met Eli and encouraged him to expand into organic produce. Eli hadn't seemed interested, though Thomas had begged to stay longer.

John slowly passed another black buggy going along the side of the rode. And it reminded him of an incident when he'd given Thomas and his older sister Ruth a ride back to the farm that day. Before they left the market, Thomas had cajoled John to install a game app on his cell phone so he could play it. During the drive, Ruth acted friendly, until her admonishing Thomas for playing the game app on John's phone had fallen on deaf ears.

This late afternoon, as John turned into the parking lot, he marveled how Amish kids seemed to know of such technology. What he saw by the store amazed him even more. The parking lot was teeming with large and small buggies, the horses lined up at the rail, waiting patiently, their tails a-twitching. John's heart grew full of his mother's letter to him. He began to have an inkling of her life in a similar community.

He found an empty spot in a far corner where his car would be out of the way. At last he spotted Thomas' youthful face in a black buggy turning into the lot. Ruth sat beside him on the seat. John figured she might be the same age as John's mother when she married John's father. Thomas pulled up to the rail, scurried out, and tied his horse. Ruth also climbed out.

With a slight dip of her head, she greeted John with a smile. "Hello, John Lapp. It is pleasant to see you again."

"Hello, Ruth," John replied, hesitant to shake her hand.

She lifted up a basket covered with a green cloth. "Mother asked me to deliver jars of apple butter to the market. I will be right back."

Ruth walked away with John wishing Thomas would make the delivery so he had time to know her better. Instead, Thomas showed up at his elbow.

"John Lapp, do you like licorice? They have the best buttons here."

"Sure, if it's black licorice," John told the teen.

"Do you have three dollars? I will get you some."

John grinned. Was he being hustled? He handed Thomas a five-dollar bill and the boy shot off like a rabbit. Ruth returned with an empty basket and got into the buggy, motioning for John to join her on the front seat.

"Thomas will be along," she said, ties hanging down from the starched gauze bonnet that framed her pretty face. "Father hopes your ideas will help our farm."

John scrambled up into the buggy, telling her, "I'll do all I can."

Thomas appeared suddenly to untie the horse. He slid in front of Ruth and sat in the middle, forcing John to scoot down. Thomas gave John two dollars and change.

He held up a paper bag of licorice and smiled. "I'll give you the candy if I can see your phone."

"Hey," John objected. "Didn't I just buy these candies?"

Ruth corrected her brother. "No, Thomas. You may not have his phone."

Thomas gave John the licorice and relinquished the reins to his sister. She lightly tapped the reins on the horse's haunches, saying softly, "Back, back."

Ruth expertly backed the horse while occasionally glancing in a small rearview mirror mounted near the buggy's roof to see behind her. John quietly handed Thomas the phone. The teenager instantly navigated to a bird cartoon app and hid the phone between his knees.

"Thomas, you will have Father's wrath if someone sees you," Ruth warned while stopping the buggy at the street's edge.

Thomas slid farther back into the seat, keeping his eyes focused on the phone between his knees. Traffic cleared. Ruth dropped the reins on the horse's haunches and guided the buggy onto the road. Soon, they were going down the asphalt to the rhythm of the horse's hooves clip-clopping on the road.

"Have you visited Walnut Cove since we saw you last month?" Ruth asked John.

"No, and I'm so happy to return."

"Truly?" Ruth asked, holding the reins. "Our life is quite different from you and your family."

"That's true. I have more than forty brothers and sisters."

From opposite ends of the buggy, Ruth and Thomas glanced at John in surprise.

"They live all over the country," he explained. "That's because I was raised by Mom and Pop DeVroom who adopted me."

"You are not married then?" Ruth asked.

John tapped the edge of his beard. "I am single. My job at the college keeps me busy. Though once my life was like yours. I was born on an Amish farm."

"Was it a tourist farm where your family went to see our ways?" Ruth asked, edging the buggy to the right and letting a car pass.

"No. My parents were Amish as were my grandparents. My father died when I was small. My mother brought me to the city to live."

Thomas raised his head a fraction from John's phone muttering, "Really?"

"That is sad," came Ruth's reply as they neared the farm. "Thomas, give John Lapp the phone."

Her brother did so in a flash. Ruth swung the buggy across the oncoming lane and into the drive. She stopped near the barn, prompting John to add to his story.

"Coming to your farm gives me a chance to reconnect with the life I was denied," he told her.

"Does our father know this?"

"About my birth? Not yet. I will tell him."

Ruth motioned to her chin while looking at John's beard. "You look different than when we saw you before. You look like one of us. I hope you will feel wilkom here."

She turned over the reins to Thomas and stepped down from the buggy. Ruth walked toward the farmhouse, swinging her basket.

Thomas lowered his voice to ask John, "You lived in the city and now want to come back to the farm. Why?"

"Thomas, it's like a part of me is missing," John answered, pocketing his phone. "Something inside of me comes alive when I work with the soil and coax healthy plants to grow. I want to grow closer to God just as my mother did before she died."

Chapter 15

John used the basin and water pitcher to wash up for the evening meal. Unease dogged him while he sat on a hard bench outside the barn's guest room, waiting to be called for supper. He wanted to spend time with Eli and family yet didn't want to burden Mrs. Miller.

He scrolled through a few apps on his phone to pass the time. Most he couldn't use with only a single bar from the distant cell tower. He put away his muted phone and tried to live in the moment. Different smells and sounds from horses and cows in the barn pleased him more than his austere apartment.

John leapt up at sounds of someone walking on the gravel. Thomas raised an arm beckoning him to the farmhouse.

"Father says it is time to eat."

"What's for dinner, Thomas?" John asked, eager for a home-cooked meal.

"Mama fixed canned beef, applesauce, and fresh asparagus from the garden. I think you will like Ruth's baked bread as much as I."

At the screen door, John caught a whiff of fragrant baking bread. He entered the spartan kitchen with a glad heart. This was the first time he'd ever set foot in an Amish home. He admired everything he saw, from the painted wooden floors to a wooden floor-to-ceiling cupboard built high along one wall. The large table, which took up most of the room, looked inviting covered with a white cloth and arranged with eight chairs.

Mrs. Miller sliced bread at the cupboard. Ruth placed glasses of water by each place setting. Mother and daughter were the picture of a contented home life in their white aprons tied around their waists and matching simple blue dresses. String ties from their gauze bonnets swayed below their chins.

"Mama, this is John Lapp." Ruth gave a nod to John.

When Mrs. Miller turned to smile at him and said, "Welcome, John," he relaxed his shoulders.

"Sit on this side of our table," she added, pointing to a chair. "We eat soon."

"Thank you, Mrs. Miller," he replied. "It smells wonderful in here."

Eli arrived in the kitchen along with three other children John had not met. Two girls and one boy were younger than Thomas. John noticed Eli's beard had no gray in it and his wife looked youthful. Ruth might be seventeen or eighteen, he calculated.

Except she seemed mature. He wondered if she'd be getting married soon.

Mrs. Miller took her seat last in a chair next to her husband and across from John. Eli bowed his head and prayed in Pennsylvania Dutch before switching to English for John's benefit.

"We give Thee thanks for John who is here to help us. Bless him too. Amen."

Mrs. Miller stood and served the children before giving Eli the platter of beef. He took a portion before passing it down the table to John. Unsure what to expect, he spooned out a modest amount.

John felt his phone vibrating in his pocket. As he slid his hand in to stop the buzzing, he noticed a daughter and Mrs. Miller both reacted to the alert sound by looking at him with concern. He continued eating.

The children chattered with their mother in their customary tongue. John was offered bread kept warm by a towel wrap. He spread butter upon it and watched the butter melt. His mouth moistened and he tried a bite. It was as good as he'd imagined.

Soon their plates were emptied. Eli selected another slice of bread while keeping up a banter in English with John, urging him to have another helping.

Eli gazed at him intently. "Ruth tells me that your mother was a plain woman."

"Yes," John answered, measuring Eli's reaction. "I told Ruth my mother placed me with an adoptive Christian family when she was dying. Only recently have I learned I was born on a farm like yours. After my father was killed in a farming accident, my mother left for the city. That's probably why I find your farm so interesting."

Once again, John's pocket erupted with his vibrating phone. Every eye at the table focused upon him. He slid his hand into his pocket and turned off the phone.

"Sorry to interrupt," John said with a sheepish smile. "I left my phone on by mistake."

Eli addressed his family in their language. Each one abruptly rose and left the table. Ruth gathered dirty dishes and walked them to the sink where she joined her mother. Eli stroked his beard while glancing at John's beard.

"You want to learn more about plain people. Is that why you offer to help us?"

"No, Eli, that isn't why," John insisted, respecting Eli's directness. "I've studied hard to learn the best ways to assist you as an Amish farmer, and also English farmers. Organic farming and organic food help people to eat healthier and live more productive lives. That's what I aim to do."

Eli nodded while staring at John as if expecting him to continue.

John chose his words carefully, wanting to assure Eli that his motives were honest. "I have questions about my childhood, such as why did God permit me to be taken from the farm into an English city. I begin to realize perhaps God stirred my interest in farming so I can help my mother's people."

"Do you wonder if you should be plain?" Eli probed.

John folded his hands on the table and decided to tell the truth. "Yes, sir, I do."

"Do you know why your mother left her family and faith?"

"No," John admitted, feeling the heat of Eli's examination. "Only that she left her community after my father died. She never left her faith. A letter she wrote me says so. And she placed me with Christian parents who adopted me. Eli, I have accepted Christ's gift of forgiveness and have a restored relationship with God."

Eli's brown eyes shone. "That is good, John. But you have lived a different life from how we live here. We are simple people who work very hard and avoid becoming entangled with the world. The Bible tells us, 'Come out from among them, and be ye separate.'"

"I know those verses in Corinthians," John acknowledged.

"Our Bishop can give many examples of English who tried to become plain people, and of their failures and troubles they brought to our people."

"Are you saying I shouldn't seek to know the ways of my family?"

Eli seemed to study John's face, as a father might with his son. "I am saying you should not put too much hope in something that may never happen. Given your last name is Lapp, I believe your father and mother are from a Pennsylvania community."

"I lived in Pennsylvania with Mom and Pop until graduating from high school."

"Do you know the Bishop of your mother's church?"

"I don't."

Eli's steady eyes bore into John's. "Maybe while you help me, you will learn more about how your family lived."

"You want me to continue with the soil tests?"

"Yes. I want to know if my soil is depleted of the minerals you spoke of." Eli got to his feet. "Thomas has gone to the barn to finish his evening chores. You go see what you find to do with your hands."

He walked with John a short way to the barn, the sky painted purple and gold from the setting sun. They stopped beneath a massive oak tree where Eli brought up a serious topic.

"John, you are welcome here. I need your word you will not tempt my children with unknown things of the English. Please do not tell them of your life."

"What you ask is reasonable." John extended his hand, which Eli shook firmly. "I will try not to foster their curiosity."

Eli nodded curtly. "Good, we understand each other. My neighbor asked me to work his field with my team in the morning. You collect the soil samples and we will meet again."

Then he spun around and walked toward the house, leaving John to wonder if Eli would accept John's guidance and become an organic farmer. He went into the barn.

Friendly as ever, Thomas smiled and handed him a pitchfork. "Come, I will show you how to be a plain farmer."

They worked until dark shoveling manure and hauling loads to a manure spreader. John had noticed running water in the kitchen, and was pleased to also find it in the barn. After he and Thomas watered milk cows and horses, John leaned against support post and drew in a deep breath.

"Thomas, where does this water in the barn come from?"

The boy smiled. "It's pumped from the same well beneath the windmill, by a gas-powered pump."

The younger Miller children ran into the barn to milk the cows. John and Thomas placed new straw in the stalls and feed for the animals. Blisters began forming on John's tender hands.

As they wheeled the last load of manure to the edge of a loading dock before dumping it into a spreader, John posed another question. "Thomas, what you do with the manure?"

"Spread it on our fields," he quickly explained. "If we have too much, we trade with our neighbors who need some."

John lifted his hurting hands. "Tomorrow, I'll talk to your father about the manure and check your soil in different places."

They washed out the wheelbarrows and parked them outside the barn in the deepening twilight. Thomas took John by surprise with an invitation.

"I come down early to feed the horses. Maybe you can help me hitch them up for the neighbor's field."

"Great," John replied, then backtracked. "Wait. How early?"

"An hour before sunrise," was all Thomas said, walking away.

John hurried to check his cell phone and find out what time the sun rose. He wanted to be "the early bird who got the worm," as Pop used to tease John. His bones ached, his hands stung, and he couldn't remember feeling more alive.

JOHN AWOKE TO A SHARP RAP. The metal latch rattled on the door to his room. He leaned on his elbow to get his bearings in the dark room. A myriad of smells confirmed his new plain lifestyle. John threw off the woolen blanket, his stocking feet touching the cool wooden floor.

He used his phone's light to locate the door, and when he opened it, he heard Thomas talking to the animals. Oops. He'd forgotten to set the alarm and slept too late. It seemed as if John had just fallen asleep. Unfamiliar sounds of horses stomping their hooves and cows mooing and grunting woke him often during the night.

After changing into jeans and a long-sleeved shirt, John brought the lamp into the shadowy barn where he joined Thomas in feeding the horses. John could see out the barn door streaks of light beaming across the eastern sky. Probably it was time for breakfast on the farm.

"Should I wash up to eat?" John asked Thomas.

The boy had other ideas. "First, we harness the team. We eat after the chores."

"What else can I do?" John's empty stomach told him to work fast.

Thomas entered a stall, and bringing out a large brown draft horse into the roomy center aisle, he instructed, "Hold Tulip's halter while I fetch her brother."

John grabbed the halter and the giant horse snorted. She moved her head up and down as if greeting the new man. He stroked her velvety nose, amazed how one-half was brown and the other side snowy white. Thomas led in another grand-looking horse.

"Teddy is our gelding." Thomas gripped the halter while pointing to leather straps hanging on a wall peg. "If you bring the tack, I will let you harness Teddy."

"Okay." John eyed the massive animal. "Remind me of what a gelding is."

"It means he will not father any colts."

John had no clue how to harness Teddy. Still, he approached the tack with gusto. This was his chance! He looped an arm through the tack, and the moment he lifted it from the peg onto his shoulder, his legs buckled beneath the weight.

No doubt he'd spent too many days typing on his computer. Not wanting to appear a weakling, John staggered toward the great horse Teddy, who was even bigger around than his sister and whose nose was all brown.

Thomas gestured to the barn floor, saying, "Drop it here.

Observe how I put this collar over Teddy's head."

He picked up a large oval padded leather object. John stood in awe watching Thomas take two short curved wooden poles with brass nobs on the top end and lower these over Teddy's head, one on each side of the collar.

"These are the hames," Thomas coached. "Each hame connects to the collar."

John paid close attention to the teen lifting long straps that looked very heavy.

"I attach the tug straps to the hames," Thomas said, neatly strapping them together beneath the horse's neck.

"It's hard keeping the equipment straight," John said. "Harnessing the team is more complex than turning a key to a tractor."

Thomas shrugged. "I could do this in my sleep. You will prepare Tulip so pay attention. I have two more horses to get ready."

John memorized Thomas' method in adjusting Teddy's straps. Then Thomas strode behind Teddy and showed John a steel ring at the end of the tug strap.

"This hooks onto the plow or wagon the team is pulling. Now we connect the final strap underneath Teddy's tail."

"What's it for?" John's mind labored to keep up.

"The breech strap works like the brake if our wagon goes downhill or stops. Teddy lets the strap push against his rump and it stops the wagon."

"Thomas Miller, I have a hard time believing you're fourteen years old. Your knowledge of farming surprises me. Eli has taught you well."

"Yah, he is a good father. Just like I want to be someday," Thomas confided. "Mama tells us Papa shows the love our Father in heaven has for us."

John swatted a pesky fly buzzing his head, thinking what his Amish father might be like. He forced himself to focus. Thomas patiently taught him the precise way to drop a bridle over Teddy's head, remove the halter, and put a bit into his mouth. The teen tied the horse to a post so easily it was like he'd assembled the team of horses a hundred times. John had to admit Thomas showed the farming skills he longed to possess himself.

"Get Tulip's tack from the wall and put it on. I will fetch the other team," Thomas said.

John wrestled the other set of harnesses from the peg and readied Tulip for the day's work beside Teddy. He tried to stay away from the horse's gigantic hooves as she nervously shifted them.

"Oops!" John cried as she landed near his right foot.

He sidestepped safely. John sighed in relief and worked diligently, his brain consumed by Eli's great example of God's loving care for his family as Thomas had said.

Hold on. Hadn't Pop given John the same care since he was little? Yes! The truth hit him squarely like a punch on the shoulder. He needed to show him and Mom right away how thankful he was for them.

Thomas said loudly, "John Lapp, Papa says you test the soil. When we return, you can help me remove the tack and bed down the horses."

"All right." Disappointment laced John's words.

Apparently, Eli didn't want him to meet neighboring farmers. Perhaps Eli didn't trust him. John straightened his back, more than ready to prove his worth. Without mentioning his misgivings, he struggled with the heavy leather collar, hames, and straps, which would permit Tulip to pull a plow. Repeated trips to examine Teddy reminded John where to connect each piece.

He finally walked over to Thomas, sweat dripping into his eyes, and announced with pride, "Tulip is ready."

"She looks fine. The other team is finished," Thomas said with no hint of pride.

John wiped his face on his shirtsleeve. "I see. You've prepared two more horses to my one. I have much to learn."

Thomas shrugged off John's praise. "Let me show you what is next."

He grabbed a four-foot-long wooden pole with metal rings on each end and explained, "The neck yoke keeps the horses from walking too close to each other."

John saw the puzzle pieces coming together as Thomas connected one end of the yoke to Tulip's breast strap beneath her chin and the other end to Teddy's.

His hard work and endless dodging of flies nearly done, John thought, *This will be my life if I live on an Amish farm someday.*

Thomas wiped his hands along his pants. "You did good, John Lapp. Now we eat breakfast."

John quickly washed his hands in the water basin and they left the barn, the sun's rays bathing the farmhouse and surrounding trees in a burst of bright light. Despite his aching shoulders and torn flesh on his thumb, John envisioned his future and believed that much like a seed, he could eventually grow into a real farmer. This thought contented him more than anything else had in months, and removed the sting of not accompanying Eli and Thomas to the other farm.

Chapter 16

John quickly gathered his supplies. He stood with a shovel in one hand and a soil test kit in the other watching father and son drive their teams down the gravel drive. Eli and Thomas went down the shoulder of the road to the neighbor's. Whether Eli approved of him or not, John had his own job to do and would keep his agreement.

He walked to the center of the field stepping carefully among rows and rows of tomato plants. Eli and his family would have a colossal tomato crop to can and sell, and John wanted to help them grow the healthiest plants possible. The soil held the answers and he turned over a shovel full of rich dark earth.

Soon, the sun's heat penetrated through his shirt. Beads of sweat lined his hairline. Based on several non-decomposed stems he dug up, John determined Eli grew tomatoes here last year too.

He plunged his hands into the soil. Excitement surged through him at the idea of his father tending a rich plot of earth on his Amish farm. John broke lumps of soil into his palm before dumping the mixture into a plastic cup, and snapping on the lid. He noted the date, time, and location of the sample using a permanent marker.

Crows flew overhead. Their ruckus invaded his peaceful mood. To the tune of the birds' loud cawing, his mind whirled over Eli's caution that many English who tried adopting a plain lifestyle failed. Eli must not approve of John exploring his roots.

"But I'm not English," John grumbled aloud.

He walked thirty yards and dug up more soil to fill another container. "I was born plain and might have lived plain. I could be plowing with the team if my mother hadn't gone to the city."

A gust of wind set the tomato plants to trembling almost as if they were nodding in agreement. His hands digging in the soil, John pondered anew his many questions.

Why did God bring me here? Is it simply to give Eli new farming techniques or something deeper?

John straightened his back, and looking toward the barn, he caught a glimpse of a slight woman hanging laundry on a clothesline behind the house. He was too far away to tell if the laundress was Ruth or Mrs. Miller.

He hurried toward the barn to satisfy his curiosity, and called out in a friendly voice, "Good morning."

The lady, clothed in a green dress, apron, and white gauze cap with dangling ties, turned and waved. He knew instantly she was Ruth. Her friendly manner prompted him to walk toward her.

Perhaps God meant for him to be her special friend.

She smiled, and with a free hand, gestured to his shovel. "Are you finding what you need for soil samples?"

He lodged the shovel under his arm and showed her the containers. "These will tell us how to improve your crop conditions. It would help if someone could tell me which sections your father farms, and what he planted last year in each field."

A serious look crossed Ruth's pretty face. "Papa will not return before dark."

"That's too bad." John leaned against the shovel wishing he'd thought to ask Eli these questions last evening.

"When I finish the laundry," she said, lifting up a pair of boy's trousers from the laundry basket, "I will show you."

John grinned over this fortunate turn of events. "Great! I'll be in the barn labeling my samples."

He practically skipped to the barn. A firm belief settled into his mind. If his mother had stayed in the community, he might be married to a woman like Ruth, raising his children, and farming by now.

In a far corner of his mind, Mom DeVroom's kind voice spoke, telling him after he'd dropped an entire bowl of eggs and spoiled her plans for angel food cake, "Never mind, son. You help me make chocolate fudge instead. It doesn't need any eggs."

TEN MINUTES LATER, JOHN SAT ON A WOODEN KEG near the open barn door to wait for Ruth. His samples secured and labeled, he quickly read his emails. Less than fifty percent power remained on his cell battery. Ruth hastened toward him carrying a jacket. He stowed his cell phone in his pocket and stood to greet her.

"John Lapp, my mother agrees I may show you where my father plants the crops."

Though she dressed plain, her face reflected goodness. Ruth was pretty with no makeup. He nearly blurted, "Why aren't you the wife of an Amish farmer?" but stopped before embarrassing her and himself. He decided to find out later from Thomas.

She put the jacket on over her apron and dress, asking if he had something warmer than shirtsleeves. "Because winds are picking up and the temperature is falling. It will be breezy in the field without trees and buildings to break the wind."

After getting his jacket and putting on his straw hat, John and Ruth walked to the adjoining fields.

She raised an arm in a wide sweeping motion. "Everything you see from the road in front of the house and to the far tree line belongs to my father."

"How many acres does he own?" John asked.

In answer, Ruth pivoted, completing a full circle. "That is all Papa's property. One hundred and twenty acres."

"Wow," John exclaimed, impressed by the size of Eli's farm. "I've read many plain family farms are forty to eighty acres. Your father is doing well."

"We were smaller, but Papa keeps expanding for Thomas and my brothers."

John's brow furrowed. His thoughts flew to his own mother and her Pennsylvania family. Questions burned in his mind. Ruth was still talking and John tried to listen.

She lifted a hand to shield her eyes from the sun. "When Thomas marries, he and his future wife will live here too."

"I wonder if my mother returned to her father's farm after he died," John said. "Or if she stayed with his family for a time?"

Sadness flickered through Ruth's eyes. "I do not know what to say. There is much you may never know."

The two faced each other in the middle of a field. Trailing vines and yellow blossoms of squash plants surrounded them. A breeze stirred Ruth's cap tassels.

John studied her face. "Thinking of my mother makes me ask, what is expected of you? Must you find a plain husband and leave this farm?"

"John Lapp." Ruth blushed. "We do not know each other well, yet you ask me things I only discuss with my parents."

"I'm sorry." John looked down at his shoes to hide his embarrassment.

A chilly wind fluttered his open jacket. He zipped it to his chin, and desperate to change the subject, he pointed. "Does your father use the corner field by the tree line and creek for hay?"

"Yes." She folded her arms as if cold.

"For more than one year?"

Ruth nodded as if thinking of something else. Her possible future marriage?

John motioned to the ground by their feet. "What was planted here last year?"

"Same as this year. Cabbage, kale, and squash."

John began walking toward the barn. Ruth came alongside. He spotted up ahead where the front quarter section intersected with a side road, and asked his now-silent guide, "Was the area beyond the house where the cows graze used for grazing before?"

"For several years," she said, and started walking again.

John lagged behind, convinced he'd made her uncomfortable. One way he could mend the divide was to go above and beyond in helping her father. They neared the clothesline, a good place to part.

He thanked her for showing him the boundaries. "Now I will sample each field. Have a good day."

"You are welcome, John Lapp," was all Ruth said.

He tipped his straw hat and walked to the barn to retrieve his kits, glancing briefly over his shoulder. She reached for and felt clothes on the line. She was so nice and John wished to know her better, but that might be impossible.

On the trek to the north quadrant, he decided to ask Thomas when they worked with the team tonight if Ruth was spoken for. He wouldn't open his heart any further until he found out.

JOHN RECEIVED AN INTERESTING PROPOSAL when he finished his soil collecting. Marlow Bryson called his cell asking him to fly to Virginia.

"John, I've lost my information technology person and need to discuss my situation with you right away," Marlow said, his voice tense. "When can you get here?"

"Monday, if it works for you," John replied, excited to learn more about his brother-in-law's organic food business.

"Fine. I'll reimburse you for the flight. Try to arrive by two o'clock. My office is around back of our house."

John verified the address and they hung up. Ruth came out of the house to collect clothes from the line.

He went over and told her, "I just had a phone call and need to leave soon. Can you or someone take me to my car?"

"That is no problem, John Lapp," she said, reaching for a shirt. "Mother asked me to shop at the store. Give me about thirty minutes."

Thomas hadn't shown John how to ready the single horse for the buggy. So John didn't offer to help Ruth. Rather, he waited on the bench outside the barn seeing his hope of speaking to Thomas of Ruth's future plans foiled before his eyes.

Perhaps she'll open up on the drive into town, he thought.

That plan soon was dashed. Ruth brought along an interloper. John had to be content with Ruth driving at a good clip and talking the entire way to her younger sister who sat beside her.

He tipped his hat before getting out of the buggy at the store. "Thanks again, Ruth. Tell your father I will return once I receive the lab results."

Chapter 17

John's plane had a bumpy landing at Dulles International Airport on Monday morning. He hurried past deplaning passengers and went straight to the car rental counter, concerned he'd have trouble renting a car, given his late reservation. He shouldn't have worried. Every detail went smoothly and he found his rental car in no time.

The GPS British voice on his cell phone calling out directions, John navigated with white knuckles along a hectic Northern Virginia highway. He preferred the rural roads in Walnut Cove. Mom and Pop were expecting him for lunch any minute.

Unfortunately, an accident up ahead caused a sudden delay. He waited in a long line and called them on his cell, saying, "A police cruiser is finally here to direct traffic around a collision. I should be on my way soon."

"Drive safely," Mom said. "Lunch will keep."

At last, he sped off, arriving at their Chantilly townhouse one minute before noon. John rolled the rental to a stop, angling into a guest parking spot. He unplugged his phone, and looking up, saw Mom in the doorway waving at him with joy in her eyes.

He ran to the door. She was joined by Pop, who swung the door open wide.

"Johnny!" She enveloped him into her plump arms. "We're thrilled to see you."

After Pop embraced him, he said, "After your call last night, Mother got busy whipping up chicken salad. She even baked her famous apple pie."

"Come inside and rest your bones," Mom said, directing him to the table. "You have an important meeting with Marlow. Lunch is ready."

John spotted his favorite sandwiches on a platter and a big bowl of potato chips in the center of a small dinette table adjacent to the kitchen and overlooking the parking lot.

His mom smiled broadly. "This table is tiny compared to the monster back at the homestead with all you kids. It suits our needs."

"I recognize the table settings and your best-ever sandwiches," John quipped.

They took their usual places, Mom to his right and Pop on his left. His dad grabbed his hand and reached over for Mom's.

"Our circle of love is complete," she said softly.

His head bowed, Pop prayed, "Father in heaven, thank You for our John, and for the happiness he's added to our lives through the years. Thank You for the man he has become. Direct his meeting with Marlow. As we enjoy the gifts of Your bountiful provisions, we are grateful for them, and ask Your blessings on the food. In the name of Jesus our Lord, Amen."

"This brings back many memories of our family gatherings around that super-long table," John said, opening his eyes and accepting the sandwich platter from Mom.

She beamed a motherly smile. "Such precious times. Things are different now we're retired and near Cora. She keeps in touch, but we're farther from you."

"We're not complaining," Pop assured. "Cora kindly helped us find this townhome and get settled."

"John, try not to be overwhelmed when you see her house," Mom cautioned. "Marlow is successful in business. When he and Cora married three years ago, he found the woman who displays his achievements to perfection. She's organized and gifted with the knack of hospitality. They're well-known among the successful families there in Louden County."

"What do you hope will result from your meeting Marlow?" Pop asked, helping himself to a sandwich.

John sipped iced tea before saying, "Cora connected me to Marlow at the Biltmore. She let it slip I'm a college professor and expert in information technology."

"I thought you taught farming methods," Mom said, a question in her tone.

"I do. He may have assumed I teach information technology as well, which is much different than crop rotation. I'll straighten him out."

Their lively conversation continued. John didn't hesitate reaching for a second sandwich and piling his plate with chips. Irene's eyes sparkled with approval.

"You always had seconds growing up. Save room for pie and ice cream," she admonished.

John bit into the tasty sandwich, its creamy goodness tasting like love. When he finished, he wiped his mouth and beard with a thick paper napkin.

"I want to help Marlow for Cora's sake," John declared.

Pop filled John's iced tea, asking, "Didn't the college want you teaching computer courses based on your experience?"

"I do," John replied. "My degree isn't in computers, but I taught myself enough to teach the basic course."

His mom set before him a plate of warmed apple pie dripping with a scoop of ice cream. "You'll be amazed when you see Cora's magnificent estate. For a young girl who began life in foster care and worked hard as a teacher, she's blessed with a fortunate marriage."

"Marlow said he works from a home office." John stopped talking long enough to try the delicious dessert. "I forgot to ask if Cora will be there."

"She's at the Trumpet's Call," Mom said, shaking her head, "so we can visit. You'll see stark differences in Cora's lifestyle compared to the Amish farmer you're helping."

"Interesting you mention that comparison." John set down his fork. "The simple Amish way of life holds great appeal for me."

"It's good you're connecting with the Amish since you were born into that life," his mother replied, patting his shoulder.

John smiled knowingly. "I sought out Eli Miller and am seeing a glimpse of my mother's transition in moving from the farm to the city."

"We love catching up but won't keep you from your business." Pop pushed his chair from the table.

"I almost forgot." Mom's hands flew to her rosy cheeks. "Fritz, get the suitcase."

"You bought me new luggage? It's not my birthday," John said.

Mom touched his hand with her warm one. "We recently discovered a special suitcase your mother packed with your clothing when you both came to live with us. We're so happy you came today so we can give it to you."

John sat there speechless. Pop returned and handed him a well-used suitcase.

John smoothed a hand over the old case. He tried recalling faded memories. If only he could remember his mother's face!

"Thanks for saving this for me," he finally managed.

"Go ahead and open it," Mom urged. "There's a nice surprise inside."

He clicked open the decades-old case, and in the bottom spotted two faded color photographs. Was this woman his mother?

He gently lifted up the pictures. Unshed tears burned in his eyes.

"I was just wishing I could see her face and here she is," John said, amazed.

Mom's voice quivered as she said, "This one is of you and your mother at Sights and Sounds in Lancaster. Pop took the picture when you both moved in with us. The other one is of Sarah before we knew her."

"I've read the letter she wrote to me over and over." John's voice caught with emotion. "What else do you remember about her?

I'd love to know any little details."

His parents gathered closely around him, with his mom saying, "John, we've been waiting for you to ask."

They beckoned him to sit in the living room where they each shared memories of his mother living with John in the guesthouse on their Lancaster property.

"Sarah was working at Sights and Sounds, but also baking for us and their restaurant," Pop explained, his blue eyes twinkling. "After her death and you moved into the main house with us and the other kids, we were always hearing reports of restaurant visitors missing your mom's delicious Amish desserts."

Mom picked up where his dad left off. "She enjoyed baking our bread and pies. Peanut butter pie was her favorite. Your mother enjoyed waking up at dawn's first light to bake cinnamon rolls. She always made sure you ate one for breakfast with your oatmeal and glass of milk."

A memory stirred. The funny thing was, John could taste those cinnamon rolls while gazing at his mother's picture.

"We aren't sure why," Mom said, becoming teary-eyed, "but Sarah moved into town after your daddy was killed in a farm accident. She never talked about it, except he was driving a horse team down the road and was hit by a truck. Your mommy fought hard to raise you by herself."

John's eyes stung with tears, and before he could respond, Mom continued, "She prayed with you each night and covered you with a quilt she'd sewn as a teen. Pop and I were so upset when her cancer came."

They talked about John's life with them as a teenager, helping Pop work on cars and everything electronic, and painting rooms together. Finally, John rose, clutching his little suitcase. Reluctance over having to leave followed him to the door.

He embraced his parents. "I begin to realize my mother was a wise woman. She found godly parents to raise me. Mom and Pop, I'm thankful for your love and for teaching me to know and love the Lord."

"John." Pop clapped his shoulder. "God blessed us greatly raising foster children, but He had more love for us to experience. He brought you and Sarah to us. Son, you've never disappointed."

They walked him outside to the car where Mom hugged him tightly, saying in his ear, "You could spend the night here. I'm saving a slice of pie with your name on it."

"Perhaps another time," John said, thinking when he might return. "I teach a class tomorrow and fly back this evening."

Pop nestled the little suitcase into the backseat. They waved at him, radiant smiles shining on their faces. John drove down the road, filled with the love of his parents and a rekindled love for his birth mother.

Chapter 18

John's sore neck muscles and wired emotions calmed thirty minutes into his drive to Middleburg. The hubbub of congested traffic along westbound Route 50 gave way to expansive grassy farms, which reminded him of Walnut Cove, only more upscale. He lowered the window and inhaled. Country air invigorated him like nothing else.

John spotted the Bryson home from a distance. Or should he say *mansion*. The large three-story home, with its fieldstone façade and fountain, overwhelmed him more than he expected. Several outbuildings dotted rolling fields of fenced pastures. John turned in the driveway, winding past manicured lawns and a bubbling water fountain.

He went to the rear of the house where two additional wings extended from either end of the house, the large size surprising him. This luxurious estate with its stable, paddock, and equestrian riding ring was a Taj Mahal compared to his parents' modest townhome and John's cramped apartment. Cora's house was more luxurious than anything John desired. Still, if she was happy, who was he to complain?

He pulled into the parking area, which was more like a courtyard and big enough to fit six cars. An imposing guesthouse of field stones was set between a small barn on one side and a greenhouse on the other. Probably Cora grew her prize roses behind those panes of glittering glass. He snugged his rental into an open parking spot.

Curtains adorned the windows of both wings, and concealed the presence of the offices inside. A young woman dressed in jeans and a snug blouse that revealed her advanced pregnancy answered the doorbell. She ushered John into a foyer decorated with riding gear.

Closed doors to his right and left prompted John to introduce himself and say, "I have a two o'clock appointment with Mr. Bryson."

"He's expecting you, Mr. Lapp. I am Amy Carr, Mr. Bryson's administrative assistant. Follow me."

Opening the door on the left, she took him past several partitioned cubicles containing computers, desks, and file cabinets. He saw two women and a man working intently at their computers. Amy hesitated at an open door, giving John a glimpse into a vast room that seemed to occupy the entire width of the mansion's west wing.

This room was actually a well-equipped office. Silken curtains graced a large bank of windows. The idyllic scene of lush pastures outside put John at ease. Apparently, he and Marlow shared a love for working and spending time around God's earth.

Seated behind a sprawling executive desk, Marlow was terminating a telephone call, saying, "I expect you'll get back to me with details, pronto."

Amy rapped on his doorjamb, announcing crisply, "John Lapp to see you, sir."

She left them alone. Marlow stepped around the desk and extended a hand to John.

"I like promptness." Marlow gave him a firm handshake, and looking him straight in the eye said, "I had to leave that reception Cora had for her parents, so I didn't have a chance to delineate my needs."

John lowered his hand. "You were leaving for China. Was your trip fruitful?"

"Very much so. My suppliers are there. I've learned meeting face-to-face beats video conferencing, which is why I asked you to fly here. Let's sit and discuss how you can join my consulting staff without leaving Ohio."

Marlow pointed to a spacious sitting area adjacent to his desk. John sat on a leather chair and listened as Marlow explained how technology permitted most of his employees to work from home around the nation.

"The few staffers working here in cubicles constitute my office disguised as my home," he added, sitting in an overstuffed chair across from John.

John was still trying to get his bearings. "Marlow, it's hard to imagine your business is nationwide with you working from home."

"I love working from here," his brother-in-law said, gesturing with a hand. "The county would stop me from building corporate headquarters at this location, so we keep things low-key here. Cora praises your teaching at the college and says you're a computer genius."

"Hardly a genius, but I seem to have a knack for computers." John removed his resume from a valise.

Marlow refused it. "Not necessary. I have a particular need for your hacking ability."

Hacking?

Dread engulfed John. He envisioned sliding down into the despicable dark web. He pushed back hard.

"Marlow, I cannot help you. I have *no* experience in hacking."

"I would never ask you to hack someone else's computer

system, or do anything illegal or inappropriate," Marlow declared with a smirk. "Your sister brags nonstop about your knowledge, so I'm hoping you'll help me assess my computer security."

"How might I do that?" John's defenses were on high alert.

Marlow walked to his credenza and snatched something before reclaiming his seat. "As you see, Occidental is in the business of distributing produce, mostly organic."

"Impressive graphics," John replied, scanning the colorful brochure displaying shiny vegetables.

"Thanks," Marlow said. "I need you to assess Occidental's entire computer system. I lacked confidence in my tech guy. Charlie Riggs, who was also my buyer, took night classes to get his degree in information technology. I'm afraid in a weak moment, I made an unwise decision and named him my IT director too. Charlie was a one-man shop, handling the job from his home in Chicago."

"You speak of Charlie in the past tense. Did he leave?"

"I fired him. I discovered he was taking his girlfriend along on buying trips, paid for by my suppliers, with the hidden costs passed on to me. After I dumped Charlie, I heard from former suppliers that he favored their competitors who were the highest bidders. His firing means I lost my IT guy. I handle the buying myself, and would appreciate you finding me a new IT person, as I assume you're content being a professor and wouldn't want the job."

John nodded. "Okay, you want me to suggest Charlie's replacement."

"Yes, and I have another request."

"Namely what?"

Marlow leaned forward in the puffy chair. "Charlie often boasted our system is as secure as he could make it, but now I'm not sure he was looking after my company's best interest. I want you to test if we are truly secure by trying to hack into my system."

"Back to hacking." John stared at Marlow. "It's a tempting offer but—"

"But what?" Marlow interjected, scowling.

"I'm not sure. It sounds like a worthwhile project. What's in it for you?"

"First, you prove your skills. Second, you can better ascertain who I should hire for Charlie's replacement." Marlow smiled widely. "I pay well."

John didn't return the smile. "I'd need a contract authorizing me to penetrate your system."

"Absolutely. No problem. Let's do it."

During the next hour, they negotiated the agreement terms,

which Amy typed into a consulting contract. John left Marlow's swanky office and expansive estate in time to reach Dulles airport and turn in his rental car. He stopped at a kiosk for a coffee and blueberry muffin.

John sipped the hot brew, worrying Cora had oversold his talents to Marlow. He didn't want to disappoint his sister or her husband. Doubt consumed him as he waited for his flight to board. What had he just agreed to?

ON HIS FLIGHT BACK to Ohio, John replayed the day's events. Marlow's home was magnificent from what John saw of it. And it seemed Occidental did span across the globe distributing organic produce. The idea of hacking into their computers to test the security threatened John's sense of well-being.

He put his head back. Because he'd already signed the contract, he couldn't back out now. Yet, he lacked peace. Or was it no confidence he would successfully complete a job of this magnitude? His small consulting project on the Miller farm didn't cause him such angst and he wondered why.

For one thing, John appreciated Eli and his simple farming methods. The Amish farmer rejected many mechanical conveniences in providing for his family. Eli also sought to grow the healthiest food for everyone's benefit while Marlow profited from merely moving food to markets.

Good thing his seatmate wasn't chatty. John was on the verge of a decision, and it was best done in quiet. He closed his eyes, and to the hum of jet engines, he considered the honorable qualities Eli and Pop shared, which he wanted to emulate in his life. Each man showed their families the importance of being self-reliant and kind to their neighbors. Most importantly, the two men shared a deep faith in God as their foundation.

John suddenly realized he knew more about Eli than he did Marlow. Perhaps that's what bothered him. Today was only the third time he'd talked with Marlow in three years since he married Cora, the Biltmore being the second.

The plane landed and John retrieved his treasured suitcase from the overhead. He hurried to his car with a new understanding. Working with Marlow would be a perfect way to become better acquainted with his brother-in-law.

Back in his efficiency apartment, John brewed coffee, intending to stay up late, and then spent an hour formatting a spare laptop, which he reset to factory settings before uploading new software. He drank coffee and ate a nut bar, confident he'd leave no evidence of his visit to website.

His agreement with Marlow permitted this attempted intrusion, but first John would check what system Charlie Riggs had installed to deter hackers. He also intended to discover if the former IT guy had concocted any mischief in retaliation for being fired.

John read the public presentation and learned something he didn't expect. Marlow was actually a broker who bought, repackaged, and sold at wholesale prices many products available in supermarkets. John contemplated a further assertion—that Occidental was the largest provider of private label organic items on store shelves bearing the merchants' own labels. Could it be true?

He rubbed his hands together anticipating a final task before turning in for the night. "This should be illuminating," he muttered aloud. "I can't wait to see what happens."

He set about launching a spear-phishing expedition to penetrate any firewall installed by Charlie.

His target: Marlow's executive assistant Amy, who was expecting a baby.

His lure: An advertisement for "Mommies in the Making" John just created.

His method: Attaching a fifty-percent-off coupon.

When Amy clicked on the coupon, she would install a download of malicious malware. This would permit John to see remote key logging, steal passwords, transfer files, and more.

Once the "Mommies in the Making" email advertisement was ready, he emailed it to her using a blast of emails to:

Amy@OccidentalOrganicsInc,
Amy.Carr@OccidentalOrganicsInc.com,
Admin@OccidentalOrganicsInc,
and
contact@OccidentalOrganicsInc.

The emails sent, John shut down his computer and went to use his new electric toothbrush. In the morning, he hoped he would not see four messages back to him proclaiming "no such recipient."

JOHN HARDLY SLEPT. Adrenaline kept surging through his brain. He tossed and turned for hours, unable to settle down until he knew if he really did deceive Amy. At four a.m., he threw off the covers and scooted from bed, which gave him a stark reminder of the morning he'd risen early to help Thomas harness the horses.

Thomas will feed the horses soon, he thought, switching on the coffee pot.

John grabbed a granola bar and logged into his newly-equipped computer, eager to know if he'd caught anything during his spear-phishing experiment. His fingers sped along the keyboard, his breath coming in short bursts. Suspense heightened.

John returned to the fictitious baby gear email and cried, "Oh no!"

Three emails had bounced back. He hurried to locate the fourth email to Amy.

"Yay!" he cheered. "That one made it through."

He'd check later, after Amy was up and his morning class ended, if she resisted a bargain or clicked on his coupon. John shut down the dedicated laptop, his growling stomach insisting he eat a proper meal for a change. Oatmeal sounded good. He cooked a bowl in the microwave and toasted rye bread, slathering the slice with peanut butter.

It was hours later when John hustled back to his apartment, certain Marlow's assistant should be at work by now. He logged into the computer and looked for his bait.

"Yes!"

He pumped his fist, overjoyed. It worked.

The irresistible fifty-percent coupon he attached to Amy@OccidentalOrganics email had been opened. He typed more key strokes and was thrilled because Amy had indeed downloaded the poisoned malware to her computer.

This looked to be another good week. Besides learning more about his mother, John's consulting business was growing. He planned to reconnect with Eli who had hinted he might introduce John to an Amish neighbor. John held out high hopes the neighbor would also need his help growing certifiable organic produce.

Just then, John could picture Ruth's pretty face and a new idea lit his mind.

He went to the small suitcase where he removed the two weathered photographs of his mother. He blinked back tears of longing. How he wished he remembered more about Sarah Lapp.

John looked at the photo showing her as a teen dressed in a simple Amish dress and couldn't deny it. His mother reminded him of Ruth. He arranged the pictures on his desk, near his computer, and decided to scan them into his smart phone to look at whenever he wanted.

In that moment, he made an important decision—to forgive the past and live in the present without worry for his future life. Personal matters dealt with, he returned to Occidental's website aware he needed to tell Marlow about the breach.

THE BREACH

When should John tell him, and how would Marlow react?

Chapter 19

Eva and Scott Montanna finally took time for themselves later that evening once their kids were settled into bed. Their feet up in recliner chairs, they turned off the TV and cell phones.

"Scott, listen," Eva said in hushed tones.

He faced her with a quizzical look. "I only hear the grandfather clock ticking."

"Exactly. My dream has come true. You and I are enjoying a quiet night together."

"I've been waiting to tell you until we were alone," he replied, his tone ominous.

Her spirits plummeted. "Has Kaley's social media gone haywire again?"

"Nothing like that." Scott kept his voice low. "The Capitol was abuzz today. The FBI invaded the Senate and arrested one of Senator Easton's staffers."

"Who did the FBI arrest and for what?" Eva asked, setting her cup on the table.

"Senator Easton's China expert assigned to the Senate Intelligence Committee is a guy named Chen." Scott paused to sip his tea. "Apparently, he was spying for the Chinese Communist Government to influence legislation and gave them Classified Intelligence."

"The CCP!" Eva cried, then clapped a hand over her mouth, afraid she'd wake the kids. She whispered, "Chen has to be a U.S. citizen to receive a Senate clearance."

"Yes, he's a second-generation American. His parents immigrated here in the eighties. Chen was born and educated in Easton's home state of Washington."

Eva's mind replayed all the intrigue caused by China in the last few months. A sudden and terrible thought occurred to her. "Would Chen have access to our phone numbers and identity data?"

"Good question." Scott's handsome face was eclipsed by a serious frown. "He might have mine, given my job as press secretary to the Speaker. I don't know how he'd get yours. Of course, he could have hacked into my personnel file. Anything's possible."

"Scott, you're right. The ChiComs are one giant shopvac sucking up our data and secrets. Mom emailed an article yesterday about the little circular robotic vacuum cleaners that zoom around floors in people's homes. According to social media, those vacuums that are manufactured in China collect information from people's households, which is then beamed back to China. Mom's friends tossed theirs in the garbage."

Scott swiped his chin, asking, "I wonder if Griff knows of Chen's arrest?"

Feeling revved and ready to fight the unseen enemy, Eva said, "It wouldn't surprise me. Griff considered Li Chen a total nuisance during the Hilton case and thought he had an obsessive interest. Can't wait to hear what he has to say tomorrow."

MORNING ARRIVED FOR EVA before the sun rose. She awoke from a strange dream of Li Chen hacking into her cell phone and office computer.

Eva nudged Scott. "Do you want an early breakfast? I'll fix eggs and sausage."

"Okay," he growled, throwing off the sheet.

Eva shoved on slippers and put on her bathrobe. In the kitchen, she scrambled eggs, microwaved sausage, and made toast, her mind awhirl.

Scott joined her at the table, looking tired. "It won't hurt me to start early."

He prayed over the breakfast and dug in. Eva ate quickly, telling him in between bites, "I can't stop thinking about Chen's arrest. He's one tiny pebble in China's toxic flood of influence across the globe."

"I'll let you know if I find out any more," Scott promised.

Eva looked deep into his eyes. "You're a wonderful husband and my best friend. I'm thankful we're in this together."

She hurried to get ready, kissing Scott on the way out. Eva hopped on the freeway before the HOV restrictions went into effect and reached the office in record time.

She strode into the JTTF office on the lookout for Griff. He wasn't at his desk, which wasn't unusual at this early hour. She dumped her heavy purse in the drawer and turned the key. On the way to make coffee, she passed Brett's cubicle, and to her amazement, Griff was talking to him looking super relaxed.

"Hey, you two," Eva said. "Griff, I'm interested in your reaction to Li Chen's arrest."

He jumped to his feet. "What? Are you pulling my chain?"

She looked around for a third chair, but there was no room.

Brett stood. "Let's finish what Eva started in the conference room."

They all sat around the table with Griff insisting, "Eva, what's going on?"

"Scott broke the news to me last night," she explained. "Chen's arrest by the FBI is public knowledge on Capitol Hill. He was working for China."

"I saw nothing on the news," Brett complained, tapping his fingers on the table.

"Obviously, politicians on the Hill are embarrassed by one of their staffers being arrested," Griff said, his voice strained. "Either the media hasn't heard or won't expose the truth about Senator Easton and his staff."

"I'm guessing the Bureau didn't issue a press release," Brett observed. "What do you make of that, Griff?"

Eva jumped in, giving her two cents. "They must not intend to flip Chen, because they would have taken him aside quietly."

"You make a good point," Griff told Eva. "I wonder if the FBI has evidence Easton was up to something crooked with Darin Hilton."

"If so, wouldn't they have briefed you?" Brett asked.

"Yes, they should have," Griff shot back. "The longer I work around D.C., I see the wheels of justice aren't just grinding more slowly, sometimes they're falling off."

From the way Griff perched ramrod straight on the chair, Eva figured he was as frustrated as she was over the news and she said, "If it weren't for the pleasure of working with you guys, I'd retire when first eligible. Griff, are you shocked by Chen's arrest?"

"Not shocked," he replied, eyes blazing. "Vindicated more like. You heard me complain about him during the Hilton case. To discover Chen's a criminal or spy explains the bad vibes I got from him."

"Which is he? Criminal or spy?" Brett asked.

"That's easy," Griff said, arms folded across his chest. "I put my money on spy. When he badgered me, Chen dropped names of his State Department contacts and those in China's embassy here. He sat in a catbird seat where he learned of our secrets to help China defeat our defenses and even influence drafting laws benefiting them."

Eva dropped a rounded fist on the table. "He's probably been scooping up data on those of us whose family members are Congressional staffers!"

His eyebrows raised, Griff began humming a suspense theme song. "Eva, it's getting worse. Will you ever know who invaded your phones?"

"Yeah." Brett looked grim. "Chen probably hacked into every bit of Scott's data."

Griff's cell phone buzzed on the table. He snatched it up, and looking at it, he said, "Judah wants me to call from the SCIF. He knows about Chen's arrest."

He left the room. Eva stared at Brett, who stared back at her.

"I hope he'll tell us what Judah says," Eva intoned, alert to the ramifications of Chen's arrest. "Brett, what's new on the threat of explosives from drug smugglers?"

He headed for the door. "I may have a new informant. I'll keep you posted."

Eva rose and after getting coffee, she returned to her office where she sat staring at her cellphone. The blast of caffeine did nothing to ally her concerns. She decided to make a call and ended up leaving a message, "Call me. I need to talk about what you told me last night."

Unable to reach her hubby, Eva hung up. Worry over what Li Chen, a Chinese spy on Capitol Hill, knew about Eva and her family flooded her mind. She vowed to grill her partner Griff and make him spill whatever he discovered from Judah.

GRIFF HURRIED INTO THE SCIF at FBI Headquarters. The special room had built-in protection against eavesdropping. He hoped Agent Judah Levitt would speak freely and divulge whatever he knew about Chen. Then again, he might not.

The technician connected Griff and pointed to the blinking light. Apprehension building, Griff said hello to Judah, who answered with his customary greeting in Hebrew, "Boker Tov."

"Judah, is all well?"

"Yes, but after Chen's arrest for his secret employment with the Chinese government, I have to ask. Did you and Eva learn more about her phone being compromised?"

"I'm astonished you're already aware of Chen's arrest," Griff replied. "There's been no public release. Eva and I think Chen is the culprit to her phone incursion. After all, her husband Scott is the press secretary in the Capitol where Senator Easton serves."

The Mossad agent continued in his heavy Hebrew accent, "My friend, we must all be vigilant. Do you recall when you visited and observed our Iron Dome at work?"

"How can I forget?" Griff said. "Dawn and I were smack-dab in the range of a Syrian missile."

"The same people are responsible."

"You mean China?"

"Exactly," Judah said. "I share something classified. China recruited one of our Israeli Defense Force officers. He gave China secret intelligence on how the Iron Dome works. As we speak, China is building offensive and defensive systems based on secret technology they stole from Israel. One of their electronic warfare ships remained off our Mediterranean coast. We have uncovered how China financed Syrian rebels to launch inbound rockets just so their warship could study our defenses."

Dread bolted through Griff like an electrical current. "Judah, their aggressiveness spreads through American colleges, businesses, and our federal government. You may be privy to more than I am, just how Israel collaborates with us to safeguard our secrets."

"What we learn, we share with your people. China's thievery has gone quite far. America has no missile defense against China. Take heed, because they are building a stealth bomber based on plans stolen from your defense contractors and using spies working in your country. Expect them to release their bomber very soon."

"Your warning must be relayed higher up in our government." Griff briefly shut his eyes. "I'll pray about this, and ask Jehovah to protect you. Judah, I left Israel with a deeper faith in God's Son. You understand I believe Jesus is the Messiah."

"I do. My cousin here in Tel Aviv has discovered your faith, my friend. He asked me to read Isaiah 53, and I have, twice. Do you know it?"

"Sure do. I'll open it on my Bible app," Griff answered, fascinated by Judah's openness. He lifted up a silent prayer for Judah and scrolled to Isaiah 53.

"Judah, verse 5 says, 'But He was pierced for our transgressions, He was crushed for our iniquities; the punishment that brought us peace was upon Him, and by His wounds we are healed.'"

"Yes," Judah said. "Cousin Ari tells me this refers to Jesus. Do you know, after reading chapter 53 for the second time last night, I dreamed Jesus came to my house. He reached out an arm saying, 'I came for you, Judah, to save you. Believe in Me.'"

Griff gave thought to Judah's dream before saying, "I've heard others in the Middle East are coming to know Jesus from their dreams."

"I want to believe," Judah said, his voice a bare whisper.

"What stops you?"

Judah's sigh sounded tortured. "Family tradition, I suppose. My father always taught us children the Messiah has yet to come to save us."

"If your father is wrong, you could be missing out on the truth," Griff told his friend. "I, too, was in a similar situation. My wife believed the truth of Jesus before I did."

"Cousin Ari gave me a Bible. Griff, I do not know where to begin."

Griff felt the answer flow from his tongue. "I opened the third chapter of John. In verse 16, Jesus reveals God loved the people of the world so much that He sent His only Son. He means you, Judah. Whoever believes in Him is saved and has eternal life with Him. The truth finally sunk into my thick head, and I could no longer live in a lie."

"What should I do if I believe?"

"You know how to pray to Jehovah. Ask Him to forgive your sins, wash you white as snow, and tell Him you believe Jesus Messiah is the true way to Him."

Silence engulfed the SCIF as Griff sat back, waiting to hear Judah's response.

Finally, in earnest tones, the Mossad agent said, "Griff, you help me more than you know. Recently, I sensed my life being weighed on a balance scale. I felt all I have done for my country did not impress Jehovah. When I awoke this morning after my dream, I felt peace. I do not have to strive anymore. Talking with you, I realize I have already decided. I want you to be the first to know, Jesus is *my* Messiah. I will call Ari tonight!"

"Here I thought we had to discuss our earthly enemies," Griff said. "And all the while, God's purpose was for us to discover the two of us are no longer His enemies, but His friends."

He encouraged Judah to read the Gospel of John, offering to text him links to his pastor's sermons on walking in the Christian faith.

"Ari attends church in Tel Aviv and invited me to come this Sunday. I will go."

"Wonderful," Griff enthused. "Text me afterwards. To finish up, Eva and I will message you if it's what we suspect. My assigned time in this facility is about to expire. Goodbye for now, my brother in Christ. Stay in touch."

"Peace be with you, Griff," Judah said, and disappeared from the connection.

Griff signed out of Bureau Headquarters with a light heart. He drove to the office, knowing this day counted for eternity. He praised God for giving him the opportunity, and was glad he hadn't squandered it by merely focusing on work.

He also couldn't wait to tell Dawn of Judah's tremendous decision. She talked often of returning to Israel with Griff. He had no idea when that might happen, yet he could see how in God's sovereign plan, going where Jesus lived was fueling Griff's desire to tell others about Jesus and His saving grace.

Chapter 20

On Friday morning, Griff sat beside Patrick O'Rourke in the courtroom, impatient to find out how much prison time Judge Ginsburg would give Darin Hilton for his threat to assault Senator Easton.

Griff glanced toward Attorney Madison Stone. She sat rigid next to her client at the table on their left, focusing directly on the judge. Ginsburg pushed reading glasses to the edge of his nose. He thumbed through the file as if searching for something.

Perhaps he's checking the presentence report, Griff thought. Did that bode well for Hilton? The judge didn't keep him waiting long.

His voice stern and his face solemn, the judge intoned, "I have read the presentence report, including the prosecutor's recommendations. Attorney Stone filed an excellent response for her client. Mr. O'Rourke, do you have anything to add?"

"No, Your Honor," Patrick answered from his wheelchair.

"Ms. Stone, what do you say before I pronounce sentencing?"

Madison stood. "Your Honor, we ask the court to impose probation or the lightest sentence for the reasons stated in our reply to the presentence report."

When the judge removed his glasses, she remained standing.

Ginsburg fixed a penetrating gaze upon Hilton. "The defendant will rise."

Madison leaned down to whisper in her client's ear. Hilton lurched to his feet, buttoning his suit jacket as if following what she just told him to do. Griff noticed Hilton stood quite erect for a man who was about to have the hammer of justice fall on him.

"Mr. Hilton, you threatened to assault an elected United States Senator, which is a very serious charge," the judge said, eyeing the defendant. "The statute provides a maximum sentence of ten years; however, the sentencing guidelines and presentence report recommend you be incarcerated for up to forty-eight months and a fine of up to five hundred thousand dollars. The government recommends you receive the maximum."

Hilton jerked his head and spoke to his attorney. Griff couldn't hear. Madison immediately raised her hands and shook her head.

Ginsburg continued, "Ms. Stone presents a strong argument for the Court to deviate from the guidelines and show leniency because you have no prior record. Mr. Hilton, I hereby sentence you to twenty-four months, followed by thirty-six months of supervised release. You will pay a fine of two hundred and fifty thousand dollars."

"This is a crime!" Hilton bellowed.

Madison tugged on his suit jacket sleeve and spoke hurriedly to Hilton to shut him up. He ignored her.

"You're the crook," he yelled at the judge. "You should be impeached!"

Griff elbowed Patrick but said nothing.

The judge banged his gavel loudly, commanding, "The defendant will be silent."

A deputy U.S. Marshal stepped through the low swinging gate separating the well of the courtroom from the spectators. His lean face somber and arms crossed, the deputy marshal took up a position next to Hilton. Loud whispers erupted.

The judge rapped his gavel with force. "The defendant has just demonstrated the contempt he has for this Court and the judicial system. In view of his contempt, the Court revises his sentence to forty-eight months in custody and a fine of five hundred thousand dollars. Mr. Hilton's bond is revoked. He is remanded to the custody of the U.S. Marshal."

"Darin, not again!" a woman shouted from behind Griff.

Griff looked over his shoulder, concluding she was Jennifer Tuttle, Hilton's sister. The judge banged his gavel again for good measure and left the courtroom. The marshal wasted no time handcuffing Hilton to sounds of loud calls from the audience.

Griff saw Jennifer wiping tears from her eyes.

"I can't believe it," Griff remarked, leaning over to Patrick. "Hilton's big mouth and arrogant ways just cost him another quarter-million and doubled his sentence. Some guys never learn."

Patrick collected his file and said, "Griff, I don't know what to make of it. Hilton is his own worst enemy."

For her part, Madison Stone didn't stay to discuss the fiasco with Griff or Patrick. She stuffed papers in a valise, lifted it over her shoulder, and rushed out of the courtroom.

Griff parted with Patrick and on the way to his car, mulled over something he hadn't mentioned to Patrick. Darin Hilton must be extremely angry at Judge Ginsburg for doubling his sentence after accepting his earlier half-million-dollar bribe.

Another idea wormed its way into Griff's mind. Wasn't it possible Ginsburg was just as mad at Hilton for demanding a bench trial and then not making the required half-million-dollar payoff because Hilton's sister, Jennifer, had given the bribe by mistake to Susan Brockman?

Griff left the parking lot with one conclusion. Hilton had received his just reward.

If only Li Chen would be convicted and receive an even tougher sentence, Griff might feel as if his long hours and dedication were worth it.

GRIFF WALKED INTO THE OFFICE with mixed feelings over Hilton's sentence. It bothered him that he hadn't told the prosecutor about Hilton intending to bribe the judge.

Eva leaned her head out of her cubicle when he passed by. "Hey, aren't you going to tell me what happened at sentencing?"

"You won't believe it." Griff stepped back and leaned against the partition to her entrance. "It was routine until Hilton responded to the twenty-four months and quarter-million-dollar fine by calling Ginsburg a crook."

"And the judge heard him?" Eva interrupted.

"Oh, yeah. Ginsburg amended the sentence on the spot. Forty-eight months and a half-million-dollar fine."

Eva laughed out loud. "Half-a-million is identical to the bribe Hilton tried to pay. Do you think the judge solicited the bribe and was sending Hilton a message?"

Griff walked over and sat on Eva's empty chair.

"You thought so. I thought so, and so did Hilton's sister," he replied, not liking any of it.

Eva tilted her head. "Did you speak with Jennifer afterwards?"

"No. As soon as the judge raised the fine to five hundred thousand, she screamed, 'Darin, not again!'"

"It's too weird." Eva stared at Griff. "Maybe we should brief Patrick about Jennifer's claim and Susan Brockman's divine gift."

"I've thought of nothing else since I left the courthouse. An additional charge of attempted bribery could have resulted in a higher sentence."

"Yeah, and that would probably be the forty-eight months he received based on his misconduct in court," Eva said, her gaze direct.

"You're right, and besides, we gave Jennifer our word this wouldn't come back against her or her brother." Griff pointed at Eva's computer screen. "What are you doing?"

"I've been sitting here convinced getting the new phones and phone numbers has ended the threats against my privacy and Kaley's. And then I find an urgent bulletin warning us of another threat."

"Now what?' Griff pressed his lips together.

Eva pushed aside her writing pad. "There's been another insane hack."

"Define *insane*."

"Sophisticated hackers, probably a nation-state, are sneaking into every file at the El Paso Intelligence Center."

"Really!" Griff jerked back his head. "EPIC stores all our contact data. Each time you and I send them an alert, they document how to reach us. It could get even worse."

"I agree. During civil rioting, anarchists could retrieve our data off the dark web and run straight to our homes." Eva's eyes burned with intensity.

"Could?" Griff demanded. "Didn't you see the bulletin Justice put out? Some deputy U.S. marshals received ricin sent to their homes in the mail."

Fear engulfed Eva. "Poison with no antidote? What if their spouse or kids opened them?"

"It doesn't bear thinking about. Those same creeps can get our personal data from China. I read an article how authorities believe China's hacked into the personal data of half of all Americans. I think they are behind our hacking. Which reminds me."

"Something Judah told you?" Eva asked, her mind awhirl with future danger.

"Right," Griff said on his way out. "Judah mentioned certain classified info. China is stealing designs for our stealth bomber and building their own bomber."

"So that's what he wanted to tell you from the SCIF?"

He grinned at Eva. "You may not believe what else he shared."

"Talking with you is like playing a game of chess." She returned his smile. "Your move, I think."

"Judah wanted to check the status of our phones because Mossad discovered China stole data about their Iron Dome defensive missile system. Here's the great news. He's studying Scripture and the book of Isaiah. He, like his cousin, now believes Jesus Christ is the promised Messiah."

Eva leapt to her feet. "That's wonderful! The best ever, and takes away the sting of riots, ricin, and corruption. We should all travel to Israel and have Judah show us around."

"Dawn's praying the same thing," Griff replied with a wave. "I'm off to write up the report about Hilton's sentencing. Let's keep his attempted bribery between us, for now."

"I agree, and I'll join Dawn in praying for God to protect us all," Eva declared forcefully.

Chapter 21

John sped back to his apartment that afternoon after teaching two classes, thinking how fast the week had flown since he and Marlow signed the consulting agreement. He dropped his briefcase on the kitchen counter, breathed deeply, and rushed to start a second session of snooping. Thanks to Amy Carr's interest in digital coupons, John had recently hacked into Occidental Organic's password-protected office network.

She'd enabled the keystroke malware he installed, allowing him to retrieve critical data and wander through corporate files. After examining dozens of emails with the firm's CPA, insurance provider, and even those Marlow sent to horse breeders looking to buy Cora's anniversary gift, John found it as exhilarating as running through a corn maze when he was a kid.

This time he would scrutinize efforts by Charlie Riggs, Marlow's fired IT guy, to provide a firewall against possible intruders.

He created a list with the heading: *Charlie installed security software*, and beneath this, John wrote: *He failed to educate Marlow/staff to avoid malware.*

So engrossed with his searching, he simply drank from a super-sized glass of water by his side and forgot to eat. His concentration paid off when he stumbled upon a startling discovery. The computer screen seemed to mock him, taunting him over what to do with the information he'd just uncovered.

Riggs had installed sophisticated software on Marlow's computer to assure his boss' conversations remained private and couldn't be intercepted. Moreover, they were digitally archived. The question was, why?

Charlie certainly had computer skills and was no dummy. But what was his true motive? John checked the clock, realizing it was past time to report in. He dialed the main number listed on Marlow's business card.

Amy answered, "Occidental Organics. How can I help you?"

"It's John Lapp," he said. "I visited Mr. Bryson last week. How is your day?"

"I remember you, Mr. Lapp. Mr. Bryson is on another line and can call back when he finishes."

"Fine. He has my number."

He hit the end button on his smart phone and returned to Occidental's "About Us" page, the one adorned with bright and healthy-looking vegetables. John had barely begun to read that Marlow was the second-generation Bryson to head the company when the man's name appeared on his buzzing phone.

Marlow greeted him pleasantly, adding, "I assume you're working hard to protect me and my company."

"I checked your office network and need to tell you what I found," John replied.

"Now's a good time to talk. It's my daily lull in the effort to keep America fed with the best organic food. What are your conclusions?"

"Your website is eye-catching and user-friendly." John cleared his throat and sipped water before adding nonchalantly, "I also hacked into your computer network."

"No!" Marlow made a thumping sound as if pounding his desk.

"Yes, sir. You asked me to do it and I did."

"Wait," Marlow sputtered. "I thought Charlie built a firewall to prevent it."

John consulted his list before saying, "You hired me to test if an expert could gain access. Riggs constructed an adequate firewall, but I tricked my way in. Be careful not to open attachments or links you aren't expecting. That goes for your staff too."

"I'm horrified. Charlie insisted he made me impenetrable. Was it more of his lies?"

John lowered his voice out of caution. "I am surprised to find he installed a Firewire Cryptic Message App. Your conversations with others who use the same app are encrypted. Has that worked well for you?"

"Why ... yes." Marlow's voice turned edgy. "I was concerned competitors might try to learn of our suppliers and other company secrets. I believe it is working. Can I trust the app to avoid intercepts?"

John toggled to Cryptic Message's website. "I'm not as familiar with Firewire as I'd like. Let me download the app on my computer and try talking with you on it."

"Do it," Marlow ordered. "I'll add you to my app contact list, then you reach out to me. We'll video and voice conference and avoid phones. See if you think it's all secure."

Through his searching, John noted that Firewire claimed it couldn't be hacked, and also the voice and image of the participants couldn't be heard or recorded.

John agreed to try it. "And another thing ..." He paused, unsure if Marlow knew the videos were being stored in his system. He decided to ask anyway.

"Did Charlie install a way for you to archive or keep a record of conversations?"

"No way!" Marlow shouted. "That's the last thing I want."

"I agree. Are you going to be in your office for another hour or so?"

"I can be, although it doesn't matter. I always take the laptop into my residence."

John had momentarily forgotten Marlow's office was actually in part of his home. "Good. I'll download Firewire and contact you within the hour to test how secure it is."

"Thanks," Marlow growled. "We'll see each other and talk at the same time."

Suddenly, he was gone.

JOHN WASTED NO TIME installing the open source software for Firewire's Cryptic Message App on his dedicated laptop. He typed Marlow's info in the contact list, and it took him less than an hour and he was ready to contact his only IT client.

John hoped this experience worked more smoothly than his efforts to FaceTime with Mom and Pop. The distance between Ohio and Virginia prevented him from visiting them often, so he thought face-to-face visits on their respective smart phones would be the answer. Wrong. They had an awful time making it work.

Vowing to give them another tutorial soon, John clicked on the icon to connect with Marlow, confident the CEO wasn't afflicted with his folk's inability to master modern technology. Marlow's deep voice burst from the speaker the same moment his face filled the laptop's screen.

"John, seeing your face is a valuable benefit of this app. I didn't recall your voice, but I recognize your face. Although, your beard is longer, which I failed to notice in my office."

"True." John stroked his growing beard. "Maybe Cora never told you, but I've discovered my mother was raised Amish. I advise Amish farmers here in Ohio. Thus, the beard."

"You teach computers at the college. Are the Amish computerizing their farms?"

John saw Marlow sitting in a recliner in front of bookshelves as if in a library. He'd forgotten to edit the IT credentials on his resume so he would correct Marlow now.

"Sir, you may have a wrong impression. While I teach basic computers at the State Agricultural College, agricultural courses are mainly what I teach. The IT work I do is really my passion. I'm helping Amish farmers improve their productivity."

"Do any grow organic?"

"They do, and are looking for market outlets," John added hopefully.

"You and I should discuss that another time. Tell me about the security of Firewire and my system."

Before John could reply, Marlow interjected, "Hold on a second. Is our conversation lockbox secure?"

"It's really ingenious," John told him. "All indications are it's very secure. Charlie did well for you."

Marlow coughed out a sigh. "What a relief. Charlie called me after I signed with you. Wanted his job back. When I refused, I hate to say it, but I got the distinct impression he was threatening retribution of some kind."

"Have no fear," John assured. "I created a new password for the entire system, added two-party verification to keep Charlie out, and shared all with Amy. You can be confident he can't access your system again."

"My friend, that is great news. How about you become our new IT guy? You could do so remotely, right?"

When John nodded, Marlow continued, "Just today, my CPA insisted I install a program on our system. I am *not* gifted in technology."

"Then rely on me to take care of your computer system needs."

Marlow extended a hand on the video as if shaking John's hand. "John, you have a deal. Send me the numbers. I'll add your new fee to our earlier contract."

"Done." John reached his right hand toward the computer screen.

Marlow aimed his index finger toward the keyboard, saying, "We'll talk later."

Instantly, the screen went blank.

John had much to do. First, he disconnected from the Firewire Cryptic Message App. Then he maneuvered to Marlow's computer and a hidden digital voice file, which Charlie had previously installed. John clicked on this file and selected the file for today's date and time. The speaker on his laptop sprang to life.

Marlow's face filled the screen and his voice barked, "John, seeing your face again is a valuable benefit of this app. I didn't recall your voice, but I recognize your face. Although, your beard is longer, which I failed to notice in my office."

John closed that file immediately. A bolt of fear shot through his body. He sat staring at the computer, which had replayed the conversation word for word.

Had Charlie done this?

The former IT guy had managed to capture both audio and video cryptic message feeds in Marlow's computer to enable their digital storage and hid them in the computer's accessory files.

Marlow just admitted he possessed no computer knowledge. He couldn't accomplish something so sophisticated. John had a sudden revelation. Marlow had a recording of their revised verbal agreement. It didn't matter if John ever signed the contract. Marlow had his proof.

Two daunting questions loomed. Why did Charlie create this backup system, and did Marlow know he possessed the recordings in his computer? Perhaps so, which was how Marlow gathered evidence to fire Charlie. John considered another angle. Riggs might secretly be keeping the video recordings. Thoughts of what Riggs might still know alarmed John. He changed his and Marlow's passwords, and would give Amy's to her later.

His consulting job finished, John was bothered by what kind of retribution Riggs meant. Was the guy even now targeting John's computer?

John's phone buzzing on the table made him jump. Cora's name flashed across the screen. Puzzled by why she'd call so soon after he hung up with Marlow, John pushed the answer button.

"Cora, I'm surprised to hear from you. I'm working on Marlow's network."

His older foster sister whispered, "I overheard Marlow talking with you and was reminded to phone you with an idea. I'm in my bedroom."

"Oh? Is there a problem?" John asked, getting concerned.

"No, it's something nice. I'm planning a surprise birthday party for Marlow and I want to make sure you note it on your calendar because I'd like you there, along with our folks."

John whispered his response, "Sounds good. Text me the date."

Chapter 22

Eva was winding down late on Saturday night after their family visit with her parents. She made the two-hour drive to Richmond frequently, wanting her kids to maintain strong bonds with their grandparents. They bought sandwiches and salads at a local deli on the way down and ate lunch together. Then she and Scott played dominoes with Kaley, Dutch, and her folks. Andy worked out in the condo fitness room to build up his muscles for football.

After enjoying her mom's traditional lasagna and garlic knots for supper, Eva stifled a yawn, wishing they had planned to stay over.

"Brew some coffee, Mom." Eva pushed away her empty plate.

Her mom rose from the table. "It's all ready, and your father wants to show you his new classic BMW in the garage."

Kaley shrieked, "A Beemer? How sweet!"

Like baby ducks, the family followed Grandma to the garage where she turned on the lights. Everyone stood dumbfounded, staring at a fat little car, shaped like a deformed red tomato, its giant headlights protruding on each side of the windshield.

Andy walked around it frowning. "This isn't a BMW. There's no doors."

Eva joined Kaley in hoarse laughter.

"What is it?" Kaley giggled.

"A 1958 BMW Isetta," Grandpa declared, pulling on the one door handle.

This caused the entire front of the car and the attached steering wheel to swing open, revealing one brown leather bench seat.

Grandma pointed to the front wheels. "Look, the two front wheels are farther apart than the back wheels. So when driving through snow, it leaves four tire tracks. Your grandfather has wanted one of these since he was a teen."

"Will you take me for a ride?" Andy asked his grandfather.

Scott intervened, "It's late and we have to drive home. Next time, buddy."

"Dad, we never get to do any fun stuff," Kaley grumbled.

Eva sought to encourage her kids, saying, "Which is why we're taking a summer vacation next month. We'll discuss it on the way home. Give your hugs and jump in our car, not Grandpa's new, fun Isetta."

Hugs all around, her mother said in Eva's ear, "Dad and I love our get-togethers. Don't forget your coffee."

"We'll come back soon," Eva promised.

She filled her travel mug to the rim, and they headed for home. The three kids shouted out separate ideas for their vacation. Kaley cast the deciding vote, agreeing with her folks they should drive to Grandpa Marty's.

Once at home, with the kids finally asleep in their rooms, Eva scrolled through photos on her cell phone in the living room where Scott was absorbed in watching an overtime baseball game on TV, the sound on low.

Suddenly, Eva's phone chirped. Her fingers flew to see who messaged her. Kaley's name appeared along the top. That was odd. Wasn't she asleep?

Eva quickly read the typed message:

Please excuse. Using Kaley's # for fear you might ignore. U should know a Jiffy Peanut Movers truck will enter Laredo tomorrow from Mexico with suspect cargo. Driver is Miguel. Check it out. U won't B disappointed.

Her heart started pounding. Was this another weird intrusion?

Eva snapped down the recliner and headed straight for Kaley's room. She opened the door quietly. Her daughter was asleep, the phone plugged in a charger by her bed. Eva walked over on tiptoe, entered the passcode, and silently scrolled to Kaley's text messages.

The most recent one to Eva had been sent yesterday, and didn't match the one she just received. She read that text again on the phone in her other hand, and left the room without a sound.

Eva returned to the living room and gestured for Scott to mute the ball game. She handed her phone to him, rolling her eyes.

"Honey, I just received the spookiest text from Kaley, who is sleeping like a baby. I checked her phone. There's no evidence she sent it to me."

Scott read the message while tapping her phone. "What do you make of it?"

"It's an anonymous tip and I have no way to evaluate if it's real or if the tipster is reliable."

Scott pushed out his bottom lip. "You must admit, it's pretty creative."

"I don't agree." Eva grabbed her phone. "I feel violated. Someone again invades our privacy. This person knows my cell number and Kaley's."

Scott got to his feet, holding a finger to his lips. "Shhh. Could be the Chinese."

Eva's mind tumbled. Scott was right. She'd better keep her

voice down. What she needed was time to think about this incredible development.

"If it is the Chinese, to what purpose? Would they know anything about Mexican shipments?"

"Yes," Scott replied. "We will soon have hearings in the House about the massive amounts of illicit drugs being run out of China and through our southern border."

"Of course. What am I thinking? My mind is mired in glue. Could be some Chinese drug trafficker is turning in his or her competition."

"Or, some ChiCom official who's been providing protection didn't get paid and is setting up the drug dealer," he offered.

Eva's eyes widened. She picked up her phone, voicing her concerns about the odd tip. "If I post a border lookout and the truck's spotted, it will be surrounded by ICE personnel. A terrorist or anarchist could detonate a truck bomb and kill our agents. That's how they trick us."

"Yikes, it's a terrible dilemma," Scott said, his tone low. "What will you do?"

"I can't ignore it. I have to post a lookout."

He turned off the TV. "I'll make us tea. I could use some, and I sense we're in for a long night."

"Make mine peppermint," Eva said.

She tossed on a light jacket, gathered her cell phone and the cordless handset, and went outside to the picnic table on their patio. She felt paranoid sitting in the dark, but here she was, doing her job to keep the nation and her family safe.

Eva punched a phone number on her government-issued cell phone, and a female duty agent abruptly answered, "Immigration and Customs Enforcement."

"This is ICE Special Agent Eva Montanna calling on my issued phone. Would you phone my home number in your system? That way, you can verify my identity."

"Did you say Eva Montanna? With one 'n' like the state?" the duty agent asked.

Telling her it was two 'ns,' Eva hung up and waited, looking over her shoulder at the kitchen light shining from the window. Love for her family and for Scott, who was tending to their needs in fixing tea, filled her heart.

He was an honorable friend and husband. Inside her kids were sleeping, believing in her, trusting her to guard them. Eva vowed to accomplish everything in her power to protect her family from China, terrorists, and drug dealers. The home phone rang, startling Eva from her revelry. It was the duty officer.

"I've received a tip," Eva said, explaining the contents of the message, adding, "It's from an unknown source."

"We could place a computerized lookout with Laredo Sector," the officer suggested.

Eva had an idea. "Can you patch me through to the Sector duty officer and stay on the line?"

"Certainly. Hold on," came her answer.

After a brief pause, a new gruff voice joined the conversation, saying, "Laredo Sector. Officer Pelham speakin'."

Eva assumed command. "This is ICE Agent Eva Montanna. I've been patched through to you by our HQ Duty Officer, who remains on the line."

"Hope you've got somethin' special for me this Saturday night," Pelham drawled. "Things are slow."

Eva read him the mysterious tip from her phone, then told Pelham, "I'm unsure of the source or reliability. Because the source contacted me through means I consider nearly impossible, I'm convinced it's more than a prank."

"Usually, Laredo's a right busy port of entry," he said. "Picture this, Agent Montanna. We've got a gazillion pre-cleared and bonded truckin' companies movin' perishable goods through here every day without being inspected."

"Really? A gazillion trucks aren't inspected?" Eva shot back, incredulous. "How do you suggest we track this tip?"

Pelham chuckled with his gravelly voice. "Ha. I may have exaggerated that number a tad, but don't you worry. We know Jiffy Peanut Movers. They're a Georgia company crossin' the border every day."

"I thought the trucking company name was a joke." Eva returned the chuckle. "Do we import peanuts from Mexico?"

"To the contrary, ma'am. We export peanuts *to* Mexico. I think the PBJ trucks, that's what we call 'em here at the border, probably started runnin' reefers. I mean refrigerators, so they could haul perishables on their way back into the states."

"Can we post a lookout for this load without arousing suspicion?" she asked.

Pelham waited a few seconds as if his mental gears were turning. "Unusual, but possible. I'll order a canine team to work the lane of pre-cleared trucks. Many drivers have their names printed just below the driver's door window. We might see several PBJs but will narrow our search to Miguel."

"It's worth a try," Eva replied, not too hopeful.

Pelham agreed. "If the dogs alert to Miguel's truck or another truck, we'll send that truck to the secondary inspection station. That shouldn't arouse suspicion."

"Let's do it!" Eva pumped a fist in the night air.

Suddenly, the ICE duty officer who had stayed on the line interjected, "Agent Montanna, since you're calling from home, I will enter the lookout here at HQ, but the Sector's already alerted."

"I'll start the ball rollin' here in Laredo," Pelham assured. "We'll notify you of a positive hit."

"Sounds like a workable plan," Eva said, satisfied she'd done the right thing. "Use my office number on the lookout. I'm not confident my cell phone is secure."

Eva gave the HQ duty officer the JTTF number in northern Virginia.

Pelham declared, "Consider it done," and his line went dead.

After thanking the ICE duty officer for her help, Eva went back inside and found her tea waiting by her recliner.

"I posted a lookout at Laredo," she told Scott.

He muted the TV again. "Can you relax now?"

"You're the best." Eva lifted her teacup. "Hopefully this helps us get to sleep."

Quiet enveloped the room until he turned on the game again. She sipped her tea when a memory rippled through her mind.

"Scott, mute the television," she said crisply.

The batter nailed a home run and Scott seemed totally engrossed in the game as if he hadn't heard. That was okay. She'd learned a thing or two about patience from their twenty-plus-year marriage.

The batter ran across home plate to score, and she tried once more, "Honey, mute please."

"Huh?"

"I need to ask you something." Eva reached across her chair for the TV remote.

Scott clicked it to silent. "Okay, but it's the ninth inning and the score's tied. I'd like to see who wins."

"No problem," Eva said, trying to see his eyes from her side view. "First, tell me, did you make up your mind about returning to DoD as press secretary?"

While he swiveled his chair to face her, he clicked off the television. "This is something I've been wanting to talk to you about. And pray over."

"What about your game? You're missing the ending."

"Our future's more important than a baseball game."

Her heart leapt at his care for the family. "You're a wonder,

Scott."

"I feel the same about you, sweetheart. All you do, day by day for our family, it makes me want to jump back in the fight. The longer I'm up on the Hill, I realize it's like a reality TV show filled with sound bites and political brawling. I'm fed up."

"You want to accept the offer to return to the Department of Defense?" Eva looked to see if his eyes gave away a clue.

His eyes shone. "Yes, and I need your agreement."

"Which I happily give you." Eva smiled like it was with her whole heart. "Scott, I never thought you fit up there, trying to shape public opinion for a group distrusted by half the country."

He stood, and reaching a hand down to Eva, gently pulled her from the chair straight into his arms. "Lady, that's all I need to know. Now we agree, I'll tell them yes."

"I'm so happy right now."

He held her close in a giant hug, saying, "Have I told you lately how much I love and adore you?"

"Keep talking," Eva whispered, looking up into his eyes. "I can never hear it enough."

Chapter 23

Eva Montanna began this Monday morning like many others. Coffee in the conference room. Talking and laughing with other JTTF officers and agents. Their comradery was something she looked forward to after the weekend and to jumpstart her week.

She concealed a yawn, drained the dark roast coffee, and listened to Brett Calloway regale the group with tales of a home improvement project gone haywire. Their supervisor told of taking his twin teenage girls, who were student athletes, to compete in a track meet. Others, Griff included, shared how they finally got much-needed rest.

Eva wished she was in that group, but no. Recent and strange events had kept her and Scott awake the last two nights. The task force agents thinned, each going to their desks or out to complete investigations.

Eva urged Griff to stay behind, telling him when they were alone, "Wait 'til you hear the baffling text I received."

His eyebrows shot up and he sat back down. "More cell phone shenanigans?"

"A mysterious text came in on Saturday night disguised as Kaley's text," Eva replied, telling him the details.

"Eva, that's bizarre." Griff slid his chair closer. "Any idea who sent it?"

She shook her head. "No, which kept me up last night too."

"Are the Chinese Communists messing with your head?"

Eva fought another yawn. "Their endless tactics gave me pause about posting a lookout. I feared a terror group might pack a truck with a bomb and ambush border inspectors when they opened the truck."

"You're concerns are legit, yet in the end you did right," Griff said. "Let me know what I can do."

Eva nodded. "I'm unsure what will come of it. I need coffee and plenty of it."

He followed her to the breakroom where they refilled their coffee. Cup in hand, she returned to her desk. Eva's energy slowly rebounded after the infusion of caffeine. She settled at the computer where she analyzed the past week's terrorist threats against the U.S. and federal agents, looking for any connection to peanut-hauling trucks.

These potential threats were a constant reminder to Eva of how creative the evil mind could be in seeking to kill and maim. She'd fought off her share of villains chasing after her. The quest for justice seemed never to set, unlike the sun.

Her office phone rang, and she snatched it, thinking this might be the break she hoped for.

"Terrorism Task Force," she barked. "Agent Montanna speaking."

"Agent Montanna, it's Officer Pelham, you know, from Laredo. We spoke Saturday night."

"Any news on the lookout?"

"Yes and no. Yes, we found a PBJ truck driven by Miguel, and no contraband on board."

"Sorry I gave you bad info," Eva apologized.

"It was real early this mornin' before the sun came up," Pelham said, chuckling. "Hey, don't be discouraged. We did find a PBJ truck driven by Miguel, so part of your info was correct, just the wrong truck. I'll add, though, we occasionally get fictitious alerts filed by ex-girlfriends or spurned lovers."

"Not in this case," Eva insisted. "My phone and number are new. The tip came in on my unlisted cell phone as a spoofed text. There's no way Miguel's ex-girlfriend would have my number."

"That sounds strange. Think the tip came from someone in your contact list?"

"Anything's possible," Eva said. "My old phone got hacked after my content was compromised in Hong Kong. But I combed my list and don't see any likely suspects."

"Hey, Agent Montanna, you realize some of these shipments arrive in Mexico from China. Maybe it's a scorned Chinese business partner instead of a girlfriend."

Eva sighed. "Our plot thickens."

"I gotta run. We'll keep the lookout and hope to get lucky."

Eva ended the call with Pelham and returned to the threat summary. Her eyes read the words, yet her mind kept replaying the baffling text. Who sent it and for what nefarious reason?

TWENTY-SIX HOURS AFTER Eva last talked with Officer Pelham, Laredo Border Patrol rang her cell phone. She answered right away.

"Hey, Agent Montanna, it's Officer Pelham at Laredo, but you prob'ly knew that. I've news to get you fired up. We just detained another Jiffy Peanut Mover's truck and bingo! This time, we found the contraband."

"Terrific and fast work. I commend you." Thrilled to know her tipster was credible, Eva asked, "Is Miguel the driver?"

"That gets real interestin'. He's not. In fact, the driver we stopped is Pablo and he almost got through without us catchin' him. The dogs failed to alert."

"Maybe it's not based on my tip then," Eva said, perplexed.

"Good thing you posted it, Agent Montanna, otherwise we'd never have found nearly 800 pounds of fentanyl listed as garlic powder on the manifest."

"Wow!" Eva could hardly wrap her mind about such a huge drug bust. "You've caught a tremendous load of illegal dope. What led you to search that PBJ truck?"

Pelham laughed in her ear. "It's like I said. These pre-cleared trucks get used to movin' quickly through the border crossing. After your tip, the canine team began stoppin' trucks and lettin' the dogs take a sniff. Mr. Pablo became one agitated driver and profane. His irrational conduct alerted our people to insist on checkin' inside his trailer, even though the dog smelled nothin'."

"It's tragic how much illegal fentanyl is pouring through Mexico."

"This is our biggest seizure, but it didn't originate in Mexico," Pelham told her. "The load of garlic cloves, mushrooms, and apples were flown from China into Mexico, with the ultimate destination a packaging company in Missouri."

Eva asked him to clarify, "Did you say China? Will you investigate further?"

"Yup, the produce came from China. Laredo ICE agents will contact you. The driver claims he knows zip about the cargo."

"Do you believe him?" Eva took fast notes of everything Pelham said.

"Well ..." Pelham paused. "Pablo's agreed to deliver the load up to Missouri. Local ICE and DEA agents are headin' north in a convoy right now with the truck and driver."

Eva told Pelham she approved of the plan, adding, "I'm curious why the driver became so angry if he really didn't know."

"Apparently, Pablo promised his wife he'd be home in time for their wedding anniversary," the officer replied.

She laughed, despite the seriousness of illegal drugs being shipped across country. "Here's how I see it. Pablo realized giving his wife flowers two days late because he's helping the government is better than being ten years too late because he's in prison."

"Hah! You're right, Agent Montanna," Pelham said, grunting. "I'm gonna run. We've got our samples for lab testin' and the fentanyl is northbound. Wait for the case agent to call with updates."

Eva hung up and dashed out of her cubicle to find Griff and Brett.

"We're hot on the trail of the PBJ driver," she told them, bringing them up to speed. "This is the terrific breakthrough we've been waiting for. I just know it is."

them up to speed. "This is the terrific breakthrough we've been waiting for. I just know it is."

Chapter 24

A few days later, after teaching his classes, John Lapp assembled the test results for Eli Miller. He planned to visit his farm tomorrow afternoon. He had one project to finish this evening before fixing supper, and that was Amy Carr's support request.

The instant his Occidental laptop warmed up, John was jolted in his seat. He did a double-take. A chessboard flashed across the screen, chessmen placed strategically as if a game were in progress.

The typed message beneath the game vexed him greatly:

It's your move. Your play to send Amy a coupon was good, but not good enough. We're in this game together. I warn you not to trust Marlow. Need proof? Check device accessory files.

John stared at the screen, stunned. Someone had invaded his computer? But who?

That someone knew Marlow's cryptic messages were being copied and stored in the accessory files. The chess player even knew of the falsely named file for an IBM printer, even though Occidental had no IBM printers.

John determined it couldn't be Marlow, because he'd recently boasted to John of having no computer savvy, which led him to the most likely hacker—Charlie Riggs!

He changed his password, again. Then John logged out, his brain processing wildly. Walking over to the window, he gazed out at a few students strolling on campus under the hot sun. His mind finally quieted, and he saw truth.

Apparently, Charlie had monitored everything John did on Marlow's computers since sending Amy the spear-phishing coupon. He also must be accessing not only John's computer, but Occidental's as well through John's laptop. By changing the password, John thought he'd blocked Charlie's further attempts.

In this high-stakes game, he knew three things for sure. One, he'd been attacked. Second, Marlow would go ballistic if he learned Charlie was sneaking around in Occidental's computer system. And third, Charlie seemed bent on some kind of retribution against Marlow.

The longer John considered Charlie's chess match, a sense of calm enveloped him. The former IT guy couldn't have total access. If he did, Charlie wouldn't be telling John to go into the accessory files. He'd already know of John's recent incursion and that John already had discovered the digital recordings in the "device accessory file."

John mentally reviewed what he knew: Every one of Marlow's cryptic messages were stored in the file Charlie had created. They were hidden in plain sight by that mislabeled and nonexistent IBM printer file. And because Charlie just urged John to look in that file, he was clueless John had wandered through the enormous printer file and its hidden evidence. Charlie must be bluffing.

"What's he playing at?" John whispered, shutting down the computer.

He needed to fight this computer battle when his mind was more rested. Not tonight. John wanted to be fresh for his consulting trip to Walnut Cove tomorrow. After finding a new text from Cora with the August date for Marlow's surprise birthday party, he typed it into his calendar and readied for bed, his appetite for supper wiped out. If only John could forget about Charlie's warning and fall asleep.

JOHN AWOKE AFTER A restless night to birds chirping. Their happy songs soothed the turmoil from Charlie bursting into John's life. His feet hit the floor, and he resolved to make this journey to Eli's farm a successful one, no matter what strange games Charlie Riggs was playing.

The bowl of oatmeal topped with raspberries for breakfast tasted even better than yesterday. John taught his class with his renewed gusto, returning to his apartment to gather his gear. After eating a light lunch, he headed off with great expectation and a longing to revisit the Amish farm.

He'd last seen Eli about three weeks ago, and in the intervening weeks, he had analyzed the soil samples. He hoped Eli would be ready for him. Just then, an errant thought assailed his mind.

Was he ready to see Ruth again?

No! his brain cried. *Yes!* answered his heart.

The bigger question was if she had any interest in seeing him again. As it turned out, his impulsive decision to race to the farm a day early caused problems. John was forced to sit in his car at the general store's parking lot listening to hymns on the radio and watching his previous doubts play out before his eyes.

Mrs. Miller hadn't exactly said his visit was unwanted, but both Eli and Thomas were out helping another farmer. So Ruth had to hitch up the horse and, along with her younger brother, drive the buggy to town while John went to park his car.

John waited, the inspiring Christian music he listened to on the radio leading him to forge a new decision—never again would he impose himself on Mrs. Miller's goodwill. He'd stick to business and leave Ruth and her family to live their lives. John would be their friendly agricultural expert and nothing more.

Deciding to buy his dinner meal inside the general store, he hightailed it straight to the meat department. A young woman standing behind a deli case wore a plain green dress, and her sandy-colored hair was fashioned in a bun covered by a hairnet. She smiled at John, asking for his order.

"I'd like a sandwich on rye bread." He pointed into the case. "Is that liverwurst?"

She gave him a friendly nod. "It is delicious. What would you like on it?"

"Seeded rye bread with lettuce, mayo, and slices of the sweetest pickles you have," he replied, his stomach rumbling.

He kept a close eye on the server assembling his dinner. His mouth moistened at the memory of eating liverwurst with Pop.

"I have not seen you before," she said, layering on plenty of pickles at the end. "You must be new in the community."

John stared as she wrapped up the biggest sandwich he'd ever seen, first in waxed paper, and then in brown paper.

"Yes. My name is John Lapp. I'm advising Eli Miller on his organic crop production."

"Are you from the agricultural college?" Her eyes sparkled at him as she marked the price on the wrapper with a black crayon before handing it to him.

John tipped his new straw hat. "Yes, ma'am. Eli received permission from Jacob Nolt for me to park my car here while visiting his farm."

"Of course. He told me that you're helping Eli. Jacob is my father."

John grinned broadly, holding up his sandwich. "Thank you, Ms. Nolt. Liverwurst is my favorite sandwich."

"John, I'm no longer a Nolt. My married name is Anne Yoder. My family calls me Annie. I'm a widow, which is why I work here."

"I'm sorry," John said in sympathy.

"We're a close-knit family. God helps me each day." Annie removed her gloves. "You take care, John."

Before he could remark further about her loss and maybe mention his mother, a customer approached wanting potato salad. Annie snapped on a fresh pair of gloves and John strolled toward the cashier, wondering what else Jacob Nolt told her about him.

He grabbed a large bag of potato chips near the register. A woman with her graying hair in a bun, who he assumed was also Mennonite, rang up his order without using a barcode reader. He paid her in cash.

On the way to his car, he watched with interest as several Amish and Mennonite families arrived in buggies or cars respectively. Dressed somewhat alike, they greeted each other and chatted in the parking lot.

The black and shiny Miller buggy arrived at last. John was impressed how capably Ruth jockeyed around people and cars as she pulled to a halt near his car. He respected her, which was exactly where he'd leave it. With a brief wave at her and her brother, he collected his travel bag, valise with his papers, and fresh sandwich.

Instead of sliding over and making room for John, Ruth went to the far side, putting her younger brother to sit between them. Ruth wore no makeup, yet her cheeks shone with a pinkish glow. Maybe it was windburn, from her heavy foot.

"Hello again, John Lapp," she chimed, nodding at her younger brother. "You met Isaac before."

John climbed in next to the buffer. "Hello again, Isaac."

"Thomas said you have a phone with games," the boy said with eager eyes. "May I see it?"

Ruth tightened the right rein, snapping them both. The horse made a U-turn and walked toward the road.

John patted Isaac on the knee. "Sorry, my phone stays in my pocket. I promised your father that I wouldn't distract you by showing it to you."

"Thank you, John," Ruth said forcefully.

Had he heard correctly? Ruth had dropped her more formal way of addressing John by his family name, and he wondered. Could a friendship be developing?

"Father expected you tomorrow," Ruth said, easing into traffic and onto the right shoulder. "He and Thomas are plowing the Byler farm and will be home for dinner."

"I couldn't wait to share the soil results. Sorry to be a bother."

The brisk clip-clop of the horse's hoofs added melody to Ruth's voice as she replied, "You are right. Father will want to know your results."

"I wanted to visit again as I learned much at your farm last time," John confided.

"Is it all new to you, John?"

"Yes. As it would be if you visited where I teach college."

Ruth grew suddenly quiet. Isaac sat between them with much energy, his small legs constantly kicking up and down.

John sought to find common ground. "For me, it's discovering the life I might have known but for my father's death and my mother leaving the farm. Do you know other plain people who left the community?"

A semitruck whizzed past at great speed. The wind shook the buggy from side to side. Ruth seemed unfazed, but John's body jumped. He gripped the seat beneath him, forcing from his mind that his father had died on a road like this.

Ruth's hands stayed steady as if used to big trucks. John considered her a strong and amazing young woman, the kind of woman like his mother. How he wished he had other memories of his mother besides the aroma of cinnamon.

He clasped his sack tightly. Except for Isaac tapping his feet on the floorboard, they rode in silence. In that moment, John doubted there would be anything more between him and Ruth. She drove a buggy and her life centered around her Amish family and farm. Whereas John lived in a cramped apartment, drove a car, and worked with computers, which required electricity and WiFi.

She finally answered, her voice strained, "Yes, I know some who left. I had the opportunity to leave."

"You did?" he turned toward her in amazement.

"You seem surprised." Ruth glanced at him, a smile curving on her face. "Have you heard of Rumspringa? That is when each young plain person decides if they will stay in the community."

"Yes, I read about it online. You decided to stay?" John probed.

"Oh yes! Thomas will have a time of Rumspringa. So will Isaac. I briefly tested a worldly lifestyle and did not like it. John, I am plain. So are my people. God has blessed me for remaining with my family."

Though she said his name, John knew in his heart she didn't mean what he'd once hoped. Ruth was simply being nice and friendly. She crossed the oncoming lane and went up the drive to the Miller farm. John looked past Isaac at Ruth and saw her in a new light.

"My visiting your farm is like my Rumspringa," John said. "For a time, I leave the English life behind to try out a plain life with your family."

"Which will you choose?" Ruth asked, her eyes wide.

"I don't know. I'm comfortable in both. God will show me."

"You speak truth."

Ruth stopped the buggy by the barn, and facing John, she told him softly, "Perhaps you are meant to be Mennonite, John."

She handed her younger brother the reins before sliding from the buggy. Isaac hopped out after her.

"I will tell my mother we are home," Ruth said. "She prepares dinner for all."

John held aloft the sandwich bag. "I brought supper from the general store and will eat in the guest room."

"Save it for tomorrow's lunch. My parents will want your company for our meal."

Ruth walked to the house. Isaac began to unhitch the horse. John stowed his bag and computer in his quarters in the barn. He lost track of time sauntering through the barn enjoying rich smells and pleasing sounds of animals stomping hoofs and munching hay. Because no one yet called him for dinner, on a whim, he climbed into the seat of the large family buggy where he imagined the thrill of driving one.

He leaned out, and seeing his face reflected in the small sideview mirror, in that moment, he knew he must seriously consider what it meant to be Amish. He'd read articles online when he first learned of his mother's Amish heritage. Joining the community meant more than driving to Sunday church in a buggy with a wife and children.

Amish worshipped in homes where a large wagon brought benches and the *Ausbund*, their songbook. He'd never sung their songs, never spoken their language. He wanted to discover if he could accept an entirely new way of life, no matter the cost.

He prayed in the buggy, "Father God, reveal Your plan for my future. Is Your purpose for me to become an Amish farmer and live plain, not just for pretend? Because You allowed me to leave the Amish community, does that mean I shouldn't try to find an Amish wife who accepts my English ways?"

Sounds of approaching horses startled him. He abruptly jumped down and hurried to the rear of the buggy. Eli and Thomas came driving their teams, pulling small carts on which they sat. In a small way, when John recognized the horses, Teddy and Tulip, he had to admit he felt at home.

He walked over to Thomas, and reaching up, patted Teddy's nose. Teddy tossed his head. His glistening coat showed he and Tulip had been working hard. Thomas scrambled off the small cart.

"You are a nice surprise," he said, extending a hand.

Nodding toward the highway, John warned, "I hope you drive carefully with your team on the road. My father died driving such a team on the roadway."

"Father warns us always. It is very dangerous."

Eli walked up with his team, greeting him warmly. "John, you are a welcome sight to my tired eyes. Will you be helping Thomas with the teams?"

"Sure, and I'll explain your test results. Ruth invited me to have supper with you, but I brought my own meal."

"You eat with the family," Eli insisted, leaving John and Thomas to attend to the horses.

John recalled what he'd learned weeks earlier, and set about freeing Teddy and Tulip from their cart. Once finished, he led them into the barn where Thomas had already tied Eli's team and was removing their harnesses. John secured his team, then unfastened and lifted the heavy tack from Teddy, vowing not to collapse again under the weight.

He did just fine, then told Thomas, "Ruth said you plowed for the Bylers."

"We helped Bylers prepare the pasture for next year's planting, which we do often," Thomas said, hanging the tack on the wall.

"Are they related to your family?" John asked.

"No, but they want to be. Their son Nathan is courting Ruth."

John stumbled in the barn. Shaken by the news, he quickly straightened his back and regained his composure. "Will he be your brother-in-law?"

"I believe soon."

God used Thomas' innocent discussion to provide an answer to John, and prompt a new question. Did the connection to the Millers and their land come from God or the demands of his own heart?

He brought the two horses outside. He and Thomas rinsed down four horses, working together as close brothers. It sure seemed God arranged for John to know Eli and his family, which meant God would work out the path for his future life. Couldn't he relax and let his time on the Miller farm unfold the way it was supposed to?

"Maybe you can show me your home and the college," Thomas proposed.

"I don't think so."

"Why not, John Lapp?" Thomas sounded hurt.

"Ruth told me about Rumspringa. Perhaps when it's your turn, if you choose to experience English ways, your father will let you visit my home. Only if he approves at the right time. I promised him."

"I hope you will not forget your promise," Thomas said.

John smiled, swatting a fly. "I'll remember."

With much good will between them, they finished scrubbing and brushing Tulip. She was clean at last, and Thomas led the other two horses into the barn. John followed with Teddy and Tulip.

Supper was minutes away. John grabbed his sandwich to save in the Miller's fridge for tomorrow. On the way to the house, he wasn't thinking of food. What filled his mind was the tremendous achievement of working with his hands.

Chapter 25

John reached into his leather satchel for his papers after the family table was cleared and wiped clean after dinner. Thomas, Isaac, and younger siblings were busy reading near lanterns in the large living room while Ruth and her mother finished washing the dishes.

Eli returned to his seat at the head, asking, "John, do your soil tests reveal I need expensive treatments?"

"Let me show you what I found."

John laid a sheet from his satchel on the table. Eli took a seat beside him to look over the paper. Ruth set a lighted gas lantern near a sketch of their farm. Though she stepped back, she remained watching.

John traced the boundary lines on his sketch. "When I was last here, Ruth gave me details of what you planted on your land and where."

"It is not to scale," Eli objected. "This farm is more than one hundred acres."

John laughed good-naturedly. "My sketch is rough. I needed to understand what you planted last year since I sampled soil in various sections."

"And?" Eli asked as if anxious to reach the bottom line.

"Your soil has excellent levels of phosphorus and potassium. There's a bit too much nitrogen. I happened to see your manure spreader, which I assume you use throughout your farm."

"Correct. Never within four months of planting."

"Good." John tapped the chart east of the barn by the roadside where nothing was planted. "This quadrant is fallow. Is that part of your plan?"

When Eli nodded, his long beard trembled. Mrs. Miller spoke something in the Pennsylvania Dutch dialect. When John heard Ruth respond, he realized she was still eavesdropping from behind. Eli and John continued talking over each quadrant.

When they exhausted discussing the soil composition, John handed Eli a colorful brochure. "How would you describe your experience growing organic vegetables?"

"We do not sell much." Eli set aside the brochure without looking at it.

Ruth reached over her father's shoulder and picked it up, telling John, "Mother and I sell the organics from a roadside stand. Ours are not so pretty as these."

"Don't feel bad," John quipped. "The wholesaler paid a

consultant gobs of money to make them shiny."

Ruth handed her father the brochure. "We enjoy eating them ourselves, and can what we do not sell. Sometimes, we give them to the neighbors."

"I am consulting for this company," John said. "Occidental buys enormous amounts of organic food, which they sell in stores throughout the country. Eli, you could sell large amounts to them, even more than you could grow."

Ruth stepped closer. "Father, John has a good idea. Perhaps you, the Bylers, and others in our community could combine crops and supply them."

"Or maybe," a coy smile crept across Eli's face, "to earn more, I could buy them from all my neighbors and sell them to John Lapp's contact myself."

John smiled up at Ruth. "Your father is a wise man."

"It might be worth considering," Eli said, gazing at John's handout.

"I have other ideas." John pointed to the sketch where he'd sampled soil among the tomato plants. "I'd like to walk here with you and examine your plants in the morning light."

Eli fingered his beard before agreeing. "After you and the boys finish the chores."

John took his leave, walking back toward the barn using a lighted lamp. For some time, he watched the purple and red painted sky, and listened to sounds of crickets and the hoot of an owl in a distant tree. Life on the farm was taking root not only in his mind, but also in his heart.

EARLY SATURDAY MORNING, John's day began with a familiar rap on his door. He and Thomas watered and fed the animals before eating a hearty breakfast of apple and walnut pancakes with the family. Eli set down his fork, signaling he was ready to walk the land. He was up from the table in no time, putting on his hat.

"We go, John. Show me what the college teaches other farmers."

The two men cut through the distant field far from the road. The sun rose in the east, lighting their footsteps.

"I grew up on this farm. So did my father," Eli said, taking long strides.

John tried to keep pace. "Will Thomas choose a wife and farm here too?"

"I believe that is the Lord's plan for him," Eli replied. "My oldest son is interested in farming."

They reached the tomato field. John walked another thirty yards where he inhaled deeply, held his breath, and exhaled slowly.

"Eli, can you smell these plants?"

The farmer mimicked John's deep breathing. "I do. It is a sweet smell."

"What if I said we can make the aroma twice as intense?"

"How? Are you saying this wonderful smell can stay with them to market?"

"To control disease and pests in your plants, you use fungicides and pesticides, right?"

"True." Eli's eyes clouded. "They are not cheap. I do not like harsh chemicals, and will not let the young children come close when we spray."

"Have you battled horn worms?" John probed further.

"Of course. My neighbors too. It is a constant battle we must win to feed our families."

John stepped in front of Eli and did something he hadn't done before with his elder. He looked Eli directly in the eyes. "I suggest you switch to a new method of improving the immune system within your tomato plants. This way, your plants defend themselves. They will be free of chemicals, and this field will smell twice as good with healthier plants that are organic."

Eli kicked his toe in the dirt. "Have you tried this?"

"Yes, sir."

"You say it works?" Eli demanded.

"Yah." John stooped down and took hold of a tomato plant stem. "See how several leaves are deformed and not symmetrical?"

Eli grunted. "What is the cause?"

"Zinc deficiency." John reached for healthy-looking leaves. "See? These have no spots, meaning your phosphorus level is correct. This wrinkly one means too much nitrogen."

Eli started protesting, "Back at the house, you said my soil tested healthy."

"I did," John assured him. "I also mentioned you have excess nitrogen. More testing can reveal what is lacking in your plants' immune system."

"Explain this additional testing."

"We take a sap sample from the stem, which we test in the lab. It detects excess ammonium nitrates, which are like food for bugs. If we find this condition, we'd apply specific trace minerals like iodine or a line of ultra-micronutrients. If we do this right, we avoid dangerous chemicals. Healthy plants repel spider mites and even horn worms."

They headed toward the barn with Eli asking, "Can I afford this?"

"You'll save money by not buying fungicides and pesticides," John replied.

"And, the money you spend on testing and trace chemicals is less. After a season or two, you will reap bigger and better yields."

They discussed testing logistics and Eli agreed to the proposed plan. They shook hands on it, and John went to gather sap samples of Eli's tomato and squash plants. The realization set in. His time at Eli's farm would be over soon. He fought a tinge of sadness and busied himself collecting sap from various plants. About noon, with the sun hot overhead, John returned to the barn to wash up and collect his gear.

Ruth surprised him by meeting him on the way out. He removed his straw hat in greeting. She held out his liverwurst sandwich and a glass of water.

"Mother and I do not want you going hungry," she said. "Annie Yoder makes a delicious sandwich."

"How do you know she made this?"

Ruth smiled knowingly. "The wrapper has the price and her initials on it."

She stood watching, as if measuring his interest. "Annie is very nice. Pretty too. She is a woman who has faith in God after a tragedy."

Again, Ruth seemed intent on watching John's reaction.

"Do you know her well?" he asked, his curiosity building about Annie.

"Well enough to tell you, Annie is a widow and Mennonite, which is closer to being English."

The sun beat down on his head. John replaced his hat and began unwrapping the sandwich. "I can guess what you mean."

"Yes, John, I think you can." Ruth smiled and turned to go. "Mother and I are praying for you as if you were our family. She and I think you are too good a man to leave Walnut Cove without considering Annie Yoder as your wife."

John tried hard not to be taken aback. "Ruth, thank you for your kindness. I'll consider your hint and ask God if He is using you to help me."

She left him to eat his sandwich, and he sat on the hard bench outside the barn, deciding not to struggle over her interest in his marriage plans. Ruth called him family. And he was in a way, because he was her brother in Christ.

Some minutes later, the liverwurst sandwich a pleasant

memory, John placed his computer and small bag into the buggy. Thomas and Isaac were ready to take him to his car. His eyes closed on the way, he tried once again to envision driving his own buggy to town, and couldn't. Perhaps Ruth was right. Maybe he should see himself driving a car with a Mennonite wife by his side.

Thomas made small talk about the horses and asked John if he would come back.

John promised he would, saying, "I'll show your father new techniques to boost healthy crop production before cold weather arrives."

"Yah, winters can be hard and most tiring for us farmers."

John rode the rest of the way imagining icy and harsh winters on an Amish farm. Having enough feed for the livestock, keeping water from freezing, and even heating homes were all factors to be considered in working on an Amish farm. John had much to think about and decide.

In the general store parking lot, they said good-bye, and the boys pulled away.

John was loading his trunk when a woman's soft voice said, "Hello, John Lapp."

He turned, amazed to see Annie Yoder about to get into her car.

"My father thinks you would enjoy attending our Mennonite church," she said, looking pretty in a plain purple dress. "Has he spoken with you about it?"

John closed his trunk lid and walked nearer, interested in learning more about her and the church. "No. In fact, I would like to meet your father, Mr. Nolt. The church I attend back home is a big part of my life."

"Please join us. Our Mennonite church is right on Main Street as you drive into town from the east. Service is at ten thirty Sunday morning."

John smiled shyly, tipping his straw hat. "Thank you, Mrs. Yoder. You have made me feel welcome. I hope to come tomorrow."

"Our church has classes for children. Bring your wife and children."

"I'm not married," John said, noticing a strange sensation in telling her so.

Annie's hand flew to her chin as if deep in thought. "I am sorry. Your beard led me to believe you are married."

"I understand." John ran his hand across his Amish beard. "Eli said I might be causing confusion."

He stepped to the side to block the sun shining in her face. "I don't know what people in your community have been told, but I was adopted as a young boy. Recently, I learned my birth mother was Amish. I've been trying to experience as much as possible about her Amish life and faith."

"Is she from here in Holmes County?" Annie asked.

"No." He rubbed his hand along his pants. "My mother is, or I should say was, from Lancaster, Pennsylvania. That's where my adoptive parents raised me after she died. I began dressing plain and grew a beard hoping to be accepted here in Walnut Cove. Instead, I created confusion."

"I can understand loss." Annie eased behind the wheel of her car. "You should try our church, which has traditions like what your mother knew. Not exactly, but similar."

With a wave, she closed her door and drove off. John hopped into his car, spotting Thomas and Isaac in their buggy waiting to turn left.

He waved to them and made a right turn, his mind alive with nostalgic thoughts. His future looked bright whatever lay beyond the next curve. God promised His plans would give John hope. The Bible told him so, and John believed God's Word with all his heart.

Chapter 26

Monday morning brought Eva many frustrations. She sighed sharply. An entire container of blueberries fell from the fridge when she'd made breakfast. Scott left late as he had to move the appliance so Eva could clean up all the berries.

Now, the previously-agreed-to meeting with a contractor to discuss replacement windows on their aging house went long. Eva checked her watch as his sales pitch droned on. When he took the final measurement, Eva saw him out and hustled into her government car, forgetting her coffee mug.

Though late for work, she decided to swing by the Trumpet's Call. Eva never knew when she might need to blend in doing foot surveillance, like in public parks, so she was always on the lookout for props. Eva also wanted to donate slacks, ones too large for her newly-slimmed husband.

Irene DeVroom sat in her small office, crowded beneath a second-floor staircase, and typing on a tablet.

"I come bearing gifts." Eva held up her bag. "Scott's slightly-used slacks."

Irene laid the slacks on the counter before returning to her tablet. "You caught me trying to get this gizmo back online before some bonanza buyer walks in."

"Is your Internet down?" Eva asked.

"I rebooted the system." Irene gave Eva her cell phone. "My phone shows it's connected to WiFi, but my tablet is stubborn. It won't accept its password."

Eva agreed to try, and Irene told her the username and password John Lapp had created for her. After Eva typed these in and they were rejected, she said, "Let me see your username."

Irene toggled to another screen to reveal, *'THETRUMPETSCALL.'*

"Here's your problem." Eva quickly released the caps lock feature. "Retype your password without capital letters."

Irene typed in her password, hit the enter key, and the WiFi connected.

"Your idea worked!"

Eva clapped lightly. "Glad to help."

"Fritz and I can't figure these things out," Irene fretted. "John set up our technology. I'm glad you met him at the Biltmore."

"You're doing well, and bolder with technology than my mother."

Irene cradled her tablet in her hands. "John loaded our address book in here and updates it from Ohio."

"How does he do that?" Eva was intrigued by his abilities.

"He connects his computer to ours, and makes changes we need. John calls it syncing our computer, tablet, and phones, whatever that means."

Eva laughed. "My job requires me to keep up with technology, so any new technique interests me. It's a blessing he looks after you from Ohio."

"He's a dear boy." Irene's eyes grew misty. "When I think how God brought him to us before his mother took ill, knowing he would need to be raised in a Christian home. John called last night and was pleased by his visit to a Mennonite church. He's making new friends, which is more than he has at the church near campus."

Eva glanced at her watch. "I've a meeting to get to. Raising three kids, I understand how their futures can weigh on your heart."

"Eva, let me share good news. Marlow is the best. Not only did he hire John to care for his company's computers, he bought us a car! Fritz loves the new SUV 'cause he sits up high like his truck."

Eva opened her mouth to reply, but Irene lifted up her hands, jumping in with, "And praises be, Cora has redecorated their guesthouse before our move-in. She paid for a new kitchen. It will be nice being near her each day."

"When are you moving?"

"First, we pack up and sell our townhome," Irene said. "I need time to sort through photo albums and mementoes, which we'll send to the kids."

Eva said good-bye and reached the door when she recalled the other reason for her visit. "I need props for the trunk of my government car. Things to help me fit in with my surroundings."

Irene stood clueless, her mouth ajar.

"Fishing poles? Tennis racquets?" Eva offered.

Irene snapped her fingers. "I have just the ticket."

She headed to a sporting goods section where Eva found a tennis racquet in good condition. She feigned a practice serve and started looking for a tennis tote. They walked around looking until Irene showed her a leather bag with big loops for shoulder handles.

"The lady who donated this is into fitness," Irene said. "Will it work?"

Eva inserted the racquet into the bag and slid her arm through the handles. She walked to a mirror, nodding with approval. "Perfect. I've enjoyed catching up."

After paying, and when she was halfway to the exit, Eva spun around. "Irene, I have an idea. Our family has several computers and often needs technical support. Possibly your John can fix our problems too."

"He's a whiz," Irene said, the proud mama she was. "Here's his number."

Irene started toggling around in her tablet. Eva handed Irene her phone and said, "Type his number right here."

Irene did, handing Eva her phone. "I typed in his email address too."

The two women shared a quick hug just as a trio of ladies from church arrived. Eva tossed the racquet and tote in her trunk. She hit the accelerator hard to reach the office, more than ready to carry out some real work.

EVA TURNED ON HER OFFICE COMPUTER, wanting to check the status of last week's PBJ fentanyl seizure before meeting with Griff and Brett. She'd been distracted by Scott leaving his job on Capitol Hill.

She logged into her emails, finding a surprising message from Laredo's ICE office: *Beecher Packaging in Missouri accepted delivery of mushrooms, apples, and garlic cloves. Rejected the fentanyl labeled as 'powdered garlic,' claiming it wasn't on their manifest nor expected.*

Eva scanned additional details before hitting the print button. She hurried to collect the reports from the printer, then headed to Griff's cubicle. For a change, she had something important to share with him and Brett.

"Knock-knock," she chirped, holding the reports high like the Statue of Liberty torch. "You'll both want to hear the latest on the Laredo fentanyl seizure. Let's go confer in the conferring room. I need to spread these out."

"I'm in," Brett said.

Griff logged off his computer, and the three agents grouped around the conference room table where Eva laid out the documents.

"Brett, you'll recognize this scenario," Eva began. "Pablo, the driver, claims total ignorance of what he's hauling. After being stopped by border inspectors, he agrees to drive the load to the Missouri packaging company. With your DEA colleagues tracking him, he delivers the Chinese produce he picked up in Mexico. Beecher Packaging refuses to unload 800 pounds of 'garlic powder,' claiming they didn't expect any."

"Hah!" Brett said. "I doubt they didn't know."

Griff nodded vigorously. "That may be. The fact is, we've no one besides Pablo to arrest, and we lack evidence of his knowledge."

"I'm afraid you're right." Eva pushed out her bottom lip while scanning the report. "It says Beecher specializes in repackaging bulk shipments into retail size packages, which they then distribute to grocers."

"Okay, this shipment comes in from China, gets repackaged, and then my Dawn buys the stuff tonight at the store," Griff said, his voice edgy.

Eva snapped her fingers. "Listen to this, you guys. The shipment included reams of plastic bags printed in China, stating the Chinese produce is not only 'Organic' but 'Produced in U.S.A.'"

"There must be a law forbidding such false claims," Brett replied, scowling. "Who enforces it?"

Eva thought hard, coming up with, "ICE. We have authority over imports. Laws within the Commerce and Agriculture Departments apply as well. I'll ask our legal department."

"Face it, Eva," Brett scolded. "If it's not a terroristic threat or a dangerous drug threat, no one's got time or resources to care about fraudulent food labels."

Eva tossed her hands in the air. "I care! Dawn cares. Any of us who shop carefully to avoid dangerous foods for our families, we all care."

"Wait," Griff interrupted, holding the alert. "If you owned a packaging company and a shipment arrives from one of your regular suppliers with unexpected produce, do you send it away without checking?"

She pumped her fist. "Great point. I'd contact my supplier and ask how to handle the unwanted garlic powder. We need to find out, is Beecher Packaging involved or is one of their employees freelancing?"

"Run a computer check on the names of the packaging company and importer," Brett suggested.

Eva shuffled through the reports. "We shouldn't duplicate what the Laredo case agent is doing. After all, it's not my investigation or even a terrorism case."

"Hey, did you forget the unknown texter is connected to your cell phone?" Griff demanded, lifting his hands.

"You're right!" Eva cried. "Write down these names, Beecher Packaging Company and Occidental Organics, who is the importer."

Brett wrote fast. "Got it. I agree with Eva, we need to determine if the importer is behind the illegal drug shipment or someone at the packaging company."

"Fentanyl is scary." Griff held up his phone. "I have here a DEA press release from a recent seizure. It says an amount of fentanyl as small as three grains of salt kills a person. The illegal shipment from Eva's tip carried enough fentanyl to kill *millions* of people."

Eva snapped shut her file. "Think of it. What if this load never reached the drug dealer who expected it, and instead, the packaging company mistakenly bottled it as garlic powder? It could end up in kitchen cupboards across the country."

"A terrible thought," Brett agreed, his eyes gleaming. "I think the tipster is Occidental's competitor or a disgruntled employee who wants them to get caught selling fake organic foods."

"Good possibility," Eva said, nodding.

Griff rapped his knuckles on the table. "Next, we track down if the fentanyl came from China with the other produce or got added in Mexico for the trip into the U.S."

"There's more going on here than Laredo ICE agents can know," Eva said. "It's possible the illegal drugs aren't connected to Pablo's truck. Remember the tip was for Miguel. Our discovery might be a fluke. I'll monitor Laredo's progress, and research any areas they ignore."

"I don't trust the ChiComs." Griff stood and headed for the door. "Keep digging."

Brett rose from his seat. "The Department of Defense starts a big operation in the Caribbean next week to stop drug shipments trying to avoid our southern border. My former partner is liaison agent there and gave me a heads-up. I'll give him a call."

"Scott returns next week as DoD's press secretary," Eva told Brett. "The current one is retiring."

"I'll keep him in the loop," Brett assured.

Back at her desk, Eva prepared an investigative lead for the Laredo ICE agent: *JTTF Northern Virginia requests an attempt be made to determine if the fentanyl in the Beecher shipment arrived from China or was added to the shipment in Mexico.*

She signed her name and sent a copy to Griff and Brett, hoping she didn't have to wait too long for the results.

Chapter 27

John Lapp rose to his feet on Sunday with the rest of Walnut Cove Mennonite Church, his second time attending this congregation. The pianist played "Amazing Grace," a hymn he knew well, one of Mom and Pop's favorites.

He lifted his tenor voice to sing the first stanza, "Amazing Grace, how sweet the sound, that saved a wretch like me …"

A lovely alto voice behind him reached his ears. He turned to see who was singing the beautiful harmony, and looked right into Annie Yoder's pretty face.

Her lips curved into a smile. He kept looking at her as he sang, "I once was lost, but now am found. Was blind, but now I see."

Facing forward, John poured forth the words of the next verse with something changing inside of him. The longer he sang, the more his inner spirit came alive. In every church service he'd ever attended growing up with his folks, and then at the Bible church near his apartment, John had thought he was a Christian because his adopted parents were. Today he began to realize something much deeper. His faith in Jesus could be his own.

John sat down with the congregation following the final chord and listened intently to the silver-haired minister open the Word of God like he'd never listened before.

"In Luke 22, the Bible records Jesus' prayers to the Father on the Mount of Olives the night before His crucifixion," the pastor said. "I've returned from Israel where my wife and I visited the Garden of Gethsemane. There, our Lord knelt and prayed earnestly, asking the Father to take the cup from Him. We, too, knelt to pray beneath an ancient and gnarled olive tree.

"Jesus prayed so intently in the garden, He sweated drops of blood. We see our blood when we prick our finger on paper or a knife when cutting fruit. Imagine Jesus feeling such strain and knowing every past, present, and future sin of mankind, my sins, your sins, would be placed upon Him the next day, that blood flowed from His brow."

John shut his eyes to those around him. He'd once seen a painting of Jesus praying in the garden. The vivid scene swept into his mind, and yet, he couldn't begin to imagine the agonies Jesus suffered.

The minister was talking and John heard him explain, "The word Gethsemane means 'to press.' An olive press would have been in the garden where Jesus was betrayed and Roman soldiers arrested Him on that dark night. Dear ones, have you asked Jesus to forgive your sins, to save you? If not, today is the day. Jesus, the only Son of God, went willingly to the cross for you. He paid the price and sets you free if you give your life to Him. When you become an heir of God, you become adopted into His family. Even if you are alone, Jesus promises to never leave or forsake you."

The pastor urged everyone to sing another hymn, and said, "I'll be down front to speak with anyone who wants to give their life to the Lord."

To the strains of "Blessed Assurance, Jesus Is Mine," John's logical mind became one with his once-hurting spirit. He belonged to Jesus! Jesus belonged to him! No matter what obstacles life threw at him, John would never be alone. The message touched him powerfully. To know he was adopted into God's family because of Jesus was life-altering.

The song ended, and he raced down the aisle to talk with the minister. They shook hands, and after John explained what happened to him, the kindly man of God put an arm around him and prayed in low tones, "Heavenly Father, this young man belongs to You, body and soul. He stands here today proclaiming Jesus as his Savior. Bless him, keep him, make Your face shine on him, and give him peace."

Tears seeped from John's eyes and he swiped them away. The minister offered to meet with him in the morning, but because he would be teaching class then, John promised to contact him the next time he came to town. He walked up the aisle feeling like a freed man.

He nearly skipped out the door and down the steps where he saw Annie talking with her parents. Mrs. Nolt held the hand of a young boy who looked rather grownup dressed in dark slacks, a white shirt, and black bowtie.

"Is this your brother?" John asked, walking up to Annie.

"Meet my son, Samuel." Her eyes beamed like sunshine. "He is five years old."

John leaned down to the brown-haired boy. "May I shake your hand, Samuel?"

"Yes, sir." Samuel let go of his grandmother's hand and reach-ed out his tiny one.

After they shook hands, John straightened his back and whispered to Annie, "I was his age when my mother went to heaven."

"John, join us for Sunday lunch," Mrs. Nolt interjected. "We've plenty to share."

He gazed at Annie, saying, "I'd love to. I have no other plans."

THE NOLTS COULDN'T HAVE been more hospitable to John. Annie's father waited for him at the front door while he parked in the driveway and turned off his cell phone.

He shook John's hand firmly on the way in, telling him, "My wife Agnes and I are happy you will break bread with us."

"I'm intrigued by your ranch home, Mr. Nolt." John stopped in the foyer. "Is it all brick?"

"Yes. Every brick came from the plant down the road, in Sugarcreek. And John, call me Simon."

Agnes smiled and pointed for John to sit at Simon's left. Simon prayed the blessing, and they all began enjoying the homemade chicken noodle dish, glazed carrots, and freshly baked bread. Samuel was seated across from John without the bowtie, and looked at him with big, brown eyes.

"I helped Mama make the jam," the boy said. "Do you like to play ball?"

"Sure, when I was your age, and I'd like to with you sometime," John replied.

Samuel nodded. "Good. Not today, it's Sunday."

"Of course, not on the Lord's Day," John said, taking the dish Annie passed him.

She seemed quieter than at the store. He understood that might be due to her parents' presence. No matter. John was thankful to be here rather than alone in his apartment heating a frozen meal in the microwave.

"Samuel, your strawberry jam is very tasty," John said, accepting another slice of bread. "Everything is. Thanks for inviting me."

"Help yourself to more," Agnes suggested.

Simon also wanted him to eat more. "Wait until you sample our Annie's peanut butter pie."

"Peanut butter pie?" John repeated. "I've heard it was my mother's favorite. Can you believe I don't remember eating it?"

Agnes rose to refill his milk. "You're in for a rare treat. Our Annie is a skilled baker and cook."

"Mama, may I eat pie too?" Samuel asked, looking at Annie who sat beside him.

She ruffled his curly hair. "Yes, and an extra big piece!"

Agnes brought the pie as Annie replenished their coffee. John noticed her cheeks blushing from her parents' compliments. She passed him a sugar bowl with a shy smile. They settled into eating dessert, which John found to be a creamy delight.

Samuel declared in his grown-up sounding voice, "The bery

best, Mama."

"Annie says your mother was Amish." Simon gazed at John thoughtfully. "Your last name being Lapp, I surmise your father is from Pennsylvania."

John finished the last bite of pie before telling them about the letter his birth mother wrote before she died, and adding, "She didn't say much about my father's family. I believe her husband, my father, was an Amish farmer near Lancaster. He died when I was a few months old so I never knew him."

"We will talk more in the living room and let the ladies wash up."

With that, Simon rose and ushered John into a homey room where the two men discussed the Sunday service.

John kept an eye on Annie drying dishes while telling her father, "The minister's sermon inspired me."

"I saw you going to greet pastor," Simon said.

John noted approval in his tone and was about to comment further when Samuel came over to sit by John on the couch. The way the boy stared at him in apparent interest made John want to spend time with the youngster. A picture flashed through his mind of showing Samuel how to plant tomatoes in the garden. He would ask Annie if she and her parents kept a garden.

Annie walked into the living room wiping her hands on a towel. "Time for your Sunday nap, Samuel."

He nodded and slid off the fabric couch. He reached out his hand to John. "Shake again?"

John shook the tiny hand with a firm idea this would *not* be the last time he saw Annie's son. She took him upstairs to his room, and returned carrying a colorful leaflet, which she handed to John.

"You might enjoy reading about the Walnut Cove Heritage Museum where I work part-time as a docent."

"You stay busy," John observed. "What are your duties?"

Simon returned to the kitchen, and Annie sat in a chair across from John. "A docent is a sophisticated word for tour guide or lecturer. I'm a volunteer and could research the history of the Pennsylvania Lapps for you."

"You would do that for me?"

"I would like to."

The warmth in Annie's words and her genuine smile disarmed him.

She continued describing the museum. "It's known for oodles of information on the Amish and Mennonites who emigrated from Europe. You could visit or I could send you what I learn. I need your email or phone number to text."

"You know technology." John sat back in surprise.

"I do." Annie trilled a laugh. "It's like solving a puzzle to check computer databases to help people search for their ancestors. We have international records from Switzerland, where many Amish families originated."

"My business card has my email and phone number." John reached for his wallet. "Whatever you send me will be a treat."

JOHN DROVE HOME, leaving Annie and Samuel behind, his heart overflowing with happiness. He called his folks the moment he stepped in the apartment.

"I've something to share, Mom. Can you get Pop on speaker?"

He waited, gathering his thoughts. When they both came on, he said excitedly, "I made an important decision today."

"Tell us about it, son," Pop urged. "Take your time. We're here for you."

In those words, John heard wisdom and love, which spurred him on to share how he grew closer to the Lord in church.

"Afterwards, the Nolts invited me for Sunday lunch. You will love them both."

"They sound like fine Christian people. We've been praying you'd find close friends," Mom said, her voice cheery, inviting a deeper discussion.

Should he admit to his blossoming feelings for Annie? Or wait until things were more definite with her?

John decided to plunge ahead. "Your prayers and mine are being answered. I have found a true and special friend. Annie is Mr. and Mrs. Nolt's daughter. She's near my age and is a widow with a young son, Samuel. Mom, Pop! We haven't known each other long, but I can't stop thinking about her. Is it right to have strong feelings already? How do I know when it's more than appreciation for her being nice?"

"It's a good sign she is on your mind when you should be working," Mom answered lightly. "Did we ever tell you how your dad and I fell in love?"

"I'd been drafted and knew I was going to Viet Nam," Pop said.

"I was a bridesmaid at my cousin's wedding," Mom added. "Your dad was a groomsman when we met. I thought he was fun to be around and good-looking."

Pop interrupted, "I was so smitten by your mom and her vivacious smile that I asked her on a date while decorating the groom's car and attaching a string of tin cans."

"The rest is history." Mom laughed. "He wanted to see me

whenever I had spare time. He asked me to wait until he came home from Nam so we could marry and I did."

"Don't be bashful. Let her know how you feel," Pop advised with enthusiasm.

"Which reminds me of another matter," she said. "Being encouraged you might marry and have little ones, I want you to have the antique school desk where you and the other kids did your studies. You were the last one to use it."

"I'd love it, if you're not keeping it."

"We're downsizing to better fit into Cora's guesthouse," Pop explained. "We aren't ready to give up our independence, but we like the idea of living near Cora. She and Mom will ride to the Trumpet's Call. Marlow says I can putter around in an addition off the horse barn. We're selling our townhome and will move soon."

John wanted to encourage them during this time of change. "You've always taught me to do the right thing, and I hope it works out great for you both."

After saying good-bye, John thought long and hard about what it meant for him to do the right thing.

Chapter 28

Late that Sunday afternoon, Eva's sons, Andy and Dutch, played Frisbee-keep-away in the yard with their dad. Eva enjoyed watching their antics through the kitchen window as she washed veggies. She laughed over Scott's agility in catching his share, especially when snagging one meant for Dutch.

She put the salad in the fridge to cool, and took out boneless and skinless chicken thighs for a casserole. Eva set these on the counter when an alert blazed across her cell phone on the cupboard. The new text was from Kaley. She was in her room, supposedly studying.

Eva ignored the message and went on arranging chicken, musing about the breakdown of communication between parents and kids. Kaley was too lazy to walk twenty steps to speak to her mother. Eva nestled chicken in the baking dish, and layered artichokes and frozen mixed vegetables on top. She poured simmering cream of chicken soup over all before washing and drying her hands.

Then she retrieved Kaley's message from her phone. Unease pierced her mind. Eva instantly recognized the format:

U missed your chance to catch that load. Pablo's truck delayed 2 long. They made enough. Won't try again.

Eva rushed to Kaley's room, and finding her typing on a laptop, asked, "Will you please open your phone? I need to see your most recent text."

She kept mum about having Kaley's passcode.

"Why?" Kaley looked up from typing, her forehead crumpled.

"I received a strange text. At first, I thought it came from your phone."

Kaley got up from her built-in desk, typed in her passcode, and toggled on her cell phone. "I see none to you. Satisfied?"

Eva had expected as much. Still, she'd hoped for the impossible.

"I should have asked you before, but who has your new number?" she demanded.

Kaley withdrew half a step, as if she'd done something wrong. Counting off on her fingers, she answered, "You, the school, and Lexi. That's it."

"Are you sure?" Eva launched into interview mode. "Who else may have it?"

"Who else? Mom, that's the extent of my life." Kaley paused. "Wait, I did give it to someone else."

"Who?"

"Mrs. DeVroom, so she could call me and change my work schedule. She said my old phone number was disconnected."

"When did you give her the new one?" Eva demanded impatiently.

"Back when we changed them!" Kaley cried. "Mine and yours too. What's going on, anyway?"

"I'm not sure," Eva admitted, wishing she knew why this text was coming to their new numbers. She turned for the doorway, asking over her shoulder, "Did your phone make any noises in the last few minutes?"

"No," Kaley replied with a careless shrug.

Dinner flew by in a blur. Eva's family laughed and joked at the table. Kaley helped clear dishes afterwards. Eva had little memory of any of it, her mind playing like a broken record, going over the past texts she'd received claiming to be from Kaley.

She should have asked Kaley who had her number when that first tip came in, but Eva had focused on tracking down the PBJ truck and the suspicious cargo. Dishes finally done, and the kids tucked in their rooms, Eva wanted to relax beside Scott while he read the newspaper. Yet her thoughts wouldn't ease up. She wouldn't sleep a wink if she didn't investigate this puzzling text.

Eva grabbed her purse and told Scott, "I'm running to the office."

"Can't it wait till morning?" He folded the paper in his lap, making crinkling sounds.

"No, I'd better jump right on this." She kissed his forehead. "I won't be late."

The trip to the office was a breeze as she encountered little traffic. It didn't take Eva long to access ICE investigative files. To her disappointment, she wasn't able to get into the entire file of the Laredo seizure. She did find an unclassified chronology of events, which included the importer's name.

She scribbled the key points:

1. Occidental Organics is the importer of the organic vegetables

2. Danny Mills is plant manager at Beecher Packaging Co. in St. Louis

3. Danny Mills rejected the fentanyl

4. Wouldn't the receiving clerk usually sign for shipments?

5. Or did Danny take charge, suspecting law enforcement's involvement due to the delay at the border?

She checked a couple more things before logging out of the

secure system. Next, Eva combed through Internet files available to the public. Ha! Her instincts proved right! Occidental Organics owned Beecher Packaging Company. It was all the same company using different divisions.

Occidental's website looked quite professional. Hold on a minute … Eva peered closer at the screen. Its headquarters were in Middleburg, Virginia, the same town the DeVrooms were moving to because Cora lived there.

Eva toggled to the "Meet our Team" page, her pulse skyrocketing at the photo of a man smiling at an expensive-looking desk, a stunning horse painting behind him. The caption below the photograph stated the man was Marlow Bryson, Cora's husband. Marlow appeared respectable, a husband Cora could be proud of.

Eva rapidly blinked her drying eyes. The very idea of Marlow making a fortune importing and distributing illegal drugs, which hurt and wounded people in towns across America, filled her with disgust. Suddenly, in her heart, Eva felt sorrow for Cora and concerned for her future. Eva hadn't met Marlow, which made it easier to view him as a possible drug smuggler and purveyor of counterfeit organic foods.

Staring at his smiling face, she reviewed how she got here. The first anonymous text sent from Kaley's phone about Miguel's load had resulted in Eva getting evidence against Marlow and his company. Also, Irene recently confided that her son, the professor of organic agriculture and computer technology, now worked for Marlow.

Eva began weaving threads together and concluded John Lapp had the know-how to send her messages anonymously. He must have Eva's phone number and her daughter's as well because Kaley gave their new numbers to Irene. And John had set up Irene's cell phone contacts.

Whew! Eva's mind calculated at supersonic speed, connecting all the dots. If only she knew John's motive. Had he somehow discovered drugs were secreted in Marlow's shipments? Or was he trying to expose Marlow's counterfeit organic produce?

A question haunted Eva. Why didn't John simply phone her with his information?

Her decision made, she shut down the computer. Then she found John's contact info on her cell phone, which Irene had entered in at the Trumpet's Call.

Eva selected his cell number and typed with assurance: *Gotcha! Call me. Eva.*

She pressed *send* and locked her desk. Eva urged herself to wait patiently, at least for a time. If John truly was interested in helping right a wrong, he'd call without delay.

SWEAT POOLED ON JOHN LAPP'S FOREHEAD. Monday afternoon was sun-scorched outside and hot inside. He sat hunched over his laptop keyboard, hungry and consumed with worry. He bolted from his chair to close the drapes, hoping to lessen the heat in his apartment.

John hadn't gone out all day. And for good reason. He'd started something yesterday for which he needed wisdom before taking the next step. Fear shot through him. Had he made the worst mistake of his life?

He guzzled a cold soda. Flexing his fingers, John prepared to begin two Internet searches. Each would have a tremendous impact on his life and his future. Each grew out of what he'd already set in motion. One or both could bring him future happiness, or a painful journey.

For the hundredth time, he snatched up his phone and gaped at Eva Montanna's text from last night: *Gotcha! Call me. Eva.*

John knew little about Eva other than she'd gone far beyond the call in organizing the successful fundraiser at the Biltmore for the Trumpet's Call, where her daughter Kaley worked. For these reasons, and the fact she attended church with his parents, he considered Agent Montanna to be an honest person. He trusted her.

Yet, her cryptic and subtle message seared his conscience. How best to respond?

"Get a grip, buddy," he said out loud. "Do your research and prepare for what comes next."

John had no intention of speaking with the federal agent without doing his due diligence, which if he'd been thinking properly, he should have done before now. Finishing his soda, he looked up several search terms: Federal court witness, Federal snitch, and FBI informant.

With each one he checked, anxiety flared up and hammered in his chest. Panic squeezed his heart like a vice grip. He should have thought to hire a lawyer. Was it too late?

John's eyes bulged as he tore through one news article after another. Federal agents and prosecutors used powerful tools, enticing citizens to become their witnesses in court. If all else failed, they launched sneaky ways and forced people to cooperate.

He clicked on a link that sank him. Oh, how John wished he'd never laid eyes on what he saw. A witness named Barry Seal received immunity to testify in a federal court drug trial and was machine-gunned to death in Baton Rouge!

Machine gunned! How terrible! Killed for being a federal witness!

Sweat poured down John's armpits. Perhaps he'd been too hasty yesterday. No, that wasn't right. *Perhaps* didn't go far enough.

"I messed up!" he cried, looking upward to heaven. "Please, God, protect me!"

A measure of calm seeped around the edges of his mind, and John gathered courage to begin a second Internet search. He grasped at one amazing alternative. Rosebush was a small Amish community in Michigan. Everything he read provided an answer. He could flee there with a new name and never be found by Eva Montanna.

Then his thoughts turned to Annie and Samuel. Reality burned in his mind. She probably wouldn't marry him and live Amish any more than she'd marry him and risk retribution from mobsters.

He shut down his computer with a click. A loud knock sounded on his door. His heart collided in his chest. Had Agent Montanna sent someone to interview him already? Would they take him to jail?

John wiped sweaty palms along his jeans and tiptoed to the door. He peered out the peep hole and saw a man dressed in brown shorts and a brown shirt standing outside his door holding a box. He heaved a sigh of relief. A delivery guy!

He opened the door and signed for the box. He shut the door quickly, and using scissors, cut the tape. Mom and Pop sent him a treasure trove of photo albums and ancient school papers. On the handmade card that had a photo of sunflowers on the front, they wrote:

John, we thought you'd enjoy some mementos. The desk is too large for the box so we're saving it for you. Inside are your favorite peanut butter cookies in the tin. Praying for God to bless you in everything. We love you, son! Mom and Pop

He yanked open the tin and ate three cookies on the spot. Their delicious treats soothed his scattered brain. Having scared himself enough, he decided to research something more pleasant. From Annie's pamphlet, he typed in the website address for Walnut Cove's Historical Society and became engrossed by reading about the delightful residents who lived there.

The sight of Amish folks in their customary dress and horse-drawn buggies renewed warm feelings of kinship, as did browsing the history of local Mennonite board members. He happened upon a schedule for guided tours of the museum, and decided to follow up. One picture showed guests thumbing through many books. John couldn't believe his eyes. There was Annie holding a book.

His mind flooded with peace just seeing her sweet face. He had a sudden idea. Using his camera phone, he snapped her picture off the computer screen. What he just did would be impossible if he joined the Amish church and married an Amish woman.

Not only would he have to forsake his computers, he wouldn't be able to keep a photo of his wife. Annie wasn't Amish. He should be able to keep her photo without guilt. But would she approve?

His fun excursion over, John wiped his brow and peeked out between the drapes. Out on the campus green, students wearing backpacks walked in groups, living their lives without a care.

Here he was, holed up in his apartment stymied by nothing but worry. John dreaded having to make a difficult phone call, one that might change his life forever.

Chapter 29

For Eva, dinner hour was as hectic as her day. Scott burned the burgers on the grill. Kaley and Andy argued over social media postings by Lexi. And Dutch spilled his milk. Finally, Eva got the kids into their rooms to study or read actual books. Scott was deep into the news on TV, and Eva started ironing a linen blouse for work.

Kaley came bolting from her room, her eyes wide with fear.

She held her hand tightly over the microphone on her cell phone, and stepping close to Eva, whispered, "A man's on my phone asking for you. It said 'no caller ID.' Mom, I thought it was you. He called me Kaley and asked for you."

Eva's brain revved on high alert. This could be the call she was waiting for. She smiled knowingly at Kaley and mouthed, "It's okay."

She took the phone. After waving Kaley away and turning off the iron, Eva walked into the unoccupied den.

"I expected you'd call on my cell phone," Eva said in a friendly tone.

An unknown voice answered, "I assumed if I phoned this number, you'd know it was me."

"Because you want to remain anonymous, right?"

"Yes, for now. If there's good reason to change that, we can talk about it."

In all her years, Eva had never faced dealing with an informant who went to such extremes to remain hidden. She needed to muster all her skill.

She shut the door and kept her voice low. "You'd have more credibility if you were at least known to me."

"How so?"

Eva tried to mask her frustration. She opted to use her teaching voice rather than her command voice. "When seeking justice, we need to corroborate the information we receive, especially if we might bring charges against someone."

"You mean the reliability of a snitch or informer," he replied.

"Yes, but it's more than that." Eva went on to explain, "Sometimes information comes to us innocently, say from a man or woman on the street. We are still required to assure a federal judge the evidence is legitimate and trustworthy."

"Speaking of judges, they too must be trustworthy."

"What are you saying?" Eva demanded.

"Do you remember a witness named Barry Seal?" the man said, his voice shaky. "He was set up by a federal judge and murdered for being a witness."

Surprised by the turn of this call, Eva replied calmly, "I know of Barry Seal. He was a criminal witness testifying to reduce his own sentence for wrongdoing. Is that your motivation? If so, we can get consideration from a judge."

"No!" the caller barked. "That's what got Seal killed and it doesn't apply to me."

"Okay." Eva would shift her approach. "Perhaps we need to be more specific. What would you like to see happen in the matter of Jiffy?"

"Did you get helpful information?"

Eva considered how to remain truthful without misleading him. Still, she didn't want to lose the caller.

"Yes, we took action on the information. In the end, no one was arrested. We might have more success if we had evidence to support what you told me."

"Wait ... you should have found produce fraudulently sold as organic."

Ah hah! Eva had uncovered his motive.

"We sure did," she told him. "It's unfortunate there isn't much I can do. That's a regulatory matter for which the person faces stiff fines. I'm a criminal investigator."

"You're saying you need to know my identity or you can't use my info."

"No. I may know who you are. Because I don't want to front you out, your evidence has limited value."

"Huh," the caller grunted. "I need time to think. Meanwhile, maybe I can improve on the information I send you. I'll be in touch."

Instantly, the line went dead.

Eva returned the phone to Kaley in her room, telling her, "I may need to talk with someone again who has your phone number. If he calls, bring me the phone, okay? Don't be worried."

"Mom." Kaley sat on her bed, concern darting through her eyes. "College starts soon. You and Dad said we are taking a vacation, but when? Lexi wants me to go with her and her mom to Boston where she's starting college in the fall. She wants a fresh beginning, which I was trying to tell Andy at dinner. Conner's back in Florida."

Eva gulped, searching for words. Boston seemed light years away. At least Kaley was enrolled at George Mason University and would live at home her first year. Eva sat beside her daughter and patted her hand.

"Do you want to go with Lexi, or would you rather enjoy seeing Lake Michigan and Grandpa Marty? He's invited us to the farm. Your dad and I narrowed down some dates. We'd like to vacation as a family. You can ask Lexi to come along."

Kaley stayed quiet as if deep in thought. "Grandpa Marty promised to take me blueberry picking and is teaching me how to paint watercolors. Count me in."

TWO DAYS PASSED since Eva took the last disguised call on Kaley's phone. She suspected John Lapp was the anonymous texter and wondered if he was also a co-conspirator who was afraid of being arrested. Still, he had objected to Eva's suggestion he possessed guilty knowledge of a crime.

Her phone app buzzed, alerting her to a traffic jam on the interstate. Eva cranked the wheel and veered down a side road to avoid congestion. She trained her eyes on the road while her mind reviewed questions that needed answering. What did the tipster stand to gain by fronting out Marlow? Was the guy a snitch?

She took off aggressively when the stoplight turned green. Griff and Brett were expecting her any minute. She'd sent texts to both agents asking them to meet this morning: *JTTF meeting at 9 am. I have the most compelling new info. You need to see it!*

One red light after another slowing her progress gave her time to reflect on the caller's true motive, which she believed was to expose Marlow's violation of importing non-organic produce and selling it as organic.

A sudden thought blazed through Eva's mind. Her tipster was a superhero similar to Paul Revere, running forth and warning others about the dangers of the invasion of unsafe food. That's it. Rather than a tipster, she'd call him Paul Revere.

Apparently, her Paul Revere had decided to "spoon feed" her evidence. She gave him credit. He certainly was determined.

Eva reached the secure lot at the task force, and thankfully the security guard waved her in without delay. She parked and hustled up to the office, telling Griff as she rushed past his cubicle, "Get Brett. Bring your laptop and meet in the conferring room."

She stopped by the supervisor's office long enough to say, "Sosa, I have critical info on the Laredo case. Join us if you have time."

Eva went back to lock her gun in the desk drawer. With the home laptop under her arm, she headed to the conference room. Griff was already in there.

"Got your text last night," he barked. "You just told Sosa something about Laredo. What gives?"

Brett and Sosa entered together, their faces expectant. They each took seats at the conference table close to the door. Griff slid into a chair across the table.

Eva pulled out one for herself, then snugged up to the table and opened her computer. "Last night, I received sizzling new information. Griff, please open your browser to the webpage for OccidentalOrganics.com."

"For Sosa," she nodded at her boss, "I'll summarize what we call our Laredo PBJ case. Recently, an unidentified tipster informed me suspect cargo would enter the U.S. border at Laredo in a Jiffy Peanut Movers truck driven by Miquel."

Griff interjected, "Hence our nickname PBJ."

"Right," Eva said. "Laredo ICE confirmed the Jiffy Peanut Movers trucks, which they also call Peanut Butter and Jelly trucks, are from a trusted, bonded company with special pre-clearance due to hauling perishables."

She stopped long enough to ask if they had questions.

"No," Sosa snarled, checking his phone.

"After that tip," Eva continued calmly, "a PBJ truck driven by Pablo, not Miguel, was searched and found to be carrying garlic cloves, mushrooms, and apples, plus 800 pounds of fentanyl disguised as powdered garlic."

Brett whistled. "As I said before, that's a lot of dope."

"Despite Pablo claiming innocence, he agreed to deliver the load to Beecher Packaging Company in Missouri," Eva explained. "ICE agents tried making a controlled delivery, but Beecher refused to accept the powdered garlic or fentanyl, insisting it was unexpected and not part of their shipment. We've since learned Beecher is owned by Occidental Organics, a company in Middleburg, Virginia."

Eva looked at Griff, who read from Occidental's webpage, telling Sosa, "They import organic foods, which are then packaged for sale through wholesalers by their subsidiary, Beecher."

"Let me summarize." Sosa tented his hands. "What you have is a case based on an unreliable snitch, investigated by Laredo ICE, which resulted in seizure of contraband, but no suspects."

Eva narrowed her eyes. "True, until last night. Griff, if you'll bring up the 'About Us' page on Occidental's website. You'll find a picture of the owner, Mr. Marlow Bryson."

Griff did so and slid the computer toward the table end so Marlow faced everyone in the room.

"He looks like a successful businessman," Sosa suggested.

"Yeah," Brett said. "With his big desk, ornate fireplace, and horse painting, it looks like some high-priced photographer posed him. I see drug dealer written all over Bryson's handsome face."

Eva got up and placed her laptop next to Griff's. "Watch this audio-video file. It arrived last night in my cell phone with no caller ID, phone number, or name. The original tip came to me in the same way."

She started the video and immediately froze the picture on her computer. With Marlow's website photo on Griff's computer next to Eva's video picture, they could all see it was the same man sitting at the same desk, only wearing more casual dress in the video.

Eva pointed at the smaller image of a person at the bottom of her screen. "Notice you can see a small image of the other caller in Marlow's video session."

"The Asian-looking man and décor behind him suggests the call might be from China," Sosa declared, looking at both screens.

"I believe Marlow *is* talking to someone in China," Eva replied. "I believe these calls occurred before I received the tip. You'll be amazed."

Eva pressed *play* and Marlow became animated. The agents watched and heard him complain loudly to the Asian man, "Your last two deliveries were delayed in arriving in Mexico."

"Yes, yes … so sorry," the other man said haltingly. "Try to do better. The next load arrives in Mexico in three days."

"Everything I ordered?" Marlow growled as if fuming.

The man raised his hands and voice, "Yes! Garlic cloves, apples, mushrooms, and 365 kilos China Girl garlic powder!"

Marlow leaned closer to his computer's camera. "Listen, Wen. This is very important. You must be exact about the timing of this shipment. Advise me when it leaves Mexico. If it's not delivered to Beecher within thirty hours, Danny will refuse the girl and we won't pay for her. Do you hear me?"

"We try harder," Wen replied, bowing his head. "I call when it leaves Mexico."

The recording ended as abruptly as it began. Eva stopped the video. She left Marlow's angry-looking face staring at the federal agents from her computer screen.

She paused for the full effect to sink in before explaining, "This video proves Marlow directed Danny at Beecher to refuse the fentanyl delivery. It proves it wasn't 'unexpected' as Beecher asserted. Marlow's conversation with Wen answers most questions and provides the evidence we need to prosecute."

"I heard no mention of fentanyl. How can you tie Marlow to the drugs?" Sosa shot back.

"Boss, they both did," answered Brett, the DEA agent in the

group. "The supplier mentioned 'China Girl,' which is the street name of fentanyl. Marlow said they wouldn't accept 'the girl' if the shipment was late."

"What's it all about?" Sosa sounded confused.

Eva thought it best to let the DEA agent keep explaining. Drugs were Brett's area of expertise. She nodded for him to continue.

Brett leaned back in the chair. "Drug smugglers know the precise time it takes for drugs to transit from the point of shipment in Mexico on to our border, and how long it takes from there to their destination. They know full well a delay means American authorities discovered the load and either confiscated it, or sent it for delivery to arrest the recipient."

"Hold on." Eva held up a finger. "I received another recording."

She started the second video, showing Marlow back in his office chair. This time he wore a golf shirt. A different man's shiny bald head and austere office with streaked walls appeared in the split screen.

"Danny, I just spoke with China," Marlow intoned. "The next shipment arrives in Mexico in three days."

The man named Danny nodded. "We're ready. We can't get enough China Girl. Did you warn them not to be late again?"

"You bet. He's sending 365 kilos of the girl. I'll give you the exact date when I know it."

Ending the video, Eva stood. "Marlow instructed Danny Mills, plant manager of Beecher, to expect the fentanyl. I received two shorter videos. In one, Marlow alerts Danny to the exact time the drug load will arrive and in the final video, Danny tells Marlow that he refused the 'garlic powder' for fear U.S. Customs agents intercepted it."

"That's sufficiently incriminating," Griff opined.

Brett let out another sharp whistle. "We couldn't get better evidence if we tried for months. Too bad we have no way to introduce these dynamic videos in court."

"I've got a call to make." Sosa rose while gazing at his cell phone. "Brett's right. It's problematic. Eva, how can we verify under oath you obtained the videos legally?"

Eva lifted her chin in rebuttal, "We can—"

"We in the FBI won't bend any rules to get our man," Sosa interrupted, giving Eva a frosty stare. "Are you putting us at risk?"

"What are you saying, Sosa?" Eva glared back at her boss.

"I'm saying, I wanna know, have you done something illegal here?"

Her blood pressure soared. Eva snapped back, "I resent your

thinking I'd ever do such a thing. You should know, Griff and I have arrested many more and many bigger criminals and terrorists in our career than you ever have. We always do it legally."

"Eva." Sosa's face turned red. "I'm sorry. I don't mean to suggest you aren't trustworthy. I'm trying to understand if we can go further."

Griff stepped close to Eva and said, his voice steady, "Eva is doing everything correctly, boss."

"Think about it, Sosa," Eva replied, struggling to calm down. "An inside source with great evidence has reached out to us. Do we ignore him because we can't yet testify we know who he is?"

Sosa rubbed his neck. "Okay. We open a case, that is, if you can verify those video calls originated here in Marlow's Virginia office."

"The background on the video matches the office on his webpage," Griff insisted.

Sosa agreed. "Eva, you'll be assigned the case agent."

"It deals with drugs," she countered. "Brett should be case agent."

Sosa glanced at his phone again. "Your point is valid. Okay, I like that idea. Wen, the supplier, must be Chinese. Fentanyl of that amount could wipe out the entire East Coast in the hands of a terrorist. Brett, open the case as a Chinese terrorism threat."

Sosa hurried away. Brett followed him to begin opening the case.

Griff rolled his eyes at Eva, and said in a bare whisper, "Eva, I know why you refused to be lead agent."

"You can read my mind, can you?" she asked, clutching the laptop.

"You won't admit it publicly, but I will. You're reliving our former big terrorism case when you investigated Emile Jubayl for terrorism, and his wife went to your church. In this case, you know Marlow's wife Cora, just as you did Jubayl's wife."

"You nailed me once again." Eva sighed. "It stinks for Cora. I can't imagine she's a party to her husband's illegal schemes. I have asked myself, though, what if she is?"

Chapter 30

John Lapp drove into the quaint city of Walnut Cove after class the following day and made a wrong turn. He reached a dead end, so he consulted the instructions Annie had given him when they last spoke on the phone. Finding his mistake, he backed up and headed right at the corner.

A minute later, just as she'd described, he found the road paralleling a strip of raised land, a common indicator of an abandoned railroad track. John parked beneath a hand-painted sign, *Walnut Cove Historical Society.*

He unplugged his cell phone from the charger. Standing on the sidewalk, John stopped to admire the old brick building, which appeared to be a former train station. He walked up the steps to a wooden front door only to be startled by a sign in the side window. The museum was closed.

What? Had he mixed up the day?

Crestfallen, he plunged down the steps, prepared to return home when out of the corner of his eye, he glimpsed Annie through the window. She was inside! He watched her rise from a table and walk toward the door.

He rushed back up the steps, a smile springing from his heart. Annie swung open the heavy door. She wore a beautiful smile, and was dressed in a modest skirt and blouse, looking even prettier than when he'd seen her at church.

"Welcome to our quaint museum." Her eyes sparkled. "How was your drive?"

"Relaxing, which I needed. It's a little over an hour from the college."

"I asked you to come after closing time so we have everything to ourselves." Annie closed the door behind him. "This way, we won't be interrupted."

After showing him around, she returned to a computer, leaving John to roam around the former railroad station waiting room. He admired bucksaws, antique corn seed planters, and sickles displayed on the walls, the floor, and hanging from the ceiling.

"This is wonderful. I hadn't paid much attention to Amish history until learning of my mother's past. Since then, it's like sunshine in winter, I can't get enough."

She smiled graciously. "Then may today bring you much light. If you sit over here, I'll share something I find exciting."

Annie brought him to the table where she'd been sitting when he drove up. He took a seat by an open book.

She gestured with her arm. "You can view the displays, but first, let me show you what I've discovered about the Lapp family."

"You mean my family?" His body stiffened.

Annie reached a hand toward his arm. "I hope you aren't offended. When we first met at my father's store, I sensed you came to town to learn more of your heritage."

"What gave me away?"

Annie touched her chin. "I could tell your husband beard was a recent addition. If you hadn't explained, I would have thought you were newly married, and our conversation would never have developed."

"I've enjoyed the beard, but I need to remove it. I don't want to confuse people."

"And I don't want people to think I'm spending time with a married man," she replied, lifting her chin.

"Annie." John said her name with the reverence he felt. "I'm so glad I shared my situation with you. It's taken me time to meet my true self."

"The lost shall be found," she said quietly.

Comfortable with the direction of their talk, John leaned back in the chair and told her, "You understand me perfectly."

"I can understand a little," Annie said. "When my Jacob died, I was crushed until the Lord showed me I needed to make a new life for myself and Samuel. That experience helps me to see you need to discover more about your Amish roots."

She picked up the thick book from the table, and stuffed between its pages were pieces of folded copy paper.

"People in our community research oral history and publish their findings. That's true in other Amish and Mennonite towns, such as Lancaster, Shipshewana, and Amana. We buy copies of their publications as they do ours."

John gestured to the book. "What mysteries will be revealed, I wonder."

"You and I are on the same page." Annie smiled, and John laughed at her joke.

She continued, "I've been reading about the Lapps of Lancaster, Pennsylvania, and believe I found your family."

"How can you be sure?" A ripple of excitement flowed through his mind.

"Relatively certain."

Annie opened the book on her lap, and John inched closer, being careful not to touch her knees.

"I traced the Amish Lapp family from Switzerland to their

settlement in Lancaster, Pennsylvania, by Michael Lapp in the year 1737." She tapped an open page. "Many generations are mentioned."

She pulled out the papers from between the pages, but kept them folded. "John, here is the record for Elmer Lapp, a young farmer killed when a truck hit the team he was driving to a nearby farm. That was twenty-seven years ago."

"Oh!" John caught his breath. "My father died then. I never knew his name."

"Accidents between vehicles and horses are far too common in Amish communities, back then and even now." Annie blinked rapidly as if emotional.

John wanted to ask how her husband died, but thought better of it. He wanted Annie to share her personal life when she was ready.

"Listen to this, John," she said. "It's even more interesting."

"Really?"

"Yes!" Annie clapped her hands. "Elmer Lapp married a young woman named Sarah Stolzfus. Their infant son's name is John Lapp."

John's jaw fell. "You found me."

"This is where I made an amazing find." She rattled the folded pages. "Amish families usually wouldn't document all this, but Sarah became part of the greater Lancaster community. She took a local job and was well-known and loved by the Mennonite community. She disappeared and no one knew where she went. We may have hit a dead end."

"What are those?" John pointed to the papers she held.

Annie laughed. "I'm so enthused, I nearly forgot. This is our last hope. I copied the account from the book because it has a photo of Sarah and her son in front of Sights and Sounds where she worked."

"Here's all of our evidence." She unfolded the photocopied sheets, which she handed to John.

He studied the photo and shook the papers, yelling, "This is me! This is my mother!"

"Have we really found your mother?" Annie's hands flew to her face.

John pulled his phone from his pocket, his hands shaking and heart throbbing.

"Look here!" He scrolled to his photos. "I have the same picture."

Annie stared as if awestruck. "How did you get your picture?"

"I have much to share. Do you have time?"

"Samuel is with my grandparents," she replied. "I'd love to hear."

John confided to Annie the story of his life, from his adoption by Mom and Pop, the letter his mother wrote him, to the little suitcase that held his total belongings in his early years. When he showed her the two pictures, including the one identical to Annie's, he could hardly believe the circle of his fragmented life was being connected in such a profound way.

He sat back, exhausted. John briefly took hold of Annie's hands, and released them to wipe tears from his eyes.

"How can I ever thank you? You've found the missing pieces in my life. Things I never would've found. I may be an expert of everything on the web, but Amish history and genealogy aren't online."

"You're welcome, John," Annie said, her smile suddenly shy. "I enjoy the unconditional love of my family. That's why I started working at this museum, to bring people's past together with their future."

"You do more than that, Annie. At least for me. You know me without me telling you much. Your kindness also assures me how much the Heavenly Father cares for me."

They looked into each other's eyes. John had no idea how long. Time stood still. Gazing into her twinkling light-brown eyes, it was like he was seeing into the eyes of his future.

He clasped her hand in his again. "Annie, could you care for me? Like I care for you? I know this is moving pretty fast. Tell me now if you consider me just a friend you want to help. Because my feelings for you are running as deep as the ocean."

"I do care for you, John," Annie said, a sweet lilt in her voice. Her gaze never wavered. "Will you join us for supper tonight? Mother and Father have told me they care for you too."

John saw it was God's hand guiding him to not only turn the car around, but also to hurry back up the step today when he'd spotted Annie in the window. He brought him to this blessed museum and to Annie, the woman he would cherish the rest of his life.

Chapter 31

At eleven o'clock on Tuesday morning, the conference room was humming with the preparation of investigators, their nostrils tingling with the scent of justice. Eva and Brett had spent the last chaotic hour arranging for a secure video conference with their JTTF office and other agencies including ICE in Laredo and ICE and DEA offices in St. Louis.

Eva checked her watch. It was time to begin, and she wondered when Patrick O'Rourke, the AUSA from Alexandria, would arrive. In less than a minute, Brett held the door open, and Patrick rolled in his wheelchair. He proceeded to the end of the conference room table and removed a briefcase from his lap.

Eva's supervisor, Sosa Garcia, puckered his brow and told her, "I'm changing my mind about our JTTF getting tangled up in a fentanyl smuggling case. I see no terrorism connection."

"Why not wait and see," Eva replied, livid at her boss prejudging the results of her meeting.

Griff said in a low tone as he passed her, "You've got this, partner."

Eva appreciated his vote of confidence and told him so. Griff grabbed a seat next to Sosa. Patrick tapped his pen on the table to get everyone's attention. The room grew quiet.

"Before we connect to the other offices," Patrick intoned, "I'll summarize. St. Louis seized the fentanyl, but has no evidence to indict anyone. We in Virginia have no seized fentanyl, but we have Eva's tipster whose identity and motive are unknown."

"Not exactly true," Eva interrupted. "I've given him the name Paul Revere, because I believe he's charging forward to warn the public about the dangers of uncertified organic produce or drugs."

"Eva, you must admit, we can't call Paul Revere to testify for the prosecution because we don't know who he really is," Patrick argued.

Eva knew Patrick was right, yet she hit back, her voice firm. "That could change."

"Admittedly, I haven't seen the video Paul Revere sent you," Patrick replied. "At this point, we can only be supportive of a prosecution, most likely in St. Louis or Laredo."

Sosa turned to Brett. "Okay, case agent, Patrick has stated his position. Connect with the other offices and we'll get their opinions."

Once the connections were secured, Eva introduced the four short videos, saying, "These were provided by my anonymous source I've named Paul Revere. I'll play them back-to-back without interruption."

The screen burst to life with Marlow's face. Eva watched Griff and Brett nodding as the videos played along, with Patrick and Sosa sitting stone-faced. Not able to read their stoic faces, at the end of the fourth one, she leaned over and stopped the video.

Before Eva could comment, the Laredo federal prosecutor blurted, "Wow! That's the best evidence I've ever seen. And from an anonymous source. Either St. Louis or Virginia has an excellent case. The only option for us here in Laredo is to go after Pablo, the PBJ driver. We can show he possessed and smuggled the fentanyl. But knowing how these drivers work and pick up their pre-cleared loads, I'm guessing he knew nothing of the crime, which is why he agreed to complete the delivery to Beecher."

"I agree," interrupted Delores Campbell, DEA in St. Louis. "The man on the video from Beecher Packaging is Danny Mills. We put his brother Randy in prison last year for distributing fentanyl. We suspected Danny after we heard him talking to Randy on our wiretap investigation, but until now, we had insufficient evidence against him. Randy was Beecher's plant manager before Danny. We'll use these videos to charge Danny and Marlow here in St. Louis."

Eva decided it was time to jump in. She wanted to pressure O'Rourke to take this case. Could she sway him?

"Given what Agent Campbell just said about Danny Mills and his admissions on the videos," Eva said, facing Patrick, "I'm curious to know what AUSA O'Rourke thinks after observing these four compelling videos."

Patrick consulted his notepad. All eyes in the room were upon him as well as those over the video feed. Eva could hardly bear the delay. Couldn't anyone make up their minds to stop drug traffickers?

Finally, Patrick cleared this throat, and said in a firm voice, "We have a strong case based on the videos alone. While watching them, I've devised a way to bolster Paul Revere's reliability and allow us to use the videos as evidence to indict Danny and Marlow."

"Terrific!" Eva said.

"My thoughts exactly." Brett slapped his palm on the table. "The phone calls originating in Virginia give us jurisdiction."

Patrick nodded curtly. "We believe Paul Revere visited Marlow's Virginia office, so he can verify that's the setting in the video. We'll lock in his real identity before the grand jury where he can also establish the foundation to introduce the videos in court. If everyone agrees, we'll prosecute this case."

Laredo agreed. Delores Campbell spoke next. "Patrick, if you indict Danny and anyone else involved at Beecher Packaging, we gladly defer to you."

"Sounds like a plan," Brett said, summing things up this way, "Laredo and St. Louis, send me reports of all your evidence. We'll proceed and bring Paul Revere before the grand jury. Thanks for participating."

Brett signaled the call was over and Griff terminated the connection.

Eva told Patrick of her new concern. "We should give more thought to getting a search warrant for Marlow's office."

"What are you implying?" he asked.

She tapped her laptop. "Paul Revere is finding evidence of wrongdoing in Marlow's computer and sending it to us. If we execute a search warrant before arresting Marlow, we may miss out on new evidence."

The others in the room fell silent.

"Eva, I'll consider your caution and send you the grand jury date," Patrick replied. "You forward it to Paul Revere."

With that, Patrick left the conference room followed by Sosa. Eva traded high fives with her team.

"Way to go, Griff and Brett," she said, satisfied with the result. "The hard part will be convincing our skittish tipster to play his part. He'll have to be identified under his true name at the grand jury, which will require deft handling."

"You're one persuasive agent when you put your mind to it," Griff reminded her.

Brett nodded. "Yeah. You'll find a way, Eva."

"I suspect Paul Revere has additional evidence to give us," she said. "No way we can be accused of directing him. He's totally uncontrollable."

Eva walked to her cubicle, definitely wanting to hold off searching Marlow's office until they arrested him. What if Patrick didn't agree?

She spotted on her desk a calendar from her kids for Christmas. Seeing the Bible verses prompted Eva to lift up a silent prayer.

Dear God, help me do the right things and to always protect my family. May Your justice prevail in every way. And please, don't let Paul Revere ruin this investigation.

AS PROMISED, THE NEXT DAY Eva received an email from Patrick with the information for her tipster's appearance before the grand jury. She used his email to prepare a text to Paul Revere:

You are expected to meet with Assistant U.S. Attorney Patrick

O'Rourke this Thursday at 9:00 a.m. at Albert V. Bryan U.S. Courthouse, 401 Courthouse Square, Alexandria, Virginia. You are to appear before the grand jury for secret testimony. The grand jury proceeding will protect your identity, but you will need to show Mr. O'Rourke your I.D. Also, bring all your relevant material. You will be reimbursed for travel, food, and lodging. You have much to tell, and will help right many wrongs.

Eva fully expected Paul Revere, who she now believed was John Lapp, would do the honorable thing and comply without pushback. Wondering if he would message her after receiving his summons, she headed to the coffee station for a quick refill. Griff had the same idea, and she told him about texting Revere.

"We'll see what his next move is," she declared.

As Griff topped off his coffee, he said, "If his anger over organic food is driving him, he'll gladly show up. Have you seen those demonstrations on the Hill involving organic food devotees?"

"No, but Kaley asks me to buy organic. Oops, I left my phone on my desk."

Eva hastened over to check. Sure enough, she read Revere's message: *Do you promise the prosecutor will keep my identity secret?*

Eva swiftly replied: *I've worked with AUSA O'Rourke for over ten years. He, like you, is honorable. You can fully trust him. Your appointment is under the name Paul Revere.*

The next text arrived ten minutes later: *I will be there. Will you?*

No. But text me any time afterwards.

Revere wrote nothing more. Eva went over to Griff and brought him up to speed.

"Yup, he's coming through." Griff arched his eyebrows. "You and I will have to decide when we arrest Marlow once Revere lays out his evidence for the grand jury."

Eva grew thoughtful, saying only, "I feel sorry for Cora being married to Marlow at a time like this. I'd like to spare her the worst."

LATE WEDNESDAY NIGHT, Eva was startled awake by her phone on the nightstand chirping. She'd kept it on in case something happened, and grabbed it before it chirped again, waking Scott.

A message, a strange and mysterious one, flashed across her cell phone like a neon sign in the darkened bedroom. Rattled, she crept from bed and went to the den where she pondered the meaning of the troubling message for over an hour. Finally, Eva went back to bed and slept little.

Just when she'd achieved an understanding of how to handle

their case, another fastball was thrown straight at her. Too bad her mind kept swinging and missing that ball all night long. Finally, at 5:00 a.m., she edged from beneath the covers and dressed quietly to not disturb Scott's peaceful sleep.

She dashed off a note: *Honey, duty calls. Please make sure the kids eat breakfast. Fruit's in the fridge and there are scones from the bakery. Love you! Eva*

Here it was a few hours later, and at 9:00 a.m., Eva stifled another yawn. She went to pour more coffee at the office, needing a fix to carry her until Griff arrived. She desperately wanted his counsel. Where was he, anyway?

She started typing reports on the computer, yet her thoughts wouldn't cooperate and kept cascading back to the disturbing text. At last, she signed off on her reports and logged into emails when Griff whizzed by.

She jumped from her chair. Cell phone in hand, she rushed to the station where he was pouring coffee.

"Good morning," she said optimistically.

Griff turned. A puzzled look spread across his face. "Is it?"

"It should be."

"You look like you've been up a while," he said. "Were you here all night?"

Eva punched him lightly on the shoulder. "That's not nice."

"Sorry to be grumpy. I got zero sleep last night. Dawn's dog-sitting for a friend. The golden retriever never stopped whining."

"Join the club," Eva said. "I had a different reason for staying awake."

Griff gestured for her to follow and she settled onto the chair in his cubicle.

"What's up, doc?" Griff asked, then sipped his coffee.

"The ChiComs are messing with me. Sent an unsettling message late last night."

Griff palmed his mustache. "How bad is it?"

"At first, I thought it was Paul Revere. But he always sends me texts disguised as coming from Kaley's phone. This new one came to my cell before midnight with no sender information. It contained my and Kaley's names and our cell phone numbers."

"Not again! Judah warned the Chinese have your cell info," Griff reminded her.

"Exactly. But Judah referred to our *old* numbers. This one's to my new number."

"Weird." Griff reached for her phone. "Let me see it."

Eva dropped her voice to a whisper and said, "Look, Chinese

language characters are written beside our names!"

"Could be Paul Revere is sending you another hint." Griff narrowed his eyes as if alert for trouble. "Doesn't he testify before the grand jury with O'Rourke today?"

"Ah!" Eva leapt to her feet. "I totally forgot! I'm calling Patrick right now."

She shot over to her desk phone and hit speed dial for his office. The receptionist advised he'd left for the courthouse. When Eva insisted it was urgent, the receptionist offered to send him a message.

"Please do so right away," Eva declared. "Tell Patrick to ask Paul Revere if he sent Eva a text last night. If so, why?"

Chapter 32

Paul Revere stepped tentatively into the reception area of the U.S. Grand Jury office with rubbery knees and sweaty palms. He looked around. Seeing three men and two women sitting in the cramped room, he stopped.

Who are all these people? he wondered. *Is one of them the federal prosecutor?*

He was supposed to meet Patrick O'Rourke. When no one greeted him, Paul wiped his hands along his pants legs, uncertain if he should sit too or wait standing up. This situation was completely foreign. Sweat began to drip from beneath his hairline.

The door swung open behind him. Paul whirled around. A man wearing a suit, white shirt, and red tie rolled into the room in a wheelchair.

"I'm AUSA Patrick O'Rourke," he said crisply. "Is someone here to see me?"

Paul raised a hand without giving his name. At least Patrick didn't mention it either. He nodded to Paul, and without a word, he spun his chair around. He cruised out the door into a long and brightly-lit corridor. Paul guessed he should follow, so he did.

Out in the hallway, Patrick looked up at him, asking, "What is your name?"

"I received a message telling me to come here and ask for Patrick O'Rourke. I'm to use the name Paul."

"We head to this next room," was all Patrick said.

His arms pushed the wheels forward, and they stopped by a sign indicating "Grand Jury Room." He opened this door and entered a cramped room with several empty chairs.

Paul didn't know what to think. This whole process seemed worse than he'd expected, a mountain he wanted to flee and not climb. He trailed behind the prosecutor, his brain overflowing with questions.

Where was the grand jury? Why wasn't O'Rourke explaining anything?

Patrick urged him to be seated and said in a friendlier tone, "We'll get acquainted. Did you bring identification?"

"Yes, sir."

Paul removed a passport from his rear pocket, which he gave to Patrick.

"You have no beard in your photo," the prosecutor intoned. "Still, there's no mistaking your blondish red hair and dark brown eyes. Plus, you're wearing the same blue striped shirt."

He reached out a hand. "Pleased to meet you, John Lapp. Thanks for agreeing to testify. Who messaged you to meet with me?"

Tension squeezed John's neck and shoulders as Patrick voiced his real name.

"Ah … Eva Montanna, sir," John managed.

He felt like an outsider. How dumb to force himself into the danger zone. He wished he'd never set foot in this place.

Patrick's face lit with encouraging smile. "You don't have to call me sir. My name is Patrick."

"Yes, sir," John replied. "I mean Patrick."

"Does Eva Montanna know your real name?"

"She knows me by my real name, John Lapp. But the tips I send her are anonymous and I think I've succeeded in hiding my identity. She messaged me that you can know my identity and will keep it confidential going forward."

Loud laughter erupted from an adjoining room and John cringed.

Could that be from the grand jury? Was another witness in there who might come out and see him sitting here? Was Cora in there?

He clasped his hands. "Sir … Patrick, why are they laughing? Is someone in there I might know?"

"No other witness is in there," the prosecutor assured. "You're the only one this morning. The grand jurors are getting their early morning coffee. They're comfortable because they serve together a few days each month for eighteen months. Are you familiar with grand juries?"

John shrugged. "Not really. I only looked them up online beforehand."

"Here's how it works. Twenty-three citizens, like you, are called from counties in the Eastern District of Virginia. They take an oath to hear evidence and decide if there's sufficient evidence to charge persons with any crimes. They're sworn to secrecy. You and I go in together. You first provide evidence of your true identity. You answer my questions and what you say could be used as evidence and for arrest warrants. For the most part, your identity remains a secret."

John reared back in his seat. "What do you mean, for the most part?"

"We may be forced to trial and you might need to testify. Although, in my years of experience, most folks charged in federal court plead guilty without a trial."

John glared at Patrick. "You're taking me by surprise."

"You're free to hire an attorney, who can be present here in this outer room with you, but not inside when you testify." Patrick nodded toward the laughter. "You should know, Eva named you Paul Revere. She sees you as shining a bright light on unsafe food and the like."

John paused to think. Hadn't he studied agriculture and even come into Cora's life for such a time as this? As Queen Esther, John decided he would not waver nor be afraid.

"No attorney is necessary," he answered boldly. "Eva is right. I trust her and I trust you. It's my duty to help others."

Patrick opened a leather writing pad on his lap. "Good. To confirm, I have your permission to enter your name, John Lapp, into the grand jury record."

"Yes."

"The clerk will copy the first page of your passport for the record. But John, the jurors inside will know you as Paul Revere, and they'll know it's a pseudonym."

"Agreed," John replied, certain he was following God's orders.

All the stress fled from his neck and shoulders.

Patrick asked him some preliminary questions, then announced, "Let's play ball."

John steeled himself for another new experience, which God seemed to be sending him daily. It couldn't hurt to lift up a fresh prayer for the Lord's help in telling the absolute truth. He didn't want to make any more mistakes.

JOHN WALKED THROUGH THE DOOR and stepped into a giant room filled with rows of risers, which held many small desks. He didn't count them, but guessed there must be twenty-three because a citizen-juror sat behind each one looking down toward a lone witness chair.

Every eye turned to stare at him. John flinched under their scrutiny. He inhaled deeply while scanning the group. Most smiled at him. One older lady with graying hair fastened in a bun nodded and beamed at him. He imagined she might be a wonderful grandmother just like his mom.

John smiled in return. Besides the witness chair up front, he saw a table against the wall brimming with a coffee urn, bowl of cut fruit, bottles of water, and small cakes, along with plates, plasticware, and napkins.

Patrick handed John's passport to a woman sitting at a small desk near the door. Only then did the AUSA direct John to sit in the witness chair.

Patrick drew his wheelchair close to him, and gesturing to a woman seated at another table beyond the witness chair, explained, "As the official court reporter, Ms. Raleigh operates the device that records everything we say. The official account of your sworn testimony is sealed by the court and can only be seen by me and a few investigators who will be sworn to keep it secret."

John tried to remain steady as a man rose from his desk in the first row and pronounced, "I'm the foreperson for the grand jury and will administer the oath. Please stand and raise your right hand."

John did as he asked.

"Do you swear or affirm to tell the truth, the whole truth, and nothing but the truth under the penalty of perjury, so help you God?"

His right hand raised, John said, "I do."

"Be seated." The foreperson returned to his seat.

John perched upon the chair's edge and observed the court reporter taking notes by the device recording everything he said. His heart began to pound even thinking what might happen.

Patrick looked at a yellow pad and began, "Please state your name."

"Paul Revere," John answered, which sounded pretty good, he thought.

"Mr. Revere, did you bring documentary evidence of your identity?'

"Yes, my passport."

"The clerk will make a copy for the record," Patrick explained, adding John would get it back before he left. "Mr. Revere, how are you employed?"

"I'm an associate professor of agriculture at a college in another state, and also teach entry level classes in computer technology."

"You know about computers?"

"Yes, a fair amount," John replied, seeking to be truthful.

"Did your knowledge of computers lead to a consulting contract with Marlow Bryson, of Occidental Organics Incorporated?"

"Yes, sir."

"Can you tell the grand jury what your contract required and what you've learned about Occidental?" Patrick motioned with his hand as if cueing John to elaborate.

John gazed at the jurors. They watched him intently. He swallowed, choosing his words carefully.

"When I saw Marlow Bryson at a fundraising event, he said he'd heard I knew about computers and asked me to help him."

Uncertain what else he should say, John quit talking.

Patrick prompted, "What happened next?"

"I went to his office in Middleburg because he'd fired his information technology consultant." John saw blank faces on several jurors and added, "The IT person keeps computer networks functioning. Charlie Riggs, Marlow's previous IT guy, claimed he made the company's computers safe from hackers. Marlow wanted me to verify they were secure and asked me to hack into his system."

"What?" the jury foreperson whispered, his eyes growing round.

Holding up a hand to quiet the jury, Patrick asked John, "What did you do next?"

"I told Marlow I needed his written authorization first. His assistant prepared one, which he and I signed. Marlow said depending what I found, he might want to hire me as his new IT consultant."

"Did you breach Occidental's system?"

"Yes. I hacked in and installed malware available on the dark web. Though my predecessor had done certain things right, I got into the system because an Occidental employee took the bait on my phishing attempt. The volume of organic foods Marlow imports and distributes impressed me. Because I teach organic farming at college, I enjoyed learning the marketing side of his business."

"Did anything concern you?"

John nodded. "I discovered Marlow or his IT guy installed an uncommon app, one that permits Marlow to talk on an encrypted Internet communication line. That means it's immune from eavesdropping or law enforcement bugging, you know, by the police."

"Did you report to Marlow how you hacked in and what you found?"

"I did. He was shocked his system wasn't secure from me. I assured him that's because I was just too good."

Muffled snickers from the jurors rippled across the room.

John smiled at the grandmother lady before explaining, "I told him about the encrypted communication app I found and he said he needs it to prevent industrial espionage. In fact, at Marlow's direction, I installed the same system on my computer so he and I can have secret conversations."

"Did you learn anything else you did not mention to Marlow?"

John lowered his voice at the gravity of what he'd unearthed. "I located something buried deep in his computer files. It's a digital recording app, which is activated by Marlow's microphone and speakers. Every time he has a conversation, including his test one with me, the app copies and stores the video and audio inside his computer where it's nearly impossible to find."

"You never mentioned this new find to Marlow?"

"I asked if he had a means of storing copies of the secret conversations," John replied, his eyes focused on Patrick.

"How did he respond?" the prosecutor demanded.

"Marlow said something like, he wouldn't want that to happen. I'm unsure who installed it. Perhaps Charlie Riggs was blackmailing his former boss, but I doubt it. If he did, Charlie would still be employed. I think Marlow had it installed to record his verbal business agreements, but lied to me."

Patrick interrupted, "Is it your sworn testimony you found the digital recording app in his system and you did not install it?"

"Yes," John answered, startled by the question. Then he backtracked. "No. I mean no. Why would I do that?"

"When you said 'yes' and then 'no,' is it your testimony you did not find it there, or that you did not install it?" Patrick asked, his voice stern.

John paused. "It's my testimony that I found it there and did not install it."

A sudden and loud rap at the closed door made John's body jump. Patrick looked over toward the door. "This is a good time for a short break."

The jury foreperson walked to the door and accepted a note, which he promptly delivered to Patrick. John remained in the witness chair, watching jurors rush down to the snack table. His stomach growled and he wished he could get up and snatch a muffin.

Probably, that wasn't allowed, so he sat and thought, *What I wouldn't give right now for one of Annie's yummy liverwurst sandwiches!*

After quietly reading the note, Patrick swiftly rolled out of the room, leaving John's mind to flood with worry. What was happening outside the room?

Chapter 33

John continued to sit in the witness chair with the jurors helping themselves to more cake and fruit. The minutes ticked by on a large round clock on the wall, and his mind was battered by his vivid imaginings of that other federal snitch who had been gunned down!

Patrick failed to return. John considered getting up and walking out. No one could stop him. He'd simply told the truth and so far, he hadn't told anything bad about Marlow.

But no. John reminded himself, he'd come here to fulfill a mission. His job wasn't done. Despite the internal pep talk, his energy level sagged from the stress. His lips were parched. He craved something to drink. No one offered him any water.

Suddenly, Patrick came back inside. The jurors scrambled into their seats. The prosecutor cast a knowing look at John and cleared his throat.

"We're resuming testimony after a short break," Patrick said. "You understand, Mr. Revere, you're still under oath?"

John said he did and Patrick started his questions again.

"Did you uncover evidence Marlow Bryson was doing something illegal?

"Ye-es," John said, swallowing a tickle. He hoped he wouldn't start coughing.

"What was it, and as a result, what did you do?"

"I'd seen things on his system making me suspect Marlow was buying agricultural products that were *not* organic, but he sold them as organic. I happened to find a video recording of him talking to a man named Wen, who I assume was in China. Wen told Marlow a shipment was going from Mexico to St. Louis and the timing of the shipment was crucial to avoid it being seized by U.S. authorities. I was shocked to hear this, and also to discover that shipment included produce bags printed in China claiming the produce was grown in the U.S. That's against all organic practices and I—"

Patrick raise a hand to stop him. "Did you share this video with anyone?

"Yes, sir." John fingered his beard. "I had the phone number for Federal Agent Eva Montanna, so sent a copy of the video and audio file to a cell phone in her household."

"Did you indicate it was from you?"

"No. I omitted any identifying data as to who sent it."

Patrick looked up from his legal pad. "Do you know Agent Montanna well?"

"Not really. I met and talked with her on one occasion."

"Then why send it to her?"

"I trusted she would forward the video to the appropriate agency to look into Marlow importing food wrongly labeled and sold as organic."

"Did Agent Montanna or any other federal employee tell you to spy on Marlow Bryson, or obtain any information about him, his company, or his activities?"

"Not at all. The only other federal person I know is my mail carrier and I haven't spoken to her about it."

With a wavering smile, Patrick asked John, "What response did you receive after sending the video to Agent Montanna?"

"At first she tried to find out who I was. When I refused to tell her because I didn't want to be a witness, or a snitch as some call it, she texted back to my pseudonym asking me to come here today."

"Do you remember what products were shipped along with the improperly labeled produce bags?"

"I sure do," John replied. "Apples, garlic cloves, mushrooms, and 800 pounds of 'China Girl garlic powder.'"

"Nooo," a juror whispered.

Another juror gasped, "Really?"

Patrick directed an icy glare at the grand jurors and shook his head to stop their outbursts. John watched, confusion rolling through his mind. Should he say something else?

"Um … perhaps I didn't get the right name. I mean, I'm not sure if it was garlic powder or concentrate. I know it was China Girl."

"Do you know anything else called China Girl?" Patrick asked, his jaw set.

"I do not."

Several jurors snickered. John gaped at the federal prosecutor, concerned what he might ask next. Why were the jurors laughing at him?

"Mr. Revere, when you sent Agent Montanna the video, did you hope she or someone in government would intercept the counterfeit organic food and falsely labeled bags?"

"Correct."

Patrick straightened something in his notebook before lifting up a small piece of paper. John figured it was the note he'd received at the door.

"Mr. Revere, did you send a text to Agent Montanna last night with Chinese language characters?"

John lowered his head toward his lap. "Yes, sir, I did."

"Did you use a pseudonym or a blocked cell phone number?"

"A blocked number."

"What prompted you to do that?" Patrick asked, looking over at the court reporter who was recording John's testimony.

"I wanted federal investigators to have this important information without me being known as the source."

"Does it relate to the Marlow Bryson matter, which we've discussed today?"

John sighed. "No, it doesn't."

"Then why send it to Agent Montanna?"

"She seems shrewd. I thought she'd discern its value and bring it to your attention."

"Please explain to the grand jurors what you sent her and why you think it's important."

"It's a bit complicated. I recently found a USB drive left in a computer port at the college's computer lab. I investigated and learned it contains sensitive research being done at our college under a federal grant. It also had all the contact information from my computer and cell phone."

"Who does the USB drive belong to?"

"I didn't know at first and since found out. After seeing its contents, I became suspicious. I made a copy, which I brought today. Professor Mao Peng came to my office the same day looking for his USB drive. I told him a student found it and gave it to me. I returned the original to Professor Peng."

"Did you notify the FBI?" Patrick asked.

John nodded. "I called them twice. I believe Professor Peng was giving away or selling our government's secrets to the Chinese government. No FBI agent returned my messages. It's been weeks, so I decided to bring it to you. Am I in trouble for waiting?"

Several jurors chuckled. Patrick told John, "I think not. Why do you believe Peng is giving or selling sensitive information to the Chinese Communist government?"

John didn't answer right away. He needed to compose his thoughts. "Here's why. The USB drive showed emails Professor Peng sent and received from people at the Ming University of Soil Science in China. Warning bells went off in my mind. That's the same university associated with prior thefts of our agricultural secrets."

"What else did Professor Peng target besides your contact data?"

"He copied on his USB drive highly sensitive data on biotech corn seed from the college's computer files."

"Do you know how Peng accessed this data?"

"I'm not certain. He teaches advanced computer classes on campus." John paused. "I suspect he used the computer lab network to hack into the school's research."

"Did he ask if you accessed his drive?"

"No!" John said forcefully. "When I gave it to him, I explained I kept it for the owner, assuming he or she would come looking for it as it had no label."

"Do you believe the professor copied Agent Montanna's phone number from your contact list?"

"When the FBI failed to call me, I searched further on the USB copy and found all my phone contacts were on there, including Agent Montanna who I have listed in there as an FBI agent. I assume Peng saw her name listed as FBI, because there was Chinese printing added next to her name. I thought maybe the note mentioned the value of her information to the Chinese government. I can't read Chinese."

Patrick nodded and asked if the grand jurors had questions for his witness.

"I do," a man hollered from the back with his hand raised. "Are there organic law violations for which this grand jury can indict someone?"

Patrick gave the answer. "It's a matter requiring more investigation." He looked around the room and this time a woman raised her hand.

"Can the witness tell us how we can know which produce is really organic?"

John immediately said, "I rely on the packaging label. Also, check out the Department of Agriculture's website that lists companies with fraudulent certificates. That's another reason why I sent the information to Agent Montanna. We should trust the food we buy and eat."

John saw the juror who reminded him of his mom impatiently waving her hand in the air.

"Go ahead with your question," Patrick declared.

"My granddaughter's single and the same age as the witness. Is he available?"

The entire room erupted in laughter, except for Patrick. He faced the group with a frown and his palms extended. "That's an inappropriate question."

"I don't mind," John volunteered with a slight smile.

This time Patrick chuckled. "Okay, go ahead."

"Until recently, I was probably like your daughter, wondering if

I'd ever meet my mate in life. Recently, I was helping farmers grow organic crops and stopped by a deli for lunch. I had no idea I'd meet a widow with a young son. Because I've been praying for God's direction in my life, I'm convinced she is the woman God has been saving for me. I have hope she feels the same way."

The jurors broke into applause and smiles. John couldn't help seeing God's hand guiding him here today, despite his initial reluctance to come.

Patrick then asked, "Did you bring copies of the video files you mentioned?"

"They're in here." John held up a ziplock baggie, with the date marked on it, and containing the USB drive with Marlow's video files.

"Do you intend to surrender these items to the grand jury?"

"Yes, sir."

"Do you also surrender the USB drive you copied from Professor Peng?"

"Correct." John held up a second labeled baggie with a second USB drive.

Patrick said the witness was excused, adding, "The jurors may take a break. The witness and I will transfer the exhibits to the clerk."

John hopped up from the chair, thrilled to escape. The clerk quickly returned his passport. Hurrying toward the door, the kindly grandmother stopped him.

"Do you have an available brother?" she asked, her face crinkled in a warm smile.

John shook his head. "But I wish you all the best for your granddaughter."

He sped away from the grand jury room, heading for his sweet and true Annie in Ohio, never once looking back.

Chapter 34

First thing Monday morning, Eva Montanna strode into the office to confront Griff, going straight into his cubicle.

With no chit-chat, she declared, "Last night you called and said you now possess a Chinese professor's USB, originally discovered by Paul Revere. What were you talking about?"

"Good morning to you, too." He slowly looked up from his computer.

"Oh yeah." Eva smiled sheepishly. "Morning, Griff. What's going on with the professor?"

He raised his chin asking, "Didn't you send a message to Patrick at the grand jury last Thursday?"

"Yes. He called me from the grand jury and I told him that Paul Revere sent data to my phone with Chinese language characters. So?"

"What Paul Revere sent you was from a USB drive belonging to a Chinese professor, which Paul copied and gave to the grand jury," Griff replied with a smirk.

"Oh great," Eva grumbled. "The ChiComs steal data from my phone at the Hong Kong airport and share it with every Chinese national in the U.S."

Griff abruptly stood. "Let's talk in the conference room."

She slung her purse, heavy with a gun, over her shoulder, and followed him into the conference room. Eva realized if Paul handed the USB over to the grand jury, its contents were secret. Would Griff divulge even one hint?

Shutting the door, he immediately asked, "Did you notice Sosa and I weren't here Friday afternoon?"

"It was pretty quiet," she admitted. "I thought you might have been doing something personal. You'd better spill whatever you're keeping from me."

"Steady on." Griff pointed to the chairs and they sat down. "I was trying to decide how to handle Paul's grand jury information, so Friday morning I entered the professor's name into our FBI computer system."

"What did you find?" Eva tried moving him along.

Griff rapped his knuckles on the table. "Nothing. It was like no one ever heard of the guy. I began preparing an FD-302 about the info that Paul, whom I identified as a 'tipster,' shared with the grand jury. Less than an hour after I queried the professor's name, Sosa rushed into my cubicle insisting we both report immediately, in person, to the FBI Counterintelligence section at Headquarters.

That's why we were gone."

"Your query about the professor ..." Eva paused to squint as if she might see inside Griff's mind, wishing she knew the guy's name. "Your query flagged the CI people, who obviously already know about him and are limiting access to those who 'need to know.'"

Griff nodded. "They warned me not to discuss 'Professor so and so' and demanded I surrender the USB."

"Paul's tip must have enormous value to them, which gives me satisfaction," Eva said keenly, adding, "Perhaps it's not crucial we know what they already know."

"*Au contraire*," Griff objected. "I informed them you have knowledge of the Chinese Communist government having your unlisted government-issued cell number, which also happens to be on the USB drive."

"Yikes! I'm dragged into their net?" Eva's mind reeled at the implications.

"They promised me and Sosa, if they find critical info, we'll be notified at the appropriate time," Griff replied, emphasizing the last four words.

"Wait, Griff. You can't give them the USB drive. It's grand jury material and must remain secret. The Bureau needs to have Patrick designate a specific agent as a representative of the grand jury before they can have it."

Griff stood. "Correct, which is why it's still in my possession. They'll contact Patrick with the name of their designated agent. Then I'll turn it over because we don't work counterintelligence cases."

"So we can't go after the Chinese professor? What can we do?"

Griff swung open the door. "You and I are supposed to find some smokin' hot terrorism case to pursue. Like Brett's case against those drug smugglers who are moving explosives across the border. I'm not happy about it either. The CI guys at the FBI acted cagey and I wonder if they'll really pursue it."

"It stinks. We should be able to track down everything related to Paul Revere if the FBI won't." Eva rose, pushing her chair in a huff. "Where is Brett, by the way?"

Griff rolled his eyes. "Oops. Glad you reminded me. While you and I need to develop an exciting terrorism case to claim as our own, Brett needs our help on Marlow Bryson's case. We're meeting Brett at Rob's Deli for lunch, where I'm sure he'll advise what fun we three will be having in the near future."

Eva returned to her desk where she locked away her purse and gun, eager to find the hot case Griff said they needed. Such a spectacular find seemed as elusive as her family's summer vacation.

EARLY THE NEXT MORNING, Eva woke to an annoying single chirp on her cell phone charging on the nightstand. She heard Scott's calm breathing, and took her phone into the closet to see who wanted her at four a.m.

Meeting at the office 6am. Don't be late. Lots happening. Griff

Wow! She had only two hours to shower, make coffee, and reach the task force office, an hour away. But wait! If she got on I-66 by 5:00 am, she wouldn't need a second person in the car for the HOV lanes and should arrive on time.

Eva slid slacks from a hanger along with a clean blouse. Taking her clothes, she hurried to the kitchen, hit "on" for the coffee pot, then tiptoed to the master bathroom. She returned to the kitchen twenty minutes later, washed and dressed for the meeting.

She dashed a note to Scott: *Honey, I figure with the all-nighter you pulled the other night, you need extra sleep. Griff texted—surprise JTTF meeting. Talk later. Luv, E*

After pouring piping hot coffee into her travel mug, she snatched a nut bar from the bowl on the counter and roared toward the office. This rushing to keep pace with events was wearing on Eva's spirit. Her entire family seemed out of touch like they were characters from some movie.

The darkness enhanced her melancholy mood. Something urgent must have occurred to warrant a six a.m. meeting. Had Paul Revere's appearance before the grand jury gone off the rails? If so, neither Griff nor Brett mentioned anything they found disturbing at lunch yesterday.

She resisted the urge to call Griff, not wanting to wake his wife Dawn. Eva exceeded the speed limit, hoping Paul Revere hadn't done something horribly wrong.

ONCE IN THE OFFICE, Eva dumped her weapon and big purse in the desk. She turned the key in the lock before hustling toward sounds of voices in the conference room, not even stopping to refill her coffee.

She strode in with no firm grasp of why Griff summoned her. He and Brett were huddled together, talking. AUSA Patrick O'Rourke sat in his wheelchair at the head of the table perusing a stack of documents in front of him.

"Morning all," Eva said, her jaw muscles tight. "Will someone please tell me what's going on? I feel like an outsider."

Griff motioned for her to sit across from him, and said grinning widely, "You're going to feel like it's Christmas in July. We're about to open a group gift."

"Whew!" Eva took her seat. "Now I can relax."

"You should be proud, Eva. I've never seen a case develop like this one," Patrick complimented, opening his folder.

Griff, too, acted upbeat, spreading his hands out on the table, saying, "This week defies everything I trained for in becoming a senior Special Agent. Our investigations usually take months or years. Eva, you've surpassed yourself."

"Yeah." Brett nodded his head vigorously. "Eva, to think it all started with your cell phone receiving strange texts."

"Hey, Eva, you're by the door," Patrick said. "Close it, okay?"

She did and resumed her seat. "I never could wait for Christmas morning. Will you unwrap this gift before Christmas disappears before my eyes?"

"First things first," Patrick intoned. "Thanks to you, Eva, while you and Brett enjoyed the last few days, I and, to a lesser degree, Griff, were working our tails off."

Eva raised her eyebrows and glared at Griff. He simply frowned in reply.

"What did I do?" she objected.

Patrick held up a hand. "Before we proceed, you're all now covered by the judge's order and considered officers of the grand jury."

"We three can now access its secret testimony, right?" Eva asked, to ensure they didn't violate secrecy rules.

"Correct," the AUSA assured. "I'll go back and add an FBI counterintelligence agent so he or she can receive the USB drive."

"Keep me in the loop," Griff urged.

Patrick nodded and consulted his legal pad. "To recap, as Brett just said, an unknown person sent tips and evidence to Eva's cell phone using a decoy caller ID. No matter what she tried, the tipster refused to cooperate or authenticate the evidence. We brought the tipster she named Paul Revere before the grand jury to obtain his evidence."

"Have you determined his true identity and motive?" Eva probed.

Patrick tented his fingers. "Yes. His real identity is John Lapp. I can't decide if he's unbelievably naïve or a brilliant strategic thinker. He delivered evidence of two intricate cases we might not otherwise have, all to expose organic fraud as Eva suspected."

"John Lapp!" Eva clapped her hands. "I thought so! He set up his mother's cell phone contact list, which includes my cell numbers and Kaley's. No doubt, he's credible."

Patrick went on to explain how John presented to the grand jury the videos he'd previously messaged to Eva. "Eva did a stellar job in getting the tipster to give secret testimony. Every bit of the evidence he has obtained lawfully."

"Way to go, partner." Griff gave her a high five.

"Brett," Patrick said, sliding over a stack of papers. "These are arrest warrants for Marlow Bryson in Middleburg and Danny Mills, manager of Beecher Packaging in St. Louis, which Bryson owns. Both are charged with importing 800 pounds of fentanyl."

Brett let out a low whistle. "Excellent. I'm ready to take both these scumbags off the street. Eight hundred pounds is worth close to 363 million dollars."

The agents stared at each other in silence. Then they fixed their gaze upon Patrick, as if asking, "What now?"

"Brett, you lead the arrest team, and my U.S. Attorney's office will issue a press release."

"How did John Lapp know about the fentanyl?" Eva asked, still amazed by how the myriad of unimaginable clues produced criminal indictments. Truth was indeed stranger than fiction. It was also on their side.

"He didn't." Patrick tapped his legal pad. "That's why I say he's naïve. He found the digital video while servicing Bryson's computer, and believed he had evidence of non-organic produce coming from China and packaged in bags claiming to be USA organic. John still thinks 800 pounds of China Girl is garlic powder."

Eva folded her arms, not liking what she was hearing. "I have a concern."

"Because he doesn't know the powder is illegal fentanyl?" Patrick asked. "That's no problem."

Eva pushed out her bottom lip. "No. The problem is, unless Bryson pleads guilty, we have to introduce the videos at trial. John will not want to testify."

"Griff, explain what you've been doing," Patrick instructed.

Griff palmed his mustache as if waiting for this moment. "Listen to John Lapp's more unbelievable luck. He finds the USB drive in the college's computer lab. Suspicious of its content, he copies it and waits. Professor Mao Peng, from another campus who teaches one class using John's lab, claims ownership."

"Now will you tell me what's so suspicious about the USB?" Eva asked, leaning forward and sensing her case was about to explode.

"For one thing, it contained every bit of contact info from John's computer, including yours and Kaley's phone numbers. Next to your name was written 'FBI.'"

Eva widened her eyes. "Which is how the ChiComs identified me, according to our Mossad friend. Why does it say I'm with the FBI?"

"Perhaps Lapp listed you that way among his contacts," Brett offered.

Eva thought that made sense. "John's mother, my friend Irene, gave him my data. She wouldn't be the first friend to think I work for the FBI."

"Sounds plausible," Brett agreed. "My aunts and uncles will say I'm an FBI agent. To some, every federal agent is FBI."

Griff continued, "Worse yet, Professor Peng was stealing agricultural research from the college and giving it to the Chinese Communist government, who paid him massive amounts of money to be their spy."

"Why are you confident Peng is working for China?" Eva asked, her mind on high alert for what might come next.

"After our talk, Eva, I felt compelled to see what I could find out." Griff stifled a yawn. "I examined the USB and spoke with an agent I respect in the FBI's CI division. He told me that they had observed Peng with a Chinese MSS officer from China's Consulate in Chicago."

Brett stopped him. "Wait. What is MSS?"

"It's China's foreign intelligence arm," Griff replied, adding, "The Ministry of State Security is like our CIA. FBI agents suspected Peng was doing something else fishy as they'd already discovered China paid him a salary. John Lapp's USB is the proof."

Eva snapped her fingers. "Peng must have passed my contact info to the Chinese, which is the same info the Israelis also found in possession of the ChiComs. We're back to square one. How do we introduce Marlow's videos without compromising John Lapp?"

"Eva," Griff said her name curtly. "Remember, the one video shows Marlow talking to a guy in China about importing the shipment. We don't know how many previous times this occurred."

"How does that help us?" she demanded.

"You're familiar with the Foreign Intelligence Surveillance Act, or FISA warrants. They permit the FBI to wiretap and search homes of Americans who contact the ChiComs."

Eva lowered her voice. "Are you suggesting what I think you are?"

"Look at it this way," Griff replied. "After I explained everything to the Bureau's CI agent, he is thrilled to have John's USB drive, and opened a case on Marlow's Chinese contact. I surmise by now, with Marlow asleep in his bedroom, he and other agents have already entered his office during the night and downloaded everything in his computer."

"Just my luck," Eva mused. "I have a source who I can't admit to having and have nobody to arrest, while Brett bags Bryson with 800 pounds of fentanyl and Griff delivers a good spy case to his FBI colleagues. I have cold steel cuffs just waiting to clamp onto some dirtbag's wrists, and I have no way to act."

Patrick turned to Eva. "I remember years ago you investigated Emile Jubayl, the husband of your personal friend. I, for one, didn't suppose you'd want to arrest Bryson, whose wife is your friend."

"I won't argue with your logic," Eva admitted. "I should be content I was the means for the source to approach us. To learn Paul Revere is John Lapp, a computer geek and college professor, still astonishes me."

"He's a regular Santa Claus," Patrick offered with a rare smile.

Eva added, "Or a gift from God."

She mentally replayed how God in His sovereignty had brought her to the Biltmore event where she and Cora honored Cora's parents and where Eva met John Lapp. There, Cora's husband Marlow asked John to do computer consulting for him. It was this computer work that caused John to unearth evidence of Marlow's crimes. God was behind it all.

Eva rose to her feet, prepared to tackle something productive. "Brett, when will you make the arrests?"

"I first thought we'd have to wait for FBI's CI people to grab Peng," Brett said. "But Griff believes, and Patrick agrees, they might not arrest Peng, but will flip him and use him to deliver bogus information to the ChiComs."

"Excellent! It's time we see justice against all this Chinese spying," Eva said hotly.

Brett stood and collected his warrants. "I'll coordinate with St. Louis DEA so we can strike simultaneously. Then we set up an arrest team, but I don't think you should be there, Eva."

Her first reaction was to fight back. She couldn't participate in even one arrest?

Brett was right, though, and she told him so. "The last thing I want is to encounter my friend while arresting her husband. I'll stay here at the office helping in any way."

As she turned to leave, Brett asked her to wait. "Patrick, before you make a press release, I suggest you check with the press spokespersons for DEA, ICE, and the Defense Department. There's an ongoing effort to disrupt China's flooding our country with illegal drugs. We don't want to cross any wires."

Eva heartily agreed. "Patrick, you'll deal with my husband Scott, who just returned to the Pentagon. He's now handling their public affairs department."

At least one Montanna will get in on the action, Eva thought as she left the others behind. What came next for her, she didn't know. She should get busy planning their family vacation to see Grandpa Marty and decided to call him tonight.

Chapter 35

John Lapp was enjoying a wonderful Wednesday afternoon as he strolled across campus toward his apartment. Redwing blackbirds flitted in trees along the sidewalk. The sun shone brilliantly overhead, which helped him to release his burdens about the summer term ending. Today, he had prepared the students for their final exams.

Thankful he could spend more time with Annie and her son during the break, his mind turned to another duty he'd successfully completed. Testifying last week before the grand jury hadn't been as terrifying as he thought it would be. John found the jurors friendly, attentive, and well-informed. One juror even asked a question about holding people accountable for fraudulent food practices.

A whistle flew from his lips, a praise song from church last Sunday. John relished seeing how God was guiding his life. He felt confident justice would be done for Marlow, and others like him who would discover there were consequences for deceiving people about organic foods.

Joy filled him as he mentally relived his recent visit to Walnut Cove, especially worshiping with Annie and her family. He'd driven with her along tree-lined roads and through lush countryside, which warmed his heart as he recalled the common interests they shared.

A festive finale had come for John on Sunday over warmed apple strudel with ice cream at Yoder's Family Restaurant, the eatery owned by Annie's former father-in-law. Mr. Yoder had given John a friendly handshake.

John unlocked his apartment door, certain Annie had wanted and received Mr. Yoder's blessing on their continuing relationship. Life's issues suddenly closed in the moment John stepped through his door.

Amy from Occidental Organics sent an urgent text during class and he needed to respond. He plunked down his leather valise and quickly punched in her phone number.

"Ah … Occidental Organics … this is Amy." Her voice sounded tense.

"It's John Lapp. I was teaching a class when your text arrived."

John heard a phone ringing in her office, but she didn't stop to answer it.

"John, I need your help," she gushed. "Our whole network's been down since I arrived this morning. It won't accept my password."

He booted up his computer dedicated to Occidental. "Let's see what I can do."

He maneuvered around his keyboard while Amy told him, "It's a strange morning around here."

"Oh?" John mumbled, his fingers working.

"Yeah. Mr. Bryson isn't here yet. His wife took something from his office and her face was all puffy. I could tell she'd been crying. She said nothing to any of us."

"I hope she isn't sick or something."

"It's totally weird. I should be home myself. My due date is tomorrow."

Trying to keep up with Amy, John replied, "I don't understand. Your due date?"

"Sure!" she chimed. "My baby girl is due tomorrow. Once you get me into the system, I'm heading home to rest."

John typed faster. "All the best, Amy. I've texted you a new password. If it works, you can create your own."

"It's here. Stay on the line while I try it."

Her keyboard clicked in his ear as she told him, "Even worse, the assistant manager at Beecher Packaging called. It's the company Mr. Bryson owns in Missouri. He said the plant manager was arrested early this morning by the DEA."

"The drug agency?" he exclaimed.

"John, I'm in! Your password works!"

"Good," he said, adding, "I'll see if you're able to get access to your system. But Amy, why was the plant manager arrested?"

"They think it's a mistake. A shipment arrived a while ago with unexpected garlic powder, and the plant manager refused it. The assistant manager suspects it was a shipment of illegal drugs."

John could hardly believe what Amy was telling him. Before he could reply to the startling news, she announced, a lilt in her voice, "John, we're back up! You're my hero. I can leave my job in the hands of the temp and not worry."

"Glad to help," he replied, anxious to hang up. "Be sure the temp has my phone number."

He terminated the call, rattled by what Amy had shared. He'd skipped breakfast and now his stomach demanded food before his brain could engage in any more work. John retrieved the makings of a hearty sandwich from the fridge, and laid out packages of sliced turkey and cheese. His cell rang and he answered right away, happy to hear from his mother.

"Hi, Mom. Wait until I tell—"

"John, I'm not calling to chat. I have terrible news," she said sounding tearful.

"Are you and Pop okay?"

"We are. Cora just called in tears. Early this morning, DEA agents came to their home and arrested Marlow."

Shock rolled through John's mind. He groped for words. "How awful! Why would drug agents arrest Marlow?"

"Dad and I are flabbergasted. It must be a mistake. Cora is going to Alexandria for a court hearing and to post his bond. Their lawyer told her what to expect."

"What can I do from Ohio?" Concern for Cora and his parents flooded his heart.

"That's why I'm calling," she said, her voice breaking. "I can't imagine he's done anything wrong. Please pray for them, John."

"I certainly will pray, Mom. Are you going to the courthouse with Cora?"

"No. I'm at the Trumpet's Call waiting for Kaley to start her shift. Then I'll head home and wait with Pop."

She agreed to call John once she knew more.

"If only I was there with you," he said, not hinting he'd been close by when he testified at the grand jury.

Mom sniffled. "Your love and prayers mean everything,"

Guilt made his heart pound. So what if grand juries were secret? He should've gone to see Mom and Pop when he'd flown to Virginia.

"Mom, I'm here for you both. I love you!"

John ended the call in a daze. Staring at his phone, he agonized over why the DEA arrested Marlow. They had nothing to do with fraudulent organic food, did they?

His appetite shriveled to nothing. He shoved the meat and cheese back into the fridge. Overcome with worry that he'd acted too hastily in going to the grand jury, John bowed his head in earnest prayer.

JOHN STAYED NEAR THE PHONE, restless to hear something, anything from his mom. Waiting without knowing was taxing. His nerves were a rubber band, stretched tight and ready to snap. John found Marlow's pretending to sell organic food outrageous. His brother-in-law deserved to be unmasked. John put those feelings aside and considered the hurt and pain his arrest was bringing to people he loved.

Could Cora's husband really be involved in drug dealing?

John decided to call Annie. Hearing her voice would smooth every rough place.

Mr. Nolt answered, saying warmly, "My daughter is on her way home. Try calling her in a few minutes."

"If I miss her, *please* tell her I phoned," John replied seriously.

"Yes, son. Her mother and I hope to see you again on Sunday."

Son? Mr. Nolt just called him son!

John put down the phone, figuring it might be his way of speaking. He shouldn't read much into it. After pouring a glass of water, John opened his Bible to the Psalms seeking answers. He knew God had helped King David during times of tremendous trial.

The words David wrote in Psalm 4 brought John much solace, and he read the first verse aloud as a heartfelt prayer, "Answer me when I call to You, O my righteous God. Give me relief from my distress; be merciful to me and hear my prayer."

The words described John's feelings exactly. How comforting to remember God cared and listened to his prayers. There was one person he could tell about the help he'd received from the Psalm. He pressed her name on his phone's contact list.

A moment later, Annie answered, "The Nolt residence."

"Annie, it's John." He kept his voice low.

"You're a pleasant surprise, and caught me just arriving home."

His body and soul relaxed hearing her melodic voice. "I phoned the store. Your father said you were heading there."

"Can I help you with something?"

"If you don't mind me saying this, I called to hear your sweet voice. This day is tumultuous. I needed your encouragement."

"Oh!" she cried. "What's happened?"

John wouldn't risk sharing too much about Marlow, not yet. He wasn't ready to admit his actions may have contributed to Marlow's problems.

"My folks are worried about their daughter, my foster sister, Cora. I'm looking for a ray of sunshine. How are you?"

"Samuel and I are going to the pediatrician for his booster shots."

"Glad I caught you in time. Samuel probably isn't too happy to see the doctor."

"He's usually a brave little man. Besides, we'll stop on the way home for an ice cream cone."

"You're a wonder, Annie. I can truthfully say, you're my booster," he said. "Be safe and say hello to Samuel for me. I have a gift for him."

"Really? I need to go, but is it a surprise?"

"Yes. Perhaps I'll bring it this weekend, if you want me to."

"I finish work Saturday at noon. Join us for lunch at one?"

John agreed and the moment he hung up, he went digging

around in the closet, and located his small fishing pole Pop used when he took John fishing. Letting his mind drift to seeing Annie and her son Samuel on Saturday eased a load of anxiety he felt for Cora.

He made another swift decision. John went into the bathroom, found his can of shaving cream, and with a new disposable blade, shaved off his beard. He wanted to assure Annie he'd said good-bye to any idea of becoming plain. Most of all, John didn't want others to see Annie in his company and think he was a married Amish man.

Chapter 36

The two days since his arrest and release on bail flew by for Marlow Bryson as he clawed his way back to getting his life on track. After forfeiting his passport to the authorities, he canceled his trip to China. Maybe that was just as well. Wen might take him hostage for the staggering amount of money Marlow owed him for the seized China Girl.

He sat by the kitchen table, sipping a mug of lukewarm coffee, and talking on his cell phone to his newly-retained criminal lawyer, Jeffrey Shields. Arriving Occidental employees drove past the window as Marlow drained the coffee to the bottom. He'd better get to his office and keep his companies afloat.

Yet, he hung onto every word and unfamiliar phrase Jeff uttered. As the attorney explained what to expect, Cora hovered nearby, listening to Marlow's side of the conversation.

"We'll receive a date to argue our motions and find out which federal judge is assigned to your case," Jeffrey said, his voice monotone like it was routine.

It certainly wasn't for Marlow. He looked up at Cora, seeing nothing but fright in her clouded eyes.

He told his lawyer, "I'm putting you on speaker so my wife can hear."

"Fine. We'll demand to know all the government's evidence to build your defense. The ten-thousand-dollar retainer you paid is insufficient. Be prepared to pay an additional fifty thousand, and soon."

"What do I get for so much money?" Marlow shot back.

"That depends on our strategy. If you want me to negotiate a guilty plea for you, we may not need the entire fifty grand."

"No way!" Marlow shouted. "I refuse to plead guilty. It's a mistake. I can't always know what my employees are doing at a distant subsidiary plant."

He glanced at Cora, hoping to comfort her with his theory. Tears plunged down her cheeks. This lawyer was the best Marlow had heard of so he needed to come up with additional cash and fast.

"We'll learn more once we receive and sift through what the government has on you," Jeff assured. "Meanwhile, Marlow, avoid any contact or discussion with Danny Mills, your co-defendant. Remember, he could make a deal with the feds for a lighter sentence and claim it was all your operation."

Cora sobbed softly. Marlow impatiently motioned for her to sit down. Her emotions were rattling him. He'd goofed big-time letting her listen to the call.

"I must keep Beecher Packaging operating," Marlow replied. "They do all my packaging and distribution, and if it shuts down, I won't have money to pay you."

"Don't you have other reliable staff at Beecher?" Jeffrey demanded. "Until Danny makes bond, you can't contact him anyway."

"Right." Marlow paused. "I've been wondering if I should fire Danny. After all, his conduct put my entire company at risk."

The lawyer growled, "That's the last thing you should do. Put him on paid leave, and avoid dealing with him. Your firing Danny will give him another reason to turn on you and cooperate with the government."

Marlow carried his cup to the sink. "Okay, Jeffrey. You've given me plenty to think on. I'm heading to earn the money I need for my defense."

He ended the call and turned to Cora, who joined him by the sink, her face tear-stained. She touched his arm.

"He didn't give us much encouragement. Are we in real trouble here, Marlow?"

"Everything will be okay," he promised. "I need you at my side fighting these outrageous charges."

"We can sell my new horse," she offered.

"Not yet. We'll find the money. If need be, I'll sell the classic Bentley and lastly, your horse."

He took Cora's hand. "Come with me into the office when I give the staff a pep talk. Your support is crucial."

"I want to know everything," she told him, her voice suddenly firm. "After we meet with your staff, I'm ordering Amy a fruit basket. She's being discharged from the hospital this morning with her new baby daughter."

"A fine idea, but hold off ordering until I pay the lawyer."

"Marlow, Amy has worked for you over three years. It's the right thing to do. I have a little savings in my name and can use that."

Cora has savings? his mind calculated furiously. It might look better if they dipped into her money.

"We'll decide later."

He led Cora from the kitchen into the office wing behind their palatial estate. Stopping at Amy's old desk, he instructed the temporary assistant to set the phones on auto-answer mode and bring the other employees into his office.

Marlow found Cora in there, straightening chairs and the pillowed sofa. The three other staffers trudged in, their faces glum.

They took seats on chairs and the leather sofa while Cora stood by an antique armchair near the corner of Marlow's desk.

"I want to explain what transpired this past week," Marlow began. "Don't rely on what you see or read in the media."

His eyes sought his wife's. She responded with an encouraging smile. He could always trust her to be loyal, and he needed to get maximum benefit from her allegiance.

He breathed in deeply before saying, "You've probably heard about my arrest and that of Danny Mills at Beecher. It comes as a huge shock to me, and I'm sure to you. We suspect Mexican drug cartels figured a way to ship drugs across the border hidden among legitimate commerce, and somehow they managed to retrieve their hidden loads before the trucks arrived at Beecher. I'm guessing there was a snafu, because when Danny discovered garlic powder on the manifest and we weren't expecting any, he refused to offload it."

Marlow stopped, wondering what his employees were thinking. No one said a word, deepening his suspicions of their commitment to remain.

"It may take time," he added, "but after our own inquiry, we are certain the government will determine they've brought an improper indictment."

Darryl, the office bookkeeper, said, "Our creditors may assume we're having difficulties and demand quicker payments. And the accounts that owe us might be slower to pay. What should we tell them?"

"Say what I just told you," Marlow snapped. "Don't volunteer, unless they begin hedging for reasons you mentioned."

"Okay, boss," Darryl replied in a somber tone.

Marlow forced his usual confident smile wanting to reassure everyone. "Listen, business continues. People need good organic food, which we'll provide. Don't worry, your jobs are secure. Let's get to work."

The employees hurriedly fled the room. Wanda, Amy's replacement, approached Marlow's desk, clasping her hands.

"A woman called earlier, and refused to give her name, insisting she speak with you. When I said you were on another call, she said she'd phone again."

"Did a caller ID number display?" Marlow asked, concerned who it could be.

Wanda dropped her hands as if defeated. "No, it was blocked."

Marlow looked at Cora and back to Wanda. "Maybe she's a tipster who knows the truth. If she calls again, put her through to me

ASAP."

"Yes, sir."

Wanda left. Cora stepped closer to him with a worried frown. He slung an arm around her shoulder.

"Don't be overly concerned. We'll go on with our lives as normal as possible."

Cora slumped against him. "We're in this together, Marlow, for better or worse. I want to order Amy's basket this afternoon. I'll pay."

"Good idea. You pay for her gift. I'll contact a car dealer and sell the Bentley." He squeezed her shoulder. "We'll get through this."

NEARLY AN HOUR PASSED with Marlow finding it hard to concentrate on work. He needed to find a way of out of this jam. Wanda buzzed Marlow on the intercom, interrupting his plan-making.

"The mystery woman's on the phone for you," she announced efficiently.

"Is her number blocked again?"

"Yes.

"I'll take the call," Marlow told her with a grunt.

The call connected, and he pressed the receiver tight against his ear. "Marlow Bryson here. Can I help you?"

"Not really," the deep alto voice responded. "I'm calling to help you."

"What makes you think I need your help?"

"Everyone inside the federal courthouse knows your need."

Marlow barked, "And anyone who watches TV or reads the news. So what?"

"I understand your suspicions, but thought you'd want to secure your freedom," she said, chuckling lightly. "You already retained Jeffrey Shields to represent you."

Marlow realized this was no ordinary call. "It's reckless to call me like this."

"You're not interested in my proposal?"

"I didn't say that. It's unwise to discuss such matters on an unsecure line. If you want to speak further, install the Firewire Cryptic Message App first. I'll give you a link to reach me on the app."

"I'm relieved to know you're a careful man."

"What do I call you?"

"Susie. Don't go anywhere. I'll contact you once I install Firewire. I'm ready for the link."

Marlow gave it to her and hung up, a million questions circling in his brain. Was "Susie" really an FBI agent? Was she someone from the Mexican mafia? How did she know he'd just hired Jeffrey Shields?

His questions were endless, but until Susie called back, no answers were in reach.

Before long, Marlow's computer screen lit up with a cryptic message connection. Susie used a darkened computer screen. Okay, he wasn't dealing with a novice. He signed on and deactivated his camera.

"Hello again, Marlow," Susie quipped.

"This is more secure," he replied. "Our call is encrypted."

Susie snickered into the phone. "Feel more comfortable now?"

"No! I do not. I have no idea who you are or why you're calling."

"Though Jeffrey Shields is a fine lawyer for your defense, you're still at great risk. I can assure your acquittal."

"You think you'll become the jury foreperson?" Marlow asked sarcastically.

"No. It's much easier and more certain. But costly."

Marlow doubted what he was hearing. Should he report this call to Jeffrey or the FBI? Still, he grasped onto hope, telling her, "I'm listening."

"You may not believe I can help you," she said, her voice smooth as a salesman. "Consider this. Your attorney won't know yet which judge or your next court date. I know Judge Ginsburg will hear your motion on the twenty-third at ten in the morning."

Marlow narrowed his eyes. "So? The judge's secretary can find that out."

"You're right. You need assurance Judge Ginsburg sympathizes with your plight."

"No," Marlow growled. "I need to know the jury is sympathetic."

"I see the problem. Know this. You're entitled to a bench trial without a jury, where the judge alone decides your fate. If the judge thinks his retirement account benefits enough, he will definitely find you *not* guilty."

"This is crazy talk," Marlow sputtered. "I can't believe you called me."

"I know you'd like to think it's possible," Susie shot back.

"I suppose you're Judge Ginsburg's financial planner, and know how much padding his account needs."

Susie's caustic laugh into the phone grated on Marlow's shattered nerves.

"An even million dollars seals the deal," she said. "You'll spend a ton for a jury trial. If convicted, you'll lose much more than a million, plus your freedom to move about for years to come."

A million bucks?!

Marlow shuddered. Such a huge amount! Still, if cash to the judge guaranteed his acquittal, then Susie was right.

"Besides the million, how much does the judge's financial adviser require?"

"Like all investment advisers, my fees are paid by the judge. I suspect you need proof I speak for the judge."

"Obviously," Marlow countered.

"Keep mum, especially to Jeffrey Shields," she ordered. "At your motion hearing on the twenty-third, Judge Ginsburg will wear the type of tie and color you choose. Then you'll know he's on board with our agreement."

"That sounds ridiculous," Marlow insisted.

"I make perfect sense. Because he wears a black robe, you can't see much of his clothing except for his shirt collar and tie. He doesn't normally wear them, but bowties are easier to spot above his robe. You choose red, blue, polka dots, or whatever. He'll wear your selection to the hearing and you'll know our offer is authentic."

"Blue with white polka dots," Marlow uttered in disbelief.

"I'll contact you after the twenty-third. So far, no one's done anything wrong. Are you on board?"

"I'll see how the hearing goes and then decide."

"There are two other considerations," she cautioned.

Marlow heard a sound outside his door. "Just a minute."

He got up and opened the door. There was no one there. Closing the door and returning to the computer conversation, he asked her, "What are they?"

"First, you must have the financial means. Secondly, your attorney offers a valid defense with sufficient evidence for the judge to declare you not guilty."

Marlow sighed with relief. "Neither is a problem, if your bowtie pans out."

"Okay, we'll talk again after the twenty-third."

Susie was gone. Marlow looked dumbly at the computer's blank screen until he had an idea. He immediately phoned the attorney's office.

"Jeff's in court," his assistant replied.

"It's Marlow Bryson, his client. I'm trying to sync my calendar and wonder if my case is set for a hearing before a judge."

"I'll check." he started clicking on a keyboard. "Your case was just assigned to Judge Ginsburg. No hearing date, but we'll notify you once it's set."

Marlow hung up and sat back, stunned. Something about a tangled web haunted him, but not for long. He called his investment banker. It was time to sell a chunk of his portfolio and have it liquid in case he needed to move money in a hurry.

Chapter 37

John Lapp ate a delicious lunch with Annie and her family around their table. After enjoying blueberry pie, he hurried to his car and returned with the small fishing pole.

Samuel's eyes gleamed. "Are you going fishing, John?"

"Not today. I will take you sometime, Samuel. This pole is for you."

"Thanks!" he squealed.

John took the young boy out onto the front porch where they had fun practicing casting out in the yard while Annie and her mother washed dishes. When Annie came outside wearing a lavender dress, her hair blew around her pretty face in the light breeze. John was smitten.

"Would you take a drive with me to the Miller farm?" he asked impulsively.

"If I'm not in the way of your business. Let me collect some rhubarb sauce for Ruth. She kindly brought chicken soup for my father's bad cold last winter."

John rejoiced having Annie accompany him to Eli's farm. He was bringing the farmer research articles and lists of local marketing outlets for organic produce since Eli couldn't research the Internet himself. John had relinquished his hope Walnut Cove Amish farmers would form a co-op and sell produce to Occidental Organics. Since uncovering Marlow's questionable methods, John was firmly against the idea.

He simply wouldn't connect any Amish farmer to a company that failed to practice the highest quality and ethics. John would say nothing of Marlow's arrest to anyone, not even Annie.

"Do you like helping Eli?" Annie asked as they headed toward the farm.

"Funny you should ask. I was just thinking how I appreciate learning the ways of his family farm. I respect their commitment to their faith in God and living plain."

John didn't tell Annie how impressed he was by Eli's sons and especially Ruth. Or how he had decided some time ago that the chasm between his life and the Amish ways was too great to be bridged.

"Could you live and farm in Walnut Cove, or are you too modern and too English?" Annie asked, catching him off guard.

John sensed his reply to her question would be as crucial as those he'd given to the grand jury. He carefully prepared his answer, in hopes of pleasing Annie.

"You ask another insightful question." John slowed the car so he wouldn't miss the driveway. "I'm too English to be as plain as Eli and his family. Yet, I've grown to love this community and feel a true kinship with you and your Mennonite family."

She glanced his way and smiled as if relieved. "John, from when I first met you, I thought you would be happy in our Mennonite culture and faith."

They rode in silence until Annie added, "I don't think you will find many Mennonites near your college."

"True," he said softly. "Annie, you haven't mentioned I shaved my beard."

John looked from the corner of his eyes and saw her cheeks turning rosy.

"You wanted me to notice?" she asked, a lilt in her voice.

He turned into the Miller drive and stopped some distance from the house. "Annie, you're astute. I shaved it for you. I think you know what I mean. We need to discuss important matters soon. I could commute to the college from Walnut Cove. Or, I might teach in the high school or local junior college."

"Will you be here long?" Annie handed him the basket with several jars. "I prefer to wait in the car."

"I promise to be quick. Should I leave the car running or roll down the windows?"

"Put the windows down please." Her eyes sparkled at him. "I love fresh air."

John did as she asked. Pocketing the keys, he happily took her basket and breezed into the Miller home where he gave Mrs. Miller the rhubarb sauce. Ruth came in the house some minutes later, as John showed Eli the leaflets and articles. To John's delight, he acted interested today in growing organics.

John noticed Ruth and Mrs. Miller trading smiles and glances as if they shared a secret. He wondered what it might be, but rather than ask, he simply excused himself abruptly when he finished talking business with Eli.

"I will walk you to your car," Eli said, then stopped in his tracks when he saw Annie in the front seat. "John, you should have invited Annie into our home."

"She needs to get back to her son, and I didn't plan to be here long," John explained, wanting Eli's blessing.

Eli held out his hand, which John grasped firmly. "John Lapp, you have given me much help for my crop rotation and growth. I will let you know of my progress after trying your ideas. If our yield improves as you suggest, maybe you can return next spring and test my neighbor's land."

"I could drive back next month to check your crops."

"You are welcome any time," Eli said. "Annie is a fine woman. Her family is highly respected. Looks like you discovered a way to get halfway back to your past."

John smiled. "I believe it is God Who is directing me. May He bless you and your family, Eli."

"And you too, John Lapp."

John eased into the car. Annie set the empty basket on her lap. "Ruth stopped to say hello and ask after Samuel. Thanks for bringing me along."

"Ah, so that's their secret," John replied, starting the car.

"What secret? Is it something I should know?"

John didn't reply. He sat watching Eli walk toward the house.

Annie broke the silence by asking, "John, is everything all right?"

"I'm sorry." He faced her. "Ruth and her mother looked at each other like they shared a secret. I guess it's because Ruth knew you came with me. And also, now as I see Eli on his farm I think of my early years. It's like I'm watching my father walk to the house where I was born."

"I see why you enjoy this consulting experience," Annie said, a light in her eyes.

John started the car and pulled back onto the highway. He drove in silence for a mile or so before asking, "Annie, could you do me a favor?"

"If I'm able. What is it?"

"I want to visit Lancaster and see where I once lived. Could you check your books at the museum and find any clue where that might be?"

She stayed quiet a long minute as if considering the possibilities and promised to search, adding, "Even better, I will call someone I spoke with at the Lancaster museum. She may have other sources to explore."

"You're a wonderful friend to me," John said.

Their conversation turned lighter as they discussed when he'd take Samuel fishing. He walked Annie to the front door, where Mrs. Nolt handed him paper bags.

"For your supper later," she said, leaving them to say good-bye.

"Annie, it's hard to find words to say how much being with you means to me." John hesitated to leave. "Let me know soon what you find at the museum."

"You asking for my help means much to me," she said sweetly.

Annie waved as he drove away. As John thought things through on the way home, he believed more than ever that his travels into Walnut Cove, and today in particular, were no coincidence. God had arranged everything.

He hung the car keys on a hook inside his apartment door. Mrs. Nolt sent along slices of blueberry pie with fresh green beans and ripe tomatoes from their garden. She'd even made a liverwurst sandwich with pickles, just how he liked it!

John stored the food in the fridge and brewed a pot of coffee to drink while working on his computer. He wanted to see if he could still access Occidental's system and if business had fallen off since Marlow's arrest. He typed in the password and a great surprise awaited him.

Marlow hadn't obstructed John's access. He still must trust him. The system remained unchanged. John found evidence of business as usual, including recent correspondence and invoices. He then decided to check if there'd been any new contacts from Danny Mills, the plant manager Amy said had been arrested in Missouri.

John toggled to the hidden digital files, the ones that recorded conversations from the Cryptic Message App. His fingers clicked away and he found no contact from Mills. John searched a bit further, only to discover something shocking, beyond anything he could have imagined.

He couldn't believe what Marlow discussed online. His brother-in-law's ideas were getting even more bizarre, more dangerous! John hurried to make copies. He banged shut his computer to avoid being caught, his heart beating wildly.

LATE ON SUNDAY EVENING, EVA MONTANNA texted her supervisor as well as Griff and Brett, insisting the three meet her tomorrow morning at nine a.m. sharp. When she arrived in the office, Eva smelled freshly-brewed coffee and made a beeline to pour a cup. Lights were already ablaze in the conference room.

Coffee in one hand and leather satchel over her shoulder, she went in, irked she was the last to arrive.

Griff hit her with a question. "Well? Did you hear from Paul Revere again?"

"Remember, gentlemen, we're authorized to discuss the true Paul Revere," Eva replied. "So yes, I heard from John Lapp last night."

Sosa Garcia asked, "Is he using the same MO, sending texts disguised as your daughter?"

"Yes and yes." Eva set her writing portfolio on the table and slid the laptop to the center, grinning at Griff. "You're gonna love this."

She tapped her keyboard, and seconds later the digital file she'd received from John began to play. Eva quickly stopped it to explain, "Remember, in the previous file we received, we saw a video picture of Marlow Bryson talking with co-conspirators. In this one, you'll notice the female caller has her camera turned off. Marlow's is off too."

Eva played the video, showing a woman named Susie offering to take a huge amount of money in exchange for fixing Marlow's case with Judge Ginsburg. They listened to the bribery scheme unfold, the entire team spellbound.

The video ended with Eva telling them what else she surmised, "Every detail Susie gave is evidence she was behind the theft of a half-million dollars from Darin Hilton."

"I don't know everything you know, but it's unbelievable," Brett bellowed. "Is it legally obtained? Can we use this?"

Eva shrugged. "It will require stellar legal research by Patrick O'Rourke."

"Wait a minute." Brett reached over, punched the speakerphone, and tapped in a number. "I'm calling O'Rourke's office."

It rang twice. "Patrick O'Rourke's office. Nancy speaking."

"Nancy, it's Brett Calloway, I'm—"

"He's not here," she interrupted.

Brett countered, "I called to speak with you."

"You're always looking for Patrick." She laughed. "How can I help?"

"I need to know if Marlow Bryson's case has a hearing date yet."

Griff whispered, "Great idea. We'll see if Susie is right."

"Oh, it just came in," Nancy proclaimed brightly as if she'd won the lottery.

Brett held up a finger, telling Nancy, "Let me guess. The first hearing is the twenty-third at ten o'clock, before Judge Ginsburg."

"Hey, wait," Nancy sputtered. "This message arrived five minutes ago. Do you have a camera installed above my desk?"

"Seriously?" Brett countered.

"Yup, five minutes ago, the clerk's office sent the notice to us and Jeffrey Shields, the defense attorney. You DEA guys never cease to amaze me. Anything else?"

"That's it. Thanks." Brett hit the end button.

Griff slapped an open hand on the table. "Eva's spot-on. Boss, we didn't tell you before, but we suspect Susie set up a bribe from

Darin Hilton and she was supposed to get a bunch of money from Hilton's sister, Jennifer Tuttle."

"And the video reveals Susie gave Marlow the hearing date before the prosecutor or his attorney knew," Brett said, his eyes darting to Eva's. "This is fantastic evidence."

"Against who?" she asked.

Sosa Garcia stayed unusually quiet. At last their boss stood. The way his lips drooped, Eva thought he looked like he'd been sucker punched.

"I can see it no other way," Sosa said. "It appears Judge Ginsburg is dirty. You three get busy briefing Patrick pronto."

He started to leave, and stopped in the doorway to glare at the group. "I'd better not learn any of you instructed John Lapp to go searching for this evidence."

"No way, boss," Eva objected, leaping to her feet. "I suspect he's snooping because he's still employed there and is determined to see justice for Marlow because he's selling falsely-labeled organic food."

"You'd better be right," Sosa snapped, leaving the agents to confer.

Eva stood with her hands on her hips. "Here we go again, you guys. I provide evidence for your cases, and meanwhile, my handcuffs grow rustier by the day."

Chapter 38

Days passed. Eva and her fellow task force agents tracked terror suspects, and even made a preemptory arrest of a radical who threatened to burn the house of a federal official who lived near Eva, which put her on edge. On the morning of the twenty-third, the instant Brett left for Marlow's hearing before Judge Reginald Ginsburg, Eva sailed into Griff's cubicle.

"Should we dash to the hearing and check if the judge is wearing a bowtie?" Eva asked, her eyebrows arched.

"I assumed we were."

She immediately grabbed her big purse, and on the way out, told him, "I don't want Marlow or Cora to see me."

"Your friend will probably be in the courtroom," Griff said, opening his car doors with a fob. "Why not look through the small window in the courtroom door?"

Eva buckled her seatbelt with a snap. "Super idea. You go in and get a sense of how things are going."

Twenty minutes later, the two federal agents were greeted by court security officers and waved around the metal detectors. They ran up the steps to Ginsburg's courtroom so Eva wouldn't bump into Cora. They walked in silence to the courtroom door where Griff peered through the window. Eva elbowed him, demanding her turn.

"Shhh," he whispered. "There's Marlow sitting with his back to us."

Eva edged beside Griff. He moved slightly to let her peek through the small window on the adjoining door. She saw Patrick sitting in his wheelchair, and he was addressing the judge. Eva's eyes flew to the judge's neckwear.

"Ginsburg's slouching," she hissed. "I can't see if he has on a blue bowtie."

Finally, the judge straightened his back. Eva elbowed her partner.

"Griff, do you see what I see?"

"I see his bowtie all right," he grunted.

Adrenaline surged through Eva. "Ginsburg's got on a blue and white polka dot bowtie," she whispered, "just as Susie told Marlow he would be."

"He's letting Marlow know he wants his cash." Griff sounded disgusted. "Brett must be going crazy sitting there."

"Yeah, he has more than a drug smuggling case now," Eva said, contempt washing over her like dirty water.

Griff stepped away from the door. "I've seen enough. I can't make out any polka dots, but I'm sure Brett can. I don't need to go inside."

He rubbed his hands together as if looking forward to nailing a crooked judge.

Eva pulled her cell phone from her purse. "Hold on. I'm taking his picture."

"Why didn't I think of that?" Griff replied, giving her plenty of room.

"We came a long way to examine his tie." Eva smiled. "I'm not leaving without proof."

She expertly held her phone up to the window and snapped a few photos using the cell's volume button.

"Griff, let's beat it before the U.S. Marshal sees us hanging out by the window."

They hustled down the hall and sprinted down the stairway. When they reached the sidewalk outside, Eva stopped to catch her breath before telling Griff, "This feels like a giant corruption case with many tentacles. How far and wide will it go?"

ONCE THE JUDGE LEFT the bench and the hearing was adjourned, Brett Calloway followed Patrick's wheelchair from the courtroom, his mind ablaze over Ginsburg's blue bowtie. He needed to tell Patrick about Marlow's bribery scheme right away. But how to convey such a weighty matter with a crowd around?

Brett was about to ask Patrick to go into a side room when a tall stranger in a business suit approached them in the hallway, and said, "Patrick, Judge Ginsburg wants to meet you in his chambers."

He jabbed a bent thumb at Brett. "You and the DEA agent."

"Forgive me, Brett." Patrick looked up at him. "Vernon Bontrager is our U.S. Marshal. Vernon, Brett Calloway is the DEA agent assigned to the Bryson case."

Brett shook Vernon's hand, knowing he had been appointed by the President as the U.S. Marshal, and supervised the deputy marshals who worked at the federal court serving subpoenas, making arrests, and jailing prisoners.

The U.S. Marshal motioned them to follow him down the hall. Brett looked at Patrick with raised eyebrows as if asking a silent question. Patrick shrugged his shoulders in a silent response. Brett felt he had no choice but to comply.

The trio entered the judge's reception area where a secretary instantly brought them to his chamber door.

"Go in, gentlemen. He's waiting for you."

Never having been in a judge's private chambers before, the

spaciousness impressed Brett. Seascape paintings and diplomas adorned every wall as did photos of the judge with past as well as the current President of the United States.

Ginsburg wasted no time walking from behind his desk, and with an extended hand, said, "Brett Calloway, I assume? Your name is on the arrest warrant."

"Yes, Your Honor," Brett replied, and with politeness he didn't feel, shook his hand.

The judge motioned for him to sit in one of two carved wooden armchairs, which were placed strategically in front of his desk, allowing room for Patrick's wheelchair.

"I asked the marshal to summon you for an important reason," Ginsburg said from behind his colossal mahogany desk.

Brett had never seen Ginsburg without a robe, and was distracted by how prominent the judge's blue and white bow tie shone against his white dress shirt. The sight of that glaring tie, and being commanded by the judge to meet in his chambers, unnerved Brett. He stiffened on the expensive chair.

The whole thing reeked and didn't sit well with Brett. At least the AUSA was here and would witness whatever shenanigans the judge concocted. Tension mounted. Brett waited for Ginsburg to quit poring over a file.

At last the judge looked up, and tenting his hands, he said in an unwavering voice, "My request is unusual. Perhaps I should provide background. Bryson is the first drug case I've had in a year. I have an aversion to them, and of late, I struggle with whether I should recuse myself from hearing any."

He paused. Brett pressed his lips together and kept staring at the blue and white polka-dotted bowtie. He wanted to shout, "You're corrupt, buddy, and need to go!"

Instead, he sat there fuming.

"As you know," Ginsburg began fumbling with a stapler on the desk, "I lost my wife to cancer nearly four years ago. During her illness, our daughter, Heather, became involved with a loser named Ricky Que. As often happens, our disapproval of him drove her into his arms. They married and her life began to descend."

Brett sensed Marshal Bontrager squirming beside him as the judge nodded to him.

Ginsburg continued, "Vernon knows the account I'm about to reveal. He first brought it to my attention. Shortly after my wife's funeral, the Fairfax police stopped Ricky for a traffic violation and discovered his outstanding arrest warrant for a bad check. The police ordered him and my daughter from the car. During a search, the police found user quantities of heroin on Ricky and some on the ground near where my daughter stood on the passenger side. Heather threatened the officers, using my name and position."

Bontrager turned slightly and explained to Patrick and Brett, "I managed to suppress any damage to this court, but Fairfax County charged Ricky with the heroin. None was found on Heather, so she wasn't charged."

Brett's mind whirled over what he was hearing. Of course, he couldn't take notes, so he concentrated on making copious mental notes.

The judge dropped the stapler onto the desk with a clatter. "I'm embarrassed the marshal had to get involved and am thankful he did. Heather divorced Ricky and moved back home with me. Though it's a challenge, I think it's helped. She has assumed her mother's role. She cooks her mother's specialties and keeps me eating healthy.

"She buys my clothes and suggests what I should wear," the judge continued, adjusting his bowtie. "Occasionally, she even insists I change up to these silly bowties."

Brett blinked. Did he hear correctly?

He stared at the judge who again grasped the small stapler. Could the Susie behind eliciting a bribe from Marlow Bryson be the judge's daughter, Heather Que? Brett forced himself to focus on everything else Ginsburg was saying.

"I find her mothering a bit stifling, and it's more than I can abide. I try to be patient because I don't want to drive Heather from my life and into the streets."

The judge's eyes drifted to a framed photograph on his desk. "Recently, my clerk told me Heather was planning my nightly meals and needed to know what was coming up on my court calendar. I feel uncomfortable with her interest, especially since I've been assigned to the Bryson drug case. This brings me to my request. First, I'd like what I've told you to remain confidential."

A forlorn look struck the judge's face as he gazed at his audience of three. All three men nodded in reply, with Patrick saying, "You have our sympathy and assurance, Your Honor."

"Secondly, if you become aware of any reason why I shouldn't hear this or any other drug case, confide in me so I can consider recusing myself," Ginsburg said, holding Brett's gaze before dropping his eyes.

Again, Patrick interjected, "Sir, I respect your caution. If Agent Calloway has any such reason, he'll share it with me and I'll alert you."

Marshal Bontrager and Brett bobbed their heads in agreement. "Fine." Ginsburg stood. "Thank you for your time."

Brett and Patrick hurriedly left the office while Marshal Bontrager stayed chatting with the secretary. The prosecutor and agent entered an empty elevator. Brett waited for the doors to close before turning to Patrick.

He exhaled the pent-up strain. "I planned to tell you immediately after Bryson's hearing. Eva received new evidence impacting the case. Given the judge's impromptu briefing, we need to discuss it at your office or the task force pronto."

"Is tomorrow morning at the task force soon enough?" Patrick asked, his glittering eyes divulging his concern.

"Make it eight o'clock," Brett decided. "I'll have everyone there."

Chapter 39

Eva pulled into the JTTF parking lot at seven thirty the next morning plenty early. She simmered over Brett's phone call last night, and wanted to be first to uncover what he was up to.

All he'd said was, "Emergency meeting with Patrick at eight a.m. Bring your recent video of Susie and Marlow," before hanging up to call Griff.

His gruff manner made Eva hungry to know more. She walked into the office where the scent of brewed coffee assailed her nose. Someone had arrived before she did. Loud voices down the hall beckoned her to get moving.

Eva rushed with her laptop into the conference room where Brett, Patrick O'Rourke, and Sosa were gathering. She snagged an empty seat.

Griff hurried in, saying, "Wait for me."

"Patrick and I met with Judge Ginsburg yesterday after the Bryson hearing, and *peculiar* is one word to describe it," Brett intoned, shutting the door behind him. "Before we get to that, I'd like Eva to play the latest message she received from her tipster, John Lapp."

Eva held up a hand. "Wait. First, tell me if the judge wore a blue bowtie with white polka dots and why your meeting was so unusual."

"Yes, he wore that exact bowtie," Brett replied, sounding riled. "Patrick will explain what happened afterwards once we all see your video."

"Fair enough."

Eva set her laptop to play. The voice recording of Susie and Marlow's cryptic Firewire conference was familiar to all in the room except Patrick. Eva observed him closely, and he seemed to be listening intently.

When the conversation about paying off the judge ended, she stopped the recording, saying, "Patrick, the digital audio is actually a video feed, but both Susie and Marlow turned off their cameras."

"Why am I hearing of this now, *after* yesterday's hearing?" Patrick demanded.

Brett looked at Sosa, who nodded for him to answer. "When we first heard the video, we had doubts. Plus, we didn't want to put you in a position of needing to act until we knew if the judge wore a blue bowtie yesterday."

"Out with it," Eva intervened. "Why did Ginsburg want to meet?"

Patrick snapped opened his legal folder on the table as if

irritated to be caught off guard. Eva knew she and Griff had another confession to make, but would wait to find out what happened behind closed doors with the judge.

"I made notes after our talk in his chambers," Patrick said. "He's concerned because his daughter Heather Que is living with him and telling him what to do."

"And that warrants a secret conference with a federal judge?" Eva snapped.

"Eva, you're interrupting my explanation," Patrick said, sounding testy. "Three years ago, Heather was arrested with her then-husband for heroin possession. Heroin was found near Heather's feet, but she wasn't charged. Ginsburg wanted us to advise him of issues related to drug cases. Eva, that video is worse than I imagined."

Brett jumped in. "Since Heather moved into the judge's house, she's taken over for her mother who died. She buys his clothes and tells him what to wear. He confided she picked out his bowtie yesterday."

"Heather could be Susie." Griff's voice exuded frustration. "I was beginning to think Ginsburg was crooked. I'm relieved it's his daughter, because I respect his judicial integrity."

"What? Have you gone soft, Griff?" Eva challenged.

Met with silence from her partner, she lit into them all. "Listen, I think Judge Ginsburg's covering his behind. He must have concocted a scheme to take a bribe using his daughter out front. Now he's come up with a fake story, throwing blame on his daughter in case we're on to him."

"You make a fair point, one that crosses my mind," Patrick conceded, raising a hand in the air. "Brett, tell us your impression of Ginsburg's comments yesterday."

Brett's eyes flashed. "Eva, this time you're wrong. You didn't see the pained look in his eyes and hear the hurt in his voice. I was so affected by what he said, he almost had me crying. It would take a skilled sociopath to tell his convincing story if he's trying to cover up his involvement in a criminal act. I believe him."

"I hate to end this love fest." Eva's voice rose. "Last night I received another message between Marlow and the same woman, who we now suspect is Heather Que. She's demanding the million dollars based on Judge Ginsburg's performance yesterday."

"The gift that never stops giving," Griff chimed.

Eva switched on the digital file, and the Firewire App appeared on her screen. No video showed the participants, but their voices were the same as the previous digital voice message Eva just played. The group listened to the new recording:

"Hello, Marlow. It's Susie."

"Why am I not surprised to hear from you tonight?" he growled.

"I said I'd get back after your hearing. Did you see the signal I promised from the judge?"

"How could I miss his blue bowtie with white polka dots?" Marlow asked sarcastically. "He kept twisting it between his fingers."

Susie's chuckle sounded like breaking glass. "I trust you're satisfied. He had to shop around for the exact tie you requested."

"Is there a timeline for Judge Ginsburg to work this out?"

"It goes like this," Susie declared. "You deliver the sum we've agreed to this coming Monday. Then, your lawyer files your motion for a bench trial, and it will be granted. At the end of your trial, the judge will find you not guilty. I warn you, it will do no good unless the judge receives the money we spoke of."

Marlow sighed. "Do I bring the cash to his office?"

"Don't be a wise guy. This is serious. Deliver it to *me* at the Red Dragon Restaurant in Alexandria, one thirty p.m. Monday."

"How will I know you?"

"I'll be sitting alone, with my blond hair in a ponytail, sunglasses on top of my head. I'm slim and nice-looking, if I do say so myself. Put the cash in stacks of hundreds and in a strong shopping bag. The judge will send me to collect the money. Likewise, you can send a messenger with your package."

"That's all? Do I get a receipt?"

"There you go again, Marlow. Running your mouth when you should use your brain. Just verify who I am and leave the cash. We don't need to know anything about each other."

"I don't like your arrangement," he grumbled.

"You don't have to," came her sharp reply. "Consider the alternative. If you're a no-show, you'd better get your affairs in order, 'cause you'll be sent to prison for a long while."

"Monday at one thirty, Red Dragon in Alexandria," he repeated. "See you there."

"Good choice," Susie said.

The call ended.

Reaching over to retrieve her computer, Eva flashed Patrick a penetrating look. "I intend to investigate this further. It may be delicate, but I don't care one whit if she's a federal judge's daughter."

"And I say we can't continue relying on tips from John Lapp if he's unwilling to be identified." Patrick folded his arms and glared at Eva.

Her boss tossed in his two cents. "Hold on. You both raise

legitimate concerns."

"I have an idea," Griff interjected. "The FBI's surveillance squad could start tailing Heather and Marlow between now and Monday. We should be able to track where Marlow gets his money to pay her. The FBI squad can follow them to the meeting."

"Yeah," Brett piped in. "The squad's unbelievable and absolutely undetectable. They use drones and undercover agents on foot."

"Here's another possibility." Eva spread her hands on the table. "We delay Heather, aka Susie Q … Hey, that name works since her last name is Que. We stop her from reaching the meeting on time. We insert our own blonde in the Red Dragon and Marlow delivers the money to her."

Patrick nodded vigorously. "Eva, I applaud your idea. You could be the blonde. Susie sounded like she was describing you."

"No way." Eva shook her head. "I know Marlow's wife, Cora."

Her partner rolled his eyes and grilled, "Did you meet Marlow when you were with his wife?"

"No," she admitted. "He was at the event I planned, but left before I arrived."

Brett quickly reminded, "Eva, you worked undercover with Griff and me."

She shut her computer, unwilling to commit to work undercover on a whim.

Griff spoke up again. "Patrick, let us finalize a plan. We'll prepare a search warrant affidavit. If Marlow delivers the money and we arrest him and Susie Q, we'll search his home and office. If we seize his computers, our experts will find the hidden digital files, which we then use in court. We won't need John Lapp."

"Couldn't have said it better myself," Eva quipped.

Sosa and Brett both echoed their agreement.

Patrick looked thoughtful scratching notes on his pad, and said, "I'll find a different court and judge to sign our search warrant since it will contain Ginsburg's daughter's name. Meanwhile, try to protect the judge's reputation as he appears to be an innocent victim. You all, including the surveillance squad, be discrete."

"Patrick, you need to know Susie has done this before," Eva said, looking hard at Griff. "Darin Hilton's sister, Jennifer Tuttle, told us of a similar bribery scheme against Ginsburg perpetuated by a woman named Susie."

Griff took over, explaining how Jennifer paid $500,000 to a woman named Sue, and added, "Eva and I believe an innocent woman, a single mom with kids who lunches at the Red Dragon, ended up with Hilton's bribe."

The prosecutor's eyes bulged. Eva and Griff spent a good chunk of the morning straightening things out. In the end, Patrick agreed with their desire for justice.

"If we get the goods on Susie in this case, we shouldn't have to dredge up the former case, but no promises," Patrick replied, stowing the file in his briefcase. "Susan Brockman may have to surrender the money."

Eva didn't argue, but voiced her disagreement with Patrick's caution about the judge's reputation. She stayed mum about her plan to let the chips fall. Later that night, Eva went to the Lord in prayer asking for His perfect justice to be revealed.

MONDAY AT NOON, the task force conference room was teeming with preparations for the upcoming money exchange at the Red Dragon. Brett and Griff, along with officers from local police departments, were keyed up and ready to catch Marlow Bryson in his attempt to bribe a federal judge.

Eva strode into the room wearing a white tennis skirt, white sneakers, and blue top. Her blond hair was caught up in a ponytail pulled through the gap in a baseball cap. She perched her sunglasses on top. A tennis racket handle protruded from the large tote tennis bag Eva placed on a chair.

"Call me Susie Q," she said, checking her watch. "Count me pumped and ready to meet Mr. Marlow Bryson, drug smuggler and corrupt businessman."

"You're about to teach Marlow how to play by the rules," Griff offered, pointing to her tennis racket.

Eva smiled. "You've got that right. Any word from the surveillance group?"

"I'm monitoring both teams," Griff said, picking up a portable law enforcement radio. "They're using light aircraft. Marlow remained home all weekend. One team is currently on Marlow's house in Middleburg and the other is staking out the judge's home. No activity at either place."

Brett looked concerned as he powered up his laptop. "That surprises me. By now, Marlow should've left to pick up the money he'll deliver to the Red Dragon."

"You're assuming it's not at his home," Griff replied, arms folded.

"With the dope he's running, it's probable Marlow's sitting on that much cash," Eva said, nodding in agreement. "I'm told his estate is enormous and his office large enough to hide gobs of money without his staff or wife ever finding it."

The radio in Griff's hands sprung to life. A surveillance agent's voice could be heard above a high-pitched whine, "Male subject walking from the main house. Something tucked under his arm. Standby."

"The FBI agent in a plane flying above Marlow's estate says there's a man on the move," Griff announced loudly to the team.

Then the same deep voice returned over the radio, "Subject entering another building ... looks like a detached guesthouse."

"That should be Marlow." Eva gestured at her watch. "He's running late. It will take him an hour to reach the Red Dragon."

Minutes ticked by. The agents and police officers chatted while Eva kept tabs on the time, waiting for the precise moment to leave.

Suddenly word erupted from the aircraft, "Guy's outta the guesthouse. Carrying a large shopping bag. Hold on ... He's in a white SUV."

"I'm typing the affidavit for a warrant to search the estate," Brett declared, his fingers flying along his keyboard. "I'll add info as it develops so we can rush it to the magistrate and get a signature."

The whining radio returned and the agent aboard the aircraft shouted, "Subject turning eastbound on Route 50. Looks like he's heading toward Alexandria."

"Things are unfolding rapidly, people!" Brett rose to address the group. "Eva will leave soon and pose as Susie at the Red Dragon. The FBI's surveillance team will delay Heather aka Susie from getting there until Eva accepts Marlow's delivery of cash and exits with the bribe."

"How can they keep Heather away long enough?" This came from Detective Adler of the Fairfax Police Department, dressed in jeans and a loose-fitting black shirt.

Another officer, Detective Sergeant Lawton from the Alexandria Police Department, spoke up. "Trust me. Our officers are gonna help surveillance deter the suspect for as long as necessary."

"Move on out." Supervisor Sosa Garcia leapt to his feet. "Eva, stay in the Red Dragon's parking lot until we know Heather is actually delayed, or we could have two blond ponytails for Marlow to choose from. Adler and I will conduct undercover surveillance inside the restaurant. The rest of you, remain in the area to arrest Marlow after he's handed Eva the money."

Sosa looked at Brett, asking him, "That's your plan, right?"

"Yeah, and I want everyone's ears glued to the radio traffic," Brett replied, heading to the door, laptop in hand. "This is the tricky part. When Eva scrams from the Red Dragon with the cash, she hands it to Griff, who races in there posing as Marlow's delivery man for Heather's late arrival."

"Good reminder," Sosa said. "Questions, anyone?"

Detective Adler lifted a hand. "How will we know for sure Eva has the money and we have enough probable cause to arrest Marlow, once he's far enough away?"

"Once I have Marlow's money and he can be arrested, I'll remove my sunglasses and ball cap when leaving the restaurant," Eva said. "You should all be able to see that."

Sosa clapped his hands once. "That works, people. We're on channel three. Monitor the surveillance channel so everyone knows where the targets are. Let's go."

He left the conference room. Eva was the first behind him, prayed up and geared up for her afternoon of action. Scott knew she had an undercover operation planned and would be praying for her from his new office at the Pentagon.

She adjusted her ball cap, lowered her sunglasses, and left the JTTF building.

Griff caught up to her. "Knock'em dead, Susie Q. We'll have you well covered."

"You, too, in meeting the real Susie Q," Eva told him, thankful for his support.

Chapter 40

Heather Que served her dad a late breakfast before sending him off to the federal courthouse to do his justice thing. Forty minutes loomed ahead for her to do her justice thing. She smothered a giggle hurrying around her father's house. It was nearly a thirty-minute drive to Alexandria where she'd meet Marlow Bryson at the Red Dragon restaurant. Time to get going.

In the recently remodeled bathroom, which she'd designed, Heather stood before the mirror approving of her appearance. She meant business and looked like it. Yesterday, she'd charged hundreds of dollars on her dad's credit card at a spa and hair salon. After applying more mascara to her lashes, Heather added a dab of lipstick to her lips. There. She smiled. The money she'd spent on her highlights was well worth it.

Heather brushed her smooth blond hair into a ponytail, and straightened the beige silk blouse beneath the jacket of a black business suit. Off to the races.

In her red Chrysler convertible with a tan top, she wound her way to the Capital Beltway, accelerating hard toward Alexandria. The increased speed fueled her unsettled nerves. That would never do. Too bad the last time she'd agreed to meet a court defendant at the Red Dragon the guy never showed up.

It was imperative this new plan succeed, no matter a past failure. Her entire future teetered on a highwire. Heather exited the interstate and forced herself not to go over the speed limit. Another giggle escaped her red lips. Marlow Bryson seemed hungrier than Hilton did, and she felt confident he'd show up for the payoff.

Heather was within a mile of the restaurant and beginning her left turn onto Duke Street when suddenly the traffic light turned yellow. No way she was stopping. She stepped on the gas. At that exact moment, the woman driver in front of her slammed on her brakes. Heather screeched to a stop just in time.

A horrible thing happened next. The crazy woman ahead of her put her car in reverse and smashed right into Heather's brand-new convertible. She tried backing up. The car behind her plowed into the rear of her car. Heather was due at the restaurant in seven minutes. Now she was stuck.

She bolted from her car, furious. The young man in the car behind her took off running through traffic and disappeared between two buildings. She stared at her crushed bumper, not believing her lousy luck. She must be at the Red Dragon for that money or her life would be ruined!

Heather spun and faced the woman who'd just backed into her.

"What a stupid boneheaded move!" Heather screamed at the woman.

The other driver stepped closer. "Are you hurt?"

"What about my new car?" Heather snapped and sped to check the front end.

This bumper was dented in even worse than the back and covered in ugly scratches. What a fiasco. Heather needed to escape right away.

Not wanting to escalate the incident, she tried calming her nerves and told the woman driver, "I'm okay. The damage isn't too bad on your car or mine."

The woman pointed to where the third driver had fled. "What's up with that weirdo?"

"He's driving without a license or drunk," Heather said, lifting her proud chin.

The woman's shoulders drooped. "I'm heading to the doctor, but we need to exchange our drivers' licenses and stuff."

"Forget that nonsense." Heather motioned to the front bumper. "Though you rammed into me, the damage is light. I'm willing to forget it so we can both leave."

Without warning, an Alexandria police car roared up beside Heather's car, its lights flashing. A uniformed officer talking into a microphone rolled down his window and asked, "I saw a guy running across the street. Did he crash into your car?"

Both women nodded.

"Don't leave the scene," he ordered. "I'll be back."

The officer's siren shrieked as he zoomed around the three cars, and blasted down the street. Two other police cars with lights and sirens blaring joined the chase of the fleeing driver.

Hands on her hips, Heather faced the other lady. "I'm late for a meeting. We have no injuries and little damage. We should just leave."

"Oh no!" The woman's eyes widened with worry. "You heard the officer. I'm not getting busted for leaving the scene of an accident, not when a cop tells me to stay."

Heather huffed and puffed to no avail. She even tried pushing the car behind her. It wouldn't budge. The guy had put it in park and taken the keys. She tried reasoning with the woman. Heather's quest for a million dollars had just come to a screeching halt. What was she going to do?

TWO FBI AIRCRAFT FLEW TIGHT COORDINATED PATTERNS over Alexandria, and Eva waited impatiently for Marlow in a booth at the Red Dragon. She fiddled with the tennis tote beside her on the torn padded vinyl bench, and adjusted the sunglasses on the ball cap. She'd already ordered two spring rolls and hot tea, which were now a distant memory.

Eva plunked down the tiny cup thinking Marlow got cold feet. It wasn't like she could call him and say, "Where are you?"

She was considering every option when Sosa sauntered out from the men's room and passed by her booth, tapping his earbud. He nodded to the entrance. Eva's mind went on extreme alert. Sosa must mean surveillance had reported Marlow was in the parking lot. The ruse to delay Heather must have worked.

Just then, a tall man wearing business casual pushed open the front door. He looked like the photo on Marlow's website, but older. Eva observed his eyes sweeping the restaurant. His gaze fell upon her, and his eyes narrowed a fraction. He headed straight for Eva's booth.

"Is your name Susie?" he spat, his voice a low growl.

"Yes," Eva smiled. "It is."

"Do you have a last name?" he asked.

He started to sit down in her booth and Eva flashed a fierce glare. "You can call me Susie Q, but don't sit down here."

"Do you have something for me?" she asked, gesturing to his shopping bag.

"You're expecting this." He slid the bag toward Eva.

"Perfect." She beamed a wide smile to signal their deal was complete.

To her frustration, Marlow didn't leave. He kept talking, asking, "What now? How will I know—"

"Quit talking," Eva interrupted. "We're done here."

She stood and hurried to the hostess station, carrying the heavy shopping bag and her tennis tote. Eva paid her bill in cash. Marlow slipped past her and walked out. She told the hostess to keep the change for the server's tip, and gripping two bags in one hand, she removed her ball cap and sunglasses. Phase 2 had begun.

SOSA GARCIA AND DETECTIVE SERGEANT LAWTON scrambled into Garcia's government-issued sedan in time to see Eva stride from the restaurant. She held a shopping bag in one hand, which should be full of cash. Sosa saw Eva use her free hand to shove her sunglasses and ball cap into the tote bag slung over her shoulder. She walked toward her undercover car.

"Get ready to act," Sosa told Detective Lawton.

Then the group's radio crackled and Griff gave a play-by-play: "Susie's taken off her cap and glasses ... Suspect left the Dragon ... Hold on ... he's in the parking lot ... I think he's holding back to follow Susie and his money."

"Eva better wait," Sosa told Lawton and keyed the microphone. "Eva, stay put. Surveillance needs time to clean off your tail. Then you and your partner meet quickly and exchange the money bag."

Sosa saw Eva in the undercover car and she appeared to be talking on her cell phone.

In a few minutes, he and Lawton heard a surveillance officer say, "Agent Montanna, you can leave now. Exit the far end of the parking lot."

Eva followed the command and drove out of the parking lot.

"Bingo!" Sosa told Lawton. "Marlow is following her. If things fall apart, he wants to reach Susie Q and even the score."

Eva made a left turn. Marlow sped toward the exit, then slowed slightly and looked left as if judging her speed and direction. He accelerated from the lot, and at that moment, Marlow slammed into a young man on a skateboard.

The guy smashed into Marlow's front passenger fender, and slid across the hood, his helmeted head lying on Marlow's windshield, almost eye to eye.

Sosa could hear Griff calling Eva on the radio, telling her, "Your tail's clean for now. Turn right at the next corner. I'll meet you two blocks down. We'd better hustle."

The radio fell silent. Lawton asked Sosa, "Is that a surveillance agent on the skateboard, tangling with the suspect?"

"Brilliant, right?" Sosa chuckled. "Look how he stands by Marlow rubbing his shoulders and yelling. Next, he'll threaten to sue him."

Sosa and Lawton watched. The two men walked around Marlow's SUV, looking for damage. The undercover agent started punching on his cell phone.

"Yup," Lawton grunted. "He's threatening to call the police."

They watched Marlow yank out his wallet. After giving the agent money, he shoved the wallet in his back pocket.

"Ha ha," Sosa laughed. "The agent isn't backing down. He's rubbing his knees like they're broken."

Marlow looked devastated and threw up his arms while the agent kept arguing with him. Lawton was laughing so hard he was holding his stomach.

"Uh oh, here it comes," Sosa said, enjoying the scene playing out, and knowing Eva and Griff should be exchanging the money about now.

Marlow peeled off more money from his wallet and handed a thicker wad to the agent. Finally, the imposter picked up his skateboard and coasted down the sidewalk, kicking his foot for speed as if nothing had happened to him.

Sosa keyed the microphone, telling the team, "Subject's back in his car. Once he arrives home, take him down. Secure everything until the search warrant arrives."

Chapter 41

While traffic zipped by Heather's minor fender bender, she checked her watch. She was twelve minutes late. This would be her second disaster at the Red Dragon. She absolutely needed Bryson's money today, or she would be in serious trouble.

Suddenly, with no apparent reason, the woman who had backed into her approached Heather. "I'm sick of waiting for the cop. If you agree, let's leave."

"My thoughts exactly," Heather replied, lifting her hand, palm out.

They traded high-fives.

The woman wrinkled her nose. "We each take care of our own damage?"

"Absolutely."

Heather waved and darted to her car.

The green arrow lit, and both women raced from the accident scene, leaving behind the empty car. Heather could care less about her car's crumpled bumpers. Once she got her hands onto Marlow's cash, she'd buy a new car more to her liking.

She sped directly to the Red Dragon and scurried inside, scarcely breathing. She'd seen a picture of the CEO on his website and she looked around expectantly. Heather's hopes were dashed. She didn't spot him anywhere in the tiny restaurant. The hostess walked toward her as did a tall well-dressed man sporting a trimmed moustache.

"Are you Susie?" He raised thick eyebrows and stared at her.

She paused long enough to calculate whether Marlow sent a runner. Deciding he had, Heather answered, "That's me."

"Good," he replied, his smile genuine. "I've been waiting for you. Why not join me in my booth?"

He walked to the back, near the kitchen. Because the professional-looking man seemed like someone who worked for Marlow, she followed, every muscle tense.

They neared a booth. Heather spied a large shopping bag with string handles.

Relief cascaded through her. She was saved!

"For me?" She pointed to the bag.

The man eyed her intently. "It depends. Who did you expect to meet here?"

"Marlow Bryson," was all she said.

"In that case, Susie," the man said, picking up the bag and

handing it to her, "this is for you and I've accomplished my task."

He snatched up his check and went up front to pay. Heather clung on to the shopping bag, her lifeline. Walking around the man, she left the restaurant.

Back in her car, Heather tore open a corner of the bag. She inserted her manicured hand and pulled out a stack of one-hundred-dollar bills. A funny thing happened. She began to giggle and couldn't stop. Finally, something was going as she planned!

Heather reached over and patted the bag, feeling happy for the first time in forever.

THE VOICE OF FAIRFAX COUNTY Detective Adler crackled over Sosa's radio. He asked him, "Boss, did anyone check to see if another police agency's working this case?"

Sosa looked around the Red Dragon parking lot and didn't spot Adler. The answer he gave sounded tentative to his own ears. "I'm not sure. Why?"

"When Susie had her little accident a bit ago, I saw a guy in a black VW Jetta two cars ahead of her," Adler explained. "He parked across the intersection while she was waiting on the police. He's in the Jetta at the Dragon parking lot now."

Sosa grunted into the radio, "That sounds bad. Can you read his plate?"

"Yup. I just requested a 10-28. Should know who owns that plate real soon."

Sosa keyed his mic again. "Good job. I don't see any other surveillance around."

"License just came back," Adler gushed. "The VW is registered to Ricky Que. Dispatch says he has an arrest record for drugs."

"Bingo!" Sosa hollered. "That's gotta be Susie Q's ex-hubby and her accomplice, doing his own counter-surveillance. The plot thickens."

"10-4," Adler responded. "Maybe he's here to make sure his lady isn't robbed."

"Or maybe to ensure she doesn't take off with the money. Stick with him. Arrest Ricky when we grab Susie," Sosa ordered.

HEATHER LOOKED ALL AROUND the Red Dragon's parking lot. Everything looked clear. Wanting to be careful with such a huge amount of cash in her car, she slowly pulled from the parking lot. Heather saw Bryson's courier leaving the restaurant. He didn't once look her way. Good.

She drove the same way back toward the Beltway, making sure

to obey the speed limit. The light turned red. Heather slammed on the brakes, realizing this was the same traffic light where she'd had her accident. Ugh!

She snugged up real close to the car ahead of her. That car suddenly backed into her crushed bumper. Not again! Before Heather could react, the car behind ran into her back bumper!

This intersection was jinxed. Why hadn't she gone a different route home? It was too late now.

Heather tossed the money bag to the floor and tried smashing it up under the passenger seat. Two men hopped out of the car in front and walked toward her. She instantly locked her doors and lowered her window a tad.

In her rearview mirror, she glimpsed Bryson's courier and a blond woman wearing a tennis outfit rush up from the car behind her.

Heather opened her mouth to scream for help. Then she saw the four would-be robbers each hold up something glittering in the sunlight. She slumped back in her seat and shut her mouth. There was no escape. All four flashed their gold badges.

The blond woman with a ponytail like Heather's reached her door and exclaimed, "We're federal agents. Heather Que, you are under arrest. Step out of the car."

Heather resisted. She would not surrender. She sat glaring at the woman and man crowding her driver's door and at the two men hovering by the passenger door.

The courier with the moustache yelled, "Come on, Heather. Open the door or we'll break out your windows."

She ground her teeth. Marlow Bryson had set her up for an arrest. He would be sorry. She'd make doubly sure of that. What choice did she have but to comply, and fight back later with all her might? Her dad being a federal judge should make a difference in her case. It had before and would again. No way Daddy would see her sink to the bottom.

HEATHER UNLOCKED THE DOOR, and Eva swung it open. She began dragging Heather from the car with her seatbelt still fastened. Eva released the seatbelt and pulled Heather's hands behind her back in one swift motion. She snapped on steel cuffs, and holding her arm, walked the arrestee to Eva's government car.

"You can't do this to me!" Heather sputtered, trying to yank her arm away.

No one responded to her outburst. Detective Adler was standing alongside Eva's G-car with an unknown male in handcuffs.

Eva stopped in her tracks.

Holding firmly onto Heather's arm, she demanded, "Detective, who is he?"

"Meet Heather's accomplice and ex-husband, Ricky Que. He's been shadowing her, keeping an eye on the money."

Heather squirmed and burst out, "Ricky, I—"

"Shut up!" he ordered.

Ah, Eva saw all clearly. Ricky Que was part of the extortion plan from the beginning and probably the brains behind the scheme. Something akin to fear blazed through Heather's eyes. Eva filed away her panicky look as she escorted the crying woman into the backseat, buckling her in tight.

"Heather," Eva said, keeping her voice low. "You're arrested for soliciting a bribe and extortion. You have a right to remain silent. Anything you say can and will be used against you in court. You have the right to an attorney and to have the attorney present when we talk to you. If you can't afford an attorney, one will be appointed to help you. Do you understand?"

Heather blinked back tears lingering on her lashes and nodded.

Eva told her, "I want to hear you say yes or no. Do you understand?"

Heather's voice cracked, "Ye-es."

"Ricky is being told the same thing. Do you understand?"

"I do, and wished I didn't," she croaked, slumping against the seat. "Do you know who my father is?"

Eva considered the implications of the question before answering, "We do. I suspect he'll be disappointed to hear about your arrest. You won't receive any special treatment because of his position. Lady Justice wears a blindfold for a reason."

Heather began to whimper loudly. Eva closed the car door, wondering if anyone had notified Judge Ginsburg. She'd leave that unenviable task to others.

Eva straightened, and turning to Detective Adler, told him, "Transport Ricky and we'll book them together. Oh, Adler ..."

She waited until the detective placed his suspect in the rear seat of his unmarked car and beckoned him over.

"You all did great," Eva said, meaning it. "Thank your uniform guys for chasing the FBI agent who rammed Heather's car. Their delaying her at the intersection and preventing her from reaching the Red Dragon too soon was perfectly executed. Bravo."

She began to walk away and turned back. "Adler. We'll be going silent on the radio with these prisoners."

"Right," he responded before entering his car.

Chapter 42

Eva reached under her dash, hitting the switch to silence her radio and prevent Heather from hearing the agents following Marlow. Heather's moans and groans on the way to the slammer didn't faze Eva. She was used to criminals being sorry, not for their misdeeds, but because they were caught.

"The handcuffs are too tight," Heather blubbered. "I can't feel my hands."

Eva felt zero pity for the judge's lawless daughter. She pulled up to the JTTF building where Griff had opened the overhead door. Eva pulled into the prisoner sally port to Heather's cries in the backseat.

"Keep me from Ricky! He's trouble. I should have listened to my dad!"

Eva ignored her outbursts, and along with Griff, took her into the elevator to their floor before locking her into a holding cell. The perp's face was streaked with tears and mascara. Eva then hurried to call AUSA Patrick O'Rourke from her cubicle.

He answered immediately saying, "Brett's here, finishing the search warrant affidavit for Marlow's estate. He told me of Ricky Que's involvement. The judge feared he'd continue to be a bad influence on his daughter."

"I've just been advised our agents arrested Marlow the second he arrived home," Eva explained. "They secured his office, home, and guesthouse, and will begin searching once they know the warrant is signed."

Patrick said Brett would head to Marlow's Middleburg estate with the signed search warrant soon.

"We have a problem," Eva replied, "One only you can remedy."

"I figured things were going too smoothly," Patrick growled.

Eva's energy level began to tank as she said, "Ginsburg needs to be told Heather's under arrest. I'm shoving that onto your plate, Patrick, like my young son does with mushrooms he doesn't like."

"Just so you know, I avoid mushrooms like the plague." Patrick also sounded weary. "As much as I hate bringing him the bad news, I'll alert Ginsburg at once. He must recuse himself from the Bryson case."

Eva vowed to grab coffee at her first chance. Meantime, she popped a peppermint in her mouth before telling Patrick, "Which brings me to Heather and Ricky's arraignments."

Griff waltzed into her cubicle, setting a cup of coffee on her desk. "Thank you," she mouthed as he went to bring over his chair.

"Patrick, Griff is here, so you're on the speaker," she said. "The arrestees will both be lodged at the Alexandria City Jail tonight."

The prosecutor agreed to ring the chief judge to see how he wanted to proceed and told the agents, "We're plowing new ground here, Eva and Griff."

Eva posed another issue. "We'll process the Ques and bring them before the U.S. magistrate in the morning. Because they'll be charged in her father's courthouse along with Marlow, who's still one of Ginsburg's defendants, it's sure to create a news frenzy."

"It's going public eventually," the AUSA said, his voice taut. "I'd like the evidence to be in our hands before that happens."

Griff leaned toward the phone. "You should ask the court to revoke Marlow's bond since he attempted to bribe the judge while on bond."

"Yes!" Patrick replied as if suddenly invigorated. "Already in my notes."

Eva ended the call. Thankful for the coffee, she enjoyed a delicious sip.

Griff rose and lingered a moment, saying, "Ricky and Heather are in separate holding cells. We need to give them food and bathroom breaks."

"Has he said anything?" Eva asked. "Between her tears, Heather is blaming him."

"Not one word from Ricky. He's glowering and looking disgusted. He should've thought about landing back in prison before launching such a hairbrained scheme."

Griff left with his chair, giving Eva time to collect her thoughts. Scott needed to know she'd wrapped up her undercover role with several arrests. His voicemail clicked on and she left a warm message, asking him to call her. He did within the hour.

Scott sounded out of breath. "After hearing your message, I rushed home, fed the kids pizza for supper, and am back at the Pentagon."

"Whew, you're the best," Eva said with feeling. "Is Kaley home with the boys?"

"They were all playing a board game when I left."

His mentioning pizza made Eva realize she was starving. "I'll be busy until after we lodge our prisoners in Alexandria. I'll phone Kaley and let her know when to expect me. Why are you back at work, or can't you tell me?"

"I can only say I'll get home after you. Remember, I love you," he echoed before saying good-bye.

"Love you too."

Eva set down her cell phone as her boss stepped into her cubicle to give her the latest report on the Bryson estate.

Sosa wore an unusual grin. "The searching began the moment the warrant was signed. Agents seized his computers and guess what else?"

"China Girl?"

"Close, but not quite." Sosa's grin beamed a mile wide. "Hidden beneath a false bottom in a kitchen cupboard at the guesthouse, they seized bundles of one-hundred-dollar bills. They're nearly done counting the money. Guess how much they found?"

"You're forcing my mind to work overtime," Eva said, playing along. "Let's see, a million dollars?"

"They just passed twelve million!" Sosa announced proudly. "All because of Paul Revere. Can you imagine it, Eva? Your guy deserves a medal."

She gulped. "Wow! Twelve million dollars in cash hidden in his guesthouse? That load of fentanyl the agents grabbed on our lookout obviously wasn't his first. He's a major dealer."

"Exactly," Sosa declared. "We owe it all to crank texts to your cell phone. We've collared the kingpin, and will turn the rest over to DEA while we search for terrorists."

Sosa tossed a friendly wave and headed back to his office. Eva laughed aloud, vividly recalling her boss' initial reluctance to work this case. She lifted the coffee cup to her lips and relished the last cold swallow.

Eva strode to the coffee station where, finding the pot empty, she came up with a better idea.

She dashed to Griff's desk. "I'm calling for pizza delivery. What do you want?"

"Pepperoni. Make sure mine has extra mushrooms," he said, chuckling. "You might as well order enough for the two prisoners, and submit an expense voucher for theirs. Order me a diet cola, a biggie size. This is going to be a long night."

"But so worth it, partner," Eva said, her stomach growling. "Want to take a stab at how much cash Marlow was hiding on his grand estate?"

Griff stared at her, coming up with, "Another cool million?"

"That's what I guessed, but no. Sosa says it's over twelve million and counting. We may end up with a record-setting money seizure by anti-terrorism agents."

IN BETWEEN EATING SLICES of pizza at her desk, Eva banged out a report of their takedown of the king of organic foods, Marlow

Bryson. All the while she tried to suppress creeping concerns for his wife Cora. Eva had executed hundreds of search warrants and knew even now, Cora would be frantic.

She'd be confined in her home, being forced by agents to sit in an assigned seat. If the agents felt she posed a risk, she might even be handcuffed. Cora would be watching the agents comb through every room and every drawer. Worse yet, she must be anxious about where she would live if Marlow were convicted and sent to prison.

It was a prickly problem. Eva knew what she must do. She yanked her cell from her purse and sent a message to John Lapp: *John, phone me ASAP. It's URGENT.*

Eva slid the phone in her pocket in case John called back, and headed to the holding cells. She peered through the solid steel door's peepholes to check on Heather. That's when her phone buzzed.

Paul Revere was calling. Eva hurried to the conference room and shut the door.

"Let me bring you up to date on what's happening," she told him.

"Frankly, I'm shocked to get your text addressed to me," he replied, his tone terse. "Especially one asking me to speak with you."

"The urgent matter involves a certain case you know about."

John pushed back. "What do you want me to do? I've done all I can to avoid you and avoid being a snitch."

"Sometimes we mere mortals can't control destiny," Eva said calmly. "This is one of those times. Evidence I received from a disguised tipster has led to Marlow being arrested a second time, and his computers and all his money are being seized. He and Cora may lose their home."

"How am I involved?" John challenged.

Eva inhaled deeply, and choosing her words carefully, said, "For one thing, his arrest today will be life-altering for Cora. Your sister may be homeless and penniless. Your parents, Irene and Fritz, were planning to move into the guesthouse on the estate. That can't happen now. I have a way for you to help Cora."

"I'm sorry my sister married a deceitful liar." John's sigh was long, ragged.

"Well … I could add her present situation is thanks to you."

Eva let the truth sink in. When he remained silent, she pressed forward strongly. "John, you can do something big, but it may not remain anonymous."

"You're making me feel like the ogre here. I don't appreciate the guilt you're heaping on me."

"Let's start over. I sense you want to help Cora."

"I do," he insisted, his voice breaking. "I never once thought my sending you tips would harm her. I wanted to stop Marlow from hurting people who bought his food. I had no way of knowing he was deceiving Cora. What do you propose?"

Eva hoped to answer his concerns with truth and empathy. "It might get complicated. When someone deals in illegal drugs, federal law allows the government to seize from them all monetary proceeds from the deal and property purchased with drug proceeds. Also, any property real or personal used to facilitate drug trafficking, or as in Marlow's case, drug smuggling."

"Illegal drugs?!" John interrupted, his voice screeching. "He deals drugs?"

"We believe you didn't know and you're not in trouble. Remember when you saw the manifest for garlic powder? That is actually fentanyl, the most dangerous of drugs, which is called China Girl."

"How terrible! I feel sick!" he groaned.

Eva agreed, adding, "After Marlow's arrest today, one million dollars was initially seized. Then we located and seized another twelve million at his home. His entire estate can be taken and auctioned off because he's hiding proceeds there. Plus, he owns Beecher Packaging in Missouri, which can also be seized and auctioned off by the government. All the money flows into the Treasury Department's coffers."

After a pause and more groans, John said, "I'm speechless. My poor sister."

"Here's where you come in," Eva said, catching her breath. "Any person who gives us tips leading to asset seizures is entitled to be paid a percentage as a reward. Based on the thirteen million already in hand, you could apply for moiety. Your reward would be nearly two million dollars."

"Incredible! I'm in shock. My mind is spinning. Is there a way for me to receive a reward without being identified? I don't need much myself for a simple lifestyle."

"John, I understand your dilemma," Eva soothed. "You wouldn't have to keep the money you're entitled to. Rather, you could donate it to charity. Or use it to help your sister."

"You know how hard I've tried to keep my secrecy. I even cloned my texts to keep you from knowing."

Eva lowered her voice as her boss sauntered by her cubicle. "John, you raise a key point. Because the FBI seized Marlow's computers, we hope their forensic IT people are able to locate the digital recordings you found and texted to me."

"Oh. I suppose I … uh … I mean, Kaley could text you a 'screen grab' showing where the files are hidden on his computer. It might help direct your colleagues."

"There you go again," Eva said. "Being a valuable citizen of this country in the cause of justice. Let me explore ways to keep your moiety application a secret. It might be impossible. You should consider all the good you could do with the reward."

He promised to pray about it. "Eva, I'll call Mom and Pop and let you know soon. I'll pray for Cora and ask God to help her."

After ending the call, Eva prayed at her desk for the Lord to guide Cora and meet her needs. There would be worse ramifications to come because of Marlow's illegal conduct. People like the DeVrooms were also being hurt.

Eva might be a master at investigating and arresting criminals, but she knew only God could ensure true justice and protect and provide for innocent victims.

Chapter 43

John waited to call Mom and Pop until Saturday morning. He punched in their number, filled with trepidation. He didn't want them to ever find out he was the one who gave information leading to Marlow's arrest. There should be no reason why they would know unless he slipped up.

"Johnny," Mom answered, "please tell me everything's okay with you."

Her shaky voice distressed him, and he sought to reassure her.

"I'm fine, and I hope you don't think there's a problem every time I call. I want to know how you and Pop are doing."

"Living each day in faith and staying close to home," she assured him.

"Are you putting off moving to Cora's guesthouse?"

Mom sighed. "That idea has crumbled. The good thing is, Cora will live with us a while. The judge refused to let Marlow out on bond because he travels overseas. He and Cora hope to sell their home. Even if they do, Marlow's lawyer warned the government will probably take their money."

His heart flipped. Cora was losing her home! Should he bring up his news?

Deciding it might be a balm to his folks, he said, "I want to share something amazing. If Pop's home, put him on speaker."

"He's helping Cora pack a few things. I long to hear something good."

"Maybe you can guess. It's Annie. Mom, we're serious about each other. I plan to ask her to marry me."

"Johnny! How marvelous. I'm thrilled. Dad will be too."

"Annie doesn't know yet. I'm taking her on a picnic, where I'll show her the all-in-one engagement and wedding ring. I hope she says yes!"

"We want to meet your Annie and her son Samuel very soon."

Mom sounded happy, which gave John peace in his spirit. Life was turning out so wonderfully, and he prayed the same would happen for his parents and sister.

"So, I have your blessing?"

"Unreservedly, completely, and forever," she said, her voice filled with goodness. "May you and Annie grow to love each other as deeply as your dad and I do."

"I hesitated telling you with everything Cora is going through, but I wanted to lift your spirits. I hope I have. There's more, Mom."

She laughed softly. "If you could only see my smile. Don't hold back."

"After we marry, I'm moving to Walnut Cove, and I hope to find a house big enough for the three of us, and also for you and Pop, in case you want to move in with us. I know once you meet Annie, you will love her like a daughter."

"I'm sure we will, son. We'll call later after Dad gets home. You can tell him about your fantastic future plans. I'll try keeping quiet until then."

They chatted about the Trumpet's Call, with John asking if there was anything else he could do to help them. She promised to let him know. He hung up, his heart lighter than it had been for months, even years.

IT WAS UNCOMMON FOR EVA AND SCOTT to be alone on Saturdays, but today they enjoyed every minute of being together mowing and pruning in the yard. Kaley was working at the Trumpet's Call. Their boys were enjoying a youth rally at church.

Well beyond lunchtime, Eva fixed big BLT sandwiches, which she placed on the picnic table along with celery sticks and sweet potato chips. Scott washed up and was mopping his face with a towel as Eva set a pitcher of iced sweet tea between them.

He offered a prayer, thanking God for helping and protecting them as a family. Eva had just shared her desire to rip out mature shrubs and replace them when Scott changed the subject.

"Honey, I've been waiting for a good time to talk to you about Kaley's careless use of social media."

"Careless?" Eva stopped chewing and took a swig of tea. "Is that aimed at me because I'm the one who monitors her postings and selection of friends?"

Scott wiped his mouth with a napkin. "True, and you're doing a Herculean job. As she gets older and enters college, it's impossible to know what she's up to."

"Stop. If you know something, tell me. We're in this together."

Scott finished his sandwich before admitting what bothered him. "I saw a picture of her in a convertible with a girl and two boys I've never seen before."

"Really?" Eva had to think. "I'm her friend on her accounts and insist on having passwords so I can monitor her behavior."

"You've never seen the picture of her in the convertible?" Scott sounded incredulous.

"Where did you spot this photo?"

He scowled. "I shouldn't have brought it up."

"Oh, now you're going to claim it's a Defense Department

secret and I have no need to know," Eva sneered.

"Something like that." He shrugged.

Half of Eva's sandwich and chips remained on her plate. She rushed into the house and within a minute plunked her laptop on the table.

"Let's see what happens when I type in Kaley's username and password."

Eva quickly perused Kaley's social media accounts. Scott watched patiently.

She finally had enough, saying, "I've seen all these postings and pics. Kaley's not in any convertible."

"Is it possible she doesn't share things with you?" Scott pressed. "As Kaley grows up, that's bound to happen."

Eva stared at her husband. Where was he going with this inquisition?

"I suppose she can private message a single person or small group of friends. And sometimes, photos and messages are automatically deleted after a specified time."

"Probably explains it," Scott reasoned, snatching a few of Eva's chips.

"Wait. Let me check for private messages."

She worked her magic on the keyboard, ignoring him snitching her lunch.

"What have we here?" Eva studied the picture. "Who are these kids?"

She turned the laptop toward Scott. "Is this the one? It's good Kaley tagged them so at least we know who they are."

"That's them, and she tags everyone." Concern flickered in his eyes. "She also posts pictures of our entire family with our names plastered for the whole world to see."

"What are you talking about? Where did you see those?"

"Look for yourself," he insisted. "Do you find a picture of us five in the arboretum in Richmond with our names attached?"

"Yes, I just spotted it a minute ago."

Scott stood and grabbed his empty plate. "She needs to stop it. Her reckless actions put us at risk. Once it's on social media, it spreads around the world."

Eva lost her appetite. She followed Scott into the house with her uneaten lunch and laptop. After bringing in the sweet tea, she cornered Scott.

"What is this all about?" Eva fired. "I'll have to question other parents to find out who the kids are in the convertible. How did you discover this?"

"Let's sit. I'm beat from mowing in the humidity."

Eva replenished their iced tea and joined him at the dining room table. Scott drank some before wiping his forehead again.

"Even if any of this is classified," he said, "I think we both 'need to know.'"

Eva wrapped her hands around her glass, anticipating Scott's news. She'd found through the years he wouldn't be rushed.

She looked in his tired eyes and said, "So much for our quiet Saturday. Go on."

"Because I've been away from DoD, I'm making rounds in the Pentagon to familiarize myself with newer operations I might have to explain to the media."

"Tell me more." Eva wiggled her finger.

"Whew, it's hot," he puffed. "Anyway, we have units of young analysts who gather public information like a giant vacuum cleaner. They suck social media, news articles, and opinion from the Internet. When I said hello, they saw the ID card hanging from around my neck. One analyst snapped a picture of me with his cell phone."

Eva hung on his every word. "Then what?"

"She typed into her computer and instantly, page after page of data appeared on her screen. Not from a name search, but from facial recognition software that analyzed my photo and revealed I am Scott Montanna. She found pictures from my press briefings, of you receiving an award, of us at the arboretum, and Kaley in the convertible."

Eva's hands flew to her face. "Even our private photos! How can that be?"

"Modern technology. Platforms collect the pics. Subscribers to social media accounts agree to it when they sign up for free apps. They sell the pictures and personal information to the highest bidder."

Eva had no words. Just when she thought their lives were getting back to normal, another unseen enemy swooped in and invaded their privacy once again.

"Sweetheart, you need to know the Chinese, Russians, Cubans, and even our allies collect the same publicly available info," Scott said, gazing in her eyes.

"You saw me receiving an award?"

"Yes, the award you and Griff received in the Great Hall of Justice at DOJ Headquarters some years ago."

"How could they have that?" Eva wanted to know everything Scott knew.

Scott looked around the room. "Probably someone's family

member, who was a spectator, snapped a picture on their cell phone and posted it on social media. Then some other Internet platform grabbed it and DoD analysts, the Chinese and whomever, scooped it up on the Internet."

"It's that pervasive?" Eva shook her head fiercely.

Scott reached for the laptop. "We'll put it to the test. Bring up the website for Images."

She opened her computer and Scott snatched up the novel he'd been reading. "Check out this author. Type author Vince Flynn in the query bar."

Eva typed in his name and was shocked at how many photos popped up of Vince Flynn. "Did his PR person send all these photos to be published?"

"Search engines collect them from websites where the photos are posted." Scott folded his arms across his chest.

Eva typed in her name and sat back stunned at what she found. "No! They have the same awards ceremony photo of me. It even has my name attached. How dare they."

"As I said, it's one giant intelligence vacuum cleaner. The Chinese and Russians have your photo, along with mine, and possibly our whole family at the arboretum."

"Scott, we'd better give the kids a stern talking to," Eva insisted. "I'm tempted to take away their phones and to never give one to Dutch, ever."

He leaned back. "Welcome to the new normal, Eva. We'll warn Kaley and Andy, and urge them to escape the social media jungle. I fear the future for them."

Eva picked up the tea pitcher and headed for the kitchen. "Scott, one good thing happened because of Kaley's cell phone. Paul Revere, my bashful tipster, was able to contact me with important evidence. I have no doubt God was involved. And the rest is His-story."

TWENTY MINUTES AFTER they were in bed for the night, Eva whispered, "Scott, are you sleeping?"

He didn't stir right away so she touched his arm lightly.

After several seconds, he croaked, "What's up?"

"I'm wide awake and thinking nonstop about our privacy. Aren't you bothered by the lack of it?"

"Apparently not. I was sleeping. You want some hot cocoa?"

"No." Eva rolled on her side to face him. "I'm wondering how your facial recognition software works. Did they find your pictures and info just from analyzing your facial features?"

"Yup. That's what the analysts told me."

"Can they ID people worldwide?"

"Eva, it's the Defense Department. We fight wars worldwide. Why do you ask?"

"In my computer, I have a video of a guy in China," Eva said, her voice hushed. "We know he uses the name Wen. If I get a screenshot of him, could your analysts use their software and identify him?"

Scott tossed his pillow on the floor and flopped onto his stomach. "I'll ask. Can we talk in the morning?"

Eva slid from the bed.

"Where are you going?" he muttered.

"To take a screenshot and email it to you. When you get to work on Monday, you'll have it. Then maybe I can fall asleep."

Chapter 44

E va entered her office on Tuesday morning carrying the folded sheet of paper Scott brought home from the Pentagon. Her husband had come through for Eva in a spectacular way. She parked her purse and equalizer in her desk drawer and went looking for Brett. She tapped on the partition, interrupting him from typing on his computer.

He looked up, a hopeful gleam in his eyes. "Do you have another new tipster?"

Eva unfolded the paper. "I bring you another major arrest for your case."

"My cuffs are always primed for action," he replied, smirking.

He pointed to a small chair and Eva settled in.

"I can't give you these handwritten notes because they would incriminate someone," she explained. "My new source has identified Wen in China."

Brett grabbed a pen and pad. "Okay, Eva. Let's hear it all."

"Mr. Wen Yuan is the source behind Marlow's Chinese fentanyl. He's from Wulang, China, where he sells chemicals and food additives."

"Is your new source reliable?" Brett fired back.

"For sure." She smiled. "If Paul Revere was good, we'll be naming this source George Washington."

"You have me curious."

Eva consulted the note, telling him, "My source advises the State Department has located visa applications showing Wen entered the U.S. twice in the last three years to attend a food packager's convention in Seattle."

Brett's eyebrows shot up. "Where he met Marlow Bryson, correct?"

"Right. Things are ratcheting up. The State Department found Wen's visa request to attend this year's upcoming show in Seattle."

"We go to the grand jury, supersede our indictment to include Wen, and nail him on our soil." Brett rubbed his hands together. "That would be a huge get."

Eva rose. "My research reveals Wen's company is China's largest supplier of NPP, the chemical precursor in manufacturing fentanyl."

"Now we're talking," Brett said with gusto. "Uh oh … we'd better find out if Wen Yuan is still coming to Seattle. He might cancel if he knows Marlow's in jail."

Eva reclaimed her seat. "Two more things. We'll post a Be On

The Lookout, a BOLO, with Customs to notify us if Wen enters the country. Be prepared to arrest him in Seattle."

"What's the second thing?"

"Since you do undercover work," she said, "I discovered something very concerning this weekend. All the while I've been working undercover, photos of me are floating around the Internet, which front me out as an ICE agent."

Brett's eyes widened. "Who did that?"

"I went on Images' website. They show pictures of me and maybe you. I didn't check."

Brett spun in his chair and Eva watched him type his name into the Images search bar. Pictures of several men named Brett Calloway loaded up. As the two agents scanned these, it became apparent Brett wasn't among them and hadn't been unmasked.

"Whew, I'm safe." He swept a hand across his forehead. "I can't believe this site has all these pictures."

"I've another idea, Brett. Try Marlow's name."

He did and both agents watched the screen load up dozens of photos.

Eva saw it first. "There! It's Marlow standing with a Chinese guy."

They leaned closer to the screen, and she declared, "That's him, Wen Yaun."

"How do you know? There's no name posted."

Eva scrolled through her smart phone and showed Brett the screenshot she took the other night. "I snapped this photo of Wen from Marlow's computer video."

Brett said, "Yeah, it's him," as he enlarged the photo on his computer.

"It looks like they're at a reception." Eva pointed to the new photo of Marlow and Wen. "They are both holding glasses with paper umbrellas."

"Maybe it's last year's packaging conference in Seattle," Brett offered.

He scrolled through more photos, stopping at one of Marlow and Wen standing alongside two men wearing suits and ties and raising cocktails.

"Most likely it's the same event," Eva said. "Does it say who the two men are?"

Brett squinted and read, "Senator Cambridge Easton, and his aide Li Chen."

"Unbelievable!" Eva exclaimed. "Easton's a crook too. He received large donations from Darin Hilton, the defendant in Griff's case."

Brett stared at Eva, his mouth ajar. "Where's our case going next?"

"Marlow will want to plea bargain." Eva raised her chin decidedly. "You and Patrick make sure he tells everything he knows about Senator Easton and his Chinese connections. Brett, our team's weeding out corruption one dandelion at a time."

JOHN LAPP WAS WATCHING a documentary about the Dust Bowl on television when his cell phone vibrated. He snatched it up from the table next to his chair. Annie's smiling picture greeted him.

He was thrilled to hear from her and told her so. "Annie, your call is the best thing to happen all day."

"John, I hope I'm not interrupting anything important, but I have wonderful news."

The sound of her lyrical voice cheered him. He quickly muted the TV.

"Forget rivers of dust," he said, grinning down to his socks. "I'd rather talk with you, Annie. Call anytime, day or night, even without news."

Her sweet laugh in his ear made him wish she was here and not merely talking on the phone.

"I'm at the museum," she said, "and took advantage of a lull to phone Lancaster."

"I didn't realize until now I forgot about checking into Lancaster," he replied.

"John," she trilled his name. "I found your family's farm."

His mind tumbled. "For real? Do you know how amazing you are?"

"Guess what else, John? I found your Aunt Bethel."

"I have an Aunt Bethel?" he repeated with no clue to what she meant.

"Yes. I spoke with the museum director in Lancaster who is familiar with the Lapps. She lives a quarter mile away from them. Your widowed Aunt Bethel Lapp still lives there. She married your father's brother."

"Hooray!" John leapt up from the chair. "My hopes are coming true. I'm unsure what to do next."

"Watch for my text with the director's phone number. She is Mennonite and wants to tell you about your family."

John's life had changed for the better since he met Annie. Words stuck in his throat and he sipped some water to collect himself.

"Annie, you're the best," he managed. "And you bring me the most happiness I have ever known."

"As you do for me," she said, her voice gentle in his ear. "Samuel is eager to go fishing with you tomorrow."

"I'm excited to take him on his birthday. I also can't wait to see my family's farm in Lancaster. I should wait until after our wedding. Then I can visit there with my new wife. Would you mind exploring the Pennsylvania Dutch countryside on our honeymoon?"

"Secretly, I hoped you would ask me," Annie said, giggling.

John laughed heartily. "I'm getting to know your thoughts and am glad it won't be too long before I can call you my own dear Annie Lapp."

Chapter 45

The following Sunday, John could hardly sit quietly next to Annie in the second row of her church in Walnut Cove. Not when his heart was bursting with such great love for her. He was ready and eager to see his heartfelt desire come true with his folks as witnesses.

Mom and Pop had driven up with Cora from Virginia. His sister brought Annie and Mom each a single yellow rose to mark the occasion. Yesterday afternoon they'd enjoyed a fun picnic at the park with Annie and her son Samuel.

Pastor Frederick finished his message and began praying for everyone to follow Christ's command to love your neighbor as yourself. John opened his eyes and saw his mom give a glowing smile to Samuel sitting beside her. She and Pop already loved him as their grandson. As John noted the joyous look in her eyes, he wondered if perhaps the boy reminded Mom of him when he was six years old.

The congregation stood for a final hymn. John and Annie lifted their voices, and standing side by side, sung in harmony the old hymn "No One Ever Cared for Me Like Jesus."

As the piano played the last tender note, John squeezed her hand, whispering, "It's almost time, dearheart."

"Yes, it's our time," Annie said, crinkling her nose and smiling.

The pastor announced in a friendly manner, "Please be seated. We are having a special marriage ceremony between John Lapp and Annie Yoder. Many of you have known her since she was born. Annie and John, please join me at the altar."

John squeezed her hand once more. Her cheeks blushed prettily. She looked gorgeous in her lavender dress. Annie gave Irene her rose to hold, and hand in hand, they walked up front. John's heart swelled in his chest.

He felt like shouting, *This is the most blessed day of my life!*

Their ceremony was reverent and simple. They exchanged vows, pledging to honor and cherish each other and serve the Lord Jesus in their marriage.

Pastor Frederick told the congregation, "The couple asked me to read verses in First Corinthians chapter 13 where the Apostle Paul teaches, 'Love always protects, always trusts, always hopes, always perseveres. Love never fails.' This biblical truth is a strong foundation upon which to build a marriage."

John's spirit soared as he slid a sparkling diamond wedding band onto Annie's slim finger. She put a polished gold band onto his, a sign of her love for him.

The pastor held onto the Bible, asking, "Do you John Lapp, and do you Annie Yoder, covenant to keep the love of Jesus in your hearts and your marriage as long as you both shall live?"

"We do!" they echoed in unison.

"John and Annie, you both pledge your Christian faith each to the other in the presence of God, your family, and friends. By the authority vested in me, I now pronounce you husband and wife. You may kiss your bride!"

OUTSIDE THE CHURCH, Mr. and Mrs. John Lapp were joined by Annie's parents. Simon and Agnes Nolt both held unto Samuel's little hands. Mom and Pop, their faces luminous, walked up and embraced Annie. Cora kissed her cheek.

John introduced the parents one to the other. His joy bubbling over, he told the Nolts, "Mom and Pop befriended the formerly Amish Sarah Lapp, my mother. They adopted me after her terminal illness. I'm one of the many kids they rescued."

Annie reached for Samuel's hand, and smiling up at John, said, "And now Samuel is *our* son. I hope everyone understands that John and I chose to have the simple and traditional Mennonite wedding ceremony."

"Everything was precious," Mom said. "Annie, you are a beautiful bride and our new daughter."

John laughed. "Having you all here is extraordinary, like Christmas morning."

Other friends crowded around wishing the newlyweds well.

Annie's mother leaned over to Irene, and John heard her say, "We're so happy to meet you. Dinner is ready at our home. We hope to know you and Fritz better."

They proceeded to gather around the Nolt's large dining room table. John saw before his eyes the two families becoming one that day, forging the bond of Christian fellowship. Only God could have orchestrated and woven such a beautiful tapestry from their many frayed and broken strands.

Chapter 46

Eva dashed over to Irene's townhome the following Saturday afternoon. She parked in front, and after opening the passenger door, removed two shopping bags. Cora surprised Eva by opening the door instead of Irene.

"Come in, Eva." Cora's eyes were puffy like she'd been crying. "My folks ran to an emergency dental appointment for Dad. They mentioned you might stop by."

"Do you feel like company?"

"Absolutely. I've been in the house by myself too long."

Eva stepped in, lifting up one bag. "Goodies from Kaley and me. We baked up a storm last night. Hope you like zucchini bread. There's cinnamon rolls and chocolate chip cookies too. In the other bag are containers of spaghetti with meat sauce, salad, and garlic bread for supper."

"You're very kind." Tears hovered on Cora's lashes. "Dealing with Marlow's legal case is difficult."

In the kitchen, Cora stored the cooked food in the fridge and made green tea. She offered Eva one of the cookies, but Eva waved off a treat.

"Those are for you and your folks. Do you live here now?"

Cora sipped her tea. "Yes. Our Middleburg house is up for sale."

"Cora," Eva said her name softly. "I pray for you, asking God to bring you a new beginning and help you in everything."

She broke down sobbing. Eva wrapped arms around her and breathed a prayer over her, "Father in heaven, Cora needs to know how much You love her, and how much she's loved by her family and friends. Please guide her through this time of pain and trial. Jesus, be the lifter of her head. We trust in You, Amen."

Cora scurried away. Eva sat on the sofa, worrying she might have discovered Eva's involvement in Marlow's arrest. Eva batted down rising concerns. Marlow was negotiating a guilty plea and Eva shouldn't have to testify against him. Most likely the Brysons would never learn the details of her undercover role.

Dabbing her eyes with a tissue, Cora sat next to Eva saying, "You and Mom's other church friends are faithful in praying and bringing food. I don't know why I quit church. Perhaps it was after Marlow and I married nearly four years ago, and he lost interest. I let him talk me out of going. That's my mistake. One of many, I'm afraid."

"You couldn't know what he was involved in with his business,"

Eva replied vaguely.

"No." Cora blinked back more tears. "I was too busy decorating a gigantic house and planning social events. I've asked God to forgive my selfish ways. I know He has. I still hear a voice inside saying, 'You volunteered at the Trumpet's Call and that counts for something.' I know now my works are nothing. It is all Jesus and His shed blood that saves me."

"Cora! I call you my sister in Christ." Joy flooded Eva's heart. "The Bible promises God works everything for our good when we are called to Him and His purposes. I pray He brings you much good on this rocky road."

"I once believed Marlow's decisions were influenced by his faith in God and he lived his life accordingly. I can only pray he'll repent and be reconciled to God."

Eva decided to share with Cora something God had shown her recently. "I've been reminded when we accept Jesus' sacrifice for our sins, God sees us as not guilty. I hope Marlow will see Jesus paid it all for him. Others have found Jesus while incarcerated."

Eva's thoughts turned to Marlow making money by smuggling drugs and ensnaring others into a life of woe. She felt no guilt for doing her job in exposing a lowlife who scammed and lived a lie. Yet, she hoped he would find spiritual rebirth.

Cora was talking and Eva listened.

"He has sunk so low." Cora wiped her eyes. "The lawyer said we shouldn't talk about the case with anyone, but you're not just anyone, Eva. With your job, you understand more than most people the pain of being charged with crimes."

Eva sensed she shouldn't discuss Marlow's case at all. Still, that didn't prevent her from encouraging Cora before leaving.

She patted Cora's hand. "I won't come between you and your legal counsel. Another verse comes into my mind. In the tenth chapter of John, Jesus teaches that He came so we might have life to the full. He knows your deepest need. The more you turn your cares over to Him, He promises to make a way forward."

"My mom keeps giving me verses to read and they are helping. She's invited me to your next ladies' prayer group and I plan to come."

"We ladies open our hearts and cry out to the Lord in prayer for our families and needs," she told Cora. "You are most welcome to join us."

With that Cora dissolved into fresh tears. Eva gave her a tender hug and rose.

"Thanks for your support," Cora said, wiping her eyes again

and walking Eva to the door. "Mom and Dad will be sorry to have missed you. I'll look up the verse in John and bring it to Marlow next time I see him at the jail."

"May you find strength in the love of family and your faith," Eva said with feeling.

She went to her car where she sat a moment before starting the engine. Eva knew it was wrong, but she felt like she'd just left a dental appointment. Whenever she'd see Cora in the future, she would remember her own involvement in Marlow's arrest. God needed to help Eva to move forward in the strength she'd just commended to Cora.

IT WAS LATE AUGUST. Eva wiggled her toes in white Lake Michigan sand, watching Scott laughing and flying stunt kites with Dutch. Kaley had gone to the car with her brother Andy to fetch the lunch cooler.

"It's marvelous we're finally together," Eva told Grandpa Marty, who sat in a beach chair beside her. "Life with three kids has a way of stretching beyond my grasp sometimes."

Her grandfather looked fit and healthy for his advanced age. His wife Rebecca sat next to him in a colorful beach chair. They held hands looking out upon the rolling waves with white foam curling on top.

He turned to Eva, his blue eyes sparkling. "I've learned a secret through the years."

"Please share," she urged.

"God makes everything beautiful in its time," he answered with a bright smile, and went back to looking at the silvery-blue water.

Eva realized his "secret" was in the Bible and she made a note to look it up later. For now, contentment and delight merged together in her heart. Kaley and Andy delivered the cooler and dashed off to fly kites. Scott handed his soaring kite to their daughter, who would begin college the day after they returned from vacation.

Eva smiled as Scott coached, "Kaley, pull the right line when you want the kite to turn right. The left line makes it go left."

"It's going to crash!" Kaley squealed. "I can't fly this."

"Yes you can. Pull them both back together so the kite climbs higher."

Kaley followed her dad's instructions, and the kite ascended high.

"Good!" Scott called. "Now pull and hold the right line and make it go in a loop."

Kaley obeyed. The stunt kite spun into a fast dive, then turned skyward to complete a loop. Eva cheered. Kaley laughed. With her phone, Eva snapped a few pictures. This glorious day in the sand brought her much peace. She knew for certain Kaley would fly in life just as her kite did.

A chirp on Eva's cell phone startled her. Brett Calloway was sending her a text message. He knew she was vacationing, so he must have something she needed to know.

She swiped across the message to open it: *Eva, congrats. Yen Wuan was arrested getting off the plane in Seattle from China. A search of his luggage revealed incriminating evidence, and hundreds of packets of unknown mystery seeds. Marlow's lawyer phoned to hurry his client's guilty plea. Call when you have time.*

Eva sent Brett a thumbs-up emoji and brief reply: *On the beach with family. Will call after lunch from the car.*

Sliding her phone into her beach bag, she wondered just what "mystery seeds" Yen Waun had in his luggage. Perhaps John Lapp could examine them and give his opinion. Eva chuckled over the surprising turn of events.

"Good news?" Scott ran up, dropping in his chair beside her under the umbrella.

"Brett sent me the most satisfying message. The Chinese chemical salesman you found using facial recognition software has been arrested. Nabbed him deplaning in Seattle."

Scott winked his approval. "What's for lunch? I'm starving."

Eva pulled the cooler closer and unpacked sub sandwiches and sodas.

"Lunch, everyone," she called, waving an arm at the kite flyers.

After supplying Grandpa Marty and Rebecca their lunch, she handed Scott a plate of food. Before he tasted one bite, his cell rang. He placed the soda can in a cup holder, and balancing his chips and sandwich on his knee, he took the call. Eva heard his tense back-and-forth, concluding it was his office at the Pentagon.

"That *is* serious," Scott said into the phone, flashing Eva a concerned look. "I need to know what the White House intends to do before we release anything to the press. Text me the President's proposal. Then we'll write something supporting their position."

He shoved his phone into her beach bag, his face a picture of raw emotion.

"What's so vital to interrupt your vacation?" Eva asked quietly.

Scott leaned close to whisper in her ear, "At this very moment, while our Navy and Coast Guard conduct anti-narcotics operations in the Caribbean, Chinese warships are patrolling off California's Southern coast. Two day ago, DoD satellite surveillance spotted a

Chinese warship transferring cargo onto a Colombian submersible vessel near the coast of Mexico. This morning, the Coast Guard caught the submersible near San Diego smuggling five tons of fentanyl."

"I'm glad they caught that massive amount of drugs," Eva said decidedly.

"It's more than drugs." Scott kept his voice low despite the kids laughing and throwing sand. "They found not only paper on board with Chinese markings, but also a Chinese Communist spy with his computer, who was being smuggled into the U.S."

"Will you announce any details in a press release?"

Scott held her glance for a long moment. "We'll let the policymakers decide what to release. I think China patrols near our coastline to draw America into conflict. They oppose our presence in the South China Sea and our Justice Department arresting so many Chinese professors for spying. The ChiComs are hurling new threats against us by the hour."

"I suppose we'll cut our vacation short," she said, sighing.

"Perhaps. War with China is imminent." Scott also breathed a sigh before taking a swig of his cola. "Our seizing their huge shipment of drugs and catching their spy just might put a crimp in their propaganda campaign and quest for power."

Worry over a future war with China sizzled through Eva in a flash. She didn't want to overreact with Grandpa Marty and kids nearby. Then her grandfather's earlier wise counsel overpowered her fears. God would take care of everything.

She put her hand over Scott's, telling him, "We need the Lord's help more than ever. He knows the future and we can depend on His faithfulness."

"Do you agree there's not much we can do from here on the beach?" he said, shrugging his shoulders.

"Yes, and I'd rather not leave yet," Eva urged. "Eat your lunch. Enjoy this precious time together. Something Grandpa Marty mentioned makes me realize we should relax and recharge. We'll have time later to help secure our nation for our family."

Chapter 47

Eva checked her outfit in the back-hall mirror. Her black jacket, worn over her purple blouse and black dress slacks, would have to suffice for the event. She hadn't shopped in ages, not with the heavy work demands. The weather forecast for this fine October day was for plenty of sunshine and seventy-degree temperatures.

As she searched for her small purse, Eva mulled over the happenings since Marlow's guilty plea to drug smuggling a few weeks back. He'd waived all right to fight the seizure of real property owned by him and his companies as well as the seized cash and other assets. Cora kept her car and small savings account from before their marriage. She'd become active in Eva's ladies' prayer group and seemed to be coping with her husband's three-year prison sentence.

AUSA Patrick O'Rourke had dropped the bribery charges against Marlow in exchange for his agreement to testify against Judge Ginsburg's daughter, Heather Que, and also Senator Easton. The senator awaited trial where Marlow was expected to testify about funneling China's illegal campaign contributions to Easton.

In the end, Marlow never testified against Heather because she plead guilty to extortion, after convincing O'Rourke that her father never was wise to her scheme. She'd begun serving her eighteen-month sentence and would be released from prison six months before Ricky, her ex-husband.

Eva tossed a scarf around her neck, and after gathering her purse and keys, she declared herself ready. Kaley waited outside by the SUV. Eva waved to her hubby while he leaned on a rake, no doubt enjoying a respite from yard work with the boys. Scott fired off a mock salute and went back to raking pine needles from beneath the trees.

"We've dodged hard work for once," Eva said to Kaley, easing down the driveway. "This will be fun. You're so busy with college, we rarely see each other."

Her daughter stared at the cell phone in her hand as if she hadn't heard a word, until she finally said, "Tell me again how Mrs. DeVroom saved part of the girl's school."

"It's an inspiring story of God using Irene to turn ashes into something beautiful," Eva replied. "I'll share details if you put away your phone."

Kaley laughed and shoved the cell into her purse. Eva's spirit danced. She'd scored one tiny victory in the battle against tech tyranny.

Turning the corner, she explained, "The former exclusive all-girls prep school went bankrupt. Developers bought the campus to build high-end homes. They decided not to tear down the home of the school's founder or the original quaint colonial-style building, which was a dormitory."

"Why are we going there?" Kaley asked. "Exams have turned my mind into knots."

"Then it's a perfect afternoon to enjoy the house and dormitory being dedicated as a new foster home. It's being established by the Trumpet's Call Foundation."

"Is that Mr. and Mrs. DeVroom's foundation?" Kaley sat clutching her purse.

"Exactly, and here we are."

Eva turned up the long driveway lined with trees blushing autumn red. Casually-dressed guests strolled across the campus towards a large tent. Chairs were arranged in between the founders' house and dormitory.

"I love seeing how God restores what is broken," Eva said earnestly.

Kaley cried, "Look! The tent's enormous! I smell barbeque and am starving, Mom. Thanks for inviting me."

Eva laughed. Her daughter sure had become talkative without the cell phone. As they drove past the house, Irene rushed toward them. Eva stopped the SUV to roll down her window. Irene's face lit up bright as sunshine.

She leaned down, saying, "Eva and Kaley, I'm thrilled you both made it."

"Can we help?" Eva asked, looking around.

"Not at all." Irene gestured over her shoulder. "Did you know the Trumpet's Call Foundation is designating the house for the new executive director? Fritz and I will be consultants for whoever is chosen."

"It's a pretty setting, and conveniently close to the thrift store," Eva noted.

"God is working wonders beyond what we could ever imagine, especially given what Marlow put us through," Irene said, her voice catching. "We thank the Lord with all our hearts."

She hurried away. Eva went to park, telling Kaley, "We should both remember how Irene and Fritz are a good example of living strong in times of trouble."

"All these people here today know how kind they are," Kaley observed.

They scurried from the SUV, hoping to make the reception in time.

Attorney Madison Stone pulled alongside their car, so Eva greeted her with a cheery, "Madison, it's great seeing you."

"Eva!" Madison exclaimed. "It's been forever. You're with your daughter, who I met at the Trumpet's Call."

"Because of you, Kaley's studying pre-law in her freshman year at college." Eva then told her daughter to go ahead, adding, "I need to speak with Maddie confidentially."

"You do?" Maddie asked, looping her arms through straps on her backpack.

Eva drew Maddie toward the cars to keep their conversation private. "I recently discovered information you may not know, but should."

"Really?" Maddie stopped in her tracks, alarm filling her eyes.

"It's about Darin Hilton."

Maddie's eyes snapped fire. "I'll never forget my client's shock when Ginsburg declared him guilty. I never approved of the judge deciding the case. We had a solid defense."

"Hilton got scammed," Eva said, selecting her next words with care. "A schemer convinced him to pay a half-million dollars in cash for a bench trial, promising Ginsburg would find him not guilty. Hilton paid a fortune and still was convicted."

"Are you sure?" Maddie asked, her forehead etched in a deep frown.

"One hundred percent," Eva assured. "Agent Griff Topping and I worked another case where the same scammer tried it again and we caught her. She plead guilty and is in federal prison."

"Which explains Darin's insistence to reject my advice. You know what?" Maddie's lips curved upward.

Eva folded her arms, a smile growing on her face. "From your tone, I sense another twist."

"Serves him right. He went to prison and never paid the balance of what he owes me."

Eva smirked. "Sorry to hear you were cheated by your client. I assume what money he had went to Senator Easton."

"What do you mean?" Maddie took a step back.

"It's been on the news. Senator Easton received campaign contributions from a Chinese donor that were laundered through Marlow Bryson. I've since wondered if that same Chinese donor was source for the money Darin Hilton donated to Easton."

"How is that connected to my former client?" Maddie looked perplexed.

Eva moistened her lips. "We discovered a photo of Marlow at a Seattle conference, smiling and shaking hands with Senator Easton and Marlow's Chinese source for fentanyl, Wen Yuan. In Wen's plea proffer, he admitted China's Communist government passed money through him to Marlow, which Marlow then illegally gave to Easton as domestic political contributions."

"Let me guess. You convicted Yuan, and Marlow's cooperation is behind the bad publicity I saw about Senator Easton."

"Washington plunges farther into corruption every day," Eva declared. "Scott and I may move after our son Andy starts college in a few years."

Maddie adjusted her backpack. "Since I began practicing law here, I'm saddened to learn the deviousness of some people. Do you think Easton will be convicted?"

"He'll be tried by a jury, so you never know."

"Eva, one more thing." Maddie reached out a hand. "A friend of mine teaches at a medical school and is on loan to the National Institute of Health. She told me yesterday she's been contacted by a professor from China, offering my friend a pre-paid trip to China to teach a fellowship. She's concerned. Will you talk to her?"

"Have your friend call me on Monday," Eva said as they hurried to catch up with Kaley. "Some officials say war with China is inevitable, which keeps me up praying many nights. Let's forget trouble and find out how God is blessing the Trumpet's Call."

"It's my favorite place to shop," Maddie said, walking alongside Eva. "Look at all these people Irene and Fritz are helping."

The reception started moments after Eva and Maddie hastened into the tent. The DeVrooms' friends and grown foster kids mingled together, eating plates of BBQ beef, corn on the cob, and hot baked potatoes.

Eva finished her spiced apple cider when a man with white hair, and wearing a tailored suit, stepped to a podium. He introduced himself as the board chair and asked everyone to take seats. The chairs began to fill.

"The DeVrooms continue to love children," he said, motioning to Fritz and Irene. "The board is honored to dedicate Genesis House, which we hope will create a new beginning for orphaned children and those who need a home."

The audience applauded. Eva and Kaley slipped into seats next to Maddie.

The chairman's voice resounded as he explained, "When I learned the prep school would close, I contacted the developer who had an option to purchase the property, telling him we hoped to buy the dormitory and founder's house for a foster home. God's handiwork comes to fruition because none of us could have done this on our own."

Kaley leaned over to Eva. "I'm glad he said that, Mom. I'll tell you later why."

Eva nodded and lifted a finger to her lips, listening to what else the chairman was revealing.

"The developer wanted a tax break," he said. "And he donated both buildings. More amazing things are happening. A generous person, who remains anonymous, has pledged two million dollars for matching funds. Guess what? The other two million dollars were matched and donated!"

Eva and Kaley clapped vigorously along with the rest of the group.

"That's not all," the chairman proclaimed. "We raised enough money to hire a full-time executive director and refurbish the dormitory to add a dining area and offices on the first floor. Rooms for ten children on each of the second and third floors, along with apartments for two couples serving as foster parents, were updated. I'm pleased to announce the executive director for Genesis House is one of the early children fostered by the DeVrooms and eminently qualified to run this place."

It was his turn to applaud. "Please welcome Cora Bryson."

Eva gasped. Cora walked tentatively to the podium. A moment of silence morphed into joyful sounds of applause and cheers. Eva knew God was using the most illogical of circumstances to accomplish His divine purposes.

Cora was well into her comments when Eva realized her mind had wandered. She only heard Cora say, "Lastly, I thank my brother, John Lapp, who I'm told has done far more than he'll ever get credit for." She stopped.

"Not that John ever seeks attention. He and his new wife, Annie, flew here today on their way to South Sudan, where he'll teach several villages to grow drought-resistant corn. John is donating computers for Genesis House and wiring it for full Internet access. Please tour the new facilities and help yourselves to coffee and homemade desserts."

People stood and clapped. The crowd began to disperse. Eva spotted the newlyweds talking with the DeVrooms. She and Kaley wound their way to them.

Irene enveloped Eva in a hug. "Can you see the depths of God's love?"

"Vast beyond all measure, like the old hymn," she offered.

"Just when Fritz and I dreaded moving to Middleburg and being too far from the Trumpet's Call, God intervened and did all of this." Her hand made a sweeping gesture.

Eva smiled at her dear friend. "Cora will achieve much as executive director."

"We were sworn to secrecy," Irene confided. "Now I can say, Cora asked us to move into the founder's house with her. It will be wonderful to work so closely together. Fritz and I will be her consultants while operating Trumpet's Call. I'm bringing in more help, Kaley for one."

"Sure, on all my school breaks," Kaley said.

Eva saw John Lapp approaching and smiled.

With great thanksgiving in her heart for his generosity, Eva gestured around the campus, telling him, "John, how marvelous it is someone donated the seed money to give boys and girls a home who need one."

"And Eva," he flashed her a knowing nod, "how marvelous God used a certain someone to inspire the other someone to make such a donation."

Irene sauntered up, interrupting, "Sorry, I failed to introduce you to John's new bride. Meet our sweet Annie."

Eva and Kaley greeted Annie, who had a special way of making one think they'd been friends for years. Eva hoped Kaley saw the natural beauty in Annie's countenance.

"Will you continue living in Ohio?" Eva asked her.

"Yes, we're in Walnut Cove, not far from the college where John teaches. My son Samuel will stay with my folks while John and I travel to Africa on a mission trip."

Nearby, John was conversing with Fritz, but Eva could see Annie was comfortable talking about her Amish and Mennonite community.

"In fact, John learned some time ago he was born in an Amish home," Annie told them. "Only recently did we discover more about his parents."

"Annie, I need to ask," Kaley interjected, "was it through a picture?"

Annie's eyes twinkled in surprise. "You are clever. We found a picture of him with his birth mother in Pennsylvania, which matched the one she'd left in his suitcase."

"I found that photo in Mrs. DeVroom's thrift shop!" Kaley chirped.

"Honey." Annie turned to John. "Kaley is the one who located your picture in the little suitcase."

John gave Annie his full attention as she said, "I was about to tell Eva and Kaley of your desire to live a plain life. John realized he's too 'wired,' excuse the pun. He is made to further the positive side of technology, so it was a step back too far."

"True." John gave Annie an adoring glance. "I've found my home with Annie and her family at their Mennonite church. Have you tried the peanut butter pie? It's my Annie's favorite recipe."

After Kaley and Eva enjoyed their pie, Eva said her farewells. Maddie slipped a note into her hand when they reached their cars.

"My friend's name and number," she said with a wave.

Eva promised to follow up. The moment she started the car, her cell phone alerted. Griff sent an interesting message:

Eva, here's an idea to consider. Dawn and I just booked a second trip to Israel with our pastor. It's a family tour. Still several openings if you and Scott want to come with the kids. New discoveries we want to see. Will email full details.

"What's up, Mom?" Kaley asked, bucking her seatbelt.

"Something fun we can discuss later," Eva said. "Did you enjoy the celebration?"

Rather than answer, Kaley asked in a puzzled tone, "I wonder if someone really donated two million dollars."

"Yes. The first donation was conditioned on others donating matching money, which is why Genesis House was actually born with four million."

"Mom, back at home, I heard you talking on a call to someone about donating. Were you involved? Do you know who is?"

"It's from an anonymous person who doesn't want to be known. I can only guess. What's nice about anonymous donors is God receives all the credit."

Kaley leaned her head back. "When the man said God made it all happen, I can see He is working in my life too. That's what I wanted to tell you. Crazy stuff is swirling in our country, it's hard growing up. When I see something good, like today, I'm happier."

"Me too," Eva agreed. "Think about all we've witnessed. Because Cora's husband made bad choices and went to prison, they lost their home and money. Yet, God used the circumstances to bring Cora a new home where she'll help kids needing a family."

"Is that why you didn't want me and Lexi around Connor, because he wasn't choosing wisely?"

Eva kept her eyes on the road. "Dad and I believe God gives us crucial insights to help protect our children. It's not like we want to control your life. I wasn't a perfect teen. My mother often told me, 'Eva, be sure, your sins will find you out.'"

"I find that hard to believe," Kaley snapped.

"Ask Grandma," Eva said, grinning. "The more you mature, the more you need to question opportunities and seek wisdom. Cora's husband never learned to, causing much damage to himself and others."

"You're helping me to understand my faith is my foundation. It's more than Bible stories I learned in youth group. I want to find a man like Dad to love. One who shares my love for Jesus."

"Honey, you've just made me one happy mama," Eva said. "How about music?"

She turned on a CD. Kaley began singing softly and Eva tapped her fingers on the steering wheel. Would Scott agree to take a trip to Israel? With Kaley sharing how her faith was becoming more important, Eva knew this was the perfect time for them to take her. Andy and Dutch might be too young to enjoy such a historic trip.

One more important thing Eva knew. God had totally healed the breach in her relationship with Kaley. Mother and daughter were fully restored. Eva drove home with a song on her lips and in her heart for all of God's incredible gifts and blessings to her and her family. She could rest secure knowing their future was in His loving and sovereign hands.

ABOUT THE AUTHORS

ExFeds, Diane and David Munson write High Velocity Suspense novels reviewers compare to John Grisham. The Munsons call their novels "factional fiction" because they write books based on their exciting and dangerous careers.

Diane Munson has been an attorney for more than thirty years. She has served as a Federal Prosecutor in Washington, D.C., and with the Reagan Administration appointed by Attorney General Edwin Meese as Deputy Administrator/Acting Administrator of the Office of Juvenile Justice and Delinquency Prevention. She worked with the Justice Department, U.S. Congress, and White House on policy and legal issues. More recently she has been in a general law practice.

David Munson served as a Special Agent with the Naval Investigative Service (now NCIS), and U.S. Drug Enforcement Administration over a twenty-seven year career. As an undercover agent, he infiltrated international drug smuggling organizations, and traveled with drug dealers. He met their suppliers in foreign countries, helped fly their drugs to the U.S., feigning surprise when shipments were seized by law enforcement. Later his true identity was revealed when he testified against group members in court. While assigned to DEA headquarters in Washington, D.C., David served two years as a Congressional Fellow with the Senate Permanent Subcommittee on Investigations.

As Diane and David research and write, they thank the Lord for the blessings of faith and family. They are collaborating on their next novel and traveling the country speaking/appearing at various venues.

Check out their website at:
www.DianeAndDavidMunson.com

The Camelot Conspiracy

"The Camelot Conspiracy" rocks with a sinister plot even more menacing than the headlines. Former DC insiders Diane and David Munson feature a brash TV reporter, Kat Kowicki, who receives an ominous email that throws her into the high stakes conspiracy of John F. Kennedy's assassination. When Kat uncovers evidence Lee Harvey Oswald did not act alone, she turns for help to Federal Special Agents Eva Montanna and Griff Topping who uncover the chilling truth: A shadow government threatens to tear down the very foundation of the American justice system. The Munsons' thrillers are companion books, with characters reappearing in other novels, but each begins and ends a new story.

ISBN-13: 978-0982535523
352 pages, trade paper
Christian Fiction / Mystery and Suspense
14.99

Hero's Ransom

Could Chinese espionage disrupt your home town? CIA Agent Bo Rider (The Camelot Conspiracy) and Federal Agents Eva Montanna and Griff Topping (Facing Justice, Confirming Justice, The Camelot Conspiracy) return in Hero's Ransom, the Munsons' fourth family-friendly adventure. When archeologist Amber Worthing uncovers a two-thousand-year-old mummy and witnesses a secret rocket launch at a Chinese missile base, she is arrested in China for espionage. Her imprisonment sparks a custody battle between grandparents over her young son, Lucas. Caught between sinister world powers, Amber's faith is tested in ways she never dreamed possible. Danger escalates as Bo races to stop China's killer satellite from destroying America, and with Eva and Griff's help, to rescue Amber using a unexpected ransom.

ISBN-13: 978-0982535530
320 pages, trade paper
Christian Fiction / Mystery and Suspense
14.99

Redeeming Liberty

In this timely thriller by ExFeds Diane and David Munson (former Federal Prosecutor and Federal Agent), parole officer Dawn Ahern is shocked to witness her friend Liberty, the chosen bride of Wally (former "lost boy" from Sudan) being kidnapped by modern-day African slave traders. Dawn tackles overwhelming danger head-on in her quest to redeem Liberty. When she reaches out to FBI agent Griff Topping and CIA agent Bo Rider, her life is changed forever. Suspense soars as Bo launches a clandestine rescue effort for Liberty only to discover a deadly Iranian secret threatening the lives of millions of Americans and Israelis. Glimpse tomorrow's startling headlines in this captivating story of faith and freedom under fire. The Munsons' thrillers are companion books, with characters reappearing in other novels, but each begins and ends a new story.

ISBN-13: 978-0982535547
320 Pages, trade paper
Fiction / Mystery and Suspense
14.99

Joshua Covenant

CIA agent Bo Rider moves to Israel after years of clandestine spying around the world. He takes his family, wife Julia, and teens, Glenna and Gregg while serving in America's Embassy using his real name. While Glenna and Gregg face danger while exploring Israel's treasures, their father is shocked to uncover a menacing plot jeopardizing them all. A Bible scholar helps Bo in amazing ways. He discovers the truth about the Joshua Covenant and battles evil forces that challenge his true identity. Will Bo survive the greatest threat ever to his career, his family, and his life? Glimpse tomorrow's startling headlines as risks it all to stop an enemy spy.

ISBN-13: 978-0-983559009
336 Pages, trade paper
Christian Fiction / Mystery and Suspense
14.99

Night Flight

When CIA Agent Bo Rider adopts a retired law enforcement dog for his family, teenagers Glenna and Gregg are surprised to discover Blaze's special skills. They put the dog to work solving crimes, but a captured criminal seeks revenge forcing the kids to hide out at their grandparents' Florida home. In Skeleton Key powerful villains connive to stop the teens from discovering their criminal enterprise. As Glenna and Gregg face high stakes, they find courage to keep pursuing justice. In Night Flight, the Rider family learns the true meaning of loving your neighbor as yourself. This is the debut thriller for young adults and grand parents by these best-selling ExFeds who write factional fiction based on their careers.

ISBN-13: 978-0983559023
224 Pages, trade paper
Fiction / Mystery and Suspense
9.99

Stolen Legacy

Stolen Legacy, by Diane and David Munson, tells the daunting tale of Germany invading Holland, and the heroes who dare to resist by hiding Jews. Federal agent Eva Montanna stops protecting America long enough to visit her grandfather's farm and help write a memoir of his dangerous time under Nazi control. Eva is shocked to uncover a plot to harm Grandpa Marty. Memories are tested as secrets from Marty's time in the Dutch resistance and later service in the Monuments Men of the U.S. Army fuel this betrayal. The Munsons' eighth thriller unveils priceless relics and a stolen legacy, forever changing Eva's life and her faith.

ISBN-13: 978-0983559047
336 pages, trade paper
Christian Fiction / Mystery and Suspense
14.99

Embers of Courage

ICE Special Agent Eva Montanna discovers the world is ablaze with danger when militants capture her task force teammate, NCIS Special Agent Raj Pentu, during a CIA operation in Egypt. She risks her life to defeat tyrants oppressing Christians, and is plunged into a daring rescue mission. Eva's faith is tested like never before as mysterious ashes, her ancient family Bible, and fifteenth century religious persecution collide with modern-day courage under fire. This riveting novel, the ninth by ExFeds Diane and David Munson, is their third linking true historical events with their signature High Velocity Suspense.

ISBN-13: 978-0983559061
336 pages, trade paper
Christian Fiction / Mystery and Suspense
14.99

The Looming Storm

Tomorrow's headlines leap from the pages of *The Looming Storm* when Federal Agent Eva Montanna uncovers a menacing threat to harm Eva and her family. When daughter Kaley travels to Eastern Europe on a class trip, Eva's Christian faith is challenged, and their lives are altered in the blink of an eye. Tensions skyrocket as Eva and Griff Topping, her FBI partner, use every trick to infiltrate a band of Florida smugglers. The agents are shocked when their undercover charade reveals the criminals have sinister plans for America. Secrets are shredded in the Munson's tenth 'stand alone' thriller, as this spousal duo rips the veil from a labyrinth of covert criminal enterprises.

ISBN-13: 978-0-983559085
305 pages, trade paper
Christian Fiction/Mystery and Suspense
15.99

North by Starlight

After ten best-selling thrillers, Diane and David Munson launch *North by Starlight,* their first romantic suspense with Attorney Madison Stone racing to Starlight, Vermont from her D.C. law firm to save the inheritance of Jordan Star, sole heir of his late grandfather's Star Mountain ski resort. Maddie arrives in the winter wonderland ready to defeat the claim of Jordan's mystery relative. Instead, she finds surprising struggles and diversions in the idyllic town during the Christmas season when her ex-boyfriend, attorney Stewart Dunham shows up to represent the interloper. Maddie sharpens her legal skills in outwitting him and a greedy mining enterprise bent on changing Starlight forever. She and Jordan form an alliance, and the ensuing legal battle leaves her emotionally vulnerable until Trevor Kirk, a geologist, focuses her mind back to what is important, saving the town and finding her heart.

ISBN-13 : 978-1732582309
291 pages, trade paper
Christian Fiction/ Mystery and Suspense
14.99